一次戰勝新制多益

TOEIC
必考閱讀

攻略 ➕ 解析
➕ 模擬試題

SINAGONG 多益專門小組、金富露（Peter）、趙康壽／著

林雅雰／譯

要學就學必考的！

NEW TOEIC READING

保證高分、實戰取向的工具書！

學習在「多益實戰」時，可以立刻活用的理論。

準備多益前，必須先了解自己的實力水準，定好目標分數，然後在短期內集中火力學習。英文能力不足的新手們，會因為不知道該從哪裡開始著手準備，所以習慣一個一個文法慢慢學，但這可能是在浪費時間。因為多益是考試，考試不是紙上談兵，而是「實際作戰」。如果考生不知道該如何將文法應用於解題上，而是填鴨式硬背文法理論，將無法提升考試時的解題能力。因此，為了改善這一點，本書透過解題，帶出文法講解，讓考生可同時學習文法理論與解題技巧，並抓取重點。同時，本書也提供比任何一本初級文法書都還要豐富的模擬試題。

這是一本專門針對「自學」考生的工具書。

本書完全針對沒有參加補習班、線上課程，打算自己念的考生們而規劃。內容包含最適合自學的學習步驟，以及易於理解的清楚說明和詳細解答。

短期內就能讓分數急速上昇。

英文文法能力不足可能是無法作答多益考試的原因之一，但一般來說，主要原因是沒有掌握到多益出題的基本模式。多益出題有一套既定模式，只要熟悉此模式，便能輕鬆獲得高分。本書除了提升多益考生的文法能力，也同時讓考生熟悉出題模式與方向，完整分析十年來多益的出題趨勢，精選收錄考取高分的「文法與解題技巧」。

SINAGONG 多益專門小組

獲得解題的自信！

全書內容架構依照出題類型完整分析，我覺得很好，既可充實基礎，內容也非常豐富。書中不僅提及文法，也同時說明如何應用在解題上。對於像我一樣的多益新手們，能一邊順利解題，一邊提升自信心。強烈推薦給考生們！

金武元（上班族）

可以快速應用在實際考試上！

在攻略解題法的單元中，我學到如何掌握解題線索，並實際運用到考試中快速解題。像我這樣需要快速提升多益分數的初學者，也能夠把握解題要領，這點讓我很滿意。另外，單字整理的部分，就算沒有另外列出單字表，透過例題的解說，也能讓我學到裡面的單字，對我的幫助非常大。

裴慧妍（大學生）

可以被稱作「多益法典」的一本書！

如果準備多益考試有所謂的「法典」，那麼我認為多益的學習法典就是這本書。因為這本書即時反映了多益出題趨勢，並將出題類型細分，收錄精華部分，是一本適合在短時間內衝高分數的工具書。

黃仁德（大學生）

適合自學的一本書！

對於第一次考多益、多益基礎能力不足，或是想輕鬆自學的人來說，是一本非常適合的工具書。本書將出題類型做出細分，同時系統性地整理出應試時所需的解題重點、基本字彙、基礎文法，以及出題模式等。

李碩昊（大學生）

適合不懂解題技巧的人的工具書！

我因為沒有時間去補習班，所以選擇自學，但卻無法將學過的文法理論實際應用在解題上，因此成績不見好轉。而這本書，對於像我這樣不懂解題技巧的人來說，是本非常適合的工具書。跟一般市面上的工具書不同，本書最大的優點是以解題說明為主，可以讓人立即運用到實際考試之中。此外，不拖泥帶水的重點解析，以及不生硬的設計，讓人讀了不乏味。拿到本書，讓我非常期待之後的分數能夠提升到什麼程度呢！

趙雅蘭（大學生）

同時學習「基本觀念＋解題要領」！

本書是以「基本觀念＋解題要領」為主的一本工具書。一個章節結束後，解析同類型模擬試題的同時，讓人能夠重新複習剛剛學到的內容，這點非常好。讓人有種在閱讀一本整理得很完善的筆記的感覺，可以瞬間領會到重點。如果已經厭倦了市面上強調文法的工具書，那麼請翻翻看這本書。

李沼庭（上班族）

獲得解題的自信！

透過題型來掌握解題重點，再帶入文法概念的教學方式很不錯。因此自己一個人也能輕鬆地準備多益。這是一本處處皆有體貼自學者之處的工具書，雖然市面上也有不少針對初學者的書籍，但沒有一本能像這本書一樣讓人輕鬆上手。

趙雅拉（大學生）

自學中，卻仍像是上了一堂猜題精準的名師課程！

透過本書，讓第一次準備多益的人可以很快掌握考試中需要注意的部分。另外，本書也系統性地整理出解題的步驟，對於像我這種初次面對多益的人，也能很快學到解題方法。如果老是在某題型出錯的人，也非常適合透過本書學習。明明是自學，卻讓人如同在上補教名師的課，無論是針對各題型需注意之處的叮嚀，或是拆解問題方法的教導，對於考試時快速進入狀態非常有幫助。內容囊括了單字、基本文法、模擬試題，讓我對之後的多益考試無後顧之憂。

金允熙（上班族）

可以同時學習到文法與解題技巧！

如同書名的「攻略」二字，為了讓入門者能夠把握重點，針對問題的解析非常詳盡。同一題型會反覆練習，因此對於自學者來說，學習時不費吹灰之力。相較於市面上的多益工具書，本書收錄了更多例題，並且，讀者除了可以學習到文法外，同時也能學到解題技巧，我非常喜歡。

金夏蓮（研究生）

不只是多益分數，我的英文能力似乎也跟著提升了！

在倉促的準備時間下，光是讀了這本書，在我考試時就已經有很大的助益了。當我閱讀完本書後，不僅加強了我的多益解題功力，英文實力也似乎跟著提升。這是一本整理出所需重點，讓初次應考生也能快速上手的工具書。希望大家也能透過此書，增加對自己英文能力的自信心。

朴南洙（公務員）

共同完成書籍的各位：林卞碩、姜成模、蔡秀妍、李燦宇、徐宇振、裴智賢、鄭秀鎮、姜泯、徐宥拉、金小爾、林恩熙、鄭恩周、金聖祿、李仁善、金秀庭、李瑟琪、朴智賢、崔賢浩、延正模

並非以文法填鴨
而是增強解題能力的基礎工具書！

　　撰寫本書時，我們訪談了一百多位多益考生。大部分的考生，都提出了儘管整日都在閱讀、死背他人推薦的參考書，但實際考試時卻仍然有無法解題的困擾。無法運用在解題上，只會將文法倒背如流，又有何意義呢？雖然學文法確實重要，但「能夠順利解題」才是學習的理由。

　　因此，本書將重點放在考試時會出現的文法。書中的架構，是一邊解題，一邊檢閱解題步驟中所用到的文法，將必要文法挑出來做深度學習。剔除不常用到的文法，只留下重點文法。只要跟著本書的步調，初次應考生也能在解題中得到樂趣，並可望在短期內讓分數得到不小的進步。

1. 先解題，再講解文法的架構！

　　比起長篇大論的文法，本書更著重在培養考生的解題能力。因此先進行解題，透過作者推薦的解題方法，掌握解題的靈敏度，接著再去了解該題必要的文法概念。再安插幾題模擬試題，讓考生能夠一邊解題，一邊試著應用前面所學到的解題方法與文法。

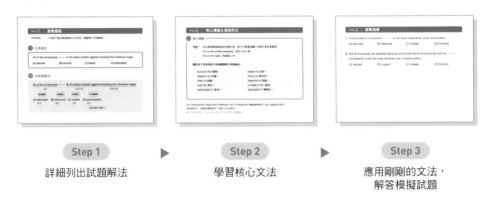

Step 1	▶	Step 2	▶	Step 3
詳細列出試題解法		學習核心文法		應用剛剛的文法，解答模擬試題

2. 精簡出解題時相關的重點文法！

　　本書並不會為了累積基礎，就讓考生死背大量的文法理論。對於考生而言，不僅不需要如此大量的文法理論，就算背起來，無法解題也是沒有任何用處的。為了多益考生，本書精簡收錄可以考取高分的精華文法於一頁之內。

3. 高命中率又豐富的模擬考題＋深究錯誤答案的詳盡說明＋免費下載多益模擬試題

　　本書秉持著自學也能夠享受解題樂趣的宗旨，因此比起其他多益參考書，本書收錄了更多試題，並且都是根據最新的出題趨勢所設計。除了書中的試題，另外還提供了一份多益閱讀模擬試題，讓考生免費下載。請掃描 QR 碼直接下載試題與解析。

　　為了讓考生獨自解題後，也能充分理解，本書將正確答案與錯誤答案的理由，都仔細地分析、說明。

📖 第一冊：**攻略本**　　　　　　　📖 第二冊：**解析本**

4. 把握文法基礎概念的單元：　「文法概念前導」

　　在正式進入多益文法教學前，為了讓考生能夠理解各個文法形式，本書規劃了「文法概念前導」單元。透過本單元，考生更能理解各類詞性，以及多益考題中出現的文法相關題型。請確認已掌握文法重點後，再接續下一章節。

多益是什麼呢？

　　TOEIC 是 Test of English for International Communication 的縮寫，為針對英語非母語人士的測驗，以語言中最主要的「溝通」為重點，評價出工作或是日常生活上所需的英文能力。考題主要為商業用，或是日常生活中的用法。

考題的出題領域與特徵

一般商務	契約、談判、行銷、銷售、商業企劃、會議
製造業	工廠管理、生產線、品管
金融／預算	銀行業務、投資、稅務、會計、帳單
企業發展	研究、產品研發
辦公室	董事會、委員會、信件、備忘錄、電話、傳真、電子郵件、辦公室器材與傢俱、辦公室流程、文字簡訊、即時通訊、多人互動線上聊天
人事	招考、雇用、退休、薪資、升遷、應徵與廣告
採購	比價、訂貨、送貨、發票
技術層面	電子、科技、電腦、實驗室與相關器材、技術規格
房屋／公司地產	建築、規格、購買租賃、電力瓦斯服務
旅遊	火車、飛機、計程車、巴士、船隻、渡輪、票務、時刻表、車站、機場廣播、租車、飯店、預訂、脫班與取消
外食	商務／非正式午餐、宴會、招待會、餐廳訂位
娛樂	電影、劇場、音樂、藝術、媒體
保健	醫藥保險、看醫生、牙醫、診所、醫院

　　多益中會避免出現適用於特定文化的考題，而同時，各個國家的名稱、地名都有可能出現在考題中。另外，美國、英國、加拿大、澳洲、紐西蘭的口音，也都有可能出現在聽力考題中。

多益題型架構

類型	Part	內容		題目數量	時間	配分
聽力測驗	1	照片描述		6	約45分鐘	495分
	2	應答問題		25		
	3	簡短對話		39	100題	
	4	簡短獨白		30		
閱讀測驗	5	句子填空（文法／字彙）		30	75分鐘	495分
	6	段落填空		16		
	7	閱讀	單篇	29	100題	
			多篇	25		
Total	7 Parts			200	約120分鐘	990分

考試時程

時間	行程內容
9:30～9:45	分發答案用紙並進行考試說明
9:45～9:50	休息時間
9:50～10:05	第一次身分證檢查
10:05～10:10	分發考題紙並確認是否有破損或缺頁
10:10～10:55	進行聽力測驗
10:55～12:10	進行閱讀測驗（第二次身分證檢查）

＊上表僅供參考，實際時程依多益考場規則而定。

多益報名方式

報名期間與報名方式：多益官方網站（www.toeic.com.tw）／**報名費用**：1,600 元
　　　　　　　網路報名、通訊報名、臨櫃報名、APP 報名／須附上照片

＊追加報名　　開放追加報名期間，只能透過網路報名，報名費用為 1,900 元。

考試準備注意事項

■合格身分證件　本國籍年滿 16 歲（含）以上之考生，僅限「中華民國國民身分證」正本或有效期限內之「護照」正本。未滿 16 歲之考生則可攜帶「健保 IC 卡」正本。若無身分證明則無法應試，請務必攜帶入場。

■文具　　　　　2B 鉛筆（推薦考生將筆尖削粗，比較方便使用。一般鉛筆或自動筆也可以，但原子筆是不能使用的）、橡皮擦都必須攜帶入場。

成績查詢與成績單寄送

在成績查詢開放期間可透過多益官方網站，或是使用 APP 來查詢多益成績。紙本成績單則會於測驗結束後 16 個工作日（不含假日）以平信方式寄出。若未收到成績單，可於測驗日起兩個月內致電多益測驗中心詢問，洽詢專線：(02)2701-7333。

Part 5 句子填空（30 題）

將正確的單字填入句子的空格中。題型主要為文法、詞形變化或是字彙。

考題範例

1. 文法相關

------- we need to do is contact our regular customers and let them know about the new refund policy.

(A) When　　(B) Where　　(C) What　　(D) That

翻譯　我們需要做的是聯絡我們的常客，告知他們新的退款政策。

解析　這是詢問連接兩個子句時，何者為最適當連接詞的題型。由於空格後的子句，是不具備受詞的不完整子句，因此應選擇同時可作為受詞以及連接詞的 What 為答案。　　**答案 (C)**

2. 詞形變化相關

------- are the results of the latest residents' survey on the proposed shopping mall construction project.

(A) Enclose　　(B) Enclosed　　(C) Enclosure　　(D) Enclosing

翻譯　隨信附上居民們對於提出的購物中心建案，最新的問卷調查結果。

解析　be 動詞前方，一般來說是主詞的位置，很容易將名詞 Enclosure 視為答案。但實際上 be 動詞後方的 the results 才是本題中的主詞，因此本題應選擇主詞補語 enclosed，意思為「隨信附上的問卷調查結果」。總結來說，如果一個很長的主詞移動到後方，便可將本句視為倒裝句，出現 enclose、attach 以及 include 時，須注意是否為以過去分詞形態出現的倒裝句。　　**答案 (B)**

3. 字彙相關

Bain Management Systems, one of the global management consulting firms, ------- new personnel polices on hiring last month.

(A) performed　　(B) implemented　　(C) achieved　　(D) convinced

翻譯　全球性管理顧問公司之一的 Bain Management Systems，上個月針對人才招募實施了新的人事方針。

解析　此題主旨在詢問適合填入空格的動詞。而空格後連接的是 new personnel policy（新人事方針），因此應選擇 implemented（實施）。　　**答案 (B)**

Part 6 段落填空（16 題）

　　與 Part 5 相同，都是選出適合填入空格的選項。差別在於，Part 6 的問題是安插在一整段文章中。另外，將適合的句子放入文章的空格中，也是 Part 6 獨有的題型。

考題範例

Questions 135-138 refer to the following announcement.

Rodrigo Seria Exhibition

------- on May 15, the Bledgile Gallery will be exhibiting a selection of
135.
paintings by Rodrigo Seria. The exhibit will showcase Seria's recent series of portraits and also provide an overview of his earlier works. The exhibit is ------- by loans from the artist, the Veril Foundation, and the
136.
Metro Art Museum. -------. Discussions with the curator will be held
137.
every Thursday evening, with topics ranging from Seria's inspiration to the recent spotlight on Latin American art. The exhibit will run -------
138.
June 29 and will be located on the first floor of the gallery on Rumdau Street.

---

135. (A) Started
(B) Starting
(C) Starter
(D) Start

136. (A) contacted
(B) nominated
(C) supported
(D) proposed

137. (A) A book featuring Seria's portraits will be available for sale at the gallery.
(B) The Bledgile Gallery building was previously a French restaurant.
(C) The gallery's exhibit that attracted the most attention this year was Andy Vardy's.
(D) Mr. Gagliardi, the gallery's curator, is new to the style of Rodrigo Seria.

138. (A) by
(B) on
(C) after
(D) until

Rodrigo Seria 展覽

5 月 15 日起，Bledgile 畫廊將展示一系列 Rodrigo Seria 的畫作。此次展覽將會展出 Seria 新的人像畫系列，以及早期作品一覽。本次展覽作品由畫家自己、Veril 財團以及 Metro Art 博物館所贊助。<u>Seria 新的人像畫系列書籍，將在畫廊中販售。</u>每週四晚上皆會舉辦策展人的座談會，囊括了從 Seria 的創作靈感，一直到近期受注目的拉丁美洲藝術等主題。展期至 6 月 29 日為止，地點位於 Rumdau 路的畫廊一樓。

---

135. 詞形變化－分詞

解析　常見的「從～（日期）開始」的用法中，其中有個句型是「starting (from) ＋日期」，因此此題答案為 (B)。　　　　　　　　　　　　　　**答案 (B)**

136. 字彙－動詞

解析　空格中的選項皆以被動語態（be 動詞＋ p.p.）出現，此時，將選項轉為主動語態，比較易於理解。因此，帶入 (C) 後變成「Loans support the exhibit~」，比較符合上下文意。另外，(A) 的主詞與受詞應為「人物／公司／機關」，(B) 則應是「人物／作品」，而 (D) 的主詞必須是人物，因此這三個選項都不適合。
　　　　　　　　　　　　　　　　　　　　　　　　　　　　　　答案 (C)

137. 從上下文意，找出適合句子

解析　空格前後的句子，都與 Rodrigo Seria 的展覽有關，因此空格內的內容，也不會相去甚遠，因此 (A) 為最適合的答案。　　　　　　　　　**答案 (A)**

(A) Seria 新的人像畫系列書籍，將在畫廊中販售。

(B) Bledgile 畫廊建築物的前身，為一間法式餐廳。

(C) 今年最受矚目的畫廊展覽是 Andy Vardy 的展覽。

(D) 畫廊策展人 Gagliardi 先生並不熟悉 Rodrigo Seria 的風格。

138. 文法－介系詞

解析　空格後方接續的是 6 月 29 日，考慮到前方的動詞 run（跑、經營、運行），可解讀為展覽最終日的日期，因此應選擇有「到～為止」意義的選項。符合此意涵的選項有 (A) 跟 (D)。如果搭配的是 run、stay、continue、keep 這類有延續性的動詞，必須使用 until；而 finish、complete、break、arrive 這類終止的動詞，則使用 by。因此此題應選擇 (D)。　　　　　　　　　　**答案 (D)**

Part 7 單篇及多篇閱讀（54 題）

　　此題型須先閱讀完一篇 e-mail、報導、廣告、訊息對話、公告等文章後，再進行答題。文章種類與問題類型如下。

1. 文章種類

1) **單篇閱讀**：針對 1 篇文章內容，提出 2～4 個相關問題，共有 29 題。
2) **雙篇閱讀**：針對 2 篇文章內容，提出 5 個相關問題，共有 10 題。
3) **三篇閱讀**：針對 3 篇文章內容，提出 5 個相關問題，共有 15 題。

2. 問題類型

1) **找出主旨**：詢問文章的目的或是意圖。

   ex) Why was the e-mail sent? 寄此封 e-mail 的原因？

2) **文章細節**：針對文章內容細節做詢問。

   ex) Who has to pay for the ordered items? 誰必須支付此筆訂單？

   ex) When did Ms. Taylor make her purchase? Taylor 小姐是什麼時候購買的？

3) **類推、推論**：文章中並沒有直接提及，而是透過各種狀況推論出來。

   ex) According to the e-mail, who most likely is Mr. Brian?
   根據 e-mail，誰最有可能是 Brian 先生？

4) **事實掌握**：根據文章提到的部分，詢問事實內容。

   ex) What is mentioned about the meeting? 關於會議，下列哪個情況有被提及？

5) **同義詞**：選出與文章中某特定單詞相似意義的選項。

   ex) The word "contribution" in paragraph 2, line 2 is closest in meaning to
   與第二段第二行中「contribution」意思相近的單字是？

6) **要求、提案**：詢問提出的要求或是提案為何。

   ex) What is Mr. Hong asked to do? 洪先生被要求做什麼？

7) **掌握意圖**：詢問特定文句中，所蘊含的意義。

   ex) At 2:21 P.M., what does Ms. Jane mean when she writes, "I'll find out."?
   下午 2:21，Jane 太太寫下了「I'll find out」，是什麼意思？

8) **句子置入**：為問題中提供的句子，找出其最適合放置的位置。

   ex) In which of the positions marked [1], [2], [3], and [4] does the following sentence best belong? 在標示 [1]、[2]、[3]、[4] 的地方，哪處最適合放入下列句子？

   "The yacht was renovated to reflect the iconic Lamada Hotel's facilities and service." 「帆船被予以改造，以體現出象徵 Lamada 飯店的設施與服務。」

|第一冊|攻略本

PART 5&6 GRAMMAR

類型分析 1　五大基本句型

類型分析 2　名詞

類型分析 3　動詞

類型分析 4　時態

類型分析 5　形容詞

PART 6　從屬連接詞&
填入正確句子

PART 7 閱讀文章類型分析

| 第二冊 | 解析本

8 週進度表（一週 5 天，總共 40 天）

　　此進度表推薦給初次準備多益，或是已經考過多益，分數在 300 分上下，想要仔細地、認真準備的考生們。這是針對那些不熟悉多益考題常見用法，以及幾乎無法了解題目意思的人所設計的進度表。此外，如果覺得本書難易度偏高，請按照下列進度表學習，兩個月內便可讀完本書，並且累積多益的基礎能力。

	Day 1	Day 2	Day 3	Day 4	Day 5
第 1 週	UNIT 01 - 02 UNIT 73	UNIT 03 - 04 UNIT 73	UNIT 05 - 06 UNIT 74	UNIT 07 -08 UNIT 74	UNIT 09 - 10 UNIT 75
	Day 6	Day 7	Day 8	Day 9	Day 10
第 2 週	UNIT 11 - 12 UNIT 75	UNIT 13 - 14 UNIT 76	UNIT 15 - 16 UNIT 76	UNIT 17 - 18 UNIT 77	UNIT 19 - 20 UNIT 77
	Day 11	Day 12	Day 13	Day 14	Day 15
第 3 週	UNIT 21 - 22 UNIT 78	UNIT 23 - 24 UNIT 78	UNIT 25 - 26 UNIT 79	UNIT 27 - 28 UNIT 79	UNIT 29 - 30 UNIT 80
	Day 16	Day 17	Day 18	Day 19	Day 20
第 4 週	UNIT 31 - 32 UNIT 80	UNIT 33 - 34 UNIT 81	UNIT 35 - 36 UNIT 81	UNIT 37 -38 UNIT 82	UNIT 39 - 40 UNIT 82
	Day 21	Day 22	Day 23	Day 24	Day 25
第 5 週	UNIT 41 - 42 UNIT 83	UNIT 43 - 44 UNIT 83	UNIT 45 - 46 UNIT 84	UNIT 47 -48 UNIT 84	UNIT 49 - 50 UNIT 85
	Day 26	Day 27	Day 28	Day 29	Day 30
第 6 週	UNIT 51 - 52 UNIT 85	UNIT 53 - 54 UNIT 86	UNIT 55 - 56 UNIT 86	UNIT 57 -58 UNIT 87	UNIT 59 - 60 UNIT 87
	Day 31	Day 32	Day 33	Day 34	Day 35
第 7 週	UNIT 61 - 62 UNIT 88	UNIT 63 - 64 UNIT 88	UNIT 65 - 66 UNIT 89	UNIT 67 -68 UNIT 89	UNIT 69 - 70 UNIT 90
	Day 36	Day 37	Day 38	Day 39	Day 40
第 8 週	UNIT 71 - 72 UNIT 90	複習（01 - 18） UNIT 91	複習（19 - 36） UNIT 91	複習（37 - 54） UNIT 92	複習（55 - 72） UNIT 93

4 週進度表（一週 5 天，總共 20 天）

　　推薦給曾準備過多益卻中途放棄的人，或是多益分數在 400 ～ 500 分之間的考生。這是針對那些稍微熟悉多益考題常見用法的人所設計的進度表。此外，如果覺得本書難易度與自身能力相差不遠，請按照下列進度表學習，可於四週內讀完本書，並培養解題能力。

	Day 1	Day 2	Day 3	Day 4	Day 5
第 1 週	UNIT 01 - 04 UNIT 73	UNIT 05 - 08 UNIT 74	UNIT 09 - 12 UNIT 75	UNIT 13 - 16 UNIT 76	UNIT 17 - 20 UNIT 77
	Day 6	**Day 7**	**Day 8**	**Day 9**	**Day 10**
第 2 週	UNIT 21 - 24 UNIT 78	UNIT 25 - 28 UNIT 79	UNIT 29 - 32 UNIT 80	UNIT 33 - 36 UNIT 81	UNIT 37 - 40 UNIT 82
	Day 11	**Day 12**	**Day 13**	**Day 14**	**Day 15**
第 3 週	UNIT 41 - 44 UNIT 83	UNIT 45 - 48 UNIT 84	UNIT 49 - 52 UNIT 85	UNIT 53 - 56 UNIT 86	UNIT 57 - 60 UNIT 87
	Day 16	**Day 17**	**Day 18**	**Day 19**	**Day 20**
第 4 週	UNIT 61 - 64 UNIT 88	UNIT 65 - 68 UNIT 89	UNIT 69 - 72 UNIT 90	複習（1 - 36） UNIT 91	複習（37 - 72） UNIT 92 - 93

PART
5&6

GRAMMAR

類型分析

1

五大基本句型

根據動詞的不同，完成一個句子的組成要素也會有所不同。根據組成句子的要素，將句子分類，便是接下來要提到的基本句型。在英文中，大致上可以將句型分成五類。

WARMING UP

1) 句子的主要元素：主詞、動詞、受詞、補語

各個單字組成句子的同時，有各自扮演的角色。句子的主要元素如下：

句子要素	意思	相關詞性	例句
主詞	作為句子的主體	名詞、代名詞	They are students. 他們是學生。
動詞	表示主詞的行為或是狀態	be 動詞、一般動詞	I study English. 我學英文。
受詞	作為主詞行為的對象	名詞、代名詞	He has a car. 他有車。
補語	補充說明主詞	名詞、代名詞、形容詞	He became an engineer. 他當上了工程師。

2) 句子的附加元素：修飾語

用來修飾句子中主要元素的主詞、受詞、動詞的話語，就稱為修飾語。修飾語可能是副詞或是介系詞片語等等，用來將句子描述地更加詳細，適用於任何句型。

修飾語	功用
副詞	Tom runs fast.（副詞 fast，便是用來修飾動詞 run。）
介系詞片語（介系詞＋名詞）	Linda lives in Canada.（介系詞片語 in Canada 是用來修飾動詞 live。）

3) 五大基本句型

英文的句子，根據句子主要元素的排列組合，基本有以下五大句型。

① 第一種句型：主詞（S）＋完全不及物動詞（V）

只利用主詞與動詞，表達最簡潔語義的句型。

ex) I work. 我工作。
　　主詞 動詞

② 第二種句型：主詞（S）＋動詞（V）＋補語（C）

只靠主詞與動詞無法完整表達，必須依靠補語來完善語義的句型。

ex) He is a doctor. 他是名醫生。
　　主詞 動詞　補語

③ 第三種句型：主詞（S）＋完全及物動詞（V）＋受詞（O）

只靠主詞與動詞無法完整表達，必須加上動詞的目標對象，才能完善語義的句型。

ex) Mike loves his family. Mike 愛他的家人。
　　主詞　動詞　　受詞

④ 第四種句型：主詞（S）＋授與動詞（O）＋間接受詞（I.O）＋直接受詞（D.O）

因動詞表達的意思，必須要有「間接受詞（對象）」跟「直接受詞（事物）」才能完善語義的句型。

ex) I gave his wife some money. 我給他太太一些錢。
　　主詞 動詞　間接受詞　　直接受詞

⑤ 第五種句型：主詞（S）＋不完全及物動詞（V）＋受詞（O）＋受詞補語（O.C）

對受詞補充描述，以完成句子的句型。此處的受詞補語，必須為（代）名詞、不定詞、形容詞，或是分詞。

ex) He made his family happy. 他使家人幸福。
　　主詞　動詞　　受詞　受詞補語

02 暖身例題

請試著寫出各句子的句型分類，並將標示出的單字在句中的元素名稱，寫在下方括號中。

1　Tom came into the office.
　　（ 主詞 ）（ 動詞 ）　　　　　　　　　　　　　　　　第 **1** 種句型

2　Mr. Medvedev is sincere.
　　（　　　）　（　　）（　　　）　　　　　　　　　第　種句型

3　He has made a significant contribution to the program.
　　　　　　　　　（　　　　　　　）　　　　　　　　第　種句型

4　You must give me your comments.
　　（　　　）（　　）（　　）　　　　　　　　　　第　種句型

5　We considered him a manager.
　　（　　　）（　　）（　　）　　　　　　　　　　第　種句型

03 例題解答

1　Tom came into the office. Tom 進到了辦公室。
　　主詞　動詞　　介系詞片語

▶ 此句型中的基本架構為「主詞＋動詞」，因此是第一種句型。動詞 came 是不及物動詞，不及物動詞後方常接續介系詞片語（into the office）或是副詞。

2　Mr. Medvedev is sincere. Medvedev 先生是真誠的。
　　　　主詞　　　動詞　補語

▶ 此句型中的基本架構為「主詞＋動詞＋補語」，因此是第二種句型。be 動詞 is，必須要跟補充說明主詞（Mr. Medvedev）的補語（sincere）同時使用。

3　He has made a significant contribution to the program. 他對這個計畫有非常大的貢獻。
　　主詞　　動詞　　　　　受詞　　　　　　介系詞片語

▶ 此句型中的基本架構為「主詞＋動詞＋受詞」，因此是第三種句型。本句包含了基本的名詞（contribution）、代名詞（He），以及用來補充的形容詞（significant）、介系詞（to）等，第三種句型中可能出現的所有元素。

4　You must give me your comments. 你必須給我你的評論。
　　主詞　　動詞　間接受詞　　直接受詞

▶ 此句型的基本架構為「主詞＋動詞＋間接受詞＋直接受詞」，因此是第四種句型。及物動詞中，有一個類型的動詞同時擁有兩個受詞，這些動詞剛好都有給予的意義，因此又被稱為授與動詞。

5　We considered him a manager. 我們視他為經理。
　　主詞　　動詞　　受詞　受詞補語

▶ 此句型中的基本架構為「主詞＋動詞＋受詞＋受詞補語」，因此是第五種句型。此時受詞與受詞補語間的關係，等同於主詞與述語。

Unit 01　五大基本句型 ── 句型 1

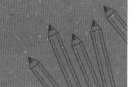

Step 1 | 實戰重點

解題策略　　介系詞片語或是副詞前方的空格,請選擇不及物動詞。

🎓 代表題型

All of the employees ------- in the latest protest against lowering the minimum wage.

(A) attended　　　　(B) informed　　　　(C) hosted　　　　(D) participated

✏️ 攻略解題法

All of the employees ------- (in the latest protest) (against lowering the minimum wage).
　　　主詞　　　　　　　　　　介系詞片語　　　　　　　　　介系詞片語

及物動詞　　及物動詞　　及物動詞　　不及物動詞

(A) attended　(B) informed　(C) hosted　(D) participated
　　參加　　　　通知　　　　主辦　　　　參加
　　　　　　　　　　　　　　　　　　participate in 參加～

文句分析　　一個句子中至少須具備主詞與動詞。題目中的主詞為 All of the employees,卻沒有動詞,由此可見空格中應填入動詞。大家可以將「participate in ＋名詞」這個用法記下來,意思是「參加～」。另外,空格後方的介系詞片語,並非構成句子的主要元素。

說明　　　　解題時,若有兩個類似或是相同語義的動詞,必須鎖定該兩個選項來解題。本題選項中,有三個是及物動詞,只有一個是不及物動詞。本題目標在於判斷空格後方是否有受詞,若無,選擇不及物;若有,選擇及物。因此,我們可以看到空格後方接的是介系詞片語(in the latest protest),所以要選擇不及物動詞 (D) participated。作為參考,請記住,擁有相同語義的 attend 為及物動詞。

翻譯　　　　所有員工都參加了最近那場反對調降最低薪資的抗議。

單字片語　　latest 最近／ protest 抗議／ minimum wage 最低薪資

解答　　　　(D)

✐ **攻略 POINT**

第一種句型的動詞後方,接續的是副詞或是介系詞片語。

核心理論

句型 1 由主詞與動詞組成的完整句型，後方可能會接續介系詞片語或是副詞。

He works **at the company**. 他在公司上班。

He works **hard**. 他認真工作。

請記住下列常用的不及物動詞與介系詞組合。

account for 解釋～	object to 反對～
depend on 依據～	focus on 集中於～
refer to 根據～	respond to 回應～
wait for 等待～	consist of 由～組成
participate in 參加～	specialize in 專精於～

An unexpected argument between two colleagues **happened** in our department.

我們部門中，兩個同事間發生了意料之外的爭吵。

▶ 介系詞片語（in our department）前方是不及物動詞。

Our company's annual profits **declined** significantly last year.

我們公司去年的年度營業額明顯地減少。

▶ 副詞（significantly）前方，是不及物動詞（decline）。

▶ 在多益考題中，句型 1 中最常出現的不及物動詞有「go 前往、come 來、work 工作、happen 發生、arrive 抵達、disappear 消失、proceed 繼續進行、fall 落下、rise 升起、function 運行、deteriorate 惡化、decline 減少」等動詞。

Mr. Martin **participated** in the company's professional development seminar.

Martin 先生參加了公司的專業發展講座。

▶ 部分的不及物動詞，如同「participate in 參加～」，必須配合固定介系詞來記。另外，也建議同時記住及物動詞中有相同語義的 attend。

Step 3 | 實戰演練

1 The success of a restaurant -------- on the food, experience, price, and location.

  (A) provides   (B) depends   (C) implies   (D) includes

2 Not all employees are satisfied because some think some of the women will not ------- competently under the new male-centered company policy.

  (A) request   (B) support   (C) release   (D) function

▶答案與解析請參考解析本第 4 頁

Unit 02　五大基本句型 ── 句型 2

解題策略　　句型 2 中的動詞後方，接續的是名詞或形容詞。

 代表題型

> The company is largely ------- for educating and training its employees to develop their skills.
>
> (A) responsible　　(B) response　　(C) responsibility　　(D) respond

 攻略解題法

修飾

The company is largely ------- (for educating and training its employees)
　主詞　　動詞　副詞　補語　　　　　　　　介系詞片語

to develop their skills.　　　副詞只用來修飾動詞與形容詞
　to 不定詞（作副詞）

respond to 回應～

(A) responsible　　(B) response　　(C) responsibility　　(D) respond
　　形容詞　　　　　　名詞　　　　　　　名詞　　　　　　　動詞

文句分析　　「be responsible for + 名詞」的意思是「對～有責任／負責～」，這個用法可以記下來。而 to 不定詞（to develop），譯成中文為「為了～」，等同於副詞的角色。

說明　　　　空格前後的副詞（largely）常常是陷阱，因此請先刪去再解題。be 動詞後方連接的是補語，補語通常是形容詞或是名詞，但通常多益考題中都不大會出現補語為名詞的情況，除非出現的是同位語。由於 be 動詞後方須為形容詞，因此 (A) 為正確解答。

翻譯　　　　公司主要負責教育、訓練員工，以提升他們的工作能力。

單字片語　　largely 主要／ develop 發展

解答　　　　(A)

攻略 POINT

be 動詞後方接續的是形容詞。

核心理論

> **句型 2** 句型為「A ＋動詞（包含 be 動詞）＋ B」，B 主要為形容詞。
>
> He became **smart**. 他變得聰明。
>
> She is **happy**. 她很開心。
>
> **句型 2 中常見的動詞**
>
> | | |
> |---|---|
> | ❶ 是～ | be 動詞＋補語 |
> | ❷ 變成／變得～ | become、get、grow、go、turn、run ＋補語 |
> | ❸ 似乎～ | seem、appear ＋補語 |
> | ❹ 仍然／維持～ | remain、stay ＋補語 |
> | ❺ 感覺起來／看起來／聽起來～ | feel、look、sound ＋補語 |

Your account information <u>is</u> **available** online, so you can access it now.

您的帳戶資料已經上線，您現在可以前往確認。

▶ be 動詞後方連接形容詞（available）。此外，online（線上的）在此句中為副詞。

The company executives expect it to <u>become</u> **profitable** within three years.

公司的管理階層預期公司在三年內可以由虧轉盈。

▶ become 後方，連接的是形容詞（profitable）。

The building <u>remained</u> **unoccupied** during the construction period.

施工期間，大樓維持淨空狀態。

▶ remain 後方為形容詞（unoccupied）。

Sonoma Company <u>is</u> a leading **manufacturer** of commercial kitchen appliances.

Sonoma 公司是商業用廚具製造商的領頭羊。

▶ be 動詞後方也可以接續名詞（manufacturer）。（Sonoma Company = a leading manufacturer）

Step 3 | 實戰演練

1 The company held the charity event, which was extremely ------- thanks to the substantial contributions that were made.

(A) successfully　　(B) succession　　(C) success　　(D) successful

2 After the factory in China was finally completed after a long period of construction, the production line became fully -------.

(A) operational　　(B) operation　　(C) operationally　　(D) operating

▶答案與解析請參考解析本第 4 頁

Unit 03 五大基本句型 — 句型 3

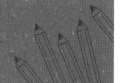

Step 1 | 實戰重點

解題策略　受詞前方的空格，不可接續不及物動詞，而必須連接及物動詞。

🎓 代表題型

All of the staff members ------- the auditorium to hear the announcement concerning the next year.

(A) looked　　　(B) prospected　　　(C) reached　　　(D) arrived

✏️ 攻略解題法

All of the staff members ------- the auditorium to hear the announcement
　　主詞　　　　　　　　　動詞　動詞（reached）的受詞　　to 不定詞（作副詞用，為了～）
concerning the next year.
　　介系詞片語

> 到 auditorium 為完整句，本段為修飾語

　　　　　　　　　　　　　　　　　　　及物動詞　　　　不及物動詞

(A) looked　　　(B) prospected　　　(C) reached　　　(D) arrived
　　看　　　　　　　　查探　　　　　　　觸及、到達　　　　　到達

文句分析　在完整句子「主語（All of the staff members）＋動詞（reached）＋受詞（the auditorium）」後方連接的 to 不定詞，在此作副詞用，表目標（為了～）。

說明　　　當題目中出現兩個意義相似的選項時，解題時請將兩個視為一組，其中必定有一方為不及物，而另一方為及物動詞。若空格後方有受詞，選擇及物動詞；若無，則選擇不及物動詞，為此題型的目的。因此我們可以得知，本題須在及物動詞 (C) 與不及物動詞 (D) 中二選一。空格後方連接受詞（the auditorium），因此本題答案為及物動詞 (C) reached。arrive 常與 at 或是 in 一起使用，(A) 則是後方須連接介系詞片語的不及物動詞，同時意義也與文句不符，(B) 也一樣與語意不合。

翻譯　　　全體工作人員來到了禮堂，為了聽明年年度的相關宣布。

解答　　　(C)

> **攻略 POINT**
>
> 若選項中出現兩個相似語義的動詞選項，必定有一個為不及物動詞，而另一個為及物動詞。本題型便是要考生選出及物動詞的選項。

核心理論

容易被誤認為不及物動詞的及物動詞

及物動詞	意思	注意事項
approach	接近～	不會與任何介系詞或是 to 一起使用
access	接近～	不會與任何介系詞或是 to 一起使用
mention	提及～	不會與任何介系詞或是 about 一起使用
discuss	討論～	不會與任何介系詞或是 about 一起使用
attend	出席～	不會與任何介系詞或是 in / into 一起使用
enter	進入～	不會與任何介系詞或是 in / into 一起使用
contact	聯絡～	不會與任何介系詞或是 to / with 一起使用

If you have any questions about our products, please **contact** me.
若您對我們的產品有任何疑問，請與我聯繫。

▶ 受格代名詞（me）前方應為及物動詞（contact）。

The personnel manager is going to **attend** the meeting on Wednesday.
人事部經理將出席星期三的會議。

▶ 名詞受詞（meeting）前方應為及物動詞（attend）。

All employees should **follow** the safety regulations while on duty.
所有的員工在上班時，都應遵循安全法規。

▶ 複合名詞受詞（the safety regulation）前方應為及物動詞（follow）。

The company **announced** that its sales revenue rose considerably.
公司宣布營業額大幅度地成長。

▶ 名詞子句（that）作為受詞時，前方須連接及物動詞（announced）。名詞子句可用來當作受詞。

Step 3 　**實戰演練**

1 The hotel will ------- them with a banquet hall, free drinks, and telephone service for the meeting tomorrow.

(A) function　　　(B) wait　　　(C) comply　　　(D) provide

2 According to the most recent financial report, reducing the employees' salaries will not ------- the problem concerning the company's deficit.

(A) deal　　　(B) address　　　(C) follow　　　(D) participate

▶答案與解析請參考解析本第 4 頁

Unit 04 五大基本句型 — 句型 4

Step 1 | 實戰重點

解題策略　在「對象（間接受詞）＋事物（直接受詞）」的前方空格，須填入句型 4 的動詞。

🎓 代表題型

All candidates must directly ------- the human resources manager their applications or send them by e-mail.

(A) sell　　　　　(B) supply　　　　　(C) give　　　　　(D) manage

✏️ 攻略解題法

　　　　　　　　　　　修飾
All candidates must directly ------- the human resources manager their applications
主詞（複數）　助動詞　　　原形動詞　　　間接受詞（對象）　　　　直接受詞（事物）
or send them by e-mail.
　動詞　受詞　　介系詞片語
對等連接詞

> manage to 勉強應付～

(A) sell　　　　　(B) supply　　　　　(C) give　　　　　(D) manage
句型 3、4 常見動詞　句型 3 常見動詞　　句型 4 常見動詞　　句型 3 常見動詞

文句分析　句型 4 中的授與動詞（give），後方必須接續「間接受詞（the human resources manager）＋直接受詞（their applications）」。另外，子句（give the human resources manager their applications）與子句（send them）間，以對等連接詞（or）並列。

說明　　　句型 4 的授與動詞 give（給～），須搭配「間接受詞（對象）＋直接受詞（事物）」，反推回來，當題目中出現「間接受詞（對象）＋直接受詞（事物）」的組合時，便可得知空格中應為句型 4 的授與動詞，因此本題答案為 (C) give。請記住，句型 4 中的授與動詞，必須搭配「對象＋事物」兩個受詞一起使用。

翻譯　　　所有應徵者都必須直接將自己的申請表交給人資經理，或是以電子郵件寄送。

單字片語　candidate 應徵者，候選人／ directly 直接地／ application 應徵（文件），申請（書）

解答　　　(C)

📌 攻略 POINT

句型 4 中的授與動詞，必須搭配「對象＋事物」兩個受詞一起使用。

📖 核心理論

句型 4 的中文解釋為「動詞＋給某人（間接受詞）某事物（直接受詞）」。

句型 4 常見的動詞

give 給	offer 提供	send 寄送
grant 准予	award 頒發	issue 發行

連接 that 子句（名詞子句）的常見授與動詞

inform 某人 that S＋V	告知某人 S＋V 的事
notify 某人 that S＋V	通知某人 S＋V 的事
advise 某人 that S＋V	建議某人 S＋V 的事
remind 某人 that S＋V	提醒某人 S＋V 的事
assure 某人 that S＋V	向某人保證 S＋V 的事
convince 某人 that S＋V	說服某人 S＋V 的事

The company **gives** excellent employees bonus at the end of the year.

= The company **gives** bonus to excellent employees at the end of the year.

公司在年終時會給予優秀的員工額外獎勵。

▶ 句型 4 中 give、send、offer、show、award 等等的授與動詞後方，連接「對象＋事物」或是「事物＋ to ＋對象」的組合。

I am pleased to inform you that I am able to attend your party.

　　　　　　　　間接受詞　　　　　　直接受詞

很高興地告知你，我可以參加你的派對。

The manager reminded all workers that they should wear safety gear.

　　　　　　　　　間接受詞　　　　　直接受詞

經理提醒所有員工必須穿上安全裝備。

▶ 句型 4 中 inform、notify、remind、assure、convince、advise 等等的授與動詞後方，連接「對象＋ that（名詞子句）」。

1 Since I am not in my office right now, Victoria will ------- David the contracts soon.

(A) negotiate　　　(B) change　　　(C) proceed　　　(D) send

2 By Monday, I will be able to ------- the plans to you about the new brand launching.

(A) assign　　　(B) show　　　(C) apply　　　(D) commence

▶答案與解析請參考解析本第 4 頁

五大基本句型 — 句型 5

Step 1 ｜ **實戰重點**

解題策略　「受詞＋受詞補語」的前方空格，應為 make、keep、find、leave、consider 其中之一。

 代表題型

> Ms. Nelson ------- the conference room empty because she has heard from Fred.
>
> (A) prepared　　　　(B) appeared　　　　(C) found　　　　(D) supervised

✏️ 攻略解題法

Ms. Nelson ------- the conference room empty because she has heard from Fred.
主詞　　動詞　　動詞（found）的受詞　受詞補語　連接詞　主詞　動詞　介系詞片語

由於空格前方為主詞，後方
為名詞，可知空格為動詞

受詞補語
形容詞

hear from ＋某人
從某人聽來

(A) prepared　　　　(B) appeared　　　　(C) found　　　　(D) supervised
句型 3 常見動詞　　句型 1 常見動詞　　句型 5 常見動詞　　句型 3 常見動詞

文句分析　find 是句型 5 中常見動詞，後方須接續「受詞（the conference room）＋受詞補語（empty）」。

說明　句型 5 中常見的動詞 find，後方必定連接「受詞（the conference room）＋受詞補語（empty）」。若選項中出現句型 5 的動詞 make、find、keep、consider，同時空格後方又是「受詞＋受詞補語（形容詞或名詞）」的組合，那麼該空格必定填入句型 5 的動詞。由於本題空格後方為「受詞（the conference room）＋受詞補語（empty）」，可知答案為 (C) found。

翻譯　Nelson 女士得知會議室目前空著，因為她從 Fred 那邊聽來的。

單字片語　empty 空的

解答　(C)

📌 攻略 POINT

「受詞＋受詞補語」的組合前方須填入句型 5 的動詞。

核心理論

> 句型 5 的語義為「動詞＋受詞＋受詞補語」。
>
> > She made me happy.
> > 她　令　我　開心
> >
> > **句型 5 的常見動詞**
> > make、keep、find、leave、consider 等等

The president **found** the merger agreement successful.
社長發現合併協議非常成功。

▶ successful（成功的）是用來補充說明受詞「合併協議」，像本例句中出現了補充說明受詞的受詞補語，便可視為句型 5。

The manager told the employees to **keep** the project secret.
經理要求員工對計畫的事情保密。

▶ 句型 5 的動詞 make、keep、find、leave、consider 後方必定接續「受詞＋受詞補語」的組合。

The company **considers** him one of its top experts.
公司認為他是公司中最頂尖的專家之一。

▶ 句型 5 的動詞 make、keep、find、leave、consider 與「受詞（him）＋受詞補語（one of its top experts）」的組合一起出現，此時的受詞與受詞補語為對等關係。

1 Changes to financial markets have ------- investors even more dependent on quality information.

(A) taken　　　(B) worked　　　(C) needed　　　(D) made

2 The success that he has had in sales makes him ------- to his company.

(A) specialize　　　(B) special　　　(C) speciality　　　(D) specially

▶答案與解析請參考解析本第 5 頁

REVIEW TEST

1. The manager ------- the employees inspired to be sure that their organization is the best in the hospitality industry.
    (A) damages   (B) holds
    (C) expires   (D) keeps

2. Jenny ------- everyone a copy of the report, which she worked on all last week at the meeting.
    (A) gave   (B) forwarded
    (C) delayed   (D) distributed

3. We must hire more employees to serve at the hall before the customers become ------- with the slow service.
    (A) anger   (B) angry
    (C) angrily   (D) to anger

4. Located in the central part of Shanghai's old city, the Shanghai Tourism Board makes local history ------- to everyone.
    (A) accessible   (B) access
    (C) accessibly   (D) accesses

5. The company announced that it will ------- responsibility for any problems that occur when people use its products.
    (A) assume   (B) search
    (C) register   (D) hand

6. We will ------- last year's sales record to that of this year and discover the differences between the two of them in order to draw up a new plan.
    (A) offer   (B) convince
    (C) match   (D) allow

7. The responses on the questionnaires that the company used to get information about the new product it had created ------- from country to country.
    (A) varied   (B) improved
    (C) suggested   (D) advised

8. The company ------- the new uniform, which was made by a foreign designer, to all of its employees, and it received a positive response.
    (A) presented   (B) showed
    (C) noticed   (D) proposed

9. I would like to ------- you that the president of the international association is looking forward to the special presentation that you have prepared for the seminar.
    (A) speak   (B) announce
    (C) inform   (D) mention

10. We ------- in networks and software, and we train people to utilize the software.
    (A) predict   (B) agree
    (C) face   (D) specialize

▶答案與解析請參考解析本第 5 頁

類型分析 2

名詞

名詞專指用來稱呼人物或是事物名稱的詞性。通常名詞的後方會以 -sion、-tion、-ance、-ment 等作為字尾，另外，名詞在句子中的位置，不可被動詞、形容詞、副詞等取代。

WARMING UP

01 文法概念前導 ·············· 正式進入文法單元前，先熟悉一下文法基本概念。

1) 何謂名詞？
用來指稱某對象名稱的單字，便是名詞，這個「對象」不僅僅是人物、動物、事物，也包含了肉眼看不到、抽象的想法等等。在句子中擔任主詞、補語或是受詞的角色。

2) 名詞的種類
根據性質的不同，大致上可將名詞分成五大類型。

① 普通名詞：肉眼可見的人物、動物或是事物的名稱

ex) cat 貓／ hand 手／ fruit 水果／ desk 桌子

② 集合名詞：針對一群人或事物的集合體所賦予的稱呼

ex) police 警察／ furniture 傢俱／ family 家人／ class 班級

③ 專有名詞：人物或地區的名稱、星期等等，針對人物或事物的特定名稱，第一個字母通常為大寫

ex) Tom 湯姆／ Sunday 星期日／ Mt. Everest 聖母峰／ the Thames 泰晤士河

④ 抽象名詞：肉眼看不到，抽象事物的名稱

ex) love 愛／ conversation 對話／ courage 勇氣

⑤ 物質名稱：肉眼雖然可以看到，但卻無法一一細數的事物

ex) salt 鹽／ sugar 糖／ coffee 咖啡

3) 名詞在句子中可能扮演的角色
造句時，各個詞彙有其固定位置，而名詞在句子中，通常扮演主詞、受詞或是補語的角色。

① 作為主詞的情況

Production will be significantly increased next year. 生產量在明年將會顯著地增長。

② 放在及物動詞後方當受詞的情況

They can't handle the demands of all of the divisions. 他們沒有辦法處理所有部門的需求。

③ 放在介系詞後方當受詞的情況

You have the right qualifications for the job. 你擁有符合這份工作的資格條件。

④ 作為補語的情況

She is the right person for this position.　▶ 主格補語
她是這個職位的最佳人選。

The president considered Mr. James a competent employee.　▶ 受格補語
社長認為 James 先生是個很能幹的員工。

02 暖身例題

請圈選出括號中正確的名詞。

1 The (transact / transaction) between the UK and Japan has been approved.

2 The employee usually thoroughly follows his manager's (instructions / instruct).

3 The manager summarized the feedback from the (customers / customizing).

4 A persuasive (argue / argument) was made at the conference.

5 Our new products will be on (display / to display) for the next three weeks.

03 例題解答

1 The ~~transact~~ (between the UK and Japan) has been approved.
　　 transaction

英國與日本間的貿易已被批准。

▶ 空格後方連接動詞（has been approved），可推測出空格為主詞，而主詞詞性必須為名詞。字尾 -tion 為名詞字尾，加上主詞詞性不能是動詞（transact），因此必須選擇以 -tion 結尾的名詞 transaction。

2 The employee usually thoroughly follows his manager's ~~instruct~~.
　　　　　　　　　　　　　　　　　　　　　　　instructions

員工通常會徹底遵從他的經理所下的指令。

▶ 名詞可填入受詞位置，此句中 follow 的受詞，便是名詞 instructions。

3 The manager summarized the feedback from the ~~customizing~~.
　　　　　　　　　　　　　　　　　　　　　　 customers

經理總結了來自顧客們的評論。

▶ 介系詞（from）後方須接上名詞，因此本題應選擇 customers。

4 A persuasive ~~argue~~ was made at the conference.
　　　　　　　　 argument

會議上，做出了一個具有說服力的論點。

▶ 形容詞（persuasive）後方須連接名詞，因此本題需選擇有名詞詞尾（-ment）的 argument。

5 Our new products will be on ~~to display~~ for the next three weeks.
　　　　　　　　　　　　　　　　　 display

我們的新產品將會在接下來三週內進行展示。

▶ 名詞可以作為介系詞的受詞，因此本題介系詞 on 的後方須連接受詞 display。

Unit 06 名詞擺放的位置 ①

解題策略　若題目中的空格位於第一格，並且後方連接動詞時，表示該空格為主詞，須填入名詞；而空格若是位於及物動詞後方，也須選擇名詞作為受詞。

 代表題型

------- about the upcoming event at the conference center will be given to all employees.

(A) Inform　　　　(B) To informing　　　(C) Information　　　(D) Informed

📝 攻略解題法

　　　　　→ 介系詞　　　　　　　→ 介系詞
------- (about the upcoming event at the conference center) will be given
主詞　　　　　　　　修飾名詞（information）的介系詞片語　　　　　動詞（被動式）
(to all employees.)
　介系詞片語
→ 主詞位置只能填入名詞或是名詞子句

(A) Inform　　　　(B) To informing　　　(C) Information　　　(D) Informed
動詞　　　　　　　to ＋動詞　　　　　　名詞　　　　　　　動詞（過去式），過去分詞

文句分析　主詞（information）與動詞（will be given）間的介系詞片語（about the upcoming event at the conference center），以及動詞後方的介系詞片語（to all employees），全都作修飾用，並不影響語句架構。

說明　　　題目空格位於首字，並且後方接續動詞時，空格即為主詞的位置，而由於主詞詞性應為名詞，必須選擇名詞選項為答案，因此本題 (C) information 為正解。(A) 動詞、(B) to ＋動詞以及 (D) 動詞（過去分詞），皆不正確。另外，請記住，當題目句型構造為「------ ＋修飾語＋動詞」時，空格須填入名詞。

翻譯　　　即將在會議中心舉辦的活動相關情報，將會發放給所有員工。

單字片語　upcoming 即將到來的／ conference 會議／ employee 員工

解答　　　(C)

📌 攻略 POINT

當句型構造為「------ ＋修飾語＋動詞」時，空格須填入名詞。

Step 2 核心理論 & 基礎形式

核心理論

名詞可作為句子中的主詞、受詞以及補語。

> Many people enjoyed the show. (Many people = 主詞，the show = 受詞)
>
> Ms. Chastain is an accountant. (Ms. Chastain = 主詞，accountant = 受詞)
>
> 等同於名詞的名詞子句，有以下幾種形式：
> (1) 從屬連接詞引導的名詞子句　(2) to 不定詞　(3) 動名詞　(4) 代名詞

- **當主詞時**

A subscription (to the magazine, Childcare Service), is necessary.
　　主詞　　　　　　修飾語（介系詞片語）　　　　動詞

訂閱 Childcare Service 這本雜誌是必要的。
▶ 當句型構造為「------ ＋修飾語＋動詞」時，空格須填入名詞詞性的主詞。請記住，此時空格前方不會出現冠詞（a / the）。

- **當及物動詞的受詞時**

The manager explained the terms of the contract carefully.
　　　　　　動詞　　　　受詞

經理仔細地解釋合約條款。
▶「及物動詞＋ ------」的句型構造中，空格為受詞。

- **當主格的補語時**

Mr. Gorman is a technician to repair your fax machine.
　　主詞　　　　　補語

Gorman 先生是來修理你傳真機的技工。
▶ be / become 後方連接的是主詞的補語，唯有在與主詞為同位關係時，才能選擇名詞為主詞補語。

Step 3 實戰演練

1 Supervisors who want to register for the workshop should make ------- of the fees promptly.

(A) pays　　　　(B) payable　　　　(C) payably　　　　(D) payments

2 ------- to the Walk to Work campaign are honored, and the CEO will announce the employee of the year at the year-end dinner.

(A) Contribute　　(B) Contributions　　(C) Contributed　　(D) To contribution

▶答案與解析請參考解析本第 6 頁

Unit 07 名詞擺放的位置②

Step 1　實戰重點

解題策略　本題型解題重點為，冠詞、限定形容詞、分詞、所有格後方須接名詞。每次多益考試中，皆會有 2～3 題本題型。

 代表題型

One of the most important responsibilities for this position is to follow specific -------.

(A) instruct　　　　(B) instructions　　　(C) instructed　　　(D) instructing

 攻略解題法

One (of the most important responsibilities) (for this position) is to follow specific -------.
主詞　修飾代名詞（One）的介系詞片語　　介系詞片語　動詞　is 的補語（to 不定詞作名詞）
one（＋複數名詞）後方接續單數動詞

to 不定詞中也可有受詞
specific 是用來修飾名詞的形容詞

(A) instruct　　　　(B) instructions　　　(C) instructed　　　(D) instructing
動詞　　　　　　　名詞　　　　　　動詞（過去式），過去分詞　動名詞，現在分詞

文句分析　「One of the ＋複數名詞」作為主詞，表「～其中之一」，視為單數，因此使用單數動詞（is）。be 動詞後方的 to 不定詞，與主詞為同位關係，意思為「～其中之一做了～」。

說明　限定形容詞（specific）後方須接續名詞，這類題型每次都一定會出現，屬於不該犯錯的題型。但這類詢問句型結構，而非詢問語意的題型中，偶爾反而會出現很棘手的選項，請多注意。本題的限定形容詞（specific）後方空格，應選擇名詞 (B) instructions，其他選項為 (A) 動詞、(C) 過去分詞、(D) 現在分詞。

翻譯　這個工作最重要的一個職責是遵守明確的指令。

單字片語　responsibility 責任，職務／ follow 遵循，跟隨／ specific 明確的，特定的

解答　(B)

攻略 POINT

限定形容詞後方的空格，百分之百是名詞。

📖 **核心理論**

冠詞、限定形容詞、分詞、所有格等等後方必定接續名詞,請記住,本題型屬於每次都會出現的基本題。

名詞的位置

冠詞、限定形容詞、分詞、所有格、名詞　　+　　名詞

- a / the ＋**名詞**（＋介系詞）　The report is about the **importance** of teamwork.
  這份報告內容是關於團隊合作的重要性。

- 限定形容詞＋**名詞**　We can't avoid making a serious **decision**.
  我們無法避免去做一個重大的決定。

- 分詞＋**名詞**　Most of our clients prefer the finished **product**.
  我們大部分的客戶比較喜歡加工完畢的成品。

- 所有格＋**名詞**　His **explanation** was clear enough.
  他的解釋已經夠清楚了。

- 名詞＋**名詞**　We checked the safety **procedures** on the board.
  我們已經確認過公告欄上的安全操作程序。

▶ 題型重點在於有劃底線的 a / the、限定形容詞、分詞、所有格以及名詞,後方須接續名詞。這類題型中,冠詞（a / the）與限定形容詞每次考試都會出現,分詞與所有格則大約 1 年出 1 題,而在名詞後方空格填入名詞的複合名詞（名詞＋名詞）題型,則是 1 年約有 6 題。

以下為常出現在考題中,名詞後方接續名詞的複合名詞:

account information 帳戶資訊	delivery service 物流服務	insurance coverage 承保範圍
job announcement 徵才公告	job opportunity 工作機會	job performance 工作表現
keynote speaker 主講者	registration form 註冊表單	renovation plan 翻修計畫
safety precaution 預防措施	sales figure 銷售數字	work environment 工作環境

1 Until the employees get final ------- from the manager at the head office, they have to postpone the decision.

(A) approve　　　　(B) approving　　　　(C) approved　　　　(D) approval

2 Customer ------- with our service will be evaluated regularly by conducting surveys at both the restaurant and on the website.

(A) satisfied　　　　(B) satisfaction　　　　(C) satisfactory　　　　(D) satisfying

▶答案與解析請參考解析本第 6 頁

Unit 08 名詞的形態

解題策略　將詞性轉變為名詞的字尾有 -er、-or、-ant、-ent、-ist、-(a)tion、-ance、ence、-(e)ty、-ity、-ment、-(a)cy 等等。

 代表題型

If you have any further questions or need special -------, feel free to contact Mr. Davidson.

(A) assistance 　　(B) assists 　　(C) assisting 　　(D) assisted

 攻略解題法

If you have any further questions or need special -------, feel free to contact Mr. Davidson.
　主詞　動詞　　動詞（have）的受詞　　動詞　動詞（need）的受詞　　　動詞片語　　　動詞（contact）的受詞

將 any further questions 與 special ------ 連接起來的對等連接詞 or

連接詞

feel free to ＋動詞
隨意地去～

(A) assistance 　　(B) assists 　　(C) assisting 　　(D) assisted
　名詞　　　　　　　動詞　　　　動名詞，現在分詞　　動詞（過去式），過去分詞

文句分析　對等連接詞（or）將兩句動詞片語（have any further questions）與（need special assistance）連接起來。後方「逗號＋原形動詞（feel）」為命令語句，表示「請～」。

說明　　　限定形容詞後方須接續名詞，本題中的空格，出現在限定形容詞（special）後方，因此答案應選擇名詞。(A) 語尾為 -ance，可推測出 (A) assistance 為答案。而 (B) 動詞、(C) 現在分詞、(D) 過去式（分詞）因詞性錯誤，不可填入空格內。

翻譯　　　如果您有進一步的疑問，或需要任何特殊協助，請聯繫 Davidson 先生。

單字片語　further 追加的，進一步的／ feel free to 隨意地去～／ contact 聯絡

解答　　　(A)

攻略 POINT

請記住名詞型語尾，當選項出現不認識的單字時，可當作解題技巧。

核心理論

多益考題中，常出現的名詞語尾：

1. **人物**：-er、-ee、-or、-ant、-ent、-ist、-ive、-ary
   例 employer 雇主、employee 員工、investor 發明家、assistant 助手、artist 藝術家
   ▶ 語尾 -ant 與 -ive 也常見於形容詞語尾。

2. **行為、性質、狀態**：-ion、-(a)tion、-ance、-ence、-(e)ty、-ity、-(r)y、al、-ure、-ment、-ness、-(a)cy
   例 introduction 介紹、appearance 外表、ability 能力、discovery 發現、approval 許可、failure 失敗

3. **資格、特性**：-ship
   例 leadership 領導能力

4. **時期、關係**：-hood
   例 childhood 孩童時期、neighborhood 鄰居

5. **主義、特性**：-sm
   例 criticism 批判主義、enthusiasm 熱情

The **objective** of this project is to stimulate the local economy.
此計畫目的在於促進當地經濟。
▶ 冠詞（the）後方應接續名詞，因此本句中可填入以 -ive 名詞語尾作結的 objective。

We require all applicants to have at least 3 years' experience in **management**.
我們要求所有應徵者須具備至少三年的管理經驗。
▶ 介系詞（in）後方應接續名詞，因此本句中可填入以 -ment 名詞語尾作結的 management。

New employees took part in the orientation program with **enthusiasm**.
新進員工都帶著熱情參加了教育訓練。
▶ 介系詞（with）後方應接續名詞，因此本句中可填入以 -sm 名詞語尾作結的 enthusiasm。

Step **3** 實戰演練

1 Despite the sales representative's explanation, Alice couldn't see any ------- between the two models.

(A) differencing   (B) different   (C) differs   (D) difference

2 His ------- for the film has encouraged the young directors to dedicate themselves to their work.

(A) enthusiastic   (B) enthusiasm   (C) enthusiastically   (D) enthuse

▶答案與解析請參考解析本第 7 頁

Unit 09　區分可數 vs 不可數名詞

解題策略　當選項皆為名詞，且其中有兩者意思相近時，通常其一為可數名詞，另一為不可數名詞。解題時請先確認空格前方是否有不定冠詞（a / an），若有，選擇可數名詞；若無，則選不可數名詞。

🎓 **代表題型**

> To have ------- to the internet for free, guests should fill out the registration card.
>
> (A) approach　　　　(B) plan　　　　(C) access　　　　(D) standard

✏️ **攻略解題法**

> To have ------- (to the internet) (for free), guests should fill out the registration card.
> 不定詞 to have 的受詞　介系詞片語　介系詞片語　主詞　動詞　動詞（fill out）的受詞
>
> to 不定詞作副詞用　修飾語句　完整句子
> 表示「為了～」
>
> (A) approach　　　　(B) plan　　　　(C) access　　　　(D) standard
> 名詞　　　　　　　動詞、名詞　　　名詞　　　　　　名詞

文句分析　當 to 不定詞句子後方接續「逗號＋主詞＋動詞」時，to 不定詞作副詞用。to 不定詞當副詞使用並作為目的時，表示「為了～」。

說明　　　空格接在及物動詞後方，可推測該空格須填入名詞。若四個選項皆為名詞，且其中有兩個選項意思相近時，請記住通常其一為可數，另一為不可數。因此要先確認空格前方是否有不定冠詞（a / an），若有，選擇可數名詞；若無，則選不可數名詞。本題中 (A) 為可數名詞，(C) 為不可數名詞，而空格前方並無 a / an，可知答案為 (C) access。另外，可以接續後方介系詞 to 的選項，唯有 (C)。

翻譯　　　要連接免費網路，訪客必須先填寫註冊卡。

單字片語　for free 免費／ fill out 填寫

解答　　　(C)

 攻略 POINT

當選項皆為名詞，且其中有兩者意思相近時，通常是區分可數與不可數名詞的題型。

核心理論

請熟記如何選擇可數／不可數名詞的解題技巧。

多益考題中常出現的不可數名詞：

consent 同意	advice 建議	information 情報	approval 許可
plan 計劃	access 存取	luggage 行李	equipment 裝備
permission 許可	furniture 傢俱	notice 通知	purchase 購買

You must obtain ~~permit~~ from your supervisor.
　　　　　　　permission

你必須要得到上司的許可。

▶ 當選項的名詞中，有兩者意思相近或相同時，通常其一為可數，另一為不可數名詞。此時，須先確認空格前方是否有不定冠詞（a / an），若有，選擇可數名詞；若無，則選不可數名詞。本例題中，permit 與 permission 意思相同，但 permit 為可數名詞（許可證），permission 為不可數名詞（許可）。而本題名詞前方並無不定冠詞（a / an），因此須選擇不可數名詞 permission。

The city council approved a construction ~~plans~~.
　　　　　　　　　　　　　　　　　　plan

市議會已通過建設計劃案。

▶ 當選項中出現單數名詞與複數名詞時，須先確認空格前方是否有 a / an，若有，選擇單數名詞；若無，則選複數名詞，因為可數名詞前方必定會加上 a / an 或是加上複數形語尾 -s。然而，若是不可數名詞的情況下，則皆用單數形態。

1 If you are anxious about the security of your computer, please visit our website for more -------.

(A) information　　　(B) detail　　　(C) entrance　　　(D) management

2 We should consider ------- of up to 70% since our competitors have started an aggressive sales plan.

(A) discount　　　(B) discounts　　　(C) discounted　　　(D) discounting

▶答案與解析請參考解析本第 7 頁

Unit 10 其他常見於考題的名詞

解題策略　人物相關名詞皆為可數名詞,但事物相關名詞,可能是可數,也可能是不可數。然而多益考題中,大多使用不可數的事物相關名詞,因此解題時,空格前方若有 a / an,選擇人物相關名詞;若無,則選擇事物相關名詞。

 代表題型

Technicians in the warehouse are advised to report directly to an immediate -------.

(A) supervise　　　(B) supervision　　　(C) supervisor　　　(D) supervisory

攻略解題法

Technicians (in the warehouse) are advised to report directly (to an immediate -------.)

主詞　　修飾名詞(Technicians)　　動詞　　補語　　副詞　　介系詞片語
　　　　的介系詞片語

be advised to
被要求～

修飾

(A) supervise　　　(B) supervision　　　(C) supervisor　　　(D) supervisory
動詞　　　　　　　　名詞　　　　　　　　名詞　　　　　　　　形容詞

文句分析　advise 後面接續「受詞+ to 不定詞」,此處的 to 不定詞視為受詞補語。因為本句的受詞(Technicians)移到主詞的位置,因此被動式(are advised)後方才會直接接續 to 不定詞(to report)。因此,原句為 advise technicians to report,改為被動式後,變成 technicians are advised to report。

說明　雖然人物相關名詞皆為可數名詞,但事物相關名詞,可能是可數,也可能是不可數。因此解題時請先確認空格前方的 a / an,若有,選擇人物相關名詞;若無,則選擇事物相關名詞。形容詞(immediate)後方的空格須接續名詞,因此須在事物相關的 (C) 與人物相關的 (B) 選項中擇一。而形容詞(immediate)前方出現了 an,可推得本題答案為人物相關名詞 (C) supervisor。

翻譯　在倉庫中工作的技工們,被要求直接回報給直屬上司。

單字片語　technician 技工/ warehouse 倉庫/ be advised to 被要求～/ directly 直接,立刻/ immediate supervisor 直屬上司/ supervise 監管

解答　(C)

攻略 POINT

當選項中出現人物相關與事物相關名詞時,若空格前方有 a / an,選擇人物相關名詞;若無,則選擇事物相關名詞。

核心理論

> 請區分出人物與事物的相關名詞,並記住以下常見的複合名詞。
>
> **人物相關名詞與事物相關名詞**
>
> | | | | |
> |---|---|---|---|
> | employee 職員 | employment 僱用 | technician 技工 | technique 技術 |
> | supervisor 監督者 | supervision 監督 | consultant 顧問 | consultation 諮詢 |
> | accountant 會計師 | accounting 會計 | analyst 分析師 | analysis 分析 |
>
> **常見的複合名詞**
>
> | | |
> |---|---|
> | application form 申請書 | pay increase 加薪 |
> | performance appraisal 績效考核 | production facility 生產設施 |
> | customer satisfaction 顧客滿意度 | replacement part 備用零件 |

James Halt is now looking for a promising ~~employment~~ to work in the new division.
employee

James Halt 正在尋找有能力的員工加入新部門。

▶ 當選項中有人物相關名詞與事物相關名詞時,須先確認空格前方是否有 a / an,若有,選擇人物名詞;若無,則選事物名詞。而本題為「a promising +_____」,因此可知道空格內須填入人物名詞 employee。

We have not fully completed the production ~~facilitated~~ in China.
facility

我們在中國的生產設備還沒完全配置好。

▶ 把兩個不同意思的名詞結合起來,當作一個名詞使用,便稱之為「複合名詞」。通常空格會在名詞前方或後方出現,屬於比較複雜的題型。複合名詞的組成是「名詞 1 +名詞 2」,如果空格填入選項後,可解釋為「為了名詞 1 的名詞 2」或是「名詞 2(動作)名詞 1(受詞)」,便可判斷為複合名詞題型。

1 The latest report suggests that the new system has improved employee -------.

(A) produce   (B) produced   (C) producing   (D) productivity

2 The ------- at Femi Business Institute helped Burn Gorman improve his communication skills.

(A) instruct   (B) instructive   (C) instructors   (D) instruction

▶答案與解析請參考解析本第 7 頁

REVIEW TEST

1. Mr. Harris wanted to find a more persuasive ------- than the previous one to quickly finish the negotiations with the agency.

   (A) arguably   (B) argue
   (C) arguable   (D) argument

2. BST Guide assures you that our professional agents will take care of all the travel ------- that you request.

   (A) arrangements   (B) arrange
   (C) arranging   (D) arranged

3. The head chef will make ------- in the menu after he develops new vegetarian dishes which customers have requested for a few months.

   (A) changing   (B) changes
   (C) changed   (D) change

4. Jessica noticed that a defective ------- had been delivered, so she had to find the receipt in order to exchange it.

   (A) product   (B) products
   (C) produced   (D) productive

5. The instructions on the bulletin board explain how to leave ------- about the project online.

   (A) suggestions   (B) suggesting
   (C) suggest   (D) suggested

6. Judge Judy, a famous American TV show, provides viewers with opportunities to hear specific ------- from lawyers.

   (A) cost   (B) hint
   (C) advice   (D) procedure

7. The ------- of Australia has been growing extremely fast due to the increasing number of immigrants.

   (A) population   (B) populate
   (C) popular   (D) popularly

8. For further -------, it is advisable for accounting clerks to duplicate some important documents when filing them.

   (A) refer   (B) reference
   (C) referred   (D) referencing

9. ------- for the secretary position have to be submitted by next week.

   (A) Applying   (B) Applied
   (C) Applications   (D) Applies

10. It is mandatory for staff members to receive ------- covered by the company for any injuries they suffer at work.

    (A) compensate   (B) compensating
    (C) compensated   (D) compensation

▶ 答案與解析請參考解析本第 7 頁

類型分析 3

動詞

主詞動詞一致性，指的是主詞與動詞間的單複數形態，須達到
一致性。

WARMING UP

1) 主詞動詞一致性

主詞若為單數，則動詞為單數動詞；主詞若為複數，則動詞也須使用複數動詞。像這樣配合主詞的單複數形態，使動詞與主詞的單複數達到一致性，便稱為「主詞動詞一致性」。

① be 動詞的主詞動詞一致性

主詞	時態	單數	複數	時態	單數	複數
第一人稱		am			was	
第二人稱	現在式	are	are	過去式	were	were
第三人稱		is			was	

Tom is our new manager. Tom 是我們新的經理。
We are working together. 我們一起工作。

② have 動詞的主詞動詞一致性

主詞	時態	單數	複數	時態	單數	複數
第一人稱		have				
第二人稱	現在式	have	have	過去式	had	had
第三人稱		has				

He has received an invitation to the party. 他收到了派對的邀請。
The goods have not arrived yet. 商品尚未抵達。

③ 一般動詞的主詞動詞一致性

主詞	時態	單數	複數	時態	單數	複數
第一人稱		動詞原形			動詞過去式	動詞過去式
第二人稱	現在式	動詞原形	動詞原形	過去式	動詞過去式	動詞過去式
第三人稱		動詞原形＋ (e)s				

She handles customer complaints. 她處理顧客的不滿。
Our marketing plan succeeded. 我們的行銷計劃成功了。

2) 被動式

被動式，是以受到該行為的人或事物，當作句子主詞時，所使用的動詞形態，以「be 動詞＋過去分詞」表現。後方可接續「by ＋做出行為的人事物」，根據句子情況，可省略。

Tom trains his manager. Tom 訓練他的經理。

His manager is trained by Tom. Tom 的經理被他訓練。

02 暖身例題

請圈選出括號中適合該句的動詞。

1 <u>Everyone</u> (was / were) preparing for the conference.

2 <u>Each member</u> (is / are) important to this project.

3 <u>This information</u> (do / does) not help us.

4 <u>Several agencies</u> (has / have) similar proposals.

5 <u>All employees</u> (works / work) on the weekend.

03 例題解答

1 <u>Everyone</u> ~~were~~ preparing for the conference. 每個人都在準備會議。
　　　　　was

▶ 主詞（Everyone）為單數，因此必須選擇單數動詞 was。

2 Each member ~~are~~ important to this project. 每個成員對這個計劃來說都很重要。
　　　　　　　　　is

▶ Each 加上主詞（member）為單數，因此須選擇單數動詞 is。

3 This information ~~do~~ not help us. 這個情報對我們並沒有幫助。
　　　　　　　　　does

▶ 主詞（information）為單數，因此必須選擇單數動詞 does。

4 Several agencies ~~has~~ similar proposals. 這幾間經銷商有著類似的提案。
　　　　　　　　　have

▶ 主詞（agencies）為複數，因此必須選擇複數動詞 have。

5 All employees ~~works~~ during the weekend. 所有員工週末也在上班。
　　　　　　　　　work

▶ 主詞（employees）為複數，因此必須選擇複數動詞 work。

動詞根據主詞來做單複數的轉換，這種主詞動詞一致性的題目，是幾乎每次考題必定會出現的基本題型。

Unit 11　主詞與動詞的一致性 ❶

Step 1　實戰重點

解題策略　動詞相關題型，只要依照「主動／被動—時態—主詞動詞一致性」的順序來解題，即可減少失誤。

🎓 代表題型

All of the managers ------- on the revision of the policy covering health insurance.

(A) are working　　　(B) works　　　(C) has worked　　　(D) are worked

✏️ 攻略解題法

All of the managers ------- on the revision of the policy covering health insurance.

| 主詞 | 動詞 | 介系詞片語 | 介系詞片語 | 關係子句 |

all of the ＋名詞，為複數

work 和 on 會一起出現

原本為 which covers health insurance，省略 which 後，covers 改為現在分詞 covering

(A) are working　　　(B) works　　　(C) has worked　　　(D) are worked
複數，現在分詞　　　單數，現在式　　　單數，現在完成式　　　複數，過去分詞

文句分析　由於 work 為不及物動詞，因此接續介系詞片語（on the revision of the policy），而後方的關係子句，則是少了主詞的主格關係代名詞，用來修飾先行詞（the revision of the policy）。

說明　記住必須依照「主動／被動—時態—主詞動詞一致性」的順序，來解動詞相關題型。本題就照這個順序來解吧！首先，不及物動詞（work）無法轉換為被動語態，因此先刪除 (D)。接著是時態，但本句中並沒有與時態有關的描述，因此直接跳到第三步，來看主詞動詞一致性。主詞（managers）為複數，因此動詞也必須選擇複數形，單數動詞的 (B) 與 (C) 可刪除，因此複數形的 (A) are working 即為答案。

翻譯　所有的經理都在努力修正與健康保險有關的政策。

單字片語　revision 修正／ cover 涉及／ insurance 保險

解答　(A)

✂️ 攻略 POINT

請記住，動詞相關題型，須依照「主動／被動—時態—主詞動詞一致性」的順序來解題。

核心理論

動詞相關題型，須依照「主動／被動—時態—主詞動詞一致性」的順序來解題。

> He (has／had) a great time last night.
> 他昨晚度過了一段美好的時光。
>
> **1. 主動／被動**：動詞後方接著受詞（名詞）a great time，因此本句為主動語態。
>
> **2. 時態**：文句中出現了涉及過去的 last night（昨晚），為過去式。
>
> **3. 主詞動詞一致性**：主詞為 He（第三人稱單數），因此只能接續 has 或是過去式的 had。

He ~~ask~~ about the new schedule.
　　asks

他詢問新的行程內容。

▶ 第三人稱單數（He、She、It）的動詞，語尾必須加上 -s 或是 -es。

I／You ~~asks~~ the manager for a new uniform.
　　　　ask

我／你跟經理要新制服。

▶ 第一人稱（I）／第二人稱（You）的動詞，維持動詞原形。

Many attendees ~~asks~~ the CEO questions about the seminar.
　　　　　　　　ask

很多與會者都向 CEO 詢問研討會相關的問題。

▶ 複數主詞（attendees）的動詞，維持動詞原形。

Step 3 | 實戰演練

1 The company ------- the most competitive food distributor since it carefully selects its supplies and concentrates on developing new services.

(A) become　　　　(B) is become　　　　(C) becoming　　　　(D) has become

2 Employees of Wowmart, one of the largest retail corporations in the world, ------- to participate in the strike against tax increases on major supermarkets starting next quarter.

(A) plan　　　　(B) plans　　　　(C) planning　　　　(D) are planned

▶ 答案與解析請參考解析本第 9 頁

Unit 12 主詞與動詞的一致性 ②

解題策略　　必須練習如何將主詞與動詞間多餘的修辭語句刪去，並找到主詞與動詞的單複數一致性。

 代表題型

The project, which still needs written approval, ------- a highly controversial topic.

(A) including　　　　(B) are included　　　　(C) includes　　　　(D) have included

 攻略解題法

The project, which still needs written approval, ------- a highly controversial topic.
先行詞（單數）　　　關係子句（插入句）　　　動詞　　　動詞（includes）的受詞

修飾先行詞（The project）的關係子句　　　　　冠詞＋副詞＋形容詞＋名詞

(A) including　　　　(B) are included　　　　(C) includes　　　　(D) have included
動名詞　　　　　　　被動語態　　　　　　　單數動詞　　　　　　複數，現在完成式

文句分析　　關係代名詞，是去掉主詞或是受詞的不完整語句。本句中的主格關係代名詞 which 子句中，是去掉動詞（needs）主詞的不完整子句，用來修飾先行詞（The project）。

說明　　　　將空格前方多餘的修飾用關係子句（which still needs written approval）忽略後，空格前後方都沒有動詞，可見空格中須填入動詞，因此可先刪去 (A)。而空格後方接續受詞（a highly controversial topic），被動語態的 (B) 也可刪去。(C) 為單數動詞，(D) 為複數動詞，接著考慮主詞動詞單複數一致性的問題。題目中的主詞（The project）為單數，因此單數動詞 (C) includes 為答案。

翻譯　　　　那份還需要書面同意的企劃案中，含有具爭議性的議題。

單字片語　　approval 許可／ highly 高度地／ controversial 具有爭議的／ topic 主題

解答　　　　(C)

✎ 攻略 POINT

忽略多餘的修飾語句後，若空格內須填入動詞，則照「主動／被動—時態—主詞動詞一致性」的順序來解題。

核心理論

主詞與動詞的單複數形態必須保持一致，因此須將修飾用的語句去掉，才能掌握住正確的主詞與動詞。

> The man, who has a car, needs a book in the library.
>
> 　　　　關係子句　　　　　　　　介系詞片語

- **主詞＋（介系詞＋名詞）＋動詞**

The final reports (for the seminar) ~~was~~ well prepared.

主詞（複數）　　　　　　　　　　were

研討會的最終報告已經準備好了。

▶ 將多餘的修飾用介系詞片語（for the seminar）去掉後，使主詞與動詞達到單複數一致性。

- **主詞＋（關係代名詞＋不完整子句）＋動詞**

Ms. May, (who visited with the staff), ~~are~~ the new manager.

主詞（單數）　　　　　　　　　　is

與工作人員一起來訪的 May 女士，是新的經理。

▶ 將多餘的修飾用關係子句（who visited with the staff）去掉後，使主詞與動詞達到單複數一致性。

- **主詞＋（現在分詞／過去分詞）＋動詞**

The schedule (explained in detail) ~~satisfy~~ the French buyer.

主詞　　　　　　　　　　satisfied

這份解釋詳盡的行程讓法國買家很滿意。

▶ 將多餘的修飾用分詞（explained in detail）去掉後，使主詞與動詞達到單複數一致性。

Step 3 | 實戰演練

1 Only the board members ------- access to the database containing the company's most important secrets.

(A) have　　　(B) has been　　　(C) was　　　(D) is

2 The manager who is overseeing the construction project ------- a sick leave, and he will be off from March 21 to 31.

(A) is taken　　　(B) has taken　　　(C) take　　　(D) taking

▶答案與解析請參考解析本第 9 頁

Unit 13 動詞的主動與被動式

解題策略　受詞前方空格為主動式，若沒有受詞的空格，則為被動式。

 代表題型

> The copies of your rental agreement ------- on time, so you can move into your new apartment.
>
> (A) were submitted　　(B) submit　　(C) have submitted　　(D) will submit

 攻略解題法

The copies of your rental agreement ------- on time, so you can move
　主詞（複數）　　修飾 The copies 的介系詞片語　　動詞　介系詞片語　　主詞　　動詞

into your new apartment.
　　　　　介系詞片語　　　　　　　　　　　　　連接句子的連接詞 so　　　　submit 為及物動詞，
　　　　　　　　　　　　　　　　　　　　　　　　　　　　　　　　　　　　是句型 3 的動詞

(A) were submitted　　　(B) submit　　　(C) have submitted　　　(D) will submit
　複數，被動語態　　　　　複數動詞　　　複數，現在完成式　　　　未來式

文句分析　so 是用來連接兩個句子的對等連接詞，通常放在句子後方。這類型的連接詞有 so、for、yet 等。

說明　　本題為動詞相關題型，一樣依照「主動／被動—時態—主詞動詞一致性」的順序來解題。除了之前提到句型 4 的動詞（give、send、offer）以及句型 5 的動詞（make、find、keep、consider）之外，剩下的都算是句型 3 的動詞。而句型 3 的動詞要分辨為主動還是被動語態，只須確認受詞的有無。主動語態中一定會接續受詞的及物動詞，在被動語態下是沒有受詞的。因此，後方有受詞的空格即為主動式，而沒有受詞的即為被動式。本題中的空格後方，沒有接續受詞，可知答案為被動式的 (A) were submitted。

翻譯　　你租屋的合約副本已經準時提交，因此你可以搬進新公寓了。

單字片語　copy 副本，複製／ rental agreement 租賃合約書／ on time 準時／ move into (= to) 移入

解答　　(A)

✏️ 攻略 POINT
後方有受詞的空格即為主動式，而沒有受詞的即為被動式。

核心理論

從主動（一般句子）轉為被動語態後，基本上意思相同，只是句子的主體有所轉換。如同下列例句：

He <u>wrote</u> the book. 他寫了書。

▶ The book <u>was written</u> by him. 書是他所寫的。

★ **將句子由主動轉為被動式的三個步驟**

❶ 將主動語態中的受詞（the book）變為被動語態的主詞。

❷ 將主動語態的動詞（wrote），改為〔be + p.p.〕was written。

❸ 將主動語態的主詞（He），配合〔by + 受格〕的句型，改為 by him。

- **被動語句**

The foundation <u>was established</u> by Judy Hall.

這個財團由 Judy Hall 創立。

▶ 動詞（establish）後方沒有受詞，所以本句使用的是被動式。

- **現在式的被動語句**

The theater <u>is being prepared</u> for the next performance.

劇院正在為下一個演出做準備。

▶ 動詞（prepare）後方沒有受詞，所以本句使用的是被動式。而將現在進行式（be + V-ing）與被動式（be + 過去分詞）結合起來的，便是現在式的被動語句（be being + 過去分詞）。

- **過去完成式的被動語句**

Our schedules <u>have been changed</u> significantly.

我們的行程被做了很大的更動。

▶ 動詞（change）後方沒有受詞，所以本句使用的是被動式。而將過去完成式（have + 過去分詞）與被動式（be + 過去分詞）結合起來的，便是過去完成式的被動語句（have been + 過去分詞）。

Step 3 | 實戰演練

1 Steak & Lobster Marble Arch will be temporarily ------- while its remodeling work is taking place.

(A) close   (B) closing   (C) closed   (D) closure

2 It's likely that the stock price of Ashley Printers ------- due to the release of its brand-new photocopier with various functions.

(A) had been risen   (B) have risen   (C) rise   (D) has risen

▶ 答案與解析請參考解析本第 10 頁

Unit 14　句型 4 的被動式

 Step 1　實戰重點

解題策略　判斷句型 4 的主動／被動語態時，若空格後方有「對象＋事物」，則為主動式，若無，則為被動式。

☺ 代表題型

The workers who were recruited recently ------- a document about the regulations at the construction site.

(A) was given　　　(B) have given　　　(C) will be given　　　(D) gave

 攻略解題法

The workers who were recruited recently ------- a document about the regulations
主詞（複數）　修飾主詞（The workers）　　副詞　動詞　　受詞　　介系詞片語
　　　　　　的關係子句
at the construction site.
　　　　介系詞片語

> give 是代表性的
> 句型 4 動詞

(A) was given　　　(B) have given　　　(C) will be given　　　(D) gave
單數，被動語態　　複數，現在完成式　　未來式，被動語態　　動詞（過去式）

文句分析　名詞（workers）同時是關係子句（who were recruited recently）的先行詞，也是動詞（will be given）的主詞。原本的主動語態 give the workers a document，改為被動語態 the workers will be given a document。

說明　首先必須確認選項中的動詞，是否為句型 4 的授與動詞。句型 4 的句子結構為「主詞＋動詞＋間接受詞（對象）＋直接受詞（事物）」，如果去掉其中之一的受詞，便須改用被動語態呈現。因此，若空格後方有連接「對象＋事物」，選擇主動語態，若無，則須選擇被動語態。本題空格後方未接續「對象＋事物」，因此可知句型 4 被動語態的 (C) will be given 為正確答案。(A) 選項錯誤的原因，是因為主詞（workers）是複數，不可使用單數動詞（was）。

翻譯　最近招募進來的工人們，將會在施工現場拿到一份相關規定文件。

單字片語　recruit 招募／ recently 最近／ regulation 規定／ construction site 施工現場

解答　(C)

 攻略 POINT

> 若題型是詢問句型 4（give、send、offer）的主動／被動式，請確認空格前方是否有「對象＋事物」。
> 若有，為主動式；若無，則為被動式。

📖 **核心理論**

> **句型 4 的被動式**　主詞＋動詞＋間接受詞（對象）＋直接受詞（事物）
>
> 與句型 3 的被動句型類似，不過只需要間接受詞（對象）或直接受詞（事物）其中之一，拉到前方當作被動語態的主詞，其餘的維持在原本位置上即可。
>
> **句型 4 ▶ 句型 3**　主詞＋句型 4 動詞（被動式）＋介系詞＋對象
>
> ➡ 主詞＋句型 4 動詞（主動式）＋事物＋介系詞＋對象
>
> **考題中常出現的句型 4 被動語態：**
>
> | | |
> |---|---|
> | 對象＋ be sent 收到 | 事物＋ be sent to 被寄給～ |
> | 對象＋ be awarded 得到 | 事物＋ be awarded to 被授予給～ |
> | 對象＋ be given 得到 | 事物＋ be given to 被給予給～ |
> | 對象＋ be offered 得到 | 事物＋ be offered to 被提供給～ |

- **句型 4 的主動式**

  The store offered new customers a 10% discount coupon. 商店提供新顧客 10% 折扣的優惠券。

  　　　　　　　　間接受詞　　　　　　直接受詞

  ▶ 句型 4 的句子中，會有兩個受詞（間接受詞、直接受詞）。

- **句型 4 的被動式**

  1. 間接受詞作為主詞的情況

  New customers were given a 10% discount coupon (by the store).

  新顧客會得到 10% 折扣的優惠券。

  ▶ 當間接受詞（new customers）作為主詞時，句子結構為「be given N」，意思為「得到～」。

  2. 直接受詞作為主詞的情況

  A 10% discount coupon was given to new customers (by the store).

  會提供 10% 折扣的折價券給新顧客。

  ▶ 當直接受詞（a 10% discount coupon）作為主詞時，間接受詞的前方，須接上介系詞（to）。

1 Electricians working at Walton's Warehouse ------- all of the details about the new procedure from the head of the Management Department.

(A) sent　　　　　　(B) has been sent　　(C) have sent　　　　(D) were sent

2 Ms. MacDowell was ------- a special bonus in recognition of her constant contribution to the project.

(A) award　　　　　(B) awarding　　　　(C) awarded　　　　　(D) awards

▶ 答案與解析請參考解析本第 10 頁

Unit 15　句型 5 的被動式

Step 1　實戰重點

解題策略　　句型 5 的被動式中，動詞後方的受詞補語位置不變。

🎓 代表題型

James Badge Dale ------- Best Emerging Journalist for his writing on the recent election.

(A) was named　　　(B) has named　　　(C) named　　　(D) are naming

✏️ 攻略解題法

James Badge Dale ------- Best Emerging Journalist for his writing on the recent election.
主詞（單數）　　　　　受詞補語　　　　介系詞片語　　　　介系詞片語

> name 是代表性
> 的句型 5 的動詞

(A) was named　　　　(B) has named　　　(C) named　　　(D) are naming
單數，被動語態　　　單數，現在完成式　　動詞，過去式　　　複數，主動語態

文句分析　　名詞 James Badge Dale 是動詞 was named 的主詞，原句主動式為 named James Badge Dale Best Emerging Journalist，改為被動式 James Badge Dale was named Best Emerging Journalist。

說明　　　　首先必須確認選項中的動詞是否為句型 5 的動詞。句型 5 的句子結構為「主詞＋動詞＋受詞＋受詞補語」，如果改為被動語態，句子會變成「被動式＋名詞」。由於本題空格後方為名詞（Best Emerging Journalist），因此可知被動語態的 (A) was named 為正確答案。此外，name 當動詞時，屬於後方會接續名詞當作受詞補語的句型 5 動詞，「name A B」意思為「將 A 任命為 B」。

翻譯　　　　James Badge Dale 在最近的選拔中，因他的文章而被頒發為最具前景的記者。

單字片語　　journalist 記者／ writing 文章／ recent 最近的／ election 選舉

解答　　　　(A)

✏️ 攻略 POINT
> 句型 5 改為被動式後，方受詞補語不變。受詞補語的詞性，則跟用的是哪一個句型 5 動詞有關。

核心理論

句型 5 的被動式 主詞＋動詞＋受詞＋受詞補語

與句型 3 的被動句型類似，不過當受詞變成主詞時，受詞補語維持在原本位置上不變。

1) 名詞作為受詞補語的情況	2) 形容詞作為受詞補語的情況	3) to 不定詞作為受詞補語的情況
be considered N 'N' 被認為是 N	be considered 形容詞 被認為～	be required to 被要求～
be called N 'N' 被稱作 N	be made 形容詞 被做成～	be advised to 被建議～
be appointed N 'N' 被指派為 N	be found 形容詞 被發現～	be asked to 被要求～
be elected N 'N' 被推選為 N	be kept 形容詞 被維持～	be allowed to 被允許～

• **句型 5 的主動式與被動式**

He considers <u>Mark</u> the most competent employee. （主動式）他認為 Mark 是最有能力的員工。
受詞補語

Mark **is considered** the most competent employee (by him). （被動式）Mark 被認為是最有能力的員工。
受詞補語

The company will make <u>a selected list of applicants</u> available on the web. （主動式）

公司會把選中的應徵者名單放在網路上。 受詞補語

A selected list of applicants will **be made** available on the web (by the company). （被動式）
受詞補語

選中的應徵者名單將會被放在網路上。

We allow <u>only authorized employees</u> to enter the office for security reasons. （主動式）
受詞補語

基於安全考量，我們只允許被授權的員工進入辦公室。

Only authorized employees **are allowed** to enter the office for security reasons (by us). （被動式）
受詞補語

基於安全考量，只有獲得授權的員工才被允許進入辦公室。

Step 3 實戰演練

1 Unauthorized workers are not ------- to access confidential customer information without manager's approval.

(A) permitted　　　(B) permitting　　　(C) permit　　　(D) permittance

2 Chris Jeong, the winner of the employee of the year award, ------- the leading authority in the field of corporate communication strategy.

(A) have appointed　　(B) has been appointed　　(C) will appoint　　(D) had appointed

▶答案與解析請參考解析本第 10 頁

Unit 16 被動式＋介系詞慣用法

Step 1 實戰重點

解題策略　　須記住常與介系詞連用的被動語態的片語。

 代表題型

> The attractions near the Eiffel Tower have been ------- for a lot of street artists seen around it.
>
> (A) dedicated　　　(B) believed　　　(C) known　　　(D) received

 攻略解題法

The attractions near the Eiffel Tower have been ------- for a lot of street artists
主詞　　　　　　介系詞片語　　　　　　動詞　　　　　介系詞片語

seen around it.
關係子句

> 由於後方連接的是介系詞片語而非名詞，可知空格為被動語態

(A) dedicated　　　(B) believed　　　(C) known　　　(D) received
常與 to 連用　　常與 that / to be 連用　　常以 be known for 出現　　放在句中意思不符

文句分析　　介系詞片語（near the Eiffel Tower）並不影響句子結構，因此可知名詞 the attractions 為主詞，為達成與主詞單複數的一致性，動詞必須使用複數動詞（have）。請注意，勿將 the Eiffel Tower 誤認為主詞。

說明　　被動語態的慣用片語題型中，空格多介於 be 動詞與介系詞中間，因此必須牢記動詞被動語態搭配的介系詞。通常這類題型的四個選項皆是過去分詞，因此答案需選出可搭配後方介系詞的動詞。本題中，與空格後方介系詞（for）搭配的動詞為 (C) known。

翻譯　　艾菲爾鐵塔附近的景點，因到處可見的街頭藝術家而聲名大噪。

單字片語　　attraction 觀光景點／ be known for 因～而有名

解答　　(C)

✎ **攻略 POINT**

被動語態的慣用片語題型，是選出適合後方介系詞的過去分詞填入空格中，因此必須牢記動詞被動語態搭配的介系詞。

核心理論

請記住句型 4 的被動式，會留下一個受詞不變；而句型 5 的被動式，則是受詞補語不變。

被動語句常見片語——情感相關

* be pleased with 滿足於～、對～感到開心
* be contented with 滿足於～、對～感到開心
* be satisfied with 滿足於～
* be shocked at 被～驚嚇到
* be amazed at 被～驚豔
* be alarmed at 被～驚動
* be disappointed at 對～失望
* be interested in 對～有興趣
* be amused at 被～娛樂到
* be worried about 對～擔心

被動語句常見片語——狀態相關

* be tired with 因～感到累
* be exhausted with 因～感到疲憊
* be fatigued with 對～感到厭倦
* be worn with 對～感到厭倦

被動語句常見片語——其他

* be absorbed in 專心於～
* be involved in 被牽扯至～
* be indulged in 沈迷於～
* be based on 根據～
* be dressed in 穿著～
* be covered with 被～覆蓋
* be crowded with 擠滿～
* be possessed of 擁有～
* be worn out 精疲力盡
* be devoted to 獻身於～
* be annoyed at 被～干擾、對～生氣
* be committed to 致力於～
* be convinced in / of 確定～

Neal **is absorbed in** conducting the experiment. Neal 專注於進行實驗。

TJ Ltd. **is devoted to** the development of new materials. TJ 公司致力於新材料的開發。

Step 3 | **實戰演練**

1 The pay raise is ------- on the employees' performances and the bimonthly evaluations submitted by their supervisors.

(A) introduced   (B) entitled   (C) avoided   (D) based

2 Since its foundation, Animals' Friends has been committed to ------- the importance of animal protection worldwide and helping people adopt abandoned dogs.

(A) promoted   (B) promoting   (C) promote   (D) be promoted

▶答案與解析請參考解析本第 11 頁

REVIEW TEST

1. The instructions on making copies ------- above the copy machine, and if you need any help, you can dial the number next to it.

   (A) have posted   (B) are posted
   (C) post   (D) posted

2. The two companies must ------- contracts to expedite the merger between them before their competitors dominate the American market.

   (A) be signed   (B) signs
   (C) signature   (D) sign

3. The executives involved in production management ------- to keep up to date with new technology and trends all over the world so that they do not get left behind.

   (A) tries   (B) have tried
   (C) has been tried   (D) be trying

4. We assure you that sensitive information such as contact details and ID numbers ------- secure with no exceptions.

   (A) are keeping   (B) kept
   (C) is kept   (D) to keep

5. Usually, John Harrison's research results ------- online, not in journals, so that he can get prompt feedback and people can easily access the information.

   (A) are published   (B) published
   (C) have published   (D) publish

6. The meal that will be served to passengers ------- beverages and a main dish with soup or salad, and there is an additional charge for other options.

   (A) include   (B) has been included
   (C) includes   (D) are being included

7. Those who were randomly selected by lot ------- a discounted rate on the Deluxe Suite Package at our hotel in addition to two round-trip tickets to Rome.

   (A) has offered   (B) offered
   (C) offers   (D) have been offered

8. The limited edition toys released by Playtime ------- by people around the world, and the sales volume rose extraordinarily during the Christmas season.

   (A) ordered   (B) are being ordered
   (C) have ordered   (D) orders

9. They all agreed to ------- their primary goals before the evaluation, which is scheduled in two weeks' time.

   (A) have examine   (B) be examined
   (C) examining   (D) examine

10. William and Alice, the new editors, ------- to our department since we are having difficulty meeting our deadline due to the staff shortage.

    (A) have been added
    (B) added
    (C) has added
    (D) are adding

▶答案與解析請參考解析本第 11 頁

類型分析 4

時態

時態，是根據該事情或是狀態發生的時間，分成現在、過去、未來等等類型。

WARMING UP

01 文法概念前導 ················· 正式進入文法單元前，先熟悉一下文法基本概念。

1) 時態的基本概念

所謂的「時態」，是針對事件或是該事實發生的當下，所使用的文法表現。跟中文文法不同的是，英文在時間相關的文法表現上，有著非常詳細的劃分。英文除了「過去、現在、未來、過去進行、現在進行、未來進行」這幾種時態的分別之外，還有「完成式」這個時態，是該語文文法的特徵之一。

2) 時態的種類

① 現在式：動詞原形／動詞原形＋ -(e)s

用於描述一般已知的事實，或是具規律性的行為。

This price includes service charges. 這個價格包含了服務費。　▶ 一般已知的事實

② 過去式：動詞原形＋ -ed ／動詞過去式的不規則變化

描述過去曾發生過的事件或是狀態，通常句子中會出現明確指出過去時間的副詞或是子句。

I attended the meeting yesterday. 我參加了昨天的會議。

③ 未來式：will (be going to) ＋動詞原形

描述未來將發生的事件或是狀態，通常句子中會出現明確指出未來時間的副詞或是子句。

A reception will be held next month. 下個月將會舉辦一場招待會。

④ 現在完成式：have (has) ＋ P.P.（過去分詞）

描述過去發生，卻一直影響至今的事情。

I have worked for the company since 2001. 我從 2001 年起就為公司服務至今。

⑤ 過去完成式：had ＋ P.P.（過去分詞）

用來描述比過去發生的某件事，還要更早發生的事件或事實。

Before I arrived at the venue, the meeting had started. 在我抵達會場前，會議就已經開始了。

⑥ 未來完成式：will have ＋ P.P.（過去分詞）

針對過去或是現在發生的事情，去預測未來可能的情況時使用。

I will have finished it by the time she comes back. 當她回來後，我應該就已經完成了。

02 暖身例題

請圈選出括號中正確的動詞。

1 They always (work / worked) on weekends.

2 They (work / worked) last weekend.

3 They (will work / worked) next weekend.

4 They (have worked / worked) since last weekend.

5 They (have worked / had worked) for a long time when I arrived.

03 例題解答

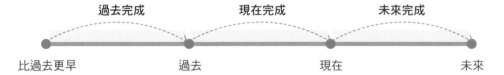

| 過去完成 | 現在完成 | 未來完成 |

| 比過去更早 | 過去 | 現在 | 未來 |

▶ 注意，未來完成式的時間帶中，也有包含到比現在更早的時間點。

1 They always **work** on weekends. 他們總是在週末工作。

　　▶ 針對平常也會發生的事件，使用現在簡單式（work）。always、usually 通常也會一起出現於句中。

2 They **worked** last weekend. 他們上週末在工作。

　　▶ 發生在過去某個特定時間點的事件，使用過去簡單式（worked）。

3 They **will work** next weekend. 他們下週末將會工作。

　　▶ 發生在未來某個特定時間點的事件，使用未來簡單式（will work）。

4 They **have worked** since last weekend. 他們從上週末開始就一直在工作。

　　▶ 描述從過去某個時間點開始，一直延續到現在的動作或是狀態，使用現在完成式。

5 They **had worked** for a long time when I arrived.
在我抵達之前，他們就已經工作好長一段時間了。

　　▶ 描述比過去某個特定時間點，還要更早發生的事情，使用過去完成式。

Unit 17 現在式

Step 1 · 實戰重點

解題策略　當描述某種習慣或是一般的事實時，使用現在式。通常會跟 usually、often、every day、every year 等等時間副詞一起使用。

 代表題型

> According to the report, people know that Miss Mason usually ------- high fees for her services.
>
> (A) charges　　　(B) charged　　　(C) had charged　　　(D) will charge

✏️ 攻略解題法

According to the report, people know that Miss Mason usually ------- high fees
介系詞　介系詞片語　主詞　動詞　連接詞　主詞　副詞　動詞　動詞（charge）的受詞
for her services.
介系詞片語
　　　　　　連接子句與子句　　表示現在的副詞

(A) charges　　　(B) charged　　　(C) had charged　　　(D) will charge
現在式　　　　　過去式　　　　　過去完成式　　　　　未來式

文句分析　動詞 know，常以 be known for、be known that 句型出現。be known for，是表示「以～而聞名」，而 be known that，則是「因～事實而聞名」。

說明　空格前方表示現在的時間副詞（usually），常用於現在式。因此可知只要空格前方有 usually，選項中的動詞現在式便為正解，由此推論，(A) charges 為答案。

翻譯　根據報告指出，人們都知道 Mason 小姐針對她自己的服務經常收取高額費用。

單字片語　according to 根據～／charge 收費／fee 手續費

解答　(A)

✂️ 攻略 POINT
表示現在的時間副詞 usually、generally、often、every day / month / year 等等，常見於現在式。

核心理論

現在式的題型，通常會在空格的前後，或是句首、句尾放上表示現在的時間副詞，平均每次考題中都會出現一題。

> **• 代表性的現在式時間副詞**
>
> usually, often, every / each year, at the moment 等等頻率副詞
>
> now, today, nowadays, at present, each year / day / month 等等時間副詞
>
> The company <u>usually</u> hires new employees at the beginning of the year.
> 公司通常會在年初招募新人。
>
> <u>Each year</u>, many regions in Africa suffer from famines.
> 每年，非洲都會有很多區域飽受飢荒之苦。
>
> **• 在以下的子句中，會以現在式代替未來式**
>
> | 時間副詞子句的連接詞 | when 當～的時候　　after ～之後　　before ～之前
as soon as 只要一～就～　　until 到～為止 |
> |---|---|
> | 條件句的連接詞 | if 如果～　　once 一旦～　　unless 除非～
providing / provided 萬一～ |

<u>When</u> she **comes** to the party, I will talk with her.
當她來到派對的時候，我會去跟她說話。
▶ 在時間副詞子句裡，即便主句是未來式，副詞子句裡也會使用現在式。

<u>If an accident</u> **happens**, the emergency center will help.
如果有意外發生，緊急救援中心將會協助。
▶ 在條件句中，即便主句是未來式，條件子句內也會使用現在式。

1 All of the three service elevators in the Francis Coast Hotel ------- out of order at the moment.

(A) were　　　　　(B) are　　　　　(C) had been　　　　　(D) will be

2 Customers in the shop often ------- about what free gift is given on that day and how much they have to spend in order to be eligible for it.

(A) inquires　　　　　(B) had inquired　　　　　(C) will inquire　　　　　(D) inquire

▶答案與解析請參考解析本第 13 頁

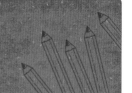

Unit 18 過去式

Step 1 **實戰重點**

解題策略　過去式的句子中，句首或句尾通常會出現表過去的時間副詞。

代表題型

The Eco-Friend Foundation ------- an awards banquet to celebrate its 10th anniversary last week.

(A) had held　　　(B) will hold　　　(C) holds　　　(D) held

攻略解題法

The Eco-Friend Foundation ------- an awards banquet to celebrate its 10th anniversary
　　　主詞　　　　　　　　動詞　　動詞（held）的受詞　　to 不定詞（作副詞用，表示為了～）

last week. ◁ 表示過去的副詞
　副詞

(A) had held　　　(B) will hold　　　(C) holds　　　(D) held
　過去完成式　　　　未來式　　　　　　現在式　　　　　過去式

文句分析　在主詞跟受詞都具備的完整子句（The Eco-Friend Foundation held an awards banquet）後方連接的 to 不定詞，作副詞「為了～」用。

說明　　當題目只有一個長句，並且是問時態類型時，要從句首、句尾或是空格前後方來找尋時間相關副詞再解答，因為當句子的動詞只有一個時，通常會在這幾處給予時態的提示。若出現 last 等過去相關時間副詞，可知答案為動詞過去式，因此本題選 (D) held。

翻譯　　Eco-Friend 基金會在上週為了慶祝十週年，舉辦了一場頒獎典禮。

單字片語　foundation 基金會／awards banquet 頒獎典禮／celebrate 慶祝

解答　　(D)

攻略 POINT

若表過去的時間副詞出現句首或是句尾，空格必定填入過去式。

核心理論

過去時態的句子，會與下列時間副詞一起使用。

> yesterday 昨天　　recently 最近　　時間＋ago　　last ＋時間　　in ＋過往年份

My supervisor **finished** reviewing the financial budget <u>yesterday</u>.

我的主管已經在昨天完成了財務預算的審核。

▶ 句尾出現了表過去的副詞（yesterday），因此使用動詞過去式（finished）。

My first exhibition at Gallery M **ended** <u>two weeks ago</u>.

我首次在 Gallery M 的展覽已經在兩週前結束。

▶ 句尾出現了表過去的副詞（two weeks ago），因此使用動詞過去式（ended）。

Nicolas **was expected** to attend university <u>last year</u>.

Nicolas 本來預計在去年上大學。

▶ 句尾出現了表過去的副詞（last year），因此使用動詞過去式（was）。

The system errors **occurred** <u>while Jack was away</u>.

當 Jack 外出時，系統發生了錯誤。

▶ 當有兩個子句（主詞＋動詞）時，必須讓動詞時態保持一致。當其中有一動詞為過去式，則另一個動詞必為過去式，或是過去完成式。

1 According to some recent research results, the number of travelers using Delot Air, a low-cost airline, ------- its peak last year.

(A) will reach　　　(B) have reached　　　(C) had reached　　　(D) reached

2 Even though Mr. Henry Kim earned an engineering degree at the University of Florida, he ------- to work as a film director or film scriptwriter.

(A) wants　　　(B) wanted　　　(C) will want　　　(D) have wanted

▶答案與解析請參考解析本第 13 頁

 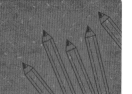

Unit 19 未來式

解題策略　若在句首或句尾出現表未來的時間副詞，空格內必填入動詞未來式。

代表題型

A new policy on the company dress code ------- to improve the work environment beginning next week.

(A) will be implemented　　(B) implemented　　(C) implements　　(D) is implemented

攻略解題法

A new policy on the company dress code ------- to improve the work environment
　主詞　　　　　　　　　介系詞片語　　　　動詞　　to 不定詞（作副詞用，表目的）

beginning next week.　　　完整句子
不定詞（表示未來）

(A) will be implemented　　　　　　(B) had been implemented
　未來式，被動語態　　　　　　　　　　過去完成式，被動語態

(C) was implemented　　　　　　　(D) is implemented
　過去式，被動語態　　　　　　　　　　現在式，被動語態

文句分析　前方句型 3 的被動式，即為一個完整句子（A new policy on the company dress code will be implemented），後方的 to 不定詞作副詞用。

說明　　　當題目只有一個完整句（主詞＋動詞），句首或句尾一定會有代表時態的相關副詞。而本題只有一個完整句，並且在句尾出現表未來的副詞（beginning next week），可知答案為 (A) will be implemented。

翻譯　　　為了改善工作環境，下週開始針對公司的服裝儀容，將會實施新的政策。

單字片語　policy 政策／ dress code 服裝規定／ implement 實施／ work environment 工作環境／ beginning 開始

解答　　　(A)

攻略 POINT

未來式的句子中，通常會跟表未來的時間副詞一起使用。

核心理論

未來時態的句子，會與下列時間副詞一起使用。

> soon　shortly　next ＋未來時刻　as of ＋未來時刻　when / if ＋主詞＋動詞現在式

Some properties near City Hall **will be** available soon.
市政廳附近一部分的土地，即將開放使用。
▶ 出現了表未來的副詞（soon），因此要使用動詞未來式（will be）。

Many employees **will** soon **enjoy** a new environment.
很多員工就快要可以享受到新的工作環境了。
▶ 詢問時態的題型，對考生來說，也可能同時是副詞的字彙考題。

All employees **will wear** protective clothing next Monday.
所有員工將會在下週一穿上防護衣。
▶ 出現了表未來的副詞（next Monday），因此要使用動詞未來式（will wear）。

A new return policy **will come** into effect as of next month.
新的退貨政策將會從下個月開始實施。
▶ 出現了表未來的副詞（as of next month），因此要使用動詞未來式（will come）。

If I meet him, I **will give** him this note.
如果遇到他，我會把這個便條交給他。
▶ 在 If 子句中，會用現在式代替未來式，而主句則維持未來式（will give）。

Step 3 | 實戰演練

1 The guidelines revised by the technical support team ------- into effect next year.

(A) had come　　(B) comes　　(C) came　　(D) will come

2 Many temporary employees ------- in the job fair hosted by the Ministry of Employment and Labor shortly.

(A) had participated　(B) will participate　(C) participate　(D) participated

▶答案與解析請參考解析本第 13 頁

Unit 20 現在完成式

解題策略　若在句首或句尾出現「since ＋某過去時間點」，空格內必填入現在完成式。

 代表題型

> The workers at B&G, Inc. ------- the construction of the fountains since they got permission from the city council.
>
> (A) will finish　　　(B) finishing　　　(C) have finished　　　(D) finish

 攻略解題法

The workers at B&G, Inc. ------- the construction of the fountains since
　主詞　　　　介系詞　　　動詞　　　　　動詞（finish）的受詞
they got permission from the city council.
　since＋主詞＋動詞過去式　　　介系詞片語

> 表示現在完成的
> 連接詞 since

(A) will finish　　　(B) finishing　　　(C) have finished　　　(D) finish
　未來式　　　　　現在分詞　　　　　現在完成式　　　　　現在式

文句分析　時間連接詞 since，句型為「since ＋主詞＋動詞過去式」，與現在完成式（have finished）一起使用，解釋為「從～以來，自～之後，從～開始」。

說明　　　當有兩個子句（主詞＋動詞）時，必須讓動詞時態保持一致，要記住「since ＋過去式（since they got）」與現在完成式是成對出現的。這裡的 since，既可作為介系詞，也可作為連接詞，意思是「從～以來，自～之後，從～開始」。因此本題答案為 (C) have finished。

翻譯　　　自從 B&G 的員工獲得市議會批准後，便完成了噴泉的建設。

單字片語　construction 建造／fountain 噴泉／since 自～之後／permission 許可／city council 市議會

解答　　　(C)

攻略 POINT

「since ＋過去某時間點」、「for / in / over ＋期間」，會與現在完成式一起出現在考題中。

核心理論

現在完成式，用來描述在過去某一時刻做的動作延續至今，或是影響至今，因此會伴隨著表過去的時間副詞一起出現。特別要記住常與現在完成式搭配出現的 since（從～開始），句型為「since ＋過去某時間點」。

| since ＋過去 | in the last / past ＋期間 | for / over the ＋期間 | recently |

We **have planned** the travel schedule <u>since yesterday</u>.
我們從昨天就開始制定旅遊行程。

Working conditions **have improved** <u>since the new CEO joined Grolano Groups</u>.
自從新的 CEO 加入了 Grolano Groups 後，工作環境便獲得改進。

The revenue of the company **has risen** considerably <u>in the past ten years</u>.
在過去十年來，公司的營收顯著地提升了。

<u>For the last three years</u>, Mr. James **has been participating** in a variety of seminars.
過去三年來，James 先生參加了各式各樣的研討會。

The editors **have changed** the draft <u>over the weeks</u>.
幾個星期以來，編輯們修改了草稿。

He **has** <u>recently</u> **been promoted** to a senior marketing director.
他最近被晉升為資深行銷主任。

1 His latest album, Feel Your Move with James, ------- at the top on the Billboard Chart as well as the UK pop charts during the past three months.

(A) will rank   (B) ranks   (C) ranked   (D) has ranked

2 Tamia's credit card ------- since the company failed to withdraw the payment from her bank account.

(A) was suspended   (B) has been suspended

(C) is valid   (D) had been invalid

▶答案與解析請參考解析本第 13 頁

Unit 21　過去完成式

解題策略　　若兩個動詞中有一個為過去式，則空格內須填入過去完成式。

 代表題型

The organizer ------- an ideal place for the party before his assistants reserved a room at the nearby hotel.

(A) will book　　　　(B) books　　　　(C) had booked　　　　(D) has booked

✏️ 攻略解題法

The organizer ------- an ideal place for the party before his assistants reserved a room
　主詞　　　　動詞　動詞（book）的受詞　介系詞片語　連接詞　時間副詞子句（主詞＋動詞過去式＋受詞）
at the nearby hotel.

> 因為主句是發生在 his assistants 所做的
> 事情之前（before），所以用過去完成式

(A) will book　　　　(B) books　　　　(C) had booked　　　　(D) has booked
　未來式　　　　　　現在式　　　　　　過去完成式　　　　　　現在完成式

文句分析　　before 是時間連接詞，因此後方必須接上「主詞（his assistants）＋動詞（reserved）」的完整句型。

說明　　　　當有兩個子句（主詞＋動詞）時，必須讓動詞時態保持一致。不過，雖然兩個句子都是過去發生的事件，但如果有一方先行發生，便須分開使用過去式和過去完成式，因為過去完成式是用來描述比過去更早發生的事件。因此本題答案為 (C) had booked。

翻譯　　　　早在他助理預定附近的飯店房間前，主辦人就已經先預約了派對的理想場地。

單字片語　　organizer 主辦人／ book 預約／ ideal for 對～來說理想的／ assistant 助理

解答　　　　(C)

✒️ 攻略 POINT

當兩個事件都在過去發生，而其中之一又較早發生時，使用過去完成式。

📖 核心理論

過去完成式使用在比過去某個特定時間點，更早發生的事件上。

引導時間子句的連接詞＋主詞＋動詞過去式，主詞＋ had p.p.
　　　　　過去的事件　　　　　　　　　　比過去更早發生的事件

主詞＋ had p.p. 引導時間子句的連接詞＋主詞＋動詞過去式
比過去更早發生的事件　　　　　　　　過去的事件

主詞＋動詞過去式 名詞子句連接詞＋主詞＋ had p.p.
　　過去的事件　　　　　　　　比過去更早發生的事件

The train to London **had already left** before our team <u>arrived</u> at the station.
在我們隊伍抵達車站之前，前往倫敦的火車早就開走了。

▶ 在過去某個特定時間點（抵達）之前，火車就已經離開了，因此使用過去完成式。

I <u>was relieved</u> that the mechanic **had already tested** my car.
我對於技術人員已經測試過我的車，感到安心。

▶ 當有兩個完整句（主詞＋動詞）時，一方為過去式，則另一方須使用過去式或是過去完成式。此時過去完成式，是用來描述比過去更早發生的事件。在過去某個特定時間點（感到安心）之前，車子就已經經過測試，因此使用過去完成式。

The Angle Corporation <u>announced</u> that its quarterly sales **had increased**.
Angle Corporation 宣布他們的季營收上升了。

▶ 在過去某個特定時間點（宣告）之前，季營收已經上升了，因此使用過去完成式。

1 The attendees were informed that their ID badges -------.

(A) are already issued　　　　　　　　(B) will already be issued

(C) have already been issued　　　　　(D) had already been issued

2 Sales representatives at Smart Connection ------- to welcome their foreign buyers half an hour before their planes turned up at the international airport.

(A) arrive　　　　(B) had arrived　　　　(C) will arrive　　　　(D) have arrived

▶答案與解析請參考解析本第 14 頁

Unit 22 未來完成式

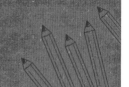

 Step 1 　**實戰重點**

解題策略　　當題目出現副詞子句「by the time ＋主詞＋動詞現在式」時，空格內須填入未來完成式。

 代表題型

The personnel director ------- searching for a replacement for Andrew by the time he

transfers to the head office in September.

(A) finished 　　　(B) finishes 　　　(C) will have finished 　　　(D) had finished

---

✏️ 攻略解題法

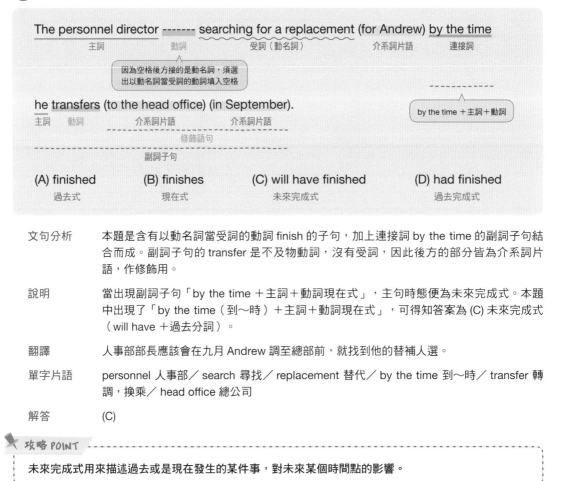

The personnel director ------- searching for a replacement (for Andrew) by the time
　　　　主詞　　　　　　　　動詞　　　　　受詞（動名詞）　　　　　介系詞片語　　　　連接詞

因為空格後方接的是動名詞，須選
出以動名詞當受詞的動詞填入空格

he transfers (to the head office) (in September).
主詞　動詞　　　介系詞片語　　　　介系詞片語
　　　　　　　　　　　修飾語句
　　　　　　　　副詞子句

by the time ＋主詞＋動詞

(A) finished 　　　　(B) finishes 　　　　(C) will have finished 　　　　(D) had finished
　過去式　　　　　　　現在式　　　　　　　未來完成式　　　　　　　　　過去完成式

文句分析　　本題是含有以動名詞當受詞的動詞 finish 的子句，加上連接詞 by the time 的副詞子句結
　　　　　　合而成。副詞子句的 transfer 是不及物動詞，沒有受詞，因此後方的部分皆為介系詞片
　　　　　　語，作修飾用。

說明　　　　當出現副詞子句「by the time ＋主詞＋動詞現在式」，主句時態便為未來完成式。本題
　　　　　　中出現了「by the time（到～時）＋主詞＋動詞現在式」，可得知答案為 (C) 未來完成式
　　　　　　（will have ＋過去分詞）。

翻譯　　　　人事部部長應該會在九月 Andrew 調至總部前，就找到他的替補人選。

單字片語　　personnel 人事部／ search 尋找／ replacement 替代／ by the time 到～時／ transfer 轉
　　　　　　調，換乘／ head office 總公司

解答　　　　(C)

✎ 攻略 POINT

未來完成式用來描述過去或是現在發生的某件事，對未來某個時間點的影響。

核心理論

> 未來完成式用來描述過去或是現在發生的某件事，將會一直影響到未來某個時間點的情況。通常句子中會出現 by next month、by the end of the week 等時間副詞，或是連接詞 by the time 等等。

They **will have finished** the job completely <u>before the general manager arrives</u>.
他們會在總經理抵達之前完成工作。

▶ 因為是在抵達之前會把事情完成，因此使用未來完成式。

<u>By next year</u>, Mr. Smith **will have served** as the CEO for 10 years.
到了明年，Smith 先生擔任 CEO 就要滿十年了。

Mr. Benkovic **will have worked** here for 10 years <u>by the end of next year</u>.
到了明年年底，Benkovic 先生在這裡工作就滿十年了。

Her colleagues **will have been waiting** for her for two hours <u>by the time she comes back</u>.
到了她回來的時候，她的同事們大概就已經等她兩小時了。

▶ 若出現副詞子句「by the time（到～時）＋主詞＋動詞現在式」，或是「as of（從～起）＋未來時間」，主句中的空格須填入未來完成式。多益中的出題，多以 by the time 為主，而近期的考題中，不只用來判斷空格是否為未來完成式，甚至會直接將 by the time 作為選項出題。

1 The special promotional event held by Fly Walk ------- by the time it launches its new line of women's walking shoes.

(A) had ended   (B) ended   (C) have ended   (D) will have ended

2 The budget problems of a few divisions will have been solved ------- the negotiations between JC Sesco and Betty Patisserie come to an end next quarter.

(A) by the time   (B) no later than   (C) at the latest   (D) no more than

▶答案與解析請參考解析本第 14 頁

Unit 23 假設語氣

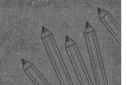

 Step 1 | **實戰重點**

解題策略　若條件句中出現「had＋過去分詞」，則答案需選擇「助動詞過去式＋have＋過去分詞」。

🎓 代表題型

If the artist had accepted the proposal by the museum, his works ------- in the main hall.

(A) had been displayed　　　　　　(B) were displayed

(C) would have been displayed　　　(D) have been displayed

✏️ 攻略解題法

If the artist had accepted the proposal by the museum, his works ------- in the main hall.
連接詞　主詞　　動詞　　accept 的受詞　　介系詞片語　　主詞　　動詞　　介系詞片語

↘ 連接兩個句子

> 過去完成的假定語句中使用
> would / could / should / might + have + p.p.

(A) had been displayed
　　過去完成式，被動語態

(B) were displayed
　　過去式，被動語態

(C) would have been displayed
　　助動詞＋過去完成式，被動語態

(D) have been displayed
　　現在完成式，被動語態

文句分析　名詞 proposal 的後方，通常會接上介系詞（from）一起使用，表示「來自～的提案」。而 display 的後方沒有受詞，可推斷應為被動語態。

說明　　假設語氣的題型與時態題型類似，都是要統一前後兩句的動詞時態，而無論是選項，或是前後方的句子中，只要出現了助動詞過去式（would、could、should、might），便是假設語氣的題型。若條件句中出現了「If＋主詞＋動詞過去式」，主句必須使用助動詞過去式（would / could＋動詞原形）；若條件句為「If＋主詞＋had＋過去分詞」，主句則必須使用助動詞過去完成式（would / could have＋過去分詞）。例如本題中出現的是「If＋主詞＋had＋過去分詞」，可推論出這是過去完成假設語句，主句須使用助動詞過去完成式（would / could have＋過去分詞），因此 (C) would have been displayed 為正解。

翻譯　　如果當初藝術家接受了博物館的提案，他的作品便會展示在大廳。

解答　　(C)

✎ **攻略 POINT**

當 If 子句結構為「If＋主詞＋動詞過去式」，為過去假設語句；「If＋主詞＋had＋過去分詞」時，則為過去完成假設語句。

📖 **核心理論**

假設語氣是用來假設與現實相反的狀況。

過去假設語句：假設與現在事實相反。
If ＋主詞＋動詞過去式，主詞＋（would / could / should / might）＋動詞原形

過去完成假設語句：假設與過去事實相反。
If ＋主詞＋ had p.p., 主詞＋（would / could / should / might）＋ have ＋ p.p.

未來假設語句：描述未來可能發生的狀況（機率不高）。
If ＋主詞＋ should ＋動詞原形，祈使句或主詞＋（will / shall）＋動詞原形

- **過去假設語句**

If the magazine **were published**, it **would** be a sensation.
要是雜誌發行了，一定會造成轟動。
▶ If ＋主詞＋ were / 動詞過去式，主詞＋ would / could ＋動詞原形。
省略 If ▶ Were the magazine published, it would be a sensation.

- **過去完成假設語句**

If he **had canceled** the trip, he **would have met** Eve.
如果他取消旅行，就會遇到 Eve 了。
▶ If ＋主詞＋ had ＋過去分詞，主詞＋ would / could have ＋過去分詞。
省略 If ▶ Had he canceled the trip, he would have met Eve.

- **未來假設語句**

If you **should ask** for an estimate, it **will be free** of charge.
如果你要求報價，將不會另外收費。
▶ If ＋主詞＋ should ＋動詞原形，主詞＋ will / may ＋動詞原形或是 please ＋動詞原形。
省略 If ▶ Should you ask for an estimate, it will be free of charge.

Step 3 **實戰演練**

1 If the posters had been posted in conspicuous places, more customers ------- the upcoming sale at our shopping complex.

(A) had noticed   (B) noticed   (C) had noticed   (D) would have noticed

2 Had they fixed the heavy machinery used at the construction site at the right time, the repairs cost ------- that costly.

(A) haven't been   (B) wouldn't have been   (C) hadn't been   (D) will have been

▶答案與解析請參考解析本第 14 頁

REVIEW TEST

1. If the musician ------- to rent the Luise Concert Hall situated in downtown, she will use it at a reduced price and will receive additional hours.

   (A) decided
   (B) had decided
   (C) will decide
   (D) decides

2. Some members of the administrative team ------- together to discuss a few possible changes as soon as they heard that the final draft could be modified.

   (A) will gather
   (B) gathers
   (C) have gathered
   (D) gathered

3. City officials in Singapore usually ------- to work in their own cars rather than use public transportation in spite of the extremely high gas prices.

   (A) will commute
   (B) commute
   (C) had commuted
   (D) have commuted

4. The unnecessary labels on the shipment had been removed before the inspectors ------- during the examination.

   (A) find
   (B) found
   (C) had found
   (D) will find

5. If you were to call the real estate agency early this morning, Mr. Taylor ------- you a tour of the property and nearby facilities.

   (A) would give
   (B) gave
   (C) gives
   (D) had given

6. To prepare for the demonstration of the new laser printer, the representatives ------- it next week.

   (A) had rehearsed
   (B) rehearsed
   (C) will rehearse
   (D) rehearse

7. About three weeks ago, specially designed security software ------- on all of the computers to keep them from getting infected with viruses.

   (A) installed
   (B) will be installed
   (C) had installed
   (D) was installed

8. The staff member informed the participants that the free consultation sessions with business leaders ------- earlier than expected.

   (A) had been booked
   (B) are booked
   (C) booked
   (D) have booked

9. If Ms. Turner had checked the weather conditions ahead of time, she ------- the outdoor flea market in Rosa County on a snowy day.

   (A) had attended
   (B) wouldn't have attended
   (C) attended
   (D) have attended

10. By the time there is a thirty-minute intermission for the musical, The Titanic, the actors ------- for an hour.

    (A) performed
    (B) will have performed
    (C) had performed
    (D) have performed

▶答案與解析請參考解析本第 14 頁

類型分析 5

形容詞

形容詞是用來表示人物或是事物性質、狀態的一種詞性，用來修飾名詞或是作為名詞補語。

WARMING UP

01 文法概念前導 ─────────── 正式進入文法單元前，先熟悉一下文法基本概念。

1) 形容詞的基本概念

所謂「形容」一詞本來的意義，是用一段話、一行字或是一個動作等等，來修飾、描述人事物外觀的樣子。因此「形容詞」，便是指用來表示人事物性質或是狀態的詞彙。

2) 形容詞的功用

① 限定用法→位於名詞正前或正後方，作修飾用。

位於名詞前修飾　It is a profitable business.

這是一個有利可圖的事業

位於名詞後修飾　It is a business profitable for them.

這對他們來說是個有利可圖的事業。

▶ 若形容詞後方連接修飾語，便移至名詞後方作修飾。

② 敘述用法→用來敘述主詞或是受詞的狀態。

用來補充主詞　The renovation was complete.
翻修作業已經完成。

用來補充受詞　Please keep your belongings safe.
請保管好自己的私人物品。

3) 形容詞的形態

形容詞通常是「名詞或動詞 + 形容詞字尾」的結構，常見的字尾如下：

字尾	範例
-able	considerable 相當的，重要的　payable 應支付的
-ible	accessible 可使用的　possible 可能的
-al	environmental 環境的　formal 正式的
-sive	expansive 廣闊的，膨脹的　impressive 令人印象深刻的
-tive	protective 具保護性的　attractive 有吸引力的
-ic	economic 經濟的，經濟學的　realistic 實際的，現實的
-ical	economical 節儉的　historical 歷史性的
-ful	beautiful 美麗的　respectful 尊敬的
-ous	conscious 有意識的　numerous 大量的，多數的
-ent	confident 有自信的，確信的　different 不同的
名詞 + ly	costly 昂貴的　friendly 親切的

02 暖身例題

請圈選出括號中最適合的詞彙。

1 All (document / documents) are stored in the cabinets.

2 He is dedicated to preparing for (this / these) event.

3 Instruction manuals will be distributed to each (division / divisions).

4 A (large / several) variety of tools are required for this job.

5 The product will become (available / availability) next month.

03 例題解答

1 **All** <u>documents</u> are stored in the cabinets. 所有文件都被收在檔案櫃裡。

> ▶ 形容詞 all 放在可數複數名詞前使用。

2 He is dedicated to preparing for **this** <u>event</u>. 他竭盡全力去準備這次的活動。

> ▶ 定冠詞 this 放在可數單數名詞前使用。

3 Instruction manuals will be distributed to **each** <u>division</u>. 操作手冊將會發送給各個部門。

> ▶ 形容詞 each 放在可數單數名詞前使用。

4 A **large** <u>variety</u> of tools are required for this job. 這份工作需要用到大量不同的工具。

> ▶ 形容詞 large、wide 跟 broad 經常跟名詞 variety 一起使用。

形容詞的種類有數量形容詞（all、both、double、twice）、指示形容詞（this、that、these、those）、分配形容詞（each、every、any、no），以及性質形容詞（大小、模樣、顏色、材料、新舊）等等分類，雖然在造句時，形容詞彼此的排序上為數量形容詞、指示形容詞、分配形容詞、性質形容詞，但此順序並非必然。

5 The product will <u>become</u> **available** next month. 下個月這個產品就出來了。

> ▶ 形容詞也會接在句型 2 動詞（become）的後方作補語。

Unit 24 形容詞擺放的位置

Step 1 | 實戰重點

解題策略　be、become 動詞後方空格，請選擇形容詞的選項填入。

 代表題型

All of the computers in the city library are ------- to the public, but there are fines for using them roughly.

(A) availability　　(B) availably　　(C) available　　(D) avail

 攻略解題法

All of the computers in the city library are ------- to the public, but there are fines
　　　主詞 (複數)　　　　　　介系詞片語　　動詞　補語　　介系詞片語　　　　　　主詞　動詞　補語 (名詞)

for using them roughly.
介系詞片語　受詞　副詞

> 補語的位置只能填入名詞或形容詞

> 將所有修飾語句刪去後，原句為 All of the computers are available, but there are fines

(A) availability　　(B) availably　　(C) available　　(D) avail
名詞（語意上不符）　　副詞　　　　　形容詞　　　　動詞

文句分析　介系詞片語（in the city library）完全不影響整個句子結構，因此千萬不要將介系詞片語錯當主詞。主詞為 All of the computers，為複數，因此後方需接續複數動詞（are）。

說明　句型 2 動詞 be、become、remain、stay 後方空格，為形容詞補語的位置，多益出題大多以 be、become 為主。而本題正是「be / become（＋副詞）＋ ------」的句型，空格中須填入形容詞，可知答案為 (C) available。

翻譯　市立圖書館的所有電腦都可供大眾使用，但不當使用時將課以罰金。

單字片語　available 可使用的／ public 大眾／ fine 罰金／ roughly 粗暴地，大略

解答　(C)

★ 攻略 POINT

形容詞可置於 be 動詞或是 become 後方，作補語用。

核心理論

形容詞用來修飾名詞，或作為補語。

> 動詞 + **形容詞** + 名詞
> 主詞 + be / become + **形容詞（補語）**
> 主詞 + 句型 5 動詞 + 受詞 + **形容詞（受詞補語）**

The human resources department spent a **considerable** time training new employees.
人事部花了相當多的時間來訓練新員工。
▶ 名詞（time）前方是形容詞（considerable）的位置。

According to a recent survey, our customer service is the most **reliable**.
根據最近的調查，我們的顧客服務是最值得信任的。
▶ be / become 後方是形容詞（reliable）的位置。

The entertaining advertisement made our new products **popular**.
這個具娛樂性的廣告，讓我們的產品變得熱門。
▶ 受詞補語位置可放上形容詞（popular）。

Step 3 | 實戰演練

1 Since the article about the presidential election by Janet Ayre is -------, it is expected to draw more readers to the website than before.

(A) excluding   (B) exclusion   (C) exclusively   (D) exclusive

2 The ------- booklet helps you to learn about scholarships, tuition, and exchange student programs, and it provides many helpful tips for new students.

(A) informatively   (B) informative   (C) information   (D) informing

▶答案與解析請參考解析本第 16 頁

Unit 25　形容詞的形態

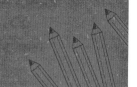

解題策略　　請熟悉形容詞中常見的字尾。

 代表題型

> It is obvious that the success of the system remains ------- on employee productivity.
>
> (A) contingently　　(B) contingence　　(C) contingent　　(D) contingenting

攻略解題法

It　is　obvious that the success of the system remains ------- on employee productivity.
主詞動詞　補語　　　　　連接詞＋主詞＋動詞　　　　補語　　　介系詞片語
→主格 it

句型 2 動詞 remain 後方
通常接續形容詞

(A) contingently　　(B) contingence　　(C) contingent　　(D) contingenting
　副詞　　　　　　　　名詞　　　　　　　形容詞　　　　　　動名詞

文句分析　　當兩個名詞結合在一起，呈「名詞＋名詞」的狀態，便稱之為複合名詞。employee productivity「員工生產力」，是個常見的複合名詞。主格 it 用來代表 that 子句，由於主詞必須簡短，因此使用 it 來代替。

說明　　　　句型 2 動詞（remain）後方空格，為形容詞補語的位置。雖然本題的選項 contingent 並非常見字彙，但我們可由空格須填入形容詞，以及常見的形容詞字尾 -ent 來推斷，答案呼之欲出，為 (C) contingent。

翻譯　　　　很明顯地，系統的成功與否，視員工生產力而定。

單字片語　　obvious 明顯的／remain 保持／contingent on 視～而定／employee productivity 員工生產力

解答　　　　(C)

攻略 POINT

必須記住形容詞常見的字尾，面對形容詞字彙的難題，才能輕鬆解開。

核心理論

請記住以下常見的形容詞字尾。

> -tive, -ive, -tile, -ous, -ful, -ing, -ed, -ate, -ary, -ar,
> -ory, -ical, -ial, -ic, -id, -ish, -ant, -ent, -able, -ible

We are currently interviewing candidates for the **vacant** position.
我們為了這個職缺,目前正在面試應徵者。
▶ 字尾 -ant 是形容詞的常見字尾。

Mr. Robert in the marketing department was considered a **versatile** candidate.
行銷部門的 Robert 先生,被視為是個多才多藝的候選人。
▶ 字尾 -tile 是形容詞的常見字尾。

The company has served only **healthy** food to its customers for over 10 years.
超過十年以上,這間公司只提供健康的食物給消費者。
▶ 字尾 -y 是形容詞的常見字尾。

The interior design company located in the heart of downtown remains **authentic**.
位於市中心的室內裝潢公司很值得信任。
▶ 字尾 -ic 是形容詞的常見字尾。

Our product catalog is **available** upon request without any charge.
我們的產品目錄在您申請後,即可免費提供。
▶ 字尾 -able 是形容詞的常見字尾。

Step 3 | 實戰演練

1 The purpose of this outdoor event is to give ------- clients chances to try our new cosmetics and to provide feedback.

(A) potentialize   (B) potentiality   (C) potentially   (D) potential

2 The process of the company reimbursing all business travel expenses after the receipts are submitted is now -------.

(A) prevalency   (B) prevalent   (C) prevalently   (D) prevalencies

▶答案與解析請參考解析本第 16 頁

Unit 26　形容詞＋名詞常見組合

解題策略　　請熟記考題中常出現的「形容詞＋名詞」組合。

 代表題型

The CEO emphasized that the sales of the newly released car have exceeded those of

former models, thanks to the company's ------- employees.

(A) reliable　　　　(B) satisfying　　　　(C) rapid　　　　(D) real

 攻略解題法

The CEO emphasized that the sales of the newly released car have exceeded those of
　主詞　　　動詞　　　連接詞　　　　　　　　主詞　　　　　　　　動詞　　受詞
　　　　　　　　　　　　　　　　　動詞（emphasized）的受詞（名詞子句）

former models, thanks to the company's ------- employees.
　　　　　　　　介系詞片語　　　　介系詞（thanks to）的受詞

> 在 the company's（所有格）與 employees
> （名詞）間，只能填入形容詞或是名詞

(A) reliable　　　　(B) satisfying　　　　(C) rapid　　　　(D) real
　值得信賴的　　　　　滿足的　　　　　　　迅速的　　　　　　實際的

文句分析　　that 是名詞子句的連接詞，名詞子句必須要完整符合「主詞＋動詞＋受詞」的結構。

說明　　　　與空格後方名詞（employees）語意符合的形容詞，只有 (A) reliable。reliable employees
　　　　　　是「值得信賴的員工」，常在考題中出現。此外，reliable 還會跟 analysis（分析）、
　　　　　　products（產品）等名詞，經常一起出現。

翻譯　　　　CEO 強調新上市的車款銷售量已超過前一代舊款，這都要感謝公司內這群值得信賴的員
　　　　　　工們。

單字片語　　emphasize 強調／ sales 銷售量／ newly 新的／ release 上市／ exceed 超過／ former 之
　　　　　　前的／ thanks to 感謝～／ reliable 值得信賴的

解答　　　　(A)

✎ 攻略 POINT

請務必記住常與名詞成雙出現的形容詞。

核心理論

以下是常見的「形容詞＋名詞」組合：

additional information 補充資料	adequate component supply 足夠的零件供給
prior notice 事前通知	affordable price 可負擔的價格
annual budget 年度預算	comparable experience 不相上下的經驗
complete list 完整清單	comprehensive knowledge 綜合知識
confidential information 機密資訊	considerable amount / effect 相當的數量／影響
continuous improvement 持續的改善	discontinued appliance 停產的家電
drastic change 急劇的變化	economic progress 經濟發展
effective technique 有效率的技術	exact shipment date 確切的配送日期
excellent service 優秀的服務	exceptional contribution 特殊貢獻
extensive damage 大規模的傷害	favorable circumstance 有利的情況
final approval 最終批准	financial analyst 財務分析
further detail 進一步的細節	general contractor 總承包商
high temperature 高溫	immediate supervisor 直屬上司
important consideration 重要的考量	impressive qualification 令人印象深刻的經歷
improper transaction 不正當交易	inclement weather 惡劣的天氣

WalMeat is well-known for its **affordable prices** and good quality.
WalMeat 以實惠的價格與良好的品質而聞名。

Without **prior notice**, we cannot provide enough information for the event.
如果沒有事前通知，我們無法提供該活動足夠的資訊。

Step 3　實戰演練

1 The record-breaking rain in Queensland also resulted in ------- damage to residential areas and plenty of farmhouses in the region.

(A) useful　　(B) careful　　(C) coming　　(D) extensive

2 One of the reasons why the AOS Shopping Mall has become the best shopping center on Maple Street is that customers can purchase high-quality goods at ------- prices there.

(A) annual　　(B) affordable　　(C) discontinued　　(D) inclement

▶ 答案與解析請參考解析本第 17 頁

Unit 27 形容詞＋介系詞常見組合

Step 1 實戰重點

解題策略　當考題中出現「be 動詞＋形容詞＋介系詞」時，通常是詢問形容詞字彙的考題。

 代表題型

> Apart from cooking, all chefs at Blue Wave are ------- for following sanitary standards.
>
> (A) clear　　　　　　(B) true　　　　　　(C) responsible　　　　　　(D) active

 攻略解題法

Apart from cooking, all chefs at Blue Wave are ------- for following sanitary standards.
介系詞片語　　　主詞　　介系詞片語　動詞　補語　介系詞　動名詞　動名詞（following）的受詞

介系詞後方多接續名詞或動名詞

(A) clear　　　　　(B) true　　　　　(C) responsible　　　　　(D) active
清楚的　　　　　　真正的　　　　　　有責任的　　　　　　　活潑的，積極的

文句分析　apart from 是介系詞，表「～之外」。介系詞（for）與受詞（sanitary standard）間，是動名詞（following）的位置。

說明　　　當空格後方接的是介系詞時，通常是詢問該介系詞應搭配哪一個形容詞的題型。而接續介系詞 for 的選項，只有 responsible，其餘的選項語意不合，也無法搭配 for 使用，因此 (C) responsible 為正解。responsible for 表示「對～有責任」。

翻譯　　　除了做菜之外，Blue Wave 的所有廚師都有責任去遵循衛生標準。

單字片語　apart from 除了～／ chef 廚師／ be responsible for 對～有責任／ follow 遵照，跟隨／ sanitary standard 衛生標準

解答　　　(C)

攻略 POINT

記住常見的「be 動詞＋形容詞＋介系詞」組合後，務必注意介系詞的搭配。

📖 核心理論

以下是常見的「形容詞＋介系詞」組合：

be associated with 與～有關	be complete with 具有～，連同～
be comparable with 與～相較之下	be compatible with 與～相容
be consistent with 與～符合	be consonant with 與～一致
be correspondent with 與～一致	be faced with 面對～
be pleased with 對～感到開心	

be accessible to 可連接至～，可使用～	be accustomed to 習慣於～
be adjacent to 與～鄰接的	be affordable to 可負擔～
be attractive to 對～有吸引力	be available to 可以～
be beneficial to 對～是有利可圖的	be close to 與～很接近
be comparable to 與～不相上下	be comprehensible to 對～充分理解
be devoted to 致力於～	be entitled to 有資格～
be equal to 與～平等	be equivalent to 相當於～
be exposed to 暴露在～	be harmful to 對～有害
be integral to 對～是不可或缺的	be liable to 對～有責任
be responsible for 對～有責任的	be aware of 注意到～

The chief manager of the assembly line **is** fully **responsible for** finding defective parts.
生產線的總經理必須負起全責找出不良品。

They **are faced with** a new problem.
他們面臨到新的問題。

1 Some confidential documents, such as lists of customers and financial statements, are only ------- to the agents in charge.

(A) eager   (B) accessible   (C) willing   (D) instructive

2 Through a continuous effort over a long period of time, GNS Health's brand power is now ------- with all of its competitors in Australia.

(A) liable   (B) capable   (C) responsive   (D) comparable

▶答案與解析請參考解析本第 17 頁

REVIEW TEST

1. Considering her ------- knowledge and four years of experience, Ms. Anna Paulson would be best suited for the open position in Sales.
   (A) compulsory   (B) comprehensive
   (C) respective   (D) elegant

2. The top priorities of the shipping company are to pick up and deliver products on their ------- shipment dates and to deliver parcels without any breakage or loss.
   (A) exactly   (B) exact
   (C) exacted   (D) exactness

3. The personnel director is currently seeking candidates with ------- qualifications and willingness to travel on short notice.
   (A) impressive   (B) impressed
   (C) impression   (D) impressing

4. The results of the study conducted at the Ailack Lab showed that workers who take short breaks are more ------- than those who don't.
   (A) creativity   (B) creation
   (C) create   (D) creative

5. Whenever you transfer money by mobile phone, checking your application for security is ------- to preventing hacking problems.
   (A) integral   (B) compliant
   (C) easy   (D) ready

6. The wage cuts at many firms and rising unemployment rates might be ------- with the recent failure of the country's trade policy with Australia.
   (A) punctual   (B) specific
   (C) associated   (D) equivalent

7. If any employee wants to take paid leave this month, download the necessary form from the intranet and e-mail it to your ------- supervisor.
   (A) immediately   (B) immediate
   (C) immediacies   (D) immediacy

8. Despite the fact that the TLS Agency is ------- with financial troubles, it is aggressively advertising the TLS Turbo on major portal sites.
   (A) faced   (B) official
   (C) successive   (D) indicative

9. All arrangements for the company picnic, which most employees are supposed to attend, will be ------- sooner than we estimated.
   (A) completion   (B) complete
   (C) completed   (D) to complete

10. Unlike many professors, who argue that it is not timely, a few market experts are still ------- about the Middle East investment.
    (A) aware   (B) complete
    (C) proficient   (D) optimistic

▶ 答案與解析請參考解析本第 17 頁

類型分析 6

副詞

副詞對於整個句子結構完全不會造成任何影響,就算沒有副詞,也不會破壞句子結構。雖然如此,副詞卻可以讓句子的語意變得更加完善、豐富。副詞通常位於形容詞、副詞、動詞,或是一整個句子的前方,不過在修飾動詞時,也可放在動詞後方。

WARMING UP

01 文法概念前導 ⸺⸺⸺⸺⸺ 正式進入文法單元前，先熟悉一下文法基本概念。

1) 副詞的基本概念
副詞常見於句子中，用來作為「怎麼樣」的說明，作修飾用。因此，除了某些例外的狀況，一般而言，就算將副詞省去，對句子的結構也不會有任何影響。

2) 副詞的功用
相對於形容詞的功能是用來修飾名詞，副詞則是用來修飾動詞、形容詞以及其他的副詞。

① 修飾動詞

　　ex) run 跑步 → run fast 跑得很快

　　▶ 當副詞用來修飾動詞時，通常會置於動詞後方。

② 修飾形容詞

　　ex) pretty 美麗 → very pretty 非常美麗

③ 修飾其他副詞

　　ex) always 總是 → nearly always 幾乎總是

3) 副詞的形態
雖然不一定所有副詞都符合此規則，但大部份在形容詞後方接上 -ly 後，便成為副詞。

副詞的形態	範例
形容詞 + ly	final + ly → finally 最後 current + ly → currently 現在 rapid + ly → rapidly 迅速地 short + ly → shortly 短暫地
-le + ly → -ly	simple + ly → simply 簡單地 flexible + ly → flexibly 有彈性地
-y + ly → ily	necessary + ly → necessarily 必要地 temporary + ly → temporarily 暫時地

02 暖身例題

請圈選出括號中最適合的詞彙。

1 This place can (easy / easily) accommodate over 10,000 people.

2 The company hired (approximate / approximately) 30 new employees.

3 We should make a decision about the issue (immediate / immediately).

4 The conference was (quite / quitely) successful and very useful.

5 All of our employees work (very / well) hard.

03 例題解答

1 This place can **easily** accommodate over 10,000 people.
這個地方可以輕易容納超過一萬人。

> ▶ 副詞是用來修飾動詞、形容詞以及其他的副詞，並非句子結構中的必要元素，純粹是用來加強或是補充該詞彙的語意。這題中的副詞 easily 就是用來補充說明動詞 accommodate。

2 The company hired **approximately** 30 new employees.
公司聘用了大約三十名的新員工。

> ▶ 這裡的 approximately 是特殊副詞，通常特殊副詞只能用來修飾特定的詞彙。

3 We should make a decision about the issue **immediately**.
我們應該要立刻針對這個議題做出決定。

> ▶ 本例句是將副詞放在句尾，用來修飾整個句子。

4 The conference was **quite** successful and **very** useful.
這場會議非常成功且有用。

> ▶ quite（副詞）用來修飾 successful（形容詞），very（副詞）則是用來修飾 useful（形容詞）。要注意的是，並沒有 quitely 這個字彙。

5 All of our employees work **very** hard.
我們所有的員工都非常努力地工作。

> ▶ very（副詞）修飾 hard（副詞）。

Unit 28 副詞擺放的位置 ❶

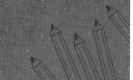

解題策略　當選項中出現副詞，並且考題的句型為「主詞＋ be ＋過去分詞」時，後方空格百分之百為副詞。

 代表題型

According to the quarterly statistical report, our income has decreased ------- compared to that of last year.

(A) consideration   (B) considerable   (C) considerably   (D) considerate

---

 攻略解題法

According to the quarterly statistical report, our income has decreased
　　　　　　　　　　　介系詞片語　　　　　　　　　　主詞　　　動詞

------- compared to that of last year.
副詞　　介系詞片語（修飾語句）　　　　　　　　　完整句子

> 當句子的構造已完整，前後方的語句都是修飾語句，而能夠用來修飾動詞的，唯有副詞

(A) consideration   (B) considerable   (C) considerably   (D) considerate
　　名詞　　　　　　　　　　形容詞　　　　　　　　　副詞　　　　　　　　形容詞

文句分析　decrease 是沒有受詞的不及物動詞。本句最主要的結構便是 our income has decreased，剩下的語句皆為修飾語。

說明　　　完整句子後方的空格，多為副詞。所謂的完整句子便是包含主詞與動詞的結構，句型 3 的被動式自然也屬於完整句，因為純粹是從「主詞＋動詞＋受詞」的主動式，變化為「主詞＋ be 動詞＋過去分詞」的被動式而已。可推論出完整句子後方，或是「主詞＋ be 動詞＋過去分詞」後方必為副詞，因此 (C) considerably 即為正解。

翻譯　　　根據每季統計報告，相較於去年，我們的收入大幅度地下降。

單字片語　according to 根據～／ quarterly 每季／ statistical 統計的／ income 收入／ decrease 減少／ compare to 相較於～／ consideration 考慮，體諒／ considerable 相當的／ considerate 考慮周到的

解答　　　(C)

 攻略 POINT

完整句子後方、不及物動詞前後、動詞＋受詞的前後方以及動詞與動詞間的空格，都是副詞的位置。

核心理論

根據句子組成的元素不同，副詞可能出現在以下幾個位置：

- **副詞**＋及物動詞＋受詞
- 不及物動詞＋**副詞**
- be 動詞＋過去分詞＋**副詞**
- 及物動詞＋受詞＋**副詞**
- be 動詞＋**副詞**＋現在／過去分詞
- have ＋**副詞**＋過去分詞

You should **carefully** review your submissions.

你應該要仔細檢查你提交的資料。

▶「動詞（＋受詞）」前方的空格百分之百是副詞的位置。

Please report the matter **immediately** to your supervisor.

請立即向你的上司報告這個問題。

▶「動詞＋受詞」後方的空格百分之百是副詞的位置。

The total income rose **dramatically**.

整體收入急劇上升。

▶ 不及物動詞後方的空格百分之百是副詞的位置。

This data was **continually** updated.

這份資料持續在更新。

▶ be 動詞與過去分詞間的空格百分之百是副詞的位置。

Our most recent order was delivered **promptly**.

我們最新的訂單有準時送達。

▶「be 動詞＋過去分詞」後方的空格百分之百是副詞的位置。

The companies have **recently** modernized their systems.

最近很多公司都已經將他們的系統現代化了。

▶ have 與過去分詞間的空格百分之百是副詞的位置。

Step 3 | 實戰演練

1 Fortunately, our hotel is close to the station, which is ------- located for us to transfer, so we don't have to worry about traffic jams.

(A) convenient   (B) convenience   (C) conveniently   (D) inconvenient

2 We have been concerning about the company's current situation, but as the country's economy stabilizes, it will also ------- stabilize.

(A) eventual   (B) eventually   (C) eventuality   (D) eventuate

▶答案與解析請參考解析本第 19 頁

Unit 29 副詞擺放的位置 ❷

 Step 1 | **實戰重點**

解題策略　當選項中出現副詞時，形容詞前方空格百分之百為副詞。

🎓 代表題型

As we mentioned before, this contract is ------- beneficial to both of our companies and will not harm any employees.

(A) mutuality　　　(B) mutualism　　　(C) mutually　　　(D) mutual

🖊 攻略解題法

As　we mentioned before, this contract is ------- beneficial (to both of our companies)
連接詞 主詞　　動詞　　　副詞　　　主詞　　動詞　　形容詞（補語）　　　介系詞片語

and　will not harm any employees.
對等　　　　動詞　　　受詞
連接詞 ⤳ 省略了 this contract

┌─────────────────┐
│ be 動詞＋副詞＋形容詞 │
└─────────────────┘

(A) mutuality　　　　　(B) mutualism　　　　(C) mutually　　　　(D) mutual
　　名詞　　　　　　　　　名詞　　　　　　　　副詞　　　　　　　形容詞

文句分析　本題中，連接兩個完整子句的連接詞用了 as，而主句中用來連接兩個動詞片語的對等連接詞，則是 and。

說明　　　副詞可以用來修飾形容詞或是分詞，而形容詞（beneficial）前方的空格百分之百是副詞位置，因此本題答案為 (C) mutually。

翻譯　　　正如同我們之前提到的，這份合約對我們兩家公司來說是互有助益的，並且不會傷害到任何員工。

單字片語　mention 提及／contract 合約／be beneficial to 對～來說有利益／mutually 互相地／mutuality 相互關係／mutual 相互的，彼此的

解答　　　(C)

✏️ 攻略 POINT
「形容詞（＋名詞）」與「分詞（現在分詞／過去分詞）＋名詞」前方的空格為副詞。

核心理論

副詞多位於形容詞或副詞前方作修飾。

> **副詞**＋形容詞（＋名詞）
> **副詞**＋現在分詞＋名詞
> **副詞**＋過去分詞＋名詞

The amended traffic regulations were **extremely** complex.
修改過後的交通條款非常複雜。

Dr. Rivera gave a **highly** interesting presentation.
Rivera 博士發表了一份非常有趣的演講報告。

This project was done by a **newly** hired employee.
這份企劃是由新招募的員工所完成。

▶ 副詞可以修飾形容詞與分詞，因此「過去分詞＋名詞（hired employee）」前方的空格，可填入副詞。

Step 3 | **實戰演練**

1 With help from the real estate investment group, he is investing in a ------- emerging real estate market.

(A) rapidities   (B) rapidity   (C) rapid   (D) rapidly

2 The city's Urban Development Department came up with the idea of luring residents from other areas with ------- new luxury apartment complexes.

(A) related   (B) relatively   (C) relation   (D) relative

▶答案與解析請參考解析本第 19 頁

常見副詞 ❶

Step 1 | **實戰重點**

解題策略　「數字＋名詞」前方的空格，多使用 approximately、nearly、almost 等副詞。

🎓 代表題型

> The corporation's new policy on the environment can provide town residents with job opportunities and can even help save ------- 3-3.50 million dollars a year.
>
> (A) approximately　　(B) approximate　　(C) approximation　　(D) approximative

✏️ 攻略解題法

The corporation's new policy (on the environment) can provide town residents (with job
　　　主詞　　　　　　　　　介系詞片語　　　　　　　動詞　　　　受詞　　　　介系詞片語

opportunities) and can even help save ------- 3-3.50 million dollars a year.　為一動詞片語
　　　　　　　對等連接詞　動詞　　　副詞 數字（形容詞）　　　　數字屬於形容詞

連接動詞片語的
對等連接詞

動詞片語

help 後方連接
原形動詞

(A) approximately　　　(B) approximate　　　(C) approximation　　　(D) approximative
　　副詞　　　　　　　　　形容詞　　　　　　　名詞　　　　　　　　形容詞

文句分析　and 用來作為連接動詞片語的對等連接詞。省略 to 的不定詞 save 作為 help 的受詞，而 save 本身另有自己的受詞。

說明　　　數字可作形容詞，也可作為名詞用，然而在多益考題中，只會出現「數字＋名詞」的組合，此時作形容詞用。形容詞必須要靠副詞來修飾，因此當考題空格出現在「數字＋名詞」正前方時，答案百分之百是副詞。由此可知本題 (A) approximately 為答案。

翻譯　　　公司對於環境的新政策可以提供城鎮居民工作機會，甚至還可幫忙減少一年大約三百到三百五十萬元的支出。

單字片語　provide A with B 提供 B 給 A／resident 居民／job opportunity 就業機會／approximately 大約／approximate 相近的／approximation 近似值／approximative 近似的

解答　　　(A)

✎ **攻略 POINT**

當數字作形容詞時，「數字＋名詞」的前方即為副詞的位置。

Step 2 ｜ 核心理論 & 基礎形式

 核心理論

> 請記住以下這些連接在「數字＋名詞」前方的常見副詞。
>
> | promptly 準時，如期 | almost (= nearly) 幾乎 | at least 至少 |
> | more than (= over) ～以上 | up to 最多至～ | approximately 大概 |

This year's annual employee awards banquet will begin **promptly** at 6:00.
本年度的員工頒獎典禮將會在六點準時開始。

Almost 25 commuters use nothing other than public transportation.
幾乎有二十五位通勤者只使用大眾運輸工具。

All candidates must submit their resumes **at least** 7 days before their job interviews.
所有應徵者都必須至少在面試七天前，提交他們的履歷表。

To get your passport, you have to wait **more than** 3 days.
要拿到護照，你至少得等三天以上。

The installation of new computer programs is scheduled to start at **approximately** 9:00 a.m.
電腦新程式的安裝，已經排好大約在早上九點開始。

Step 3 ｜ 實戰演練

1 His company has been doing business in Singapore for ------- six years, which has been a great help to his own e-commerce.

(A) ever since　　(B) and then　　(C) more than　　(D) even though

2 We are truly sorry to inform you that out of 1,000 applicants, we will only choose ------- 20 participants to take part in this project.

(A) furthermore　　(B) at times　　(C) not more　　(D) up to

▶答案與解析請參考解析本第 19 頁

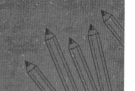

Unit 31　常見副詞 ❷

解題策略　　在句點（.）跟逗號（,）中間，必須填入連接副詞。

🎓 代表題型

In comparison with your last performance, this number seems to be reasonable. -------,
you will still have to work to increase the sales.

(A) Because　　　　(B) In addition　　　　(C) However　　　　(D) But

✏️ 攻略解題法

In comparison with your last performance, this number seems to be reasonable. -------,
　　　　介系詞片語　　　　　　　　　　　　　　主詞　　動詞　　　　不定詞　　　　副詞

you will still have to work (to increase the sales).
主詞 助動詞 副詞　　動詞　　　不定詞（作副詞用，表目的）

動詞片語

> seem to be 形容詞，
> 表示「看起來像〜」

(A) Because　　　　　(B) In addition　　　　(C) However　　　　(D) But
　連接詞　　　　　　　　連接副詞　　　　　　　連接副詞　　　　　　連接詞

文句分析　　in comparison with 是介系詞，而 seem to be~，意思為「看起來像〜」。

說明　　　　句點（.）跟逗號（,）中間，是連接副詞的位置。請記住，連接詞無法放在連接副詞的位置，因此可以先刪去選項 (A)、(D)。而 (B) 是用來對前面的句子作補充，(C) 則是與前面的句子作對照。本題的空格前方「這個數據看來很合理」，與後方「你還是需要繼續努力來提高銷售額」為對照的關係，因此 (C) However 為答案。特別要注意的是，考題中的副詞 still 常常使用在對照的語句內。

翻譯　　　　比對你上一次的表現，這個數據看來很合理，但你還是需要繼續努力來提高銷售額。

單字片語　　in comparison with 相較於〜／ reasonable 合理的

解答　　　　(C)

✏️ 攻略 POINT

請記住，連接詞無法取代連接副詞，必須分清楚連接詞與連接副詞放置的位置。

核心理論

> **連接副詞**：確認前後句的相對關係是因果、對照還是補充後，利用連接副詞將兩句連接起來，連接副詞的前方使用句號或分號，而後方則為逗號。

讓步	however 然而　　nevertheless 儘管如此　　nonetheless 儘管如此
對照	on the other hand 另一方面來說　　in contrast 相對而言
因果	therefore 因此　　thus 於是　　as a result 結果，因此 consequently 結果
時間	meanwhile 同時　　at the same time 在此同時
補充	furthermore 此外　　moreover 而且　　in addition 此外 besides 除此之外

錯誤的例子	正確的例子
連接副詞＋主詞＋動詞，主詞＋動詞	主詞＋動詞. 連接副詞，主詞＋動詞
主詞＋動詞＋連接副詞＋主詞＋動詞	主詞＋動詞；連接副詞，主詞＋動詞

The stock price decreased, **however**, the emergency protocol initiated today stabilized it.
股價跌了，然而，今天開始生效的緊急協議將其穩定住了。

We won first prize at the trade fair. **In addition**, we have the dominant position in the market.
我們在展銷會中獲得了第一名，此外，我們在市場上也獲得了優勢。

We are unable to repair the machine and **therefore** will provide a replacement.
我們無法修理好這個機器，因此，我們將會提供替代品。

Step 3 實戰演練

1 Our sales team set a remarkable record last week. -------, the president will designate us as the team of the year.

(A) Instead of　　　(B) Otherwise　　　(C) Though　　　(D) Moreover

2 It might be a good idea to call the Security Department in advance; -------, it might take days for you to get a pass card.

(A) but　　　(B) otherwise　　　(C) although　　　(D) therefore

▶答案與解析請參考解析本第 19 頁

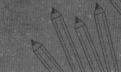

Unit 32 常見副詞 ③

Step 1 | 實戰重點

解題策略 否定句後方接 yet。

代表題型

Even though he claimed that he had gotten approval on the team project, we can't start it as the official document is not ready -------.

(A) already　　　(B) still　　　(C) yet　　　(D) never

攻略解題法

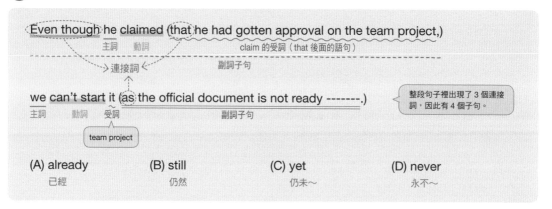

Even though he claimed (that he had gotten approval on the team project,)
主詞　動詞　　　　　claim 的受詞（that 後面的語句）
→連接詞←　　　　　副詞子句

we can't start it (as the official document is not ready -------.)
主詞　　動詞　受詞　　　　副詞子句
team project

整段句子裡出現了 3 個連接詞，因此有 4 個子句。

(A) already　　　(B) still　　　(C) yet　　　(D) never
已經　　　　　仍然　　　　仍未～　　　　永不～

文句分析　even though、that 跟 as 都是作連接詞用。類似這種結構複雜的句子，將修飾語全部刪去後，會比較能夠掌握。

說明　「副詞 yet 於否定語氣時使用」，這句話並非完全正確。因為就算是否定句，yet 仍無法放置在否定句前方的空格處。所以應該是要明確記住「yet 是放在否定句後方」，而非純粹使用在否定語氣內，這樣才能夠減少失誤的出現。本題答案為 (C) yet。

翻譯　儘管他聲稱他已拿到這個小組企劃案的批准，但因為官方文件還沒準備好，我們仍無法開始。

單字片語　even though 儘管／ claim 主張／ approval 批准／ as 因為～／ official 官方

解答　(C)

攻略 POINT

考題中常常會出現 still、yet、already、finally 等等特殊副詞的字彙題，因此須清楚了解這些副詞的特性。

核心理論

常見的特殊副詞

特殊副詞的特性	
still 仍然	否定語氣中會使用 still not。作副詞用時，偶爾也有「可是」的意思。
yet 仍未～	主詞＋ not yet ＋動詞（主要為否定語氣） （例外）have yet to 仍未～
already 已經	常常以 have already p.p. 的句型出現
finally 總算	通常出現在具連續性的動作或狀況後，用來修飾整個句子

We have <u>not</u> **yet** decided on a place for the company outing.
我們還沒決定好員工旅遊的地點。

We are waiting for the results of the last board meeting, but they have <u>not</u> come out **yet**.
我們正在等待上次董事會議的結果，但還沒出來。

She **has yet to** do anything to rectify the problem.
她還沒做任何動作來改正問題。
▶ yet（尚未）放在否定句後方，或是 has to do 的中間。

He went to London on a business trip, and he is **still** in London.
他去倫敦出差，目前人還在倫敦。
▶ still（仍然）通常用於肯定句。

The committee has **already** accepted his letter of resignation.
委員會已經受理他的辭職信了。
▶ already（已經）放置在 have（had）和過去分詞之間。

The government **finally** enacted some new regulations.
政府總算執行了一些新的規章。
▶ finally（總算）通常會跟動詞過去式一起出現。

Step **3** | **實戰演練**

1 The committee has ------- not decided whether or not Mr. Jenkins will get promoted.

(A) once   (B) already   (C) still   (D) yet

2 The general meeting will begin in a few hours, but several teams have ------- to do any research on the session's agenda.

(A) already   (B) yet   (C) still   (D) finally

▶答案與解析請參考解析本第 20 頁

Step 1 | **實戰重點**

解題策略　記住這些常與副詞一同出現的基本題型後，便可在三秒內快速解題。

 代表題型

The reason for the export decline is ------- that the cost of oil and shipping has increased greatly in the past two months.

(A) intentionally　　(B) radically　　(C) primarily　　(D) substantially

 攻略解題法

The reason (for the export decline) is -------
　　主詞　　　　　介系詞片語　　動詞

(that the cost of oil and shipping has increased greatly in the past two months.)
連接詞　　　　主詞　　　　　　　動詞　　　副詞　　　　介系詞片語
- -
　　　　　　　　　　　　名詞子句

(A) intentionally　　(B) radically　　(C) primarily　　(D) substantially
　故意地　　　　　　　徹底地　　　　　　主要　　　　　大體上，基本上

文句分析　請記住「The reason ＋（介系詞片語）＋ be 動詞＋ primarily ＋ that...」，意思是「～主要的理由，即是 that...」。

說明　　　primarily、mainly、chiefly（主要）等等的副詞，常與表理由的連接詞、介系詞片語、rely on（依靠～）、depend on（根據～）、responsible for（對～有責任）等等，出現於考題中，因此請一同背誦。

翻譯　　　外銷減少的理由，主要是由於油價與海運的成本在過去兩個月大幅上漲。

單字片語　decline 減少／ primarily 主要／ cost 費用／ greatly 大幅地

解答　　　(C)

攻略 POINT
primarily 常常與表理由的連接詞跟介系詞片語一起使用。

核心理論

請記住以下常見於考題的副詞以及基本副詞：

briefly	簡略地	originally	本來，最初
carefully	仔細地，小心地	perfectly	完美地
clearly	清楚地	permanently	永久地
closely	密切地，留心地	previously	之前
considerably	相當地	primarily	主要
consistently	一貫地	promptly	立刻
continuously	持續地	properly	恰當地
conveniently	方便地	quickly	快速地
directly	直接	quite	相當地
easily	輕易地	rapidly	迅速地
exactly	就是，準確地	rarely	很少
exclusively	專有地，唯一地	recently	最近
extremely	極度，非常	relatively	相對而言
frequently	頻繁地	routinely	慣常地
generously	慷慨地	seldom	很少
gradually	逐漸地	severely	嚴重地
heavily	嚴重地，大量地	shortly	立刻，不久後
highly	非常	specially	特別地
immediately	立即	suddenly	突然地
mainly	主要	thoroughly	徹底地，好好地
moderately	適當地	tightly	緊緊地
mutually	相互地	unexpectedly	意外地

Be sure to submit them **immediately** to the general manager. 請務必立刻將它們呈交給總經理。

The unemployment rate among graduates is **especially** high. 畢業生的失業率特別高。

Step 3　實戰演練

1 Workers ------- experience confusion when there is a change in the work system even if it does not occur suddenly.

(A) originally　　　　(B) normally　　　　(C) accessibly　　　　(D) conveniently

2 The company's success is ------- due to the president's philosophy, which is his constant persistence on the quality of the company's products.

(A) allegedly　　　　(B) formerly　　　　(C) tightly　　　　(D) mainly

▶答案與解析請參考解析本第 20 頁

REVIEW TEST

1. We are truly sorry that the particular service you asked about is ------- unavailable.
   - (A) permanently
   - (B) permanent
   - (C) permanence
   - (D) permanences

2. This product is ------- recommended to people who need fresh food ingredients every week.
   - (A) hard
   - (B) high
   - (C) hardly
   - (D) highly

3. After Mr. Rouja finished reading the woman's resume and letters of recommendation, he hired her -------.
   - (A) immediate
   - (B) immediacy
   - (C) immediately
   - (D) to immediate

4. We provide tax refunds for card purchases -------- due to the new legislation enacted by the government.
   - (A) very
   - (B) only
   - (C) once
   - (D) quite

5. On the contract above, the company ------- agreed to lead a balanced management by extensively reflecting the opinions of all board members.
   - (A) original
   - (B) originally
   - (C) origin
   - (D) originality

6. Several corporations in the industry have ------- not recovered from last month's walkouts by their employees.
   - (A) yet
   - (B) already
   - (C) besides
   - (D) still

7. The company is planning to go public this year; -------, it is unusual for a company structured like this to succeed.
   - (A) though
   - (B) however
   - (C) thus
   - (D) in case

8. Due to the strike in New York in 2017, ------- half of our market share remained frozen until last year.
   - (A) unusually
   - (B) nearly
   - (C) quietly
   - (D) randomly

9. The program was ------- easy both to upload and download, but now, due to the changed policy on piracy, people cannot do either action with a simple click of the mouse.
   - (A) generously
   - (B) previously
   - (C) carefully
   - (D) mainly

10. Currently, the position is permanently assigned to a well-qualified applicant. -------, there will not be any recruitment until further notice.
    - (A) Unless
    - (B) Otherwise
    - (C) Therefore
    - (D) Then

▶答案與解析請參考解析本第 20 頁

類型分析

7

代名詞

代名詞，是為了不反覆使用句子前面已經出現過的名詞，而用來取代該名詞的詞性。

WARMING UP

01 文法概念前導 ·············· 正式進入文法單元前，先熟悉一下文法基本概念。

1) 代名詞的基本概念
用來取代人物、事物或是動物名稱的語句，便稱為「代名詞」。例如，雖然我們周遭有非常多的男性姓名，但我們一律簡單地使用「he（他）」來稱呼。

2) 代名詞的種類
根據代名詞的特性，可分為以下幾種：

① 人稱代名詞
人稱代名詞，可以分為用來當句子主詞的主格、當作形容詞的所有格，以及當作受詞的受格。

主格　作為主詞的角色，意思為「你／我／他」。
　　　He is qualified for this position. 他適合這個職位。

所有格　放在名詞前方，結構為「所有格＋名詞」，表「～的」。
　　　Please confirm your reservation. 請確認您的預約。

受格　作為及物動詞的受詞和介系詞的受詞。
　　　We will provide you with a full refund. 我們將會提供您全額退費。　▶ 及物動詞的受詞
　　　He is afraid of them. 他很怕他們。　▶ 介系詞的受詞

② 反身代名詞
反身代名詞，在人稱代名詞中的所有格或是受格後方，加上 -self / -selves，用來表示或強調自身。

Mr. Miller showed himself to be a dependable person.　▶ 表示主詞自身
Miller 先生展現出自己是一個值得信任的人。

The manager herself reviewed the document.　▶ 強調主詞
經理自己直接審閱了文件。

③ 不定代名詞
不指出明確的人事物，而是籠統地表示是怎樣的或是多少的人事物時使用。

不定代名詞	意思	不定代名詞	意思
both	兩者皆	some	有些（肯定）
either	兩者中任一	any	任一（否定或疑問）
neither	兩者皆不	all	全部
none	皆無～	each	各個

＊ one, the other, another, the others, others 的差異

02 暖身例題

請圈選出括號中最適合的詞彙。

1 Most employees complained that (their / they) didn't have time to examine the document.

2 I saw a fashion show yesterday, and (it / its) was amazing.

3 The firm has designed (its / it) latest product.

4 Mr. Lamb always works hard, so he asked his manager to give (his / him) a raise.

5 Their proposal for the project was very smart, but (us / ours) needs to be revised.

03 例題解答

1 Most employees complained that **they** didn't have time to examine the document.

大多數的員工都抱怨過他們沒有時間去檢查文件。

▶ 以代名詞（they）代替前方出現過的名詞（employees）。

2 I saw a fashion show yesterday, and **it** was amazing.

我昨天看了場時尚秀，非常令人驚豔。

▶ 以代名詞（it）代替前方出現過的名詞（fashion show）。

3 The firm has designed **its** latest product.

企業已經設計好他們最新的產品。

▶ 以代名詞（its）代替前方出現過的名詞（firm）。

4 Mr. Lamb always works hard, so he asked his manager to give **him** a raise.

Lamb 先生總是很認真工作，所以他要求上司給他加薪。

▶ 以代名詞（him）代替前方出現過的名詞（Mr. Lamb）。

5 Their proposal for the project was very smart, but **ours** needs to be revised.

他們對這個專案的提案非常優秀，然而我們的則需要修改。

▶ 如同前方的「Their（所有格）＋ proposal（名詞）」結構，ours 則是「our（所有格）＋ proposal（名詞）」的縮寫。

Unit 34 代名詞擺放的位置 ①

解題策略　　若選項出現了代名詞，且空格在名詞前方時，請選擇所有格為答案。

代表題型

All employees must first meet ------- supervisors to fill out the application forms.

(A) they　　　　(B) themselves　　(C) their　　　　(D) them

攻略解題法

All employees must first meet ------- supervisors to fill out the application forms.
　　主詞　　　　　　動詞　　　　動詞（meet）的受詞　　　　不定詞（作副詞用，表目的）
　　　　　　　副詞　　　　　　動詞＋所有格＋名詞
　　　　　　　　　　　　　　完整句子

(A) they　　　　(B) themselves　　(C) their　　　　(D) them
　　主格　　　　　　反身代名詞　　　　所有格　　　　　受格

文句分析　　當形容詞 all 出現在肯定句中時，表示「所有的」意思，多置於可數複數名詞
　　　　　　（employees）前使用。

說明　　　　當選項中出現代名詞，且空格出現在名詞（supervisor）前方時，必須選出所有格填入。
　　　　　　請注意，不要犯下因為前方是及物動詞（meet），就選擇受格（them）的失誤。此題答
　　　　　　案為 (C)。

翻譯　　　　所有員工都必須先找他們的上司填寫申請表格。

單字片語　　fill out 填寫／application form 申請單

解答　　　　(C)

✎ 攻略 POINT

當選項出現代名詞，名詞前方的空格答案為所有格。

核心理論

代名詞的種類

人稱	單／複數	主格	所有格	受格
第一人稱	單數	I	my	me
	複數	we	our	us
第二人稱	單／複數	you	your	you
第三人稱	單數	he	his	him
		she	her	her
		it	its	it
	複數	they	their	them

- **主格**

  He didn't realize that **he** had forgotten his file.

  他沒發現他忘了他的資料。

  ▶ 動詞（didn't, had forgotten）前方是主詞的位置，因此使用主格代名詞（He）。

- **所有格**

  Her position offers a lot of possibilities for advancement.

  她的職位提供了很多升遷的可能性。

  ▶ 名詞（position）前方使用所有格代名詞。

- **受格**

  The manager instructed **them** to work.

  經理吩咐他們去工作。

  ▶ 動詞（instructed）後方是受詞的位置，因此使用受格代名詞（them）。

- **介系詞的受詞**

  Most of the employees agreed with **them**.

  大多數的員工都同意他們。

  ▶ 介系詞（with）後方是受詞的位置，因此使用受格代名詞（them）。

Step 3 | **實戰演練**

1 His passport was confiscated by the police in an attempt to prevent ------- from leaving the country.

(A) he   (B) his   (C) himself   (D) him

2 The employees are able to look beyond ------- own jobs.

(A) they   (B) their   (C) them   (D) theirs

▶答案與解析請參考解析本第 22 頁

Unit 35 代名詞擺放的位置 ②

Step 1　實戰重點

解題策略　通常，若空格出現在主詞、受詞或是補語的位置，且選項中有所有格代名詞時，答案多為所有格代名詞。

🎓 代表題型

The executives of the company forgot to bring the contract, so the secretary who was

------- sent it by facsimile.

(A) them　　　　　(B) they　　　　　(C) theirs　　　　　(D) themselves

✏️ 攻略解題法

The executives of the company forgot to bring the contract, so the secretary
　　　　　　主詞　　　　　　　動詞　動詞（forgot）的受詞　　連接詞　先行詞

who was ------- sent it by facsimile.
修飾先行詞的關係子句　動詞　受詞　介系詞

their secretary

(A) them　　　　　(B) they　　　　　(C) theirs　　　　　(D) themselves
　受格　　　　　　　主格　　　　　　　所有格代名詞　　　　反身代名詞

文句分析　關係代名詞子句（who 後方的句子）的前方，必定要加入一個先行詞（secretary）。若先行詞為人物，則須選用關係代名詞 who。

說明　be 動詞（was）後方接的是補語，而補語的位置，無法放入主格（they）、所有格（their）、受格（them）跟反身代名詞（themselves）等等，唯有所有格代名詞可填入。因此，be 動詞後方空格若為補語的情況下，答案需選擇所有格代名詞，(C) theirs 為正解。

翻譯　公司的主管們忘了帶合約，因此他們的祕書用傳真寄過來。

單字片語　executive 主管，行政人員／ bring 攜帶／ secretary 祕書

解答　(C)

✏️ 攻略 POINT

主格、受格、所有格，以及反身代名詞等，無法當作 be 動詞後方的補語。

核心理論

所有格代名詞的種類

人稱	單／複數	主格	所有格	受格	所有格代名詞
第一人稱	單數	I	my	me	mine
	複數	we	our	us	ours
第二人稱	單／複數	you	your	you	yours
第三人稱	單數	he	his	him	his
		she	her	her	hers
		it	its	it	its
	複數	they	their	them	theirs

- **置於主詞時**

  Your work is very dangerous. **Mine** isn't as dangerous as yours.

  你的工作非常危險。我的沒有你的危險。

  ▶ 所有格代名詞（Mine）可以用來當作主詞，是「所有格＋名詞」的縮寫，此題中的 mine 便是用來取代 my work。

- **置於受詞時**

  I forgot to bring my towel, but William and Kate were kind enough to lend me **theirs**.

  我忘了帶我的毛巾，不過 William 跟 Kate 非常好心，借他們的給我用。

  ▶ 所有格代名詞（theirs）可以用來當作受詞，是「所有格＋名詞」的縮寫，此題中的 theirs 便是用來取代 their towels。

- **置於補語時**

  That opportunity for advancement <u>was</u> **yours**.

  那個升遷的機會本來是你的。

  ▶ 所有格代名詞（yours）可以用來當作受詞，是「所有格＋名詞」的縮寫，此題中的 yours 便是用來取代 your opportunity。

Step 3 | **實戰演練**

1 The accommodation service the customers found more attractive was -------, for we provided free breakfast.

(A) we   (B) us   (C) our   (D) ours

2 The company tried to make a new product before the competing company could, but ------- have already been launched.

(A) them   (B) theirs   (C) their   (D) themselves

▶答案與解析請參考解析本第 22 頁

Unit 36 反身代名詞

解題策略　反身代名詞，是由人稱代名詞加上「-self（單數）、-selves（複數）」而成，有「～自己」的意思。若考題中的空格放在結構已完整的句子中，而且選項中有反身代名詞時，該選項即為答案。

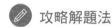 代表題型

The mayor welcomed the guests ------- until the last day of the city festival.

(A) himself　　　　(B) he　　　　(C) him　　　　(D) his

✎ 攻略解題法

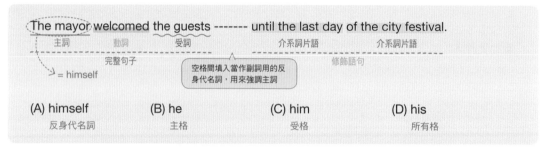

文句分析　因為前方句子結構完整，後方片語純粹用來做修飾，因此在完整句子後方的空格，須填入副詞。

說明　　　當空格出現在已經有主詞跟受詞的完整句型後方時，該空格答案百分之百為反身代名詞。上面考題的句子為「主詞（The mayor）＋動詞（welcomed）＋受詞（the guests）」，結構完整，而且後方接續空格，因此該空格須填入反身代名詞 (A) himself。這裡的反身代名詞（himself）是主詞（The mayor）的同位語，作為強調主詞的副詞。

翻譯　　　市長本人親自恭迎所有賓客，直到本市慶典的最後一天。

單字片語　welcome 歡迎，恭迎／ until 一直到～／ festival 慶典

解答　　　(A)

✗ 攻略 POINT ----------

若空格出現在結構完整的句子中，那麼反身代名詞須填入主詞或是受詞後方的位置。

📖 **核心理論**

反身代名詞的種類

人稱	單／複數	主格	所有格	受格	所有格代名詞	反身代名詞
第一人稱	單數	I	my	me	mine	myself
	複數	we	our	us	ours	ourselves
第二人稱	單／複數	you	your	you	your	yourself / yourselves
第三人稱	單數	he	his	him	his	himself
		she	her	her	hers	herself
		it	its	it	its	itself
	複數	they	their	them	theirs	themselves

- **用來表示動作行為者與承受者相同**：當表達主詞與受詞對象相同時，使用反身代名詞。

<u>He</u> recently introduced **himself** to all of the senior employees.
最近他向所有資深員工介紹自己。
  ▶ 主詞（He）與動詞的受詞（him）對象相同，因此使用反身代名詞（himself）。

<u>Ms. Connelly</u> prefers to work by **herself** rather than with a team.
比起跟團隊一起工作，Connelly 女士比較喜歡自己一個人。
  ▶ 主詞（Ms. Connelly）與介系詞的受詞（her）對象相同，因此使用反身代名詞（herself）。另外，值得注意的是，考題中常出現 by oneself，意思是「獨自一人」。

- **用來表示強調**：為了強調主詞或是受詞，通常會將反身代名詞置於主詞、受詞的正後方，或是整個句子的正後方。

Subscribers should fill out the forms themselves.
　　　　　　　完整句子
訂閱者必須自己填寫表單。
  ▶ 如果把空格去掉，句子結構仍完整，那麼空格內百分之百為反身代名詞。

1 All the employees decided that we should move the office equipment ------- when we move to the new office.

(A) our　　　　　　(B) ours　　　　　　(C) us　　　　　　(D) ourselves

2 The company prohibits its employees from attempting to make electrical repairs -------.

(A) they　　　　　　(B) themselves　　　　　　(C) their　　　　　　(D) them

▶ 答案與解析請參考解析本第 22 頁

Unit 37　不定代名詞 ❶

Step 1　實戰重點

解題策略　當選項中出現 some，同時，空格是為了指出不明確的人事物時，該選項即為答案。

🎓 代表題型

------- of the most important people at our company attended the conference to discuss buying land.

(A) Few　　　　　(B) Every　　　　　(C) Some　　　　　(D) Much

✏️ 攻略解題法

文句分析　不定代名詞（some）無論是接可數或不可數名詞，皆能搭配使用，因此「some of the」後方可接可數，也可以接不可數名詞。

說明　　　本題中的選項皆為不定代名詞，Few 表「少數的～」，有否定語氣，跟文意不符，因此 (A) 錯誤。而英文中並沒有 every of 這種用法，且 every 是形容詞，(B) 選項也非答案；Much 則主要是用在不可數名詞，(D) 選項也可刪除。本題為肯定語氣，同時文意中是要指出 of 後方不明確的 people，因此 (C) Some 為正解。

翻譯　　　我們公司裡某些最重要的人士，為了討論購買土地的事宜，參加了會議。

單字片語　attend 參加／ discuss 討論

解答　　　(C)

攻略 POINT

沒有特別指定的人事物時，可使用不定代名詞 some。

核心理論

some 與 any 的差別

這兩個不定代名詞，都有「幾個、一些」的意思，然而 some 主要用於肯定句，而 any 則用於否定句。

The company donated **some** money to charity.
公司捐了一些錢給慈善機構。

There is no difference in salary between **any** of the employees.
任何員工之間的薪水都沒有不同。

Some of the workers at the plant have been working there for at least 10 years.
有些工廠的員工已經在那裡工作至少十年以上。

▶ some 意指「幾個，一些」，句型通常為「some (of) ＋名詞」。

Any of our factories will not be closed despite the serious recession.
儘管經濟蕭條，我們任何一個工廠都不會關閉的。

▶ any 意指「任一～也不」，句型通常為「any (of) ＋名詞」。

Most of the employees have problems with the new reporting system.
大部分員工對於新的回報系統都有困難。

▶ most 意指「大部分」，句型通常為「most (of) ＋名詞」。

All of the seats in the meeting room are full.
會議室裡所有的座位都滿了。

▶ all 意指「全部」，句型通常為「all (of) ＋名詞」。

請記住上述的代名詞也可作為形容詞用。

Step 3　實戰演練

1 ------- of the employees at our company have excellent educations.

(A) Every　　　(B) Much　　　(C) Each　　　(D) Most

2 He was late for another meeting, so there were ------- of his colleagues left after the meeting.

(A) much　　　(B) no　　　(C) nothing　　　(D) none

▶答案與解析請參考解析本第 22 頁

Unit 38 不定代名詞 ❷

 Step 1 ┆ **實戰重點**

解題策略　當選項中同時出現 another 與 other 時，可數單數名詞前方為 another，而可數複數名詞前方則為 other。

 代表題型

------- stockholders need to collaborate on developing safer alternatives.

(A) Other　　　　(B) The another　　　(C) Another　　　(D) The other

攻略解題法

------- stockholders (need) to collaborate on developing safer alternatives.
　　主詞　　　　　　　　　　不定詞　　　　on 的受詞　動名詞（developing）的受詞
　　　　　　↓
　　　複數動詞

(A) Other　　　　　(B) The another　　　(C) Another　　　　(D) The other
　　複數　　　　　　　　單數　　　　　　　單數　　　　　　複數（不可數）

文句分析　當空格出現在一般名詞的前方，通常要選擇冠詞、形容詞或是動名詞等等填入。other 後方可接單複數名詞，但 another 只能接續單數名詞。另外，動詞 collaborate 跟 on 是成對使用的。

說明　　本題題型是在名詞的前方空格中，選擇 other 或 another 其一填入。此時，若名詞為單數，選擇 another；若為複數，則選擇 other。本題中的空格前方為複數名詞（stockholders），因此 (A) Other 為答案。

翻譯　　為了發展更安全的替代方案，其他股東必須一同合作。

單字片語　stockholder 股東／ collaborate on 合作～／ safe 安全的／ alternative 替代方案

解答　　(A)

✎ **攻略 POINT**

another 後方接單數名詞，other 後方接複數名詞。

核心理論

不定代名詞 other 的區分

1 個 (one)	the other 剩下的另一個
	another 另一個
	the others 剩下的全部

another vs. other

	可數名詞	不可數名詞
another	O（單數）	×
other	O（複數）	O

註 1：other 與 another 不同，不能作為代名詞使用。

註 2：若 another 後方接續的名詞是時間、重量、金額，複數形態也可以使用。

ex) for another two weeks（再兩週）、another 2 kilograms（再兩公斤）、another 10 dollars（再十元）

There is not **another** <u>editor</u> at the company.

公司裡沒有另一個編輯了。

▶ 單數名詞（editor）前方使用 another。有時候題目也會將 another 放在時間（two weeks）的前方，表「再～」。

Other <u>facilities</u> at the company were also destroyed.

公司裡其它的設施也被破壞了。

▶ 複數名詞（facilities）前方使用 other。有時考題中不可數名詞的前方，也可填入 other。

If you have a problem with <u>the copier</u>, we will exchange it for **another**.

如果你對影印機有任何問題，我們會換另一台給你。

▶ 當要表示文中出現的對象以外的另一個，便可使用 another。

Of the two copy machines, <u>one</u> is too expensive, and **the other** is relatively affordable.

兩台影印機中，一台太貴了，另一台比較便宜。

▶ 有特別指定的兩個對象時，一個為 one，剩下的另一個則是 the other。

Step **3** ┊ **實戰演練**

1 The employees are able to go to ------- branch offices located overseas and have a wide variety of experiences.

(A) one   (B) another   (C) others   (D) other

2 This internship will broaden your knowledge of the field and help you to be active in ------- organization.

(A) each other   (B) another   (C) himself   (D) other

▶ 答案與解析請參考解析本第 23 頁

Unit 39 其他常見代名詞

解題策略　　必須選擇與 of the 後方名詞單複數一致的代名詞填入空格中。

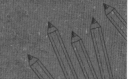

代表題型

------- of the employees are being forced to move to the new office far from the city.

(A) Much　　　　　(B) Little　　　　　(C) Some　　　　　(D) Every

攻略解題法

------- of the employees (are) being forced to move (to the new office far from the city.)

主詞　　　　　　　　動詞　　　　補語　　　　　　　修飾語句

↓
複數

(A) Much　　　　　(B) Little　　　　　(C) Some　　　　　(D) Every

修飾不可數名詞　　修飾不可數名詞　　修飾可數或不可數名詞　　形容詞

說明　　　多益考試中，經常會出現代名詞與後方名詞達到單複數一致性的考題。例如「------ + of the 名詞」的結構下，必須讓代名詞與 of the 後方的名詞單複數達成一致性。若名詞為複數，則使用複數代名詞，若名詞為不可數名詞，則選擇不可數代名詞。如本題中出現的是複數名詞（employees），因此須選擇 (C) Some。可數與不可數名詞，皆可使用 Some。(A) 與 (B) 皆必須搭配不可數名詞，而 (D) 為形容詞，不可用來當作代名詞。

翻譯　　　一些員工被迫搬到距離市中心遙遠的新辦公室。

單字片語　be forced to 被迫要～／far 遠的

解答　　　(C)

攻略 POINT

填入「------ + of the 名詞」空格中的代名詞，必須與 of the 後方的名詞達到單複數一致性。

核心理論

代名詞單數、複數之區分

搭配單數名詞的代名詞	one, either, neither, each, another, the other, much, little, someone, something, nobody, nothing, this, that 等等
搭配複數名詞的代名詞	both, several, few, others, those, these, the others, many 等等
單／複數名詞皆可搭配的代名詞	most, some, any, all 等等

Little has been done to reduce the difference.
根本沒有採取任何措施去減少差異。

▶ little 既可當形容詞，也可當代名詞。作主詞（代名詞）時，使用單數動詞。

　註：little ＋不可數名詞＋單數動詞／ little of the（所有格）＋不可數名詞＋單數動詞

Much of the success is due to the sales team.
大部分的成功都要歸功於銷售團隊。

▶ much 既可當形容詞，也可當代名詞。當代名詞時，句型為「much of the ＋不可數名詞」，使用單數動詞。

　註：much ＋不可數名詞＋單數動詞／ much of the（所有格）＋不可數名詞＋單數動詞

All of our salespeople always try to exceed sales targets.
我們所有的業務總是嘗試著超越銷售目標。

▶ all 既可當形容詞，也可當代名詞。當代名詞時，句型為「all of the（所有格）＋可數名詞複數／不可數名詞」，此時的動詞必須與 of the 後方的名詞達到單複數一致性。

One of the employees is on sick leave because of health problems.
有一位員工因健康因素而請病假。

▶ one 既可當形容詞，也可當代名詞。當代名詞時，句型為「one of the ＋可數名詞複數」，使用單數動詞。

　註：one ＋單數名詞＋單數動詞／ one of the（所有格）＋可數名詞複數＋單數動詞

Step 3 | 實戰演練

1 ------- of the employees want to request time off this summer.

(A) Another　　　　(B) Anyone　　　　(C) Much　　　　(D) Some

2 In those times, ------- of the company's products were manufactured domestically.

(A) much　　　　(B) most　　　　(C) plenty　　　　(D) almost

▶答案與解析請參考解析本第 23 頁

REVIEW TEST

1. Please let me know your phone number or email address if ------- has changed.

   (A) whatever   (B) nowhere
   (C) others   (D) either

2. Sometimes there are situations in which employees have difficulty expressing themselves during ------- presentations on stage.

   (A) theirs   (B) them
   (C) they   (D) their

3. The companies rehired ------- old staff members after getting over its financial difficulties.

   (A) theirs   (B) their
   (C) they   (D) them

4. He didn't want to give up on the project, but ------- admitted that he could not finish it by the end of the month.

   (A) he   (B) his
   (C) himself   (D) him

5. The manager was always eager to help ------- as much as she could.

   (A) their   (B) they
   (C) them   (D) theirs

6. Of the two prototypes of the new product, one was disqualified, but ------- was qualified for sales.

   (A) another   (B) the other
   (C) ones   (D) both

7. When she finishes the course, Mary must return all the office equipment except the stapler, which is ------- to keep.

   (A) hers   (B) her
   (C) she   (D) herself

8. Salaries are consistently higher for night shift workers than the salaries of ------- who work the day shift.

   (A) that   (B) whoever
   (C) those   (D) such

9. ------- of the workers agreed that they should hold another meeting about the customer's complaint.

   (A) Much   (B) Most
   (C) Each   (D) Nothing

10. ------- of the candidates is having an interview with five interviewers in the Personnel Department.

    (A) Each   (B) Most
    (C) Every   (D) Much

▶答案與解析請參考解析本第 23 頁

類型分析 8

介系詞

介系詞位於名詞前方,用來體現時間、地點或是方向的概念。
介系詞可分為一個字的簡單介系詞、兩個字組合而成的複合介
系詞,以及多個單字組成的片語介系詞等等。

WARMING UP

1) 介系詞的基本概念

除了極端的特殊情況之外，介系詞無法單獨使用，必須接續在名詞或是名詞形的前方，表時間、地點或是方向等語意。例如在 the desk 這個名詞的前方，加上 on，變成 on the desk，意指「在桌上」，表現出地點的語意。

ex) Tuesday 星期二 → on Tuesday 在星期二
a house 一間房子 → in a house 在一間房子裡
a mountain 一座山 → to a mountain 往一座山～，到一座山～

2) 介系詞的角色

在句子中，介系詞可以跟名詞結合，作為形容詞或副詞用。

① 作形容詞用的介系詞片語（介系詞＋名詞）

放在名詞後方用來修飾該名詞，或是放在 be 動詞後方作補語。

I want some information about the item. 我想要一些關於這個商品的資訊。

▶ 修飾名詞

The copier is out of order. 影印機故障了。

▶ 敘述主詞（名詞）

② 作副詞用的介系詞片語（介系詞＋名詞）

用來修飾動詞、形容詞或是副詞，或是用來修飾整個句子。

She called me after lunch. 她在午飯後打給我。

▶ 修飾動詞

Breakfast is available for free. 早餐是免費提供的。

▶ 修飾形容詞

In the end, we agreed the proposal. 最終，我們同意了提案。

▶ 修飾整個句子

02 暖身例題

請圈選出括號中正確的介系詞。

1 I have an appointment with Mr. Brown (at / in) 3 o'clock.

2 It was usually used (in / on) the offices.

3 James has left (for / by) the U.S.

4 (According to / Despite) the report, SAM showed an increase in profits.

5 (In addition to / In accordance with) teaching yoga, David films yoga DVDs.

03 例題解答

一個字的簡單介系詞

1 I have an appointment with Mr. Brown **at** 3 o'clock. 我跟 Brown 先生三點有約。

▶ 介系詞（at）置於受詞（3 o'clock）前方，表時間。

2 It was usually used **in** the offices. 這個通常會在辦公室用到。

▶ 介系詞（in）置於受詞（the offices）前方，表地點。

3 James has left **for** the U.S. James 已經前往美國了。

▶ 介系詞（for）置於受詞（the U.S.）前方，表方向。

兩個字組成的簡單介系詞

4 **According to** the report, SAM showed an increase in profits.

根據報告，可以看出 SAM 利潤的增長。

▶ 介系詞（according to）置於受詞（the report）前方，表出處。

多個單字組成的片語介系詞

5 **In addition to** teaching yoga, David films yoga DVDs.

除了教瑜伽之外，David 也拍瑜伽 DVD。

▶ 介系詞（in addition to）置於受詞（teaching）前方，表補充。

Unit 40　介系詞擺放的位置

解題策略　　當選項中有介系詞，同時，空格位於名詞或是動名詞前，介系詞即為答案。

 代表題型

> All the employees came ------- the convention to attend the seminar this morning.
>
> (A) shortly　　　　(B) there　　　　(C) to　　　　(D) when

 攻略解題法

All the employees came ------- the convention to attend the seminar this morning.
主詞　　　動詞　　介系詞片語（to + V）　　　不定詞（作副詞用，表手段或目的）
完整句子

> All the employees came 為完整句子，
> 因此空格後方須為修飾語句。

(A) shortly　　　　(B) there　　　　(C) to　　　　(D) when
副詞　　　　　　副詞　　　　　　介系詞　　　　　連接詞

文句分析　　形容詞 all 多以「all the ＋名詞」的句型出現，並不會出現「the all ＋名詞」的句型。

說明　　　　當選項中出現介系詞，同時，空格位於名詞、動名詞或是代名詞前，介系詞即為答案。本題中，空格後方為名詞受詞（the convention），因此須選擇介系詞 (C) to。(A) 副詞、(B) 副詞、(D) 連接詞，皆無法置於介系詞的位置內。

翻譯　　　　所有員工為了參加早上的研討會，都出席了這次的大會。

單字片語　　convention 大會／ attend 參加

解答　　　　(C)

⚔ 攻略 POINT

當名詞或動名詞前方加上介系詞後，便成為該介系詞的受詞。

核心理論

介系詞擺放的位置與角色

1. 介系詞＋名詞相等語（名詞、代名詞、動名詞）
   ▶ 當介系詞位於名詞前方時，該名詞便成為介系詞的受詞。

2. 介系詞後方加上名詞〈介系詞＋名詞〉的組合，在句子內，可作形容詞或副詞用。
   作形容詞：I bought a **car** for the event.（修飾前方的 car）
   我為了活動買了一台車。
   作副詞：He **takes the subway** due to the heavy traffic.
   因為塞車的緣故，他搭地鐵。（修飾前方的 takes the subway）

The employees usually use the reference books <u>at</u> the library.
員工們通常會利用圖書館的參考書。

▶ 名詞受詞（the library）前方須填入介系詞（at）。

I wonder if it would be possible <u>for</u> you to meet him this coming Monday.
我在想，你是否可以在下星期一見他一面。

▶ 代名詞受詞（you）前方須填入介系詞（for）。

The company solved the problem <u>by</u> expanding its use of waste paper.
公司藉由增加廢紙利用來解決問題。

▶ 動名詞（expanding）前方須填入介系詞（by）。

1 He cannot apply for the job ------- getting a medical examination.

(A) even   (B) though   (C) unless   (D) without

2 She wants to be friendly to the customers ------- the other members of the Sales Department.

(A) similarly   (B) like   (C) for instance   (D) together

▶答案與解析請參考解析本第 25 頁

Unit 41 時間介系詞

解題策略　　時間相關的介系詞，須整理好各類時間的介系詞組合後背誦，才能夠減少失誤。

代表題型

The meeting for the employees to discuss the new project will start ------- 10 o'clock.

(A) on (B) for (C) at (D) in

攻略解題法

The meeting (for the employees) (to discuss the new project) will start (------- 10 o'clock).

主詞　　　　介系詞片語　　　　不定詞（作形容詞）　　　動詞　　　at＋時間點

修飾　　　　　　　　　　　　　　　　　　　　　　　　　用來表時間的介系詞 at

(A) on	(B) for	(C) at	(D) in
位置，星期	目的，用途	時間	地點，時間（～時，～之後）

文句分析　　介系詞 for 最常用來表示目的，意指「為了～」。

說明　　　　時間介系詞的考題，通常是要根據文中寫出的時間類別，來選擇相對應的介系詞。本題 (A)、(C)、(D) 皆為時間介系詞，(A) 用在日期或是星期前方，(C) 用在確切的時間點，而 (D) 則是用在「月份，年度，～之後」的情況。題目中出現的是確切的時間點（10 o'clock），因此答案為 (C) at。如同本題，學習時間介系詞的方法，並非單純記下 at、on、in 是時間介系詞，而是要記住該介系詞相對應的時間型態為何。

翻譯　　　　討論新企劃案的員工會議將在十點開始。

單字片語　　meeting 聚會，會議／ discuss 討論

解答　　　　(C)

攻略 POINT

on 用於「日期、星期」，at 用於「確切的時間點」，而 in 則用於「月份、年度、～之後」。

核心理論

時間型態，以及搭配的介系詞組合

時間	自從／至	一段期間
at 短暫的時間長度、時刻 on 日期、星期 in 年度、季節等	since 自從～ by / until 一直到～	for ＋期間 during ＋活動、事件等

The interview will start **at** six o'clock.
面試將在六點開始。

▶ at（在～）接在明確的時間點（six o'clock、the end／beginning 等）之前。

He has been working at this company **since** last year.
他從去年開始就在這間公司工作。

▶ since（自從～）接在過去的時間點（last year、last week 等）之前。

You should complete the budget report **by** the end of this month.
你必須在這個月底前完成預算報告。

▶「by ＋時間點（至少在～之前）」通常跟表完成的動詞（complete、finish、submit、inform 等）一同使用。

They have to postpone the employee training session **until** June.
他們必須將員工訓練課程延到六月。

▶「until ＋時間點（到～為止，一直）」通常跟表延續（stay、remain）或延期的動詞（postpone、delay）等一同使用。

Step **3** | **實戰演練**

1 All the candidates must submit their application forms to the Personnel Department ------- September 10.

(A) for   (B) in   (C) with   (D) on

2 They have been working at this company ------- last year.

(A) toward   (B) since   (C) for   (D) on

▶答案與解析請參考解析本第 25 頁

地點介系詞

Step 1 實戰重點

解題策略　當選項皆為介系詞，且空格後方為專有名詞時，答案為 at。

代表題型

The site of the conference has been changed, so it will be held ------- Wall Street next Monday.

(A) at　　　　　　　(B) from　　　　　　(C) throughout　　　(D) after

攻略解題法

The site (of the conference) has been changed, so　it　will be held
主詞　　　　介系詞片語　　　　　　　　動詞　　　連接詞 主詞　動詞
└─────────────── 句子 ───────────────┘　　　　└── 完整子句 ──┘

------- Wall Street next Monday.
　介系詞片語　　　　副詞

changed 後方無受詞，所以是被動式

(A) at　　　　　　　(B) from　　　　　　(C) throughout　　　(D) after
　地點　　　　　　　　位置　　　　　　　地點，時間，空間　　　位置，時間

文句分析　當及物動詞（change、hold）不含受詞時，必為被動式，因此文中的兩個動詞，皆以被動式出現。

說明　　　介系詞通常會接續在住址、街道（Wall Street）、建築物（academy building）、公司（trading company）、場所（press conference）等等，具體地點的前方。具體地點的前方，須使用介系詞 at（在～），因此本題答案為 (A)。

翻譯　　　會議地點已經更動，因此，會議將於下週一在華爾街舉行。

單字片語　change 變更／hold 舉辦

解答　　　(A)

攻略 POINT

具體地點（特別是專有名詞時）的前方，使用 at。

📖 核心理論

常見的地點介系詞一覽

at	on	in
特定地點	（某種）表面之上	（某種）空間之內

throughout	within
～期間一直、～的所有區域	～之內

She applied for a position **at** a trading company.

她應徵了一個在貿易公司的工作。

▶ at（在～）接在具體地點（專有名詞、公司、建物等）之前。

The company is expected to establish a new branch **in** Europe.

公司預期會在歐洲開一個新的分公司。

▶ in 接在地名（Europe）、都市（New York）等場所之前。

They export their products to markets **throughout** the world.

他們將產品出口至全世界的市場。

▶ throughout 表「整體，到處」，通常跟 the world、the city、the country 一起使用。

He has an important position **within** the company.

他位居公司的要職。

▶ within 表「～之內」，通常跟 the company、the firm 一起出現在考題內。

1 Businesses such as restaurants and hotels are now a common sight ------- the country.

(A) next to   (B) into   (C) except   (D) throughout

2 Those wishing to transfer to different teams ------- the firm are asked to contact their supervisors first.

(A) on   (B) within   (C) beyond   (D) across

▶答案與解析請參考解析本第 25 頁

Unit 43　片語介系詞

Step 1　實戰重點

解題策略　由兩個以上的單詞組合成的片語，作介系詞用。請明確區分出片語介系詞與相似意義的連接詞。

 代表題型

------- its failure to launch the new product, the company still remains in first place in the steel industry.

(A) While　　　　(B) Due to　　　　(C) In spite of　　　　(D) Although

 攻略解題法

------- its failure to launch the new product, the company still remains in first place
　　　　　　　　　　名詞片語　　　　　　　　　　主詞　　副詞 動詞（句型 2）　補語（作形容詞）

in spite of 是表示
讓步的介系詞

in the steel industry.
　　介系詞片語

(A) While　　　　(B) Due to　　　　(C) In spite of　　　　(D) Although
連接詞（在～同時）　介系詞（因為～）　　介系詞（儘管～）　　連接詞（儘管～）

文句分析　〔介系詞＋名詞子句，主詞＋動詞〕這樣的句型結構，是每回都會出現的考題。

說明　　　從相近意義的連接詞與片語介系詞二者擇一，進行解題即可。介系詞後方必定接續受詞，而連接詞後方必定接續子句（主詞＋動詞）。本題中，空格後方連接的是受詞（its failure），可知答案為介系詞 (B) Due to 或是 (C) In spite of 其中之一。配合上下文，「新產品的上市宣告失敗，公司仍占據了鋼鐵業的首席地位」，可推論出表「儘管～」意思的 (C) In spite of 即為答案。

翻譯　　　儘管新產品的上市宣告失敗，公司仍占據了鋼鐵業的首席地位。

單字片語　failure 失敗／ in first place 第一名的／ steel 鋼鐵

解答　　　(C)

攻略 POINT
介系詞後方接的是名詞（片語）、代名詞、動名詞；而連接詞後方接的則是子句（主詞＋動詞）。

核心理論

常見的複合／片語介系詞一覽

in case of 倘若～
instead of 反而～
on behalf of 代替～
in addition to 此外～
along with 與～一同
in / with regard to 關於～

as a result of 由於～
regardless of 不論～
such as 例如～
in recognition of 為承認～
according to 根據～
except for 除了～

區分類似意義的連接詞與片語介系詞

意義	連接詞	介系詞（片語）
因果關係	because, since, as, now that	because of, due to, owing to
讓步關係	(al)though, even though, even if	in spite of, despite
目的關係	in case (that), in the event (that)	in case of, in the event of

We have received many questions **in regard to** the new safety regulations.
我們收到很多關於新安全守則的詢問。
▶ in regard to 為介系詞片語，表「關於～」。同義字有 as to / regarding / concerning 等等。

The company canceled the outdoor exhibition **because of** the bad weather.
因為天氣不佳，公司取消了戶外展演。
▶ 由於後方為名詞片語，前面須使用介系詞。同義字有 because、since 等等，可能會出現在選項中誘導考生誤答。

Step **3** | **實戰演練**

1 ------- building environmentally friendly facilities, the BICCO Center monitors all of its buildings' energy usage.

(A) In addition to   (B) Regardless of   (C) Furthermore   (D) Due to

2 The company is currently seeking applicants who are bilingual in English and Spanish ------- the new overseas expansion project.

(A) in spite of   (B) since   (C) owing to   (D) because

▶答案與解析請參考解析本第 25 頁

Unit 44 常見介系詞組合

Step 1 | 實戰重點

解題策略　背誦介系詞相關片語及慣用組合，並非單純是為了介系詞題型，解其他題型時也扮演了非常重要的角色，請留心各個單字與介系詞的搭配組合。

 代表題型

The meeting will be held soon because the increase ------- prices has driven away customers.

(A) for　　　　　(B) with　　　　　(C) in　　　　　(D) to

✏ 攻略解題法

修飾

The meeting will be held soon (because the increase ------- prices has driven away
　　主詞　　　　動詞　　副詞　　連接詞　　主詞　　　　　　　　　　　　　　　　動詞
　　　　　　完整子句　　　　　　　　　　　　副詞子句

customers.)
　　　　　　→ driven away 的受詞

(A) for　　　　　(B) with　　　　　(C) in　　　　　(D) to
　表目的、用途　　　　表陪同　　　　　　表在～其中　　　　表方向

文句分析　表因果關係的連接詞（because）作為副詞子句的連接詞，後方須接續含有主詞與動詞的完整子句。

說明　　　表增減的名詞（increase、rise、decline），與介系詞 in 搭配出現，意思為「～的增長、上升、減少」，因此本題答案為 (C) in。

翻譯　　　由於價格上升導致顧客流失，將立即召集開會。

單字片語　drive away 趕跑～

解答　　　(C)

🖊 攻略 POINT
表增減的名詞與介系詞 in 搭配出現，表示「～的增長、上升、減少」。

核心理論

〈動詞＋介系詞〉慣用形式

account for 說明～	comply with 遵守～
register for 註冊～	interfere with 妨礙～
apply for 申請～	deal with 處理～
add to 加上～	refrain / abstain from 節制～
refer to 參考～	depend / rely / count on 取決於～
subscribe to 訂閱～	concentrate / center on 專心於～
contribute to 貢獻於～	enroll in 報名～

〈動詞＋ A ＋介系詞＋ B〉慣用形式

add A to B 將 A 加入 B	replace A with B 用 B 取代 A
attribute A to B 把 A 歸因於 B	compare A with B 把 A 與 B 拿來比較
return A to B 把 A 還給 B	compensate A for B 用 B 賠償 A
transfer A to B 將 A 轉至 B	congratulate A on B 向 A 恭喜 B
provide A with B 提供 B 給 A	prevent/prohibit A from B 避免 A 去做 B

〈名詞＋介系詞〉慣用形式

access to 往～的途徑	demand for ～的需求
reaction to 對～的反應	information about / on ～相關的資訊
confidence in 對～的自信	take advantage of 利用～
increase / rise in ～的增加	at the latest 最晚～
advances in ～的進步	upon request 根據要求～

All applicants are required to **fill out** this form. 所有申請者皆被要求填寫此份表單。

We are planning to visit your office **at your convenience**. 我們打算在你方便的時候拜訪你的辦公室。

1 The manager trains the staff and keeps saying, "Do your best to keep our customers satisfied ------- all times."

(A) in   (B) from   (C) with   (D) at

2 He complained to the manager that she was interfering ------- his project, and asked her to stop doing that.

(A) to   (B) in   (C) from   (D) for

▶答案與解析請參考解析本第 26 頁

REVIEW TEST

1. All employees are asked to attend the meeting ------- 7 o'clock in order to discuss the new project.

   (A) in
   (B) on
   (C) for
   (D) at

2. Except for those in the first and second rows, which are reserved for the presenters, employees may choose any of the seats ------- the auditorium.

   (A) to
   (B) in
   (C) of
   (D) by

3. The application of the company's newly changed policy concerning better employee benefits will start ------- Monday.

   (A) at
   (B) on
   (C) for
   (D) since

4. The manager will soon be replaced to a new position, but he will remain with the Sales Department ------- next week.

   (A) by
   (B) at
   (C) until
   (D) from

5. When you take a flight to go to an overseas branch, all of your luggage should be stored ------- the seat in front of you.

   (A) beneath
   (B) over
   (C) next
   (D) under

6. Our company will open its third branch ------- the Walden Square, which will be the biggest trading company building in that area.

   (A) from
   (B) about
   (C) in
   (D) at

7. All employees in the Sales Department should finish their projects ------- the next two weeks.

   (A) within
   (B) along
   (C) into
   (D) through

8. The executive meetings concerning emergency situations usually occur more than four times ------- the year.

   (A) throughout
   (B) except for
   (C) between
   (D) except

9. Anyone interested in this position should submit a resume to the human resources manager ------- next Monday.

   (A) during
   (B) by
   (C) up
   (D) until

10. The study suggests a number of possible solutions to the conflict ------- the fields of environment and competition law.

    (A) among
    (B) of
    (C) below
    (D) between

▶ 答案與解析請參考解析本第 26 頁

類型分析

9

to 不定詞

由於在句子中沒有固定的詞性,因此被稱為「不定詞」。根據
不定詞在句子中表示的語意,可作為名詞、形容詞或副詞。

WARMING UP

01 文法概念前導 ⸺⸺⸺⸺⸺⸺⸺ 正式進入文法單元前，先熟悉一下文法基本概念。

1) 不定詞的基本概念

在英文中，要如何將動詞修改為名詞、形容詞與副詞呢？很簡單，只要在動詞前方加上 to 即可。加上 to 之後，在句子內，動詞可以變化為名詞、形容詞，甚至是副詞等等多種用法。像這樣「沒有固定詞性的字詞」，便稱為「不定詞」。

2) 不定詞的角色

① 作名詞用

當 to 不定詞在句子中當作名詞用時，可為主詞、受詞或補語，表「～這件事」或「目的」等等。

To go shopping is fun. 購物這件事很有趣。

▶ 作句子主詞

I want to go shopping with you. 我想跟你一起去購物。

▶ 作及物動詞的受詞

Our next schedule is to go shopping. 我們下一個行程是去購物。

▶ 作 be 動詞的補語

② 作形容詞用

當 to 不定詞像形容詞放在名詞後方修飾時，表「要～的」或「正在～的」。

I need a room to rest. 我需要一間用來休息的房間。

③ 作副詞用

當 to 不定詞作副詞，用來修飾形容詞、副詞、動詞或是整個句子時，表「目的、將要～」等等。

He works to provide for his family. 他為了要養活家人而工作。

We are pleased to announce the news. 我們很高興能夠宣布這個消息。

02 暖身例題

請閱讀下方題目的中文翻譯後，圈選出畫底線部分在句中的功能為何。

1 He promised <u>to call</u> me often.　　　　　　　　　　　　（主詞／受詞／補語）
他承諾會常常打電話給我。

2 <u>To obey</u> the business's bylaws is every employee's duty.　　　（主詞／受詞／補語）
遵循商業守則是每一個員工的義務。

3 Her job is <u>to research</u> the market condition.　　　　　　　（主詞／受詞／補語）
她的工作是去調查市場概況。

4 He has the right <u>to terminate</u> the agreement.　　　　　　　（副詞／形容詞）
他有終止協議的權利。

5 We decided to install an automatic system <u>to save</u> time.　　　（副詞／形容詞）
我們決定安裝一組自動化系統以節省時間。

03 例題解答

1 He promised to call me often. 他承諾會常常打電話給我。
　　　　　　　　　受詞

▶ 題目中，to call 是將動詞 call 前方加上 to，表「打電話這件事」，作受詞用。如同本例中，將 to 跟動詞（call）組合一起，便是不定詞（to call）。

2 To obey the business's bylaws is every employee's duty. 遵循商業守則是每一個員工的義務。
　　主詞

▶ to 不定詞放在主詞位置，作名詞用。

3 Her job is to research the market condition. 她的工作是去調查市場概況。
　　　　　　　　補語

▶ to 不定詞放在 be 動詞後方，作補語用。

4 He has the right to terminate the agreement. 他有終止協議的權利。
　　　　　　　　　　形容詞

▶ 不定詞放在名詞後方用來修飾名詞時，作形容詞用。

5 We decided to install an automatic system to save time.
主詞　動詞　　受詞　　　　　　　　　　　　副詞

　　　　　　　完整句子
我們決定安裝一組自動化系統以節省時間。

▶ 當 to 不定詞置於包含主詞、動詞與受詞的完整句子前後方時，作副詞用。

Unit 45　不定詞擺放的位置 ❶

Step 1　**實戰重點**

解題策略　　多益考題中，比起主詞、補語的位置，to 不定詞更容易出現在受詞的位置。

 代表題型

> I want ------- you a chance to stay at your present job, but at a higher salary.
>
> (A) offered　　　　(B) offering　　　　(C) to offer　　　　(D) offers

 攻略解題法

I want ------- you a chance to stay at your present job, but at a higher salary.
主詞／動詞　　　間接受詞 直接受詞　　不定詞　　　介系詞片語　　　　　介系詞片語
　　　　句型 4（offer 是句型 4 動詞）
　　→ 以 to 不定詞作為受詞的動詞

(A) offered　　　　　　(B) offering　　　　(C) to offer　　　　(D) offers
　動詞（過去式）／過去分詞　　動名詞　　　　　to 不定詞　　　　　動詞／名詞

文句分析　　對等連接詞（but）可以用來連接子句與子句，本題中便是用來接續介系詞片語（at your present job）與介系詞片語（at a higher salary）。

說明　　　　考題中，若選項同時出現 to 不定詞與動名詞，通常答案在兩者之中。動詞 want 是以 to 不定詞作為受詞的動詞，因此本題正解為 to 不定詞 (C) to offer。

翻譯　　　　我想提供你一個留在目前職位，但薪水更高的機會。

單字片語　　offer 提供／ chance 機會／ present 目前的

解答　　　　(C)

✎ 攻略 POINT

若考題選項同時出現 to 不定詞與動名詞，通常答案在兩者之中，只要掌握好動詞配對的受詞詞性即可。

核心理論

to 不定詞可作為名詞，置於主詞、受詞或是補語。

名詞：～的這件事	通常作為主詞或受詞用。
形容詞：要～的	通常置於名詞後方修飾。
副詞：為了～	用來修飾動詞、形容詞、副詞。

To buy a car is easy. 買車這件事很簡單。

I bought a book to read. 我買了一本要讀的書。

I worked hard to buy a house. 我為了買房子努力工作。

- **作為主格的補語**

  The aim of companies is **to maximize** their profits.

  公司的目標就是將利益最大化。

  ▶ 意思為「目的」的 purpose、aim、goal 以及意思為「任務」的 mission，常與 to 不定詞作同位關係出現於考題中。

- **作為受詞**

  The manager refused **to offer** special discounts for some products.

  經理拒絕提供某些產品特殊折扣。

  ▶ to 不定詞作為名詞，置於受詞位置。

- **作為受格的補語**

  The manager encouraged all the employees **to attend** the seminar.

  經理鼓勵所有員工參加研討會。

  ▶ to 不定詞可作受詞補語。

  ＊ to 不定詞用作主詞的例子非常少出現於考題中，因此我們不在這裡多加探討。

Step **3** | **實戰演練**

1 The donation from the United Hospital Fund will allow Baltimore Children's Hospital ------- 6 more doctors to its current staff of 32.

(A) additional   (B) addition   (C) adding   (D) to add

2 The purpose of the letter is ------- membership to those who wish to join our club.

(A) to offer   (B) offering   (C) offer   (D) offered

▶答案與解析請參考解析本第 27 頁

Unit 46 不定詞擺放的位置 ②

解題策略　當考題中的空格出現於「逗號＋完整句子」前方時，答案請選 to 不定詞。

 代表題型

------- strong relationships between its employees, the company had a two-day, one-night workshop.

(A) Established　　　(B) Establish　　　(C) To establish　　　(D) Establishment

 攻略解題法

------- strong relationships between its employees, the company had
　　　不定詞（為了～）　　　　　　　介系詞片語　　　　　主詞　　動詞

a two-day, one-night workshop. ---> to establish 的受詞
　　動詞（had）的受詞

(A) Established　　　　(B) Establish　　　(C) To establish　　　(D) Establishment
動詞（過去式）／過去分詞　複數動詞現在式　　　to 不定詞　　　　　名詞

文句分析　以及物動詞組成的 to 不定詞（to establish），後方必須接續受詞（strong relationships）。

說明　　　當空格出現於「逗號＋完整句子」前方時，空格可填入 to 不定詞，此時 to 不定詞表目的（為了～），作副詞用。(A) 若作為過去分詞，雖然就文法來說可填入空格內，但文意上未含有「目的」的語意，因此不正確，(C) To establish 才是正解。

翻譯　　　為了建立員工之間更密切的關係，公司舉辦了兩天一夜的工作坊。

單字片語　establish 建立，設立／ two-day, one-night 兩天一夜

解答　　　(C)

攻略 POINT

「------ ＋受詞／修飾語, 完整句子」的句型中，空格為 to 不定詞。

📖 **核心理論**

將 to 不定詞填入完整句子前方或後方空格，是 to 不定詞最常出現的題型。

to 不定詞作副詞用

特性	就算把 to 不定詞子句刪除，句型結構仍然完整。
位置	句子的正前方（～, 句子）或是正後方
文意	為了～，將要～

We need a sufficient number of samples **to give** a reliable analysis.

主詞　動詞　　　　　　　　受詞

完整句子

為了提供可信的分析結果，我們需要充足的樣本數。

▶ 包含主詞與受詞的完整句子後方空格，可填入 to 不定詞。此時的 to 不定詞表目的。

To gain recognition, Kentanawa carved a unique image in its products.

主詞　　　　動詞　　　　受詞

完整句子

為了增加認知度，Kentanawa 將一個特殊圖騰刻在產品上。

▶ 當空格位於句子正前方，並且後方結構為「逗號＋完整句子」時，該空格為 to 不定詞。

In order to work efficiently, establish a schedule.

為了有效率地工作，請製作一份時程表。

▶ 原形動詞前方，可填入 in order to。in order to 不定詞，是加強語氣的 to 不定詞，表「目的」。

Step **3** | **實戰演練**

1 ------- receive the best service, a customer must be polite and patient.

(A) In addition to　　　(B) As if　　　(C) So that　　　(D) In order to

2 The Maintenance Department has been working hard for weeks ------- its internal network system.

(A) update　　　(B) to update　　　(C) updated　　　(D) updates

▶答案與解析請參考解析本第 27 頁

Unit 47 搭配不定詞使用的動詞 ❶

解題策略　　請記住以 to 不定詞作受詞的常見動詞範例。

 代表題型

Despite the rainy weather, Allegheny County intended ------- the project on time.

(A) to finish　　　　(B) finishing　　　　(C) to be finished　　　　(D) finishes

✏️ 攻略解題法

Despite the rainy weather, Allegheny County intended ------- the project on time.

despite ＋名詞　介系詞片語　　　　主詞　　　　動詞　　　　finish 的受詞　介系詞片語

以 to 不定詞作
受詞的動詞

(A) to finish　　　　(B) finishing　　　　(C) to be finished　　　　(D) finishes
　to 不定詞　　　　　動名詞　　　　　to 不定詞被動語態　　　　單數動詞現在式

文句分析　　intend 後方除了接續 to 不定詞外，也可接續「受詞＋ to 不定詞」。

說明　　　通常只要選項中有 to 不定詞，該選項為答案的機率很高，因此只要有 to 不定詞的選項出現，可優先將其視為正確答案的有力候選，尤其是選項中也出現動名詞時。這類題型，只要背起來以 to 不定詞為受詞的動詞範例，即可輕鬆解題。本題中，空格前方為 intend，正是以 to 不定詞為受詞的動詞，因此只要在 (A) 或 (C) 中擇一，而空格後方緊連受詞（project），可推論出主動語態的 (A) to finish 為答案。請記住，如同本題，除了 to 不定詞以外，被動／主動語態的概念也可能會一同出題。

翻譯　　　儘管下著雨，Allegheny County 仍然試著準時完成企劃案。

單字片語　　intend to 試著～／ on time 準時

解答　　　(A)

✎ 攻略 POINT
┄┄
表「希望、計劃、約定」等等跟未來相關的動詞，後方受詞多為 to 不定詞。

核心理論

1. 以 to 不定詞作為副詞的動詞

want to 想要去～	refuse to 拒絕去～	strive to 努力去～
decide to 決定去～	intend to 試圖去～	plan to 計劃去～
fail to ～失敗了	ask to 要求～	promise to 承諾去～

2.「be 動詞＋形容詞＋ to 不定詞」常見組合

be able to 可以做～	be pleased to 很開心能～
be likely to 可能會～	be willing to 願意去～
be proud to 很驕傲能～	be eligible to 有資格去～
be ready to 準備好去～	be eager to 渴望去～

The company **decided** to reduce its employees to save labor costs.
公司決定減少員工人數以降低人力成本。

The company **plans** to increase productivity and efficiency by using new technology.
公司計劃利用新科技來增加生產力與效率。

The company **was able** to complete the construction project on time.
公司可以準時完成建設案。

We **are pleased** to introduce our new products in the market this week.
本週我們很高興地向市場介紹我們的新產品。

1 Idenis Pharmaceuticals will attempt ------- to any questions or complaints in a timely manner.

(A) responded   (B) respond   (C) response   (D) to respond

2 Some customers are willing ------- some products at significantly discounted prices.

(A) purchase   (B) purchasing   (C) to purchase   (D) to be purchased

▶答案與解析請參考解析本第 28 頁

Unit 48　搭配不定詞使用的動詞 ②

Step 1　實戰重點

解題策略　當選項中出現 to 不定詞，並且題目句型為「動詞＋受詞＋ ------」時，答案請選 to 不定詞。

🎓 代表題型

Since Miguel Perez objected to the previous budget, he has prepared a speech -------
his support of the revisions.

(A) explains　　　　(B) explanation　　　　(C) to explain　　　　(D) explained

✏️ 攻略解題法

Since Miguel Perez objected to the previous budget,

連接詞　　　主詞　　　　不及物動詞＋介系詞　　　受詞

> 不及物動詞＋介系詞等同及物動詞，後方須接續受詞

-- 副詞子句

he has prepared a speech (------- his support of the revisions.)

主詞　　動詞　　　受詞　　　　　　　to　不定詞（作副詞）

-- 完整子句

(A) explains　　　　(B) explanation　　　　(C) to explain　　　　(D) explained

單數動詞現在式　　　　名詞　　　　　　to 不定詞　　　　動詞（過去式）／過去分詞

文句分析　　「since ＋主詞（Miguel Perez）＋動詞過去式（objected）」的句型，搭配現在完成式（has prepared）一起使用。

說明　　　　多益考題中，to 不定詞為答案的機率很高。因此只要有 to 不定詞的選項出現，可優先從題目中找尋答案的線索，請記住，通常 to 不定詞的線索都會在空格的前方。本題的動詞（prepare）便是以 to 不定詞作為受詞的例子，因此答案為 (C) to explain。

翻譯　　　　由於 Miguel Perez 反對之前的預算，他已經準備好一個演講來解釋他對修訂的支持。

單字片語　　object to 反對～／ support 支持／ revision 修正

解答　　　　(C)

✎ **攻略 POINT**

to 不定詞除了可當作受詞，也可當作受詞補語。

Step 2 | 核心理論 & 基礎形式

📖 核心理論

以 to 不定詞作為受詞補語的動詞

以 to 不定詞作為受詞補語常見的動詞（動詞＋受詞＋ to 不定詞）

require 要求去～	allow 允許～
invite 邀請去～	remind 提醒～
advise 建議～	ask 要求～
expect 期待～	prepare 準備～
enable 讓～可行	permit 允許～

可將 to 不定詞作受詞以及受詞補語的動詞

want 希望～	need 需要～
expect 期待～	ask 要求 ～

The company **asked the customers** to fill out the online survey.
公司要求顧客填寫線上問卷。

The manager **advised the employees** to keep the documents in the cabinet.
經理建議員工們把文件放在檔案櫃裡。

The manager **expects the employees** to submit the proposal on time.
經理期待員工們能準時提交提案。

Step 3 | 實戰演練

1 A new training program would enable the factory workers ------- their scheduled projects much more efficiently.

(A) completed   (B) completion   (C) completing   (D) to complete

2 The new rule effective as of today will permit employees ------- their vehicles overnight in designated areas.

(A) parks   (B) to park   (C) for parking   (D) parking

▶ 答案與解析請參考解析本第 28 頁

REVIEW TEST

1. If you wish ------- this mailing service, you need to call a customer service representative and request to remove your name from the mailing list.
   (A) to cancelling
   (B) cancellation
   (C) to cancel
   (D) cancelling

2. I would like to invite all senior financial analysts ------- the meeting scheduled for April 11 in the conference room at the Botswana Corporation.
   (A) attended
   (B) attendance
   (C) attending
   (D) to attend

3. The ------- of the corporate wellness program is to give more encouragement to the newly established product development division.
   (A) source
   (B) objective
   (C) warranty
   (D) development

4. ABST support services help them ------- the needs of people who experience severe and persistent mental health problems.
   (A) meets
   (B) for meeting
   (C) meeting
   (D) meet

5. ------- the reservation of your preferred times, we recommend that you complete the registration procedure 3 weeks in advance.
   (A) To ensure
   (B) Ensured
   (C) To be ensured
   (D) To ensuring

6. You should ------- to take an alternate route because the Sacramento Bridge will be closed for repairs starting next Monday.
   (A) enjoy
   (B) plan
   (C) lead
   (D) account

7. Research shows that the average CEO in this industry took only 23.6 years ------- attain the top position.
   (A) in order to
   (B) such that
   (C) as though
   (D) regarding

8. The hospital is trying to make employees ------- their hands when the employees enter the room.
   (A) washed
   (B) washer
   (C) wash
   (D) washing

9. The notice reminds customers ------- these fragile products with care.
   (A) handles
   (B) handles
   (C) handling
   (D) to handle

10. The new CFO ------- to provide a more detailed version of the annual financial report before the next meeting.
    (A) promised
    (B) denied
    (C) discussed
    (D) canceled

▶ 答案與解析請參考解析本第 28 頁

類型分析

10

動名詞

動名詞是原形動詞加上 -ing 後，變為名詞的詞性。

WARMING UP

01 文法概念前導 .... 正式進入文法單元前，先熟悉一下文法基本概念。

1) 動名詞的基本概念
英文中，將動詞轉化為名詞的方式，是在動詞字尾加上 -ing，此詞性便稱之為「動名詞」。

2) 不定詞的角色
如同 to 不定詞，動名詞在句子中也可作為主詞、受詞以及補語。

① Studying English everyday is important. 每天念英文是很重要的。　▶ 主詞

② I continued studying English everyday. 我每天持續地念英文。　▶ 及物動詞的受詞

③ We talked about studying English everyday. 我們每天都會談論念英文這件事。　▶ 介系詞的受詞

④ My hobby is studying English everyday. 我的興趣就是每天念英文。　▶ 主詞的補語

3) 動名詞與名詞的差別
雖然動名詞在句子中扮演的是名詞的角色，但嚴格說來，動名詞是由動詞轉化而成的，因此帶有動詞特有，且跟名詞不同的特性。

① 名詞前方可加上冠詞，但動名詞不可。

　　ex) I have a <u>book</u>. 我有一本書。（O）

　　My hobby is a <u>drawing</u> a picture. 我的興趣是畫圖。（×）

② 動名詞如同動詞，可以擁有自己的受詞或是補語，並且可用副詞作修飾，但名詞不可。

　　ex) He likes studying <u>English</u>. 他喜歡念英文。

　　　▶ English 用來作為動名詞 studying 的受詞。

　　Exercising <u>regularly</u> is difficult. 規律地運動是很困難的。

　　　▶ regularly 用來修飾動名詞 Exercising。

02 暖身例題

請閱讀下方題目的中文翻譯後，圈選出畫底線部分在句中的功能為何。

1 <u>Hiring new employees</u> is my job.　　　　　　　　　　（主詞／受詞）

招募新員工是我的工作。

2 <u>Taking advantage of your location</u> is important in strategy.　（主詞／受詞）

策略上來說，活用你的位置是很重要的。

3 The company finished <u>printing the newspaper</u>.　　　　　（主詞／受詞）

公司完成了報紙的印刷。

4 They managed to finish the project by <u>conducting market research</u>.　（主詞／受詞）

他們進行了市場調查，努力地完成了這個企劃。

03 例題解答

1 <u>Hiring new employees</u> is my job. 招募新員工是我的工作。

　動名詞　　　hire 的受詞

▶ 上述句子中的主詞，是表「招募」的 Hiring。Hiring 是動詞 hire 加上 -ing 後，變化為名詞作為主詞。像 hiring 這樣的詞性，就被稱為動名詞。動名詞是動詞加上 -ing，仍可擁有自己的受詞，並用於主詞、受詞或是補語的位置。

2 <u>Taking advantage</u> of your location is important in strategy.

　動名詞　 take 的受詞　　　　　　 單數動詞

策略上來說，活用你的位置是很重要的。

▶ 主詞位置上，可置入等同於名詞的動名詞（Taking），而動名詞仍能保有動詞的受詞（advantage）。另外，請注意，動名詞為主語時，搭配的是單數動詞。

3 The company finished <u>printing the newspaper</u>. 公司完成了報紙的印刷。

　　　　　　　　動詞　　動名詞　　 print 的受詞

▶ 及物動詞後方補語的位置，可置入動名詞（printing），而動名詞仍能保有動詞的受詞（the newspaper）。

4 They managed to finish the project by <u>conducting market research</u>.

　　　　　　　　　　　　　　 介系詞　　動名詞　　　　 受詞

他們進行了市場調查，努力地完成了這個企劃。

▶ 介系詞後方的受詞位置，可置入動名詞。

Unit 49 動名詞擺放的位置 ①

解題策略　當題目的句首出現「----- ＋受詞＋（修飾語）」，且後方動詞為單數動詞時，空格多為動名詞。

 代表題型

------- to a project with commitment is important for better organizational performance.

(A) Contributed　　(B) Contributes　　(C) Contributing　　(D) Contributions

 攻略解題法

------- to a project with commitment is important for better organizational performance.

動名詞主詞 contribute to 的受詞　介系詞片語　動詞　補語　　介系詞片語（表目的）

> contribute 必須跟介系詞 to 一同使用

(A) Contributed　　(B) Contributes　　(C) Contributing　　(D) Contributions
動詞（過去式）／過去分詞　單數動詞現在式　　動名詞　　　名詞

文句分析　不及物動詞 contribute 與介系詞 to 一同使用，表「貢獻於～」。「不及物動詞＋介系詞」後，便等同及物動詞，後方可接續受詞。

說明　當空格位於題目句首，並且後方接續動詞的情況下，空格即為主詞。主詞可置入名詞或是動名詞，而動名詞視為單數，必定搭配單數動詞使用，表「做～這件事」。而本題句型為「----- ＋受詞＋（修飾語）」，且後方動詞為單數動詞，可知 (C) 動名詞為答案。雖然 (D) 也可放在主詞的位置，但與後方動詞並未達到單複數一致性，因此不正確。要注意的是「不及物動詞（contribute）＋介系詞（to）」是成對出現使用的。

翻譯　為了得到更好的組織績效表現，全心投入一個企劃案是很重要的。

單字片語　contribute to 奉獻於／ with commitment 致力／ organizational 組織的／ performance 表現，績效

解答　(C)

🖋 攻略 POINT

雖然動名詞可置於主詞、受詞以及補語的位置，但多益考題中最容易出現在主詞或是受詞的地方。

核心理論

動名詞如同名詞,可置於主詞、受詞與補語的位置,也如同動詞,後方可接續受詞。

動名詞的特性

動詞＋ -ing	原形動詞後方加上「-ing」。
扮演主詞、受詞或補語	句子中可置於主詞、受詞或補語的位置。但唯獨與主詞達到一致時,才能作為補語。
保有動詞特性	如同一般動詞,後面仍可接續受詞。

- **作為主詞**

  Making a copy is quite a simple procedure. 影印是一個很簡單的程序。

  make 的受詞

  ▶ 如名詞般,動名詞(Making)置於單數動詞(is)前作主詞。

- **作為受詞**

  Our company consultants <u>suggested</u> **reducing** unnecessary expenses.
  我們公司的顧問建議減少不必要的支出。

  reduce 的受詞

  ▶ 如名詞般,動名詞(reducing)置於動詞(suggest)後作受詞。

  We will hold a launching ceremony <u>before</u> **releasing** the new product.
  我們將會在推出新產品前,舉辦上市發表會。

  release 的受詞

  ▶ 如名詞般,動名詞(releasing)置於介系詞(before)後作受詞。

- **作為補語**

  My hobby <u>is</u> **travelling** throughout the country. 我的興趣是去全國各地旅行。

  ▶ 如名詞般,動名詞(travelling)置於 be 動詞(is)後作補語。主詞(hobby)與動名詞補語(travelling)為同位語。

1 A team of three researchers has finished ------- the first of five sets of data gathered in Colorado, New Mexico, and Brazil.

(A) analyzed　　　　(B) analyzation　　　　(C) to analyze　　　　(D) analyzing

2 ------- the enclosed survey after reading the general instructions on the back of this page is the easiest way you can get involved in the growth of Casa Adalijao.

(A) Completions　　　　(B) Completing　　　　(C) Completed　　　　(D) Completes

▶答案與解析請參考解析本第 29 頁

Unit 50　動名詞擺放的位置 ②

解題策略　　介系詞與受詞之間的空格為動名詞的位置。

 代表題型

> The Starlet safety key is now attached to a tether to discourage you from ------- the key.
>
> (A) misplaced　　　(B) misplacement　　　(C) misplacing　　　(D) misplace

 攻略解題法

The Starlet safety key is now attached to a tether to discourage you from ------- the key.
　　主詞　　　　　動詞 副詞　補語　　介系詞片語　　不定詞（作副詞）　受詞 介系詞 動名詞 動名詞的受詞
　　介系詞片語
　　　　　請記住 be attached to 的用法　　　　　　　　　　　　　　　　　（介系詞＋等同名詞的語句）

(A) misplaced	(B) misplacement	(C) misplacing	(D) misplace
動詞（過去式）／過去分詞	名詞	動名詞	複數動詞現在式

文句分析　　動詞 discourage 通常會與 prevent、keep 一同使用，句型為「受詞＋ from ＋ V-ing」，表「使無法～」。

說明　　　　介系詞後方接受詞，而名詞或動名詞皆可作為受詞。由於動名詞仍保有動詞特性，後方如動詞般，也可擁有自己的受詞。因此「介系詞＋ ------」的後方，若有受詞，空格為動名詞；若後方無受詞，則空格為名詞。例題中「介系詞＋ ------」的後方接有受詞（the key），因此答案為 (C) misplacing。

翻譯　　　　為了防止你弄丟鑰匙，Starlet 安全鑰匙被接在鏈子上。

單字片語　　be attached to 連接於～／ tether 鎖鏈／ discourage 使心灰意冷，防止／ misplace 遺落，放錯地方

解答　　　　(C)

攻略 POINT

動名詞本身當作「介系詞的受詞」的同時，也可以有自己的受詞。

核心理論

多益考試中最常出現的動名詞類型考題，便是選出位於介系詞後方，作為受詞的動名詞。

如何區分介系詞後面該接名詞或是動名詞

介系詞後方	可接名詞或是動名詞。
區分的準則	受詞的有無（名詞後方不能連接受詞，但動名詞可以）。
原因	動名詞保有動詞特性，後面仍可接續受詞。

We sincerely apologize for the delay in ~~deliver~~ your order.
delivering

對於您訂單的延遲送件，我們在此誠摯地道歉。

We can install the equipment without ~~interruption~~ the power supply.
interrupting

我們不用切斷電源供應就可以安裝裝備。

▶「介系詞＋ ------」後方連接了受詞（the power supply），因此空格內填入動名詞（interrupting）。

Without ~~pressuring~~, you can try on anything you want in this store.
pressure

沒了壓力，你可以試穿這間店裡所有你想試的。

▶「介系詞＋ ------」後方沒有受詞，因此空格內填入名詞（pressure）。

1 Richard Williamson, a spokesman for the Human Resources Department, objected to ------- staff next month due to the limited budget.

(A) adds   (B) addition   (C) added   (D) adding

2 With the aim of ------- all of our guests, Marbella recently built some holiday villas downtown, and they were designed with some very special features.

(A) satisfaction   (B) satisfying   (C) satisfied   (D) satisfactory

▶答案與解析請參考解析本第 29 頁

Unit 51　與動名詞搭配的動詞

Step 1 　實戰重點

解題策略　當選項中出現動名詞，且空格前方正是以動名詞作受詞的動詞時，答案即為動名詞。

🎓 代表題型

A significant increase in sales allowed the company to consider ------- its products.

(A) investing　　　　(B) invested　　　　(C) invest　　　　(D) investment

✏️ 攻略解題法

A significant increase in sales allowed the company to consider ------- its products.

主詞　　　　介系詞片語　動詞（句型 5）　allow 的受詞　　allow　　consider　investing
　　　　　　　　　　　　　　　　　　　　　　的受詞補語　的受詞　的受詞補語

修飾

句型 5 動詞＋受詞＋受詞補語

(A) investing　　　　(B) invested　　　　(C) invest　　　　(D) investment
動名詞　　　　動詞過去式／過去分詞　　　動詞　　　　　　名詞

文句分析　allow 的句型為「受詞＋ to 不定詞」，而此處的 to 不定詞為受詞補語，為句型 5 的文法。

說明　　　最好將以動名詞作為受詞的動詞背下來，其中最常見的例子有 consider、include、suggest、recommend 等等。本題中空格前方為 consider，因此答案應為動名詞 (A) investing。

翻譯　　　銷售量大幅的增加，讓這間公司考慮投資其新產品。

單字片語　significant 相當的／ consider 考慮／ profit 利潤

解答　　　(A)

✐ 攻略 POINT

consider、include、suggest、recommend 等等動詞，以動名詞作受詞。

📖 核心理論

以動名詞作受詞的動詞

avoid 避免～	enjoy 享受～	mind 介意～
consider 考慮～	finish 結束～	postpone 延遲～
deny 否認～	give up 放棄～	recommend 推薦～
discontinue 中止～	include 包含～	suggest 建議～

Mr. McDonnell is <u>considering</u> **applying** for the sales manager position.
McDonnell 先生正在考慮是否要應徵銷售經理的職位。

The manager <u>suggested</u> **extending** the deadline to complete the project.
經理建議延長最後期限來完成這份專案。

The manager <u>recommended</u> **using** the internet to reserve a meeting place.
經理推薦使用網路來預訂會議場地。

- **動名詞的否定型**

He suggested **not offering** customer service anymore.
他建議不要再提供顧客服務。

▶ 動詞＋ ing 的前方加上 not，便為否定型。

1 Our used ski shop is equipped with a wide selection and a great choice of equipment for skiers of every level who want to avoid ------- high retail prices.

(A) pay　　　　　　(B) paying　　　　　　(C) paid　　　　　　(D) to pay

2 The manager suggested ------- late on Friday and Saturday nights during the peak season between June 1 and August 31.

(A) closed　　　　　　(B) close　　　　　　(C) to close　　　　　　(D) closing

Unit 52 常見的動名詞相關片語

| Step 1 | 實戰重點 |

解題策略　建議記下與動名詞相關的常見片語單字。

 代表題型

> We look forward to ------- with you and hope that our relationship is mutually beneficial.
>
> (A) work　　　　(B) works　　　　(C) working　　　　(D) worked

 攻略解題法

介系詞（非 to 不定詞）

We look forward to ------- with you and hope that our relationship is mutually beneficial.
主詞 搭配動名詞的常見片語　　　介系詞片語 連接詞 動詞 連接詞　　　主詞　　動詞　副詞　　補語

介系詞後方接名詞，選項中等同於
名詞功能的唯有動名詞

(A) work　　　　　　(B) works　　　　　　(C) working　　　　　(D) worked
複數動詞現在式　　　單數動詞現在式　　　　動名詞　　　　　動詞（過去式）／過去分詞

文句分析　and 後方省略了前面已出現過的主詞 We。

說明　　　請務必盡量記住動名詞相關的片語。「期待～」的文法為「look forward to V-ing」，因此 (C) working 為答案。

翻譯　　　我們很期待與您一起工作，並願兩方的關係互惠共利。

單字片語　looking forward to -ing 期待～／ mutually 相互地／ beneficial 有益的

解答　　　(C)

攻略 POINT
必須將介系詞 to 與不定詞中的 to 分辨清楚。

核心理論

動名詞相關的常見片語

be committed to -ing 致力於～	be worth -ing 值得～
look forward to -ing 期待～	object to -ing 反對～
be accustomed / used to -ing 對～感到習慣	contribute to -ing 促成～
have difficulty (in) -ing 對～感到困難	keep (on) -ing 持續～
be busy (in) -ing 忙碌於～	on / upon -ing 一～就～
be dedicated / devoted to -ing 專注於～	feel like -ing 想要～
spend 時間／錢 (in) -ing 花時間／錢在～上	go -ing 去做～
cannot help -ing 忍不住～	

We are <u>looking forward to</u> **seeing** you soon.
我們期待盡快與您相會。

He is <u>considering</u> **accepting** the proposal.
他正在考慮接受這個提案。

All of them <u>were accustomed to</u> **working** overtime.
他們所有人都已經習慣加班。

The founder of the organization <u>is still committed to</u> **expanding** his business.
組織的創辦人仍致力於拓展他的事業。

1 The NCBA members of the beef industry are committed to ------- the safest possible products in Canada.

(A) produce   (B) production   (C) produced   (D) producing

2 Due to their sizes, small underground coal mining companies in New Zealand have difficulty ------- their productivity.

(A) increases   (B) increasing   (C) increase   (D) increased

▶答案與解析請參考解析本第 30 頁

REVIEW TEST

1. I would highly recommend ------- Paces Moving, Inc. to any business or individual that is planning to move.
   - (A) using
   - (B) usable
   - (C) use
   - (D) used

2. ------- some valid and meaningful data from surveys on behalf of a company takes time, energy, and resources.
   - (A) Collecting
   - (B) Collections
   - (C) Collected
   - (D) Collects

3. Most of the employees did not disagree with ------- parking guidelines that went into effect two weeks ago.
   - (A) follower
   - (B) following
   - (C) followed
   - (D) follow

4. The BBC reporters are accustomed to ------- all sorts of obstacles to meet their deadlines.
   - (A) be surmounted
   - (B) surmounts
   - (C) surmounting
   - (D) surmount

5. The company will be taking disciplinary action against the employee who went to the business conference without ------- his part of the presentation.
   - (A) organize
   - (B) organized
   - (C) organization
   - (D) organizing

6. Homeowners often ask what renovations are worth ------- in before selling their homes.
   - (A) invest
   - (B) investing
   - (C) to invest
   - (D) invested

7. The CEO of our company insists on ------- a new company building despite the board members' objection.
   - (A) constructed
   - (B) constructing
   - (C) construction
   - (D) constructs

8. Only authorized users identified by the Personnel Department have access to ------- about the customers.
   - (A) informed
   - (B) informs
   - (C) information
   - (D) informing

9. The Sales and Marketing Department is responsible for ------- the Sofia Hotel's unique amenities and services by advertising in the local newspaper.
   - (A) promote
   - (B) promoting
   - (C) promoted
   - (D) promotion

10. To apply for this position, remember ------- our website for details about the application requirements and deadlines.
    - (A) reviews
    - (B) reviewer
    - (C) reviewing
    - (D) to review

▶答案與解析請參考解析本第 30 頁

類型分析

分詞

分詞是原形動詞在語尾加上「-ing」或是「-ed」後,如形容詞般修飾名詞,或是用來作為補語。

WARMING UP

01 文法概念前導 ⸺⸺⸺ 正式進入文法單元前，先熟悉一下文法基本概念。

1) 分詞的基本概念

「美麗的花」、「勇敢的少年」等等，這些常見於用來修飾名詞的詞性為形容詞。但是也有像「正在睡覺的男人」、「被收集起來的郵票」等等，這些以其他詞性來修飾名詞的例子。前一句提到的「正在睡覺的」、「被收集起來的」這些詞彙，嚴格說來並非形容詞，而是動詞，應將其稱為由動詞變化而來的形容詞，這樣文法上才說得通。像這樣帶著動詞特性，卻作為形容詞使用的詞性，便稱為「分詞」。

2) 分詞的種類

分詞大致上可分為現在分詞與過去分詞兩種，各自的特徵如下方所示。

現在分詞		過去分詞	
主動語態	做～的 ex) an exciting game 令人興奮的比賽	被動語態	被～的 ex) a broken window 被打破的窗戶
進行式	正在～的 ex) a sleeping baby 正在睡覺的寶寶	完成式	已經～的 ex) fallen leaves 落下的葉子

3) 分詞的角色

雖然分詞是由動詞變化而來，但由於跟形容詞的功能相同，因此可視為同等角色。但分詞仍保留了動詞的特色，因此後方可接續受詞。

The man is watching TV. 那個男人正在看電視。

▶ 這裡同形容詞作主格補語，由於保留了動詞的特性，因此後方可接續受詞「TV」。

02 暖身例題

請圈選出括號中正確的分詞。

1 Be sure to take care of the (remaining / remained) staff.

2 By tomorrow morning, you should submit the (revised / revising) copy.

3 You have to allow for guests (waiting / waited) for a long time.

4 Ships are only allowed to dock at (designating / designated) ports.

5 When (signing / signed) the contract, read it carefully.

03 例題解答

1 the **remaining** staff （留下來的工作人員）

2 the **revised** copy （被修正過的副本）

> ▶ 如上題中，在原形動詞（remain）加上 -ing 或是原形動詞（revise）上加上 -ed，作為形容詞修飾名詞的詞性，便稱為分詞。在原形動詞後方加 -ing 的稱為現在分詞，而加上 -ed 的則稱為過去分詞。

> ▶ 被修飾的主詞與分詞的關係為主動語態時，使用現在分詞；反之，主詞與分詞關係為被動語態時，則使用過去分詞。那麼，什麼是主動語態，什麼是被動語態呢？若「修飾的名詞進行分詞的動作」，即為主動語態；若「修飾的名詞被分詞了」，則為被動語態。

3 You have to allow for guests **waiting** for a long time.

你必須要考慮到等很久的客人們。

> ▶ 「被修飾的名詞（guests）正在等待」，可見此處為主動語態，因此使用現在分詞 waiting。

4 Ships are only allowed to dock at **designated** ports.

船隻只能停泊在指定的港口。

> ▶ 「被修飾的名詞（ports）被指定好了」，可見此處為被動語態，因此使用現在分詞 designated。

5 When **signing** the contract, read it carefully.

簽合約的時候，請仔細閱讀內容。

> ▶ 當空格緊接在連接詞後方，且空格後方有受詞時，須填入現在分詞，若無受詞，則填入過去分詞。

Unit 53　分詞擺放的位置 ❶

解題策略　當主詞為人物時，主詞補語位置請填入過去分詞；若主詞為事物時，補語位置請填入現在分詞。

 代表題型

> We were extremely ------- with our stay although the hotel was beautiful and the people were friendly.
>
> (A) disappoint　　　(B) disappointing　　　(C) disappointed　　　(D) disappointment

✏ 攻略解題法

We were extremely ------- (with our stay)
主詞　動詞　副詞　　補語　　介系詞片語　　　↳ 補語的位置可放入
　　　　　　　　主句　　　　　　　　　形容詞或是名詞

although (the hotel was beautiful) and (the people were friendly.)
連接詞　　主詞　動詞　補語　對等連接詞　主詞　動詞　補語
　　　　　用對等連接詞（and）連接起來的兩個子句
　　　　　　　　　　副詞子句

(A) disappoint　　　(B) disappointing　　　(C) disappointed　　　(D) disappointment
　動詞　　　　　　　　現在分詞　　　　　　　過去分詞　　　　　　　名詞

文句分析　去掉修飾語句後，句子構造就變得比較簡單。另外，像題目中「be disappointed with（對～感到失望）」這類型前方使用be動詞，後方加上介系詞的過去分詞片語非常常見。

說明　　　放入補語位置的分詞，多為描述情感狀態的分詞。大原則是，當分詞作為主詞補語，主詞與補語互為主動關係時，使用現在分詞；互為被動關係時，使用過去分詞。不過也可以簡單劃分為：當主詞為人物時，使用過去分詞；為事物時，用現在分詞。由此可推出本題答案為 (C) disappointed。

翻譯　　　儘管飯店很美，人員也很親切，但我們對於這次住宿極其失望。

單字片語　disappoint 使失望，辜負／ stay 停留／ friendly 親切的

解答　　　(C)

✎ 攻略 POINT

當分詞語意與表達情感有關時，若主詞為人物，使用過去分詞，若為事物，則使用現在分詞。

核心理論

當主詞與補語的分詞為主動關係時，使用現在分詞；若為被動關係時，則用過去分詞。

現在分詞與過去分詞如何區分

現在分詞	當被修飾的主詞與分詞為主動關係 the smiling　　　girl 微笑的　　→　　女孩
過去分詞	當被修飾的主詞與分詞為被動關係 the offered　　　goods 被提供的　　→　　物品

Mr. Scott was **disappointed** by the quality of the entries.

Scott 先生對進口品項的品質很失望。

▶ 當分詞作為主詞補語時，若主詞為人物（Mr. Scott），表情感的動詞（disappoint）使用過去分詞（disappointed）。

The initial holiday sales were **disappointing**.

一開始的假日業績令人失望。

▶ 當分詞作為主詞補語時，若主詞為事物（holiday sales），表情感的動詞（disappoint）使用現在分詞（disappointing）。

He found Kim **exhausted** from her constant writing.

他發現 Kim 因為連續的寫作而精疲力盡。

▶ 當分詞作為受詞補語時，若主詞為人物（Kim），表情感的動詞（exhaust）使用過去分詞（exhausted）。

Stacy found the process **exhausting**.

Stacy 發現這個程序很累人。

▶ 當分詞作為受詞補語時，若主詞為事物（process），表情感的動詞（exhaust）使用現在分詞（exhausting）。

Step 3 ｜ 實戰演練

1 Current customers who are ------- with our products are likely to become regular customers.

(A) satisfy　　　(B) had satisfied　　　(C) satisfying　　　(D) satisfied

2 Eliot Dahl, an award-winning copywriter, once made a poster of his roommate running a marathon to keep his roommate ------- on race day.

(A) inspiration　　　(B) inspired　　　(C) inspiring　　　(D) been inspired

▶答案與解析請參考解析本第 32 頁

Unit 54 分詞擺放的位置 ②

解題策略　當選項中出現分詞，若空格前後方皆為名詞，填入現在分詞，若只有前方為名詞，則填入過去分詞。

 代表題型

All employees ------- in the new project are advised to participate in the world trade fair.

(A) involve　　　　(B) involving　　　　(C) involvement　　　　(D) involved

 攻略解題法

All employees	------- in the new project	are advised	to participate in the world trade fair.
主詞	介系詞片語	動詞	to 不定詞

(A) involve	(B) involving	(C) involvement	(D) involved
複數動詞現在式	現在分詞	名詞	動詞（過去式）／過去分詞

文句分析　本題中，all employees 是主詞，動詞為 are advised，而從空格開始到 project 為止皆為副詞片語。

說明　　　當選項中同時出現限定動詞與分詞時，請先確認空格前後是否有其他動詞，若有動詞，則空格內填入分詞，若無，則填入動詞。而當確定該空格須填入分詞後，前後方皆為名詞時，要選擇現在分詞；若只有前方為名詞，則選擇過去分詞。本題空格後方已有動詞（are advised），因此空格內為分詞，且空格後方接續的並非名詞而是介系詞，可知答案為 (D) involved。

翻譯　　　與這個新專案有關的所有員工，都被建議去參加世界貿易博覽會。

單字片語　be advised to 被建議～／ participate in 參加／ trade fair 貿易博覽會

解答　　　(D)

✎ **攻略 POINT**

當選項中同時出現限定動詞與分詞時，請先確認該空格須為動詞或分詞，若確定為分詞後，再辨別需填入現在分詞或過去分詞。

核心理論

一個句子只會有一個主要的動詞，必須要能夠辨別清楚何者為主要動詞，何者為分詞。通常，可以根據分詞後方其他動詞的有無來辨別。

> **主要動詞與分詞的區分**
>
> The employee conducting the survey took the day off today.
> 　　　　　　分詞　　　　　　　　　　主要動詞
> 負責問卷調查的員工今天請假。
>
> The selected employee conducted the survey.
> 　　　分詞　　　　　　　　主要動詞
> 被選定的員工負責問卷調查。

Kira Electronics delivers all orders ~~purchasing~~ through the online store within 7 days.
　　　　　　　　　　　　　　　　　purchased

Kira Electronics 公司所有的網路訂單，都會在七天內送達。

▶ 名詞（all orders）與介系詞片語（through the online store）中的空格，填入過去分詞（purchased）。

Richard starts his work by checking his company e-mail, ~~included~~ customer feedback every week.
　　　　　　　　　　　　　　　　　　　　　　　　　　　　including

Richard 每週都從確認包含顧客回饋的公司郵件開始一週的工作。

▶ 名詞（company e-mail）與名詞（customer feedback）中的空格，填入現在分詞（including）。

1 This paper is based on the outcomes of the 36 audit reports ------- by Massachusetts Printer over a period of 3 years.

(A) publish (B) published (C) will publish (D) publishing

2 Everyone ------- the USC School of Business is required to register his or her laptop on http://uscbusiness.edu.

(A) has attended (B) attends (C) attendee (D) attending

▶答案與解析請參考解析本第 32 頁

Unit 55 區分 V-ing 與 V-ed

解題策略　當分詞用來修飾名詞時，若被修飾的名詞與分詞為主動關係，使用現在分詞；若為被動關係，使用過去分詞。

 代表題型

We request that you return the completed and signed forms in the ------- envelope as soon as possible but no later than Thursday, April 11.

(A) enclosed　　　　(B) enclose　　　　(C) enclosing　　　　(D) encloser

 攻略解題法

We request that you return the completed and signed forms in the ------- envelope

主詞　動詞　　　　　　　　　對等連接詞子句　　　　　　　　介系詞片語

(as soon as possible) but (no later than Thursday, April 11.)　　冠詞（the）與名詞（envelope）之間為形容詞的位置
副詞　　　對等連接詞　　　　　副詞

(A) enclosed　　　　(B) enclose　　　　(C) enclosing　　　　(D) encloser
動詞（過去式）／過去分詞　複數動詞現在式　　　現在分詞　　　　　名詞

文句分析　that 子句是用來作為 request 受詞的名詞子句，而冠詞與名詞之間為形容詞的位置。

說明　　　冠詞（a / the）與名詞之間，可填入分詞。當分詞是用來修飾名詞的情況下，若被修飾的名詞與分詞為主動關係，使用現在分詞；若為被動關係，使用過去分詞。可推論出本題應在 (A) 或 (C) 中選擇，而被修飾的名詞（envelope）與分詞為被動關係，因此 (A) enclosed 為答案。

翻譯　　　我們要求您盡速將回郵信封中的表格填妥並簽名，並於四月十一日星期四前送達。

單字片語　completed 完成的／ signed 簽好名的／ enclose 封入，附寄／ envelope 信封／ no later than 不晚於～之前／ encloser 外殼

解答　　　(A)

攻略 POINT

冠詞與名詞之間為形容詞，而分詞可作形容詞用。

核心理論

請記住下列現在分詞與過去分詞的常見用語。

現在分詞固定用語	過去分詞固定用語
existing equipment 現有設備	attached document 附件資料
leading company 龍頭企業	detailed information 詳細資訊
growing company 成長中的公司	limited warranty 有限責任保固
lasting impression 不可磨滅的印象	damaged item 毀損的物件
promising member 有前途的成員	discounted price 折扣後價格
demanding work 高要求的工作	merged companies 合併的公司

We'll assist you in finding your **missing** luggage.

我們將會協助您找尋您丟失的行李。

▶ 請記住像「missing luggage（丟失的行李）」這類「現在分詞＋名詞」的常見用語。

Submit the **revised** project plan sometime next week.

請於下週時提交修正好的專案計畫。

▶ 請記住像「revised project（修正的專案）」這類「過去分詞＋名詞」的常見用語。

Every applicant should complete the **attached** application form.

每個應徵者都需要完成附件的應徵表格。

▶ 請記住像「attached application form（附件的應徵表格）」這類「過去分詞＋名詞」的常見用語。

Step **3** | 實戰演練

1 The ------- size of an aperture coupled microstrip antenna provides compatibility with portable communication systems.

(A) reduce   (B) reducing   (C) reduction   (D) reduced

2 In 1978, Granley Furniture organized the ------- company into three product lines and successfully expanded its business in Europe.

(A) grow   (B) growing   (C) grew   (D) grown

▶答案與解析請參考解析本第 32 頁

 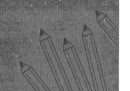

Unit 56　分詞構句

| Step 1 | 實戰重點 |

解題策略　　受詞前方的空格為現在分詞，而後方沒有受詞的空格，則為過去分詞。

代表題型

------- the survey, you'll be provided with the opportunity to enter a monthly drawing to win a $100 BKT gift card.

(A) Completely　　　(B) Complete　　　(C) Completing　　　(D) Completed

攻略解題法

------- the survey, you'll be provided with the opportunity
分詞　　　受詞　　主詞　　動詞片語　　　　受詞

分詞構句　　　　　　　　　　　完整句子
(to enter a monthly drawing to win a $100 BKT gift card.)
to 不定詞（作副詞用）

(A) Completely　　　(B) Complete　　　(C) Completing　　　(D) Completed
　副詞　　　　　　複數動詞現在式　　　現在分詞　　　　過去分詞

文句分析　　原本的句子應為 When you complete the survey, you'll...，而本題的句子將 When you 省略，將動詞 complete 變為 Completing。

說明　　　　將「連接詞＋主詞」省略後，轉化為「句首空格＋受詞或是修飾語＋逗點＋完整句子」的文法，便是分詞構句。此時，若空格後方有受詞，填入現在分詞；若無，填入過去分詞。本題中，空格後方出現受詞（the survey），因此現在分詞 (C) Completing 為正解。

翻譯　　　　完成問卷後，您可獲得參加每個月抽獎獲得 $100 BKT 禮券的機會。

單字片語　　complete 完成／ be provided with 獲得～／ enter 參加，進入／ drawing 抽籤，抽獎

解答　　　　(C)

攻略 POINT

分詞構句中，若後方有受詞，填入現在分詞；若無，填入過去分詞。

📖 **核心理論**

分詞構句是將副詞子句中的連接詞與主詞省略後，以分詞為句首的句型，功用在於讓整個句子看起來更簡潔。

When I drove the car carefully, I found a good restaurant beside the river.

①	去掉連接詞	~~When~~ I drove the car carefully, ~
②	去掉主詞	~~When I~~ drove the car carefully, ~
③	根據語意將動詞變化成分詞	~~When I~~ Driving the car carefully, ~

- **省略連接詞的分詞構句**

Removing all the previous versions of Netapp, you can lock and unlock the toolbar.

受詞　　　　　　　　　　完整子句

移除 Netapp 所有的舊版本後，你可以任意將工具列鎖定或解除鎖定。

▶「------ ＋受詞＋逗點＋完整子句」的句型中，空格內填入現在分詞（Removing）。

Located in the city's center, our hotel is within walking distance of places where

修飾語　　　　　　　　　完整子句

people can engage in cultural activities.

坐落在都市中心，我們飯店就位於民眾可以體驗文化活動地點的步行範圍內。

▶「------ ＋修飾語＋逗點＋完整子句」的句型中，空格內填入過去分詞（Located）。

- **保留連接詞的分詞構句**

When **pressing** the button on the panel, you can change the volume on the screen.

當你按下控制盤上的按鈕，就可以調整螢幕的音量。

▶ 時間連接詞（when、while、after、before）常與「V-ing ＋受詞」出現於考題內。

<u>Unless</u> otherwise **stated**, all of the images are the exclusive property of Pet Rock.

除非另有說明，否則所有的圖片都是 Pet Rock 的私人財產。

▶ 條件連接詞（if、unless）常與「V-ed」一同出現於考題內。

Step 3 | **實戰演練**

1 Before ------- the device, ensure that the system power supply is switched off; otherwise, loose cable connections may result in personal injury.

(A) check　　　　　(B) checked　　　　　(C) being checked　　　　　(D) checking

2 If ------- by a customer, Sonoma Landscape Construction will provide a personalized design of your home by a fully qualified consultant.

(A) desire　　　　　(B) desired　　　　　(C) desiring　　　　　(D) desirable

REVIEW TEST

1. Unless otherwise -------, all rates are quoted in U.S. dollars and are subject to change without prior notice.

   (A) mentioned
   (B) mentioning
   (C) mention
   (D) to mention

2. To meet the ------- demand for a skilled engineering workforce within this region, the Finisar Training and Education Center has opened an office in Kuala Lumpur.

   (A) risen
   (B) rising
   (C) rises
   (D) rose

3. If you receive a ------- item, we will send you a replacement as soon as you have returned it.

   (A) damagingly
   (B) damaging
   (C) damaged
   (D) damage

4. Enclosed are ------- instructions on how to create a simulated device with the 3D Max program.

   (A) detailing
   (B) detail
   (C) detailed
   (D) details

5. Recent research says consistent, even daily incentives work better to keep employees ------- than promised rewards at sometime in the future.

   (A) motivate
   (B) motivated
   (C) motivation
   (D) motivating

6. Stylized flowers, leaves, and butterflies are frequently used in a variety of decorations, ------- vases.

   (A) included
   (B) including
   (C) are included
   (D) includes

7. I regret to inform you that because of an ------- business trip, this week's article will be delayed until Friday.

   (A) unexpected
   (B) expecting
   (C) unexpecting
   (D) expect

8. Information regarding the career fair location and interview schedule will be emailed to the ------- applicants prior to the event.

   (A) inviting
   (B) invite
   (C) invited
   (D) invitation

9. In the job market, competition can be fierce, and an interview can provide someone with the chance to leave a ------- impression.

   (A) lasting
   (B) lasted
   (C) lasts
   (D) will last

10. All employees ------- in the office after 7 p.m. are requested to use the rear exit when leaving.

    (A) remain
    (B) remaining
    (C) have remained
    (D) remained

▶ 答案與解析請參考解析本第 33 頁

類型分析

12

連接詞

連接詞是用來連接單字與單字、片語與片語，或是子句與子句的詞性。

WARMING UP

························· 正式進入文法單元前，先熟悉一下文法基本概念。

1) 連接詞的基本概念

連接詞是在句子中，連接單字與單字，或是子句與子句的詞性。

2) 連接詞的角色

①（對等關係的）單字與單字的連接

Jane is <u>healthy</u> and <u>beautiful</u>. Jane 健康又美麗。

②（對等關係的）片語與片語的連接

I will go to work <u>by bus</u> or <u>by taxi</u>. 我會搭公車或計程車去上班。

Learn More!

＊片語是什麼呢？

片語是不含主詞或是動詞，由兩個以上的單字組合而成，表達某種語意的不完整句型。

有名詞片語、形容詞片語以及副詞片語。

名詞片語	作主詞	To err is human, to forgive is divine. 凡人皆有過，唯神能寬恕。
	作補語	My hobby is playing baseball. 我的興趣是打棒球。
	作受詞	I don't like going there. 我不喜歡去那裡。
形容詞片語	作形容詞	The bread on the table is mine. 桌子上的麵包是我的。
副詞片語	時間	He will come back on time. 他會準時回來。
	目的	I studied hard to pass the exam. 為了通過測驗，我很努力念書。
	理由	Because of you, I can't see the movie. 因為你，我沒辦法看電影。

▶ 所有片語都是以兩個以上單字組合而成，可作名詞、形容詞或副詞用。

③ 子句與子句的連接

<u>He likes her</u>, but <u>she doesn't like him</u>. 他喜歡她，但她不喜歡他。

02 暖身例題

請圈選出括號中正確的連接詞。

1 They performed the test slowly (and / but) accurately.

2 Visit our website (but / and) read the guidelines.

3 Tomorrow is a national holiday, (and / but) all stores will remain open.

4 I don't know (if / which) it is beneficial to all the staff members.

5 We should cancel the company picnic (because / that) the weather is bad.

6 He repaired the equipment (which / since) was broken last week.

03 例題解答

連接詞有對等連接詞、名詞子句連接詞、形容詞子句連接詞、副詞子句連接詞等等，而對等連接詞是用來連接對等關係的單字與單字、片語與片語，以及子句與子句。

1 They performed the test slowly **but** accurately. 他們緩慢但準準地進行了測試。
　　　　　　　　　　　　副詞　　　　　副詞

2 Visit our website **and** read the guidelines. 請上我們的網站並閱讀指南。
　　　動詞片語　　　　　　　動詞片語

3 Tomorrow is a national holiday, **but** all stores will remain open.
　　　　　子句　　　　　　　　　　　　　子句
明天是國定假日，但所有的商店還是會營業。

另外，名詞子句連接詞、形容詞子句連接詞、副詞子句連接詞只能用來連接子句與子句。

4 I don't know if it is beneficial to all the staff members.
　　　　　連接詞 主詞 動詞　補語
　　　　　作為 know 的受詞（完整子句）
我不知道這是否對所有人員來說都是有利的。

5 We should cancel the company picnic because the weather is bad.
　　　　　　　　主句　　　　　　　　　　　副詞子句（完整子句）
因為天氣很差，我們應該要取消公司郊遊。

6 He repaired the equipment which was broken last week.
　　　　　　主句　　　　　　　　　形容詞子句
他修理了上週故障的設備。

連接詞擺放的位置 ①

Step 1　　**實戰重點**

解題策略　　當選項中出現連接詞，而空格位於句首時，填入從屬連接詞。

 代表題型

------- Mr. Gensler arrived on schedule, there were unforeseen difficulties involving mechanical problems.

(A) But　　　　　(B) So　　　　　(C) Although　　　　　(D) However

攻略解題法

------- Mr. Gensler arrived on schedule, there were unforeseen difficulties involving
連接詞　主詞　動詞　介系詞片語　虛構主詞 動詞　主詞　分詞

mechanical problems.
involving 的受詞

> 含有兩個主詞與動詞（兩個子句），因此需要連接詞

(A) But　　　　　(B) So　　　　　(C) Although　　　　　(D) However
對等連接詞　　　　對等連接詞　　　　副詞子句連接詞　　　　副詞

文句分析　　以 there 作虛構主詞，構成「there ＋動詞＋主詞＋修飾語」句型的倒裝句。以 involving 為開頭的分詞構句，是 which were involving mechanical problems 原句將 which were 省略後的分詞構句。

說明　　　　對等連接詞不能放在句首，因此若空格出現現在句首時，可以先將對等連接詞選項刪除。本題中，便可先將同為對等連接詞的 (A)、(B) 選項刪去，而題目中出現了兩個子句，因此 (D) 副詞也可刪去，剩下的 (C) Although 即為答案。

翻譯　　　　儘管 Gensler 先生準時抵達了，仍有一些不可預期的困難，包含機械問題在內。

單字片語　　on schedule 準時／ unforeseen 無法預期的／ mechanical 機械的

解答　　　　(C)

攻略 POINT

對等連接詞不可放在句首位置。

核心理論

> 對等連接詞是句子中，用來連接對等關係（同位）的單字、片語或是子句等等，並可省略相同出現的內容。
>
> He purchased a TV, and **he purchased a smart phone**.
> → He purchased a TV, and **purchased a smart phone**.
> → He purchased a TV and **a smart phone**.
> 他買了電視跟智慧型手機。

~~But~~ she was in poor health, she finished her duties.
Although

儘管她身體很不好，她仍然完成了她的任務。

~~And~~ Mr. Phil resigns, the position will be vacant.
　If

如果 Phil 先生辭職了，該職位就會空出來。

▶ 對等連接詞（and、but (= yet)、or、so、for）不可放在句首。

We are going to promote **Mr. Davidson** ~~whether~~ **Mr. Nicolson**.
　　　　　　　　　　　　　　　　　　　or

我們準備提拔 Davidson 先生或是 Nicolson 先生。

He got **his driver's license** ~~although~~ **a parking permit** on the same day.
　　　　　　　　　　　　　　　and

他在同一天拿到了他的駕照以及停車許可。

▶ 對等連接詞的位置上，不可填入副詞子句連接詞以及名詞子句連接詞。

1 ------- taxation still applies to online shopping, any shoes purchased during the buy-one-get-one-free sale are exempt from shipping charges.

(A) Yet 　　　　　(B) So 　　　　　(C) Therefore 　　　　　(D) Even though

2 Basic computer word processing skills are preferred ------- not required for a part-time assistant in the San Antonio office.

(A) although 　　　(B) but 　　　　(C) which 　　　　(D) however

▶答案與解析請參考解析本第 34 頁

連接詞擺放的位置 ②

Step 1 | **實戰重點**

解題策略　當四個選項中，只有一個選項為連接詞時，該選項為答案的可能性高達 99%，所以可以
直接將該連接詞填入空格，確認文意是否通順。

 代表題型

------- the senior architect goes on a business trip, he is accompanied by his
employees.

(A) Near　　　　　(B) Yet　　　　　(C) When　　　　　(D) Always

攻略解題法

------- the senior architect goes on a business trip, he is accompanied by his employees.

連接詞　　　　主詞　　　　動詞　　goes on 的受詞　主詞　　動詞　　　　介系詞片語

> 需要填入可以連接兩個
> 主詞（子句）的連接詞

be accompanied by

(A) Near　　　　　(B) Yet　　　　　(C) When　　　　　(D) Always
介系詞　　　　　　副詞　　　　　　連接詞　　　　　　副詞

文句分析　　介系詞 by 的意思是「藉由，依靠～」，在被動語態內，句型為「be ＋過去分詞＋ by ＋
行為者」。

說明　　　　在連接詞位置中，填入副詞、形容詞、介系詞都是錯的。當四個選項中，其中之一是連接
詞，而剩下的三個為副詞、形容詞或是介系詞時，有 99% 的可能性是該空格須填入連接
詞。因此必須快速確認題目內組成子句的數量，若確認有兩個子句時，便能分辨出該空格
即為連接詞。本題中的選項，(A) 介系詞、(B) 副詞、(C) 連接詞、(D) 副詞，剛好選項中只
有一個連接詞，加上題目由兩個子句所組成，因此可立即推斷出答案為連接詞 (C) When。

翻譯　　　　當首席建築師出差時，他身邊總有他的員工一同陪行。

單字片語　　senior 資深的，年長的／architect 建築師／be accompanied by 由～陪同，伴隨著～
（某種現象）

解答　　　　(C)

✎ 攻略 POINT

當有兩個子句時，必須用連接詞連接。

核心理論

副詞子句連接詞的位置上，不可填入形容詞、副詞或介系詞。

· 副詞子句連接詞的位置

------- ＋主詞＋動詞（完整子句），主詞＋動詞（完整子句）

▶ 空格須填入副詞子句連接詞，會導致誤答的選項可能有對等連接詞／形容詞／副詞等等。

主詞＋動詞（完整子句）＋ ------- ＋主詞＋動詞（完整子句）

▶ 空格可填入副詞子句連接詞或是對等連接詞，會導致誤答的選項可能有副詞／形容詞子句連接詞／介系詞等等。

· 副詞子句連接詞的種類

表時間	表條件	表讓步	表理由
when 當～的時候 after 在～之後 while ～的時候	if 如果～ unless 除非～ once 一旦～	although / though even if / even though 儘管～	as / because since / now (that) 因為～

~~During~~ the technician finishes installing the program, we can resume our work.
 When
當技術人員安裝完程式後，我們就可以重新開始工作。

▶ 連接詞（when）的位置不可填入介系詞（during）。

The initial budget estimate was wrong ~~due to~~ it had inaccurate data.
                                        because
因為資料錯誤，最初的預算估計是錯的。

▶ 連接詞（because）的位置不可填入介系詞（due to）。

Step 3 | 實戰演練

1 ------- you agree to the program and the total price, we will make a reservation and send you an invoice with payment options via Speedpost.

(A) Later   (B) Prior   (C) Instead   (D) Once

2 ------- there is no more space on your hard drive, your computer will run slowly, and some errors will occur.

(A) Since   (B) Owing to   (C) Then   (D) Moreover

▶ 答案與解析請參考解析本第 34 頁

Unit 59　對等連接詞

Step 1　實戰重點

解題策略　當空格後方接續的是相反語意的詞彙時，答案為 but 的可能性很高。

 代表題型

> He started his own business with great expectations, ------- it turned out to be a failure.
>
> (A) but　　　　　(B) and　　　　　(C) or　　　　　(D) for

✎ 攻略解題法

He started his own business with great expectations, ------- it turned out to be a failure.
主詞　動詞　　　　受詞　　　　介系詞片語　　　　　　主詞　動詞　　　補語

因為子句有兩個，須由連接詞連接

代指前面的句子

(A) but　　　　　　(B) and　　　　　(C) or　　　　　(D) for
語意相反、轉折　　　性質一致　　　　選擇　　　　　說明原因

文句分析　own 意思為「自己的」，用來強調所有格，句型為「所有格＋own＋名詞」。

說明　　　對等連接詞中，最常出現於考題的是 but。but 用於前後句子語意相反時，因此從前後句子中找出表相對或相反語意的詞彙驗證即可。本題中，空格前方的名詞（expectation）與後方名詞（failure）互為對照，因此答案為 (A) but。(B) 表前後性質一致，(C) 表選擇，(D) 則表原因。

翻譯　　　他在眾所期待下創立了他自己的事業，但卻以失敗告終。

單字片語　great expectation 很大的期待／turn out to be 結果是／failure 失敗

解答　　　(A)

✏ 攻略 POINT

若空格前後方的單字、片語或是子句為性質一致的關係，使用 and；若為相反或是轉折關係，使用 but；若表選擇，則用 or。

核心理論

使用對等連接詞時，前後的單字、片語以及子句之間的關係必須為對等的。

單字、片語、子句 ＋ 對等連接詞 ＋ 單字、片語、子句

對等連接詞的種類

and 以及（追加說明） or 或者是（選擇） but / yet 但是／可是（相反） so 因此（結果）

All employers **and** employees should be mutually respectful. 所有的雇主跟員工都必須互相尊重。
　　　名詞　　　　　名詞

This comes with instructions for safe **and** effective use. 為了安全且有效率地使用，這個會附上說明書。
　　　　　　　　　　形容詞　　　　形容詞

The prices of materials are slowly **but** surely recovering along with demand.
　　　　　　　　　　　副詞　　　　副詞

材料價格雖然會慢一些，但一定會與需求量一起復甦。

▶ 對等連接詞可將名詞與名詞、形容詞與形容詞，以及副詞與副詞等單字之間相連。

Please complete the application **and** submit it within a week. 請在一個星期內完成申請單並提交。
　　　　動詞片語　　　　　　　　動詞片語

They agreed to expand their business **and** to strengthen their competitive position.
　　　　　　　to 不定詞　　　　　　　　　　　to 不定詞

他們決定擴張事業，並加強他們的競爭優勢。

▶ 對等連接詞也可連接動詞片語與動詞片語，或是 to 不定詞與 to 不定詞。

He was sick, **so** he couldn't go to work. 他生病了，所以沒辦法去工作。
　　子句　　　　　　　　子句

▶ 對等連接詞 so，無法連接單字與片語，只能連接子句。

Step 3 ┊ 實戰演練

1 Your customer ratings ------- comments are shared with the public and will immediately have an effect on the sales of your products and services.

(A) though　　　　(B) but　　　　(C) else　　　　(D) and

2 Stringent ------- necessary security measures at the hotel hosting the heads of SARC will be activated on March 29.

(A) otherwise　　　　(B) but　　　　(C) hence　　　　(D) so

▶答案與解析請參考解析本第 35 頁

配對連接詞

解題策略　當句子中出現 both、either、neither、between、not only 等等，請選出配對連接詞填入空格。

🎓 代表題型

PNS Officedoor can fulfill your desire to make your entrance ------- functional and beautiful.

(A) between　　　　(B) nor　　　　(C) both　　　　(D) also

✏️ 攻略解題法

PNS Officedoor <u>can fulfill</u> <u>your desire</u> <u>to make your entrance</u> ------- functional and
　　　　主詞　　　　　動詞　　　受詞　　　　　　　to 不定詞

<u>beautiful.</u>
　　　　　　　　　句型 5 的動詞（make）＋受詞（your entrance）＋
　　　　　　　　　受詞補語（both functional and beautiful）

(A) between　　　　(B) nor　　　　　(C) both　　　　(D) also
　　兩者之間　　　　neither A nor B　　both A and B　　　以及

文句分析　具有主詞與受詞的完整句（PNS Officedoor can fulfill your desire）中加入 to 不定詞，此時的 to 不定詞作副詞用。

說明　　　在配對連接詞中，最常出現於考題中的是 both，接著是 either、neither。在 both 的考題中，選項會同時出現 between 是特徵之一，因為在句子中 between、both 都會跟 and 一同出現。因此當 between 與 both 同時出現時，必須要先了解文意。both A and B 是「A 跟 B 都～」，而 between A and B 則是「A 和 B 之中～」。依照本題文意，(C) 應為答案。

翻譯　　　PNS Officedoor 可以滿足您的需求，讓您的大門兼具功能性與美觀。

單字片語　fulfill 實現，滿足／ desire 要求，渴望／ entrance 入口，大門／ functional 有功能性的

解答　　　(C)

✖️ 攻略 POINT

配對連接詞的題型，重點在於文意的理解以及句型搭配，例如 either 配 or、neither 配 nor，both 與 between 配 and，而 not only 則配上 but（also）。

核心理論

常見配對連接詞

配對連接詞	both	A	and	B	A 跟 B 都～
	either		or		A 和 B 其中之一～
	neither		nor		既非 A 也非 B
	not only		but (also)		不只 A，B 也～（＝B as well as A）
	not		but		不是 A 而是 B
	between		and		A 和 B 之間

I need **both** a TV <u>and</u> a computer in my kitchen. 我需要一台電視跟電腦在我的廚房裡。

▶ 考題中，常見 both 與 and 一同使用。

You must return it by **either** e-mail <u>or</u> fax. 你必須要透過電郵或是傳真回傳。

▶ 考題中，常見 either 與 or 一同使用。

His car is **neither** black <u>nor</u> silver. 他的車子不是黑的也不是銀的。

▶ 考題中，常見 neither 與 nor 一同使用。

They are **not only** delicious <u>but also</u> nutritious. 它們不只好吃，也很營養。

▶ 考題中，常見 not only 與 but also 一同使用。

This product is still prevalent <u>in Korea</u> **as well as** <u>the U.S.A.</u>
這個產品不僅在韓國，在美國也仍然很普遍。

▶ 請記住，as well as 是個只能連接單字跟片語，不能連接子句的連接詞。

1 If you have any inquiries, please contact ------- Jill McCarty or the Human Resources Department.

(A) only　　　　(B) not　　　　(C) either　　　　(D) so

2 Infiniti Patrol Solutions ------- monitors and sends alerts about potential bottlenecks in your system but also analyzes the system's activity in real time.

(A) no　　　　(B) not only　　　　(C) neither　　　　(D) rather

REVIEW TEST

1. Comcast is seeking a customer support manager to lead ------- the customer relations and quality assurance teams.

   (A) between   (B) both

   (C) or   (D) neither

2. Some cleaning products have ingredients that can be hazardous to users at home ------- in the office.

   (A) also   (B) nor

   (C) or   (D) but

3. The staff members were disappointed that ------- Ms. Suwarto nor Mr. Jung was able to attend the annual dinner party.

   (A) and   (B) neither

   (C) with   (D) either

4. Public schools are generally, ------- not always, less expensive than private institutions in South Dakota.

   (A) but   (B) for

   (C) so   (D) and

5. Both of these homes offer outstanding modern facilities ------- beautiful furnishings, including elegant glass lamps.

   (A) in addition to   (B) even though

   (C) instead of   (D) as well as

6. If you ordered by phone, please allow ------- one or two business days for express shipping.

   (A) both   (B) either

   (C) yet   (D) or

7. ------- you log in to use Shanghai Bank's Internet banking system, you will be asked to enter your email address in the box.

   (A) Almost   (B) Soon

   (C) Still   (D) When

8. The new product appeals not only to customers who initially bought it ------- to those who had previously paid more for a drill.

   (A) and then   (B) or else

   (C) but also   (D) other than

9. Our customer representative will contact the Shipping Department ------- the shipment fails to arrive by the date specified in the order confirmation.

   (A) instead   (B) if

   (C) moreover   (D) besides

10. His role in finance is to make sure all payments are processed not only promptly ------- also correctly and to take care of the registration of new clients.

   (A) like   (B) but

   (C) even   (D) however

▶答案與解析請參考解析本第 35 頁

類型分析

13

名詞子句連接詞

子句，是以「主詞＋動詞」的句型組合而成，而保有該種句型，同時在主體文句內擔任主詞、受詞或是補語等位置的子句，便稱為名詞子句。連接主體文句與名詞子句的連接詞，稱之為「名詞子句連接詞」。

WARMING UP

1) 名詞子句連接詞的基本概念

具有「主詞＋動詞」的要素，並在主體文句中扮演名詞角色的子句，稱為名詞子句。將該名詞子句連接至主體文句中的連接詞，便為名詞子句連接詞。

① I think. 我認為。　＋　② He is a doctor. 他是醫生。

如同上面的例子，想將兩句組合時，便需要連接詞。①句中的 think 為及物動詞，需要受詞，因此必須要將後面②的句子轉化為受詞，此時需要使用到的單字為 that。如下列方式轉化後，便能將兩句合為一句。

I think <u>that he is a doctor.</u> 我認為他是醫生。

此時，that 後方一整句，是作為 think 的受詞的名詞子句，使用 that 連接句子，並且將 that 後方一整句轉化為受詞的功能，這樣的連接詞便稱為「名詞子句連接詞」。

2) 名詞子句連接詞的角色

名詞子句連接詞在句子中擔任的角色如下所示：

① 作主詞

<u>That the Earth is round</u> is true. (= It is true that the Earth is round.) 地球為圓的是事實。

② 作補語

His problem is <u>that he is too lazy</u>. 他的問題就是他太懶了。

③ 作受詞

I believe <u>that he is honest</u>. 我相信他很誠實。

02 暖身例題

請寫出底下句子中，畫線部分所扮演的角色。

1 <u>What we need to do</u> is to hire a qualified employee.　　　　（　　　）

2 <u>Whether she can come to the party</u> is not decided.　　　　（　　　）

3 The directors know <u>that they must reach their targets.</u>　　　　（　　　）

4 We are still trying to figure out <u>what happened.</u>　　　　（　　　）

03 例題解答

名詞子句連接詞，可在句子中擔任主詞、受詞以及補語的角色。而名詞子句連接詞中，有用來連接完整子句以及不完整子句的，請將這兩種區別清楚。

作主詞

1 (**What** we need to do) is to hire a qualified employee. 我們需要做的是招募符合資格的員工。
　　　　主詞

> ▶ 名詞子句連接詞 what 加上後方子句，視為名詞，放在主體動詞 is 前面，作主詞。當名詞子句用來作為主詞時，動詞必須為單數。另外，what 是用來連接不完整子句的。

2 (**Whether** she can come to the party) is not decided. 尚未確定她是否可以出席派對。
　　　　　　主詞

> ▶ 名詞子句連接詞 whether 加上後方子句，視為名詞，放在主體動詞 is 前面，作主詞。Whether 可以連接不完整子句，也可以連接完整子句。

作受詞

3 The directors know (**that** they must reach their targets.)
　　　　　　　　　　　　　　　受詞
主任們知道他們必須達到目標。

> ▶ 名詞子句連接詞 that 加上後方子句，視為名詞，放在主體動詞 know 後面，作受詞。that 連接的是擁有「主詞（they）＋動詞（reach）＋受詞（their targets）」句型的完整子句。

4 We are still trying to figure out (**what** happened.)
　　　　　　　　　　　　　　　　　受詞
我們仍在試著搞清楚發生了什麼事。

> ▶ 名詞子句連接詞 what 加上後方子句，視為名詞，放在介系詞 out 後面，作受詞。what 是用來連接不完整子句的連接詞，如例子中少了主詞的不完整子句。

Unit 61 名詞子句連接詞的種類 ❶

解題策略　若空格出現於完整子句（主詞、動詞、受詞／補語等等，包含句子構成的要素一個也不缺）之前，選擇 that，若為不完整子句，則選 what。

 代表題型

------- the new employees need to know regarding the company's benefits has been provided in the package.

(A) That　　　　　(B) Then　　　　　(C) What　　　　　(D) However

 攻略解題法

------- the new employees **need to know** (regarding the company's benefits) **has been**
連接詞　　　主詞　　　　動詞 受詞（to 不定詞）　　　介系詞片語　　　　　動詞（被動語態）

名詞子句（作主詞）：少了 know 受詞的不完整子句

provided (in the package).
介系詞片語

為名詞子句＋動詞的簡單構造，
名詞子句在此作名詞用

(A) That　　　　　(B) Then　　　　　(C) What　　　　　(D) However
使用在完整子句前　　副詞　　　　　使用在不完整子句前　　副詞

文句分析　regarding 跟 concerning 都是常在考題中出現的介系詞，表「關於～」。

說明　　　首先，四個選項中，可以分成 (A)、(C) 連接詞組，以及 (B)、(D) 非連接詞組。接著來確認，題目是否由兩個子句組成。確認由兩個子句組成後，可將 (B)、(D) 消去，選擇 (A) 或 (C) 其中之一。若為完整子句，選 that，若為不完整子句，選 what，而本題空格後方為少了 know 受詞的不完整子句，因此答案為 (C) what。

翻譯　　　新員工需要知道跟公司福利相關的事情，都包含在這個套裝方案裡了。

單字片語　benefit 優惠，利益

解答　　　(C)

✎ 攻略 POINT

當有兩個子句出現時，必須使用連接詞將兩者連接起來。

核心理論

常以 that 子句作受詞的動詞

suggest	建議～	explain	說明～	think	認為～
show	展現～	announce	宣布～	ensure	保證～
indicate	指出～	state	陳述～	note	注意到～

常與 that 子句搭配的形容詞

aware	知道～	glad	對～很開心	likely	可能～
confident	有自信於～	delighted	對～很開心	certain	確定的～
sure	確信～	pleased	對～很開心	worried	擔心～

Employees who took the contingency training course know **what** they have to do in case of fire.

少了 do 受詞的不完整子句

接受過緊急應變訓練的員工，知道他們萬一在失火的狀況下該如何反應。

▶ what 用於少了主詞或受詞的不完整子句前方作連接。

Ms. Vikander indicated **that** she is very interested in the position of director.

完整子句

Vikander 女士表明她對主任的職位非常有興趣。

▶ that 連接了主詞（she）、動詞（is interested）以及介系詞（in）與受詞（the position of director）都具備的完整子句。

1 The Atlanta Farmer's Market announced yesterday ------- Mark Peebles, who led the state's third largest supermarket for three decades, will retire from his position as president.

(A) it   (B) that   (C) about   (D) what

2 Please be sure ------- every product manufactured at Green Factory is inspected before it is shipped to retail stores.

(A) on   (B) that   (C) about   (D) what

▶答案與解析請參考解析本第 37 頁

Unit 62　名詞子句連接詞的種類 ❷

解題策略　若選項中出現名詞子句連接詞，且題目句型為「------ ＋主詞＋動詞＋～＋動詞」，則答案為名詞子句連接詞。

 代表題型

------- our store will be open during the holiday is up for discussion.

(A) If　　　　　　　(B) Because　　　　(C) Whether　　　　(D) Although

 攻略解題法

<u>-------</u> <u>our store</u> <u>will be open</u> (during the holiday) <u>is</u> up for discussion.
連接詞　主詞　　　動詞　　　　　介系詞片語　　　動詞　　介系詞片語
- -
　　　　　名詞子句（作主詞）──完整子句

(A) If　　　　　　　(B) Because　　　　(C) Whether　　　　(D) Although
表條件　　　　　　　表理由　　　　　　表選擇　　　　　　表讓步

文句分析　「Our store will be open during the holiday.」「That is up for discussion.」，要將這兩句結合在一起，必須使用 Whether 這個連接詞。介系詞 during，是接在明確期間之前，表「在～的期間」。

說明　　　當選項中有連接詞時，要分辨清楚該連接詞為名詞子句連接詞，還是副詞子句連接詞，以及該空格為主詞位置或是副詞的位置。當句型為「------ ＋主詞＋動詞＋～＋動詞」時，為名詞子句連接詞；當句型為「------ ＋句子（主詞＋動詞）＋逗號＋句子（主詞＋動詞）」時，則為副詞子句連接詞。而本題句型為前者，因此可先將副詞子句連接詞 (B)、(D) 刪去，而 (A) 雖可以作為名詞子句連接詞使用，但在該種情況下不得放在句首，因此正確答案為 (C) Whether。

翻譯　　　我們的店是否在假日期間營業，還要再討論。

單字片語　during 在～的期間／ be up for discussion 提出討論，準備討論

解答　　　(C)

 攻略 POINT

「whether ＋主詞＋動詞」的子句，常會跟 or 一起出現於考題內。此外，拿掉 whether 後方的主詞，轉化為「whether ＋ to 不定詞」的句型，也會出現在考題中。而 if 雖可作為名詞子句連接詞，但不可用於主詞或是補語的位置，只能放在及物動詞後方作受詞。

📖 核心理論

連接詞 whether 與 if 的差別

if	只能用於及物動詞的受詞。
whether	可作為主詞、受詞以及補語，並且常與 or not 一同使用，此時，or not 位於 whether 後方或是整個句子的最後方。

常以 whether 或是 if 開頭的子句，作受詞的動詞

ask	詢問	decide	決定	see	確認
find out	了解	wonder	好奇	determine	決定

Ms. Paulson didn't decide <u>whether [if]</u> (or not) she will apply for the sales position.
　　　　　　　　　　　　 及物動詞（decide）的受詞

Paulson 女士還沒決定她是否要應徵業務的職位。

They wanted to know <u>whether [if]</u> we were satisfied with the results (or not).
　　　　　　　　　　　 及物動詞（know）的受詞

他們想要知道我們是否滿意結果。

<u>Whether [if]</u> the president can accept the merger offer or not is unknown.
　句子的主詞

還不知道董事長可不可以接受這個合併的提案。

▶ if 用作名詞子句連接詞時，不可置於主詞、補語的位置，只能放在及物動詞後方作受詞。

Step 3 　實戰演練

1 ------- or not the subway company is suffering from the deficit is not the first priority the city considers.

(A) In case　　　　(B) If　　　　(C) Even though　　　　(D) Whether

2 Our highly experienced staffing agency can decide whether ------- to hire the five new candidates through its screening process.

(A) or not　　　　(B) but　　　　(C) and　　　　(D) it

Unit 63 名詞子句連接詞的種類 ③

解題策略　選項中出現關係代名詞或關係副詞時，若空格後方為不完整子句，選關係代名詞；若為完整子句，則選擇關係副詞。

🎓 代表題型

Everyone in the division knows ------- made the preparations for the retirement party.

(A) when　　　　　　(B) how　　　　　　(C) who　　　　　　(D) where

✏️ 攻略解題法

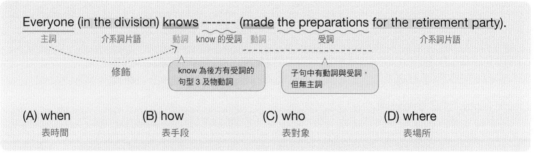

Everyone (in the division) knows ------- (made the preparations for the retirement party).

主詞　　　　　介系詞片語　　　動詞 know 的受詞 動詞　　　　受詞　　　　　　介系詞片語

修飾　　　　　know 為後方有受詞的　　　子句中有動詞與受詞，
　　　　　　　句型 3 及物動詞　　　　　　但無主詞

(A) when　　　　　　(B) how　　　　　　(C) who　　　　　　(D) where
表時間　　　　　　　表手段　　　　　　　表對象　　　　　　　表場所

文句分析　make 為及物動詞，意思為「做～」，句型為「make ＋受詞（preparations）」。

說明　　　首先，必須先分辨 who、which、what、when、where、how、why 在句中為疑問詞還是關係詞。當空格前方有先行詞時，則須將這些詞彙視為關係詞；若無，則為疑問詞。另外，關係代名詞用在不完整子句前，而關係副詞則用在完整子句前。本題中，空格後方為少了動詞（made）的主詞的不完整子句，因此唯有關係代名詞 (C) who 為正確答案。

翻譯　　　部門裡所有的人都知道是誰準備了退休派對。

單字片語　preparation 準備／ retirement 退休

解答　　　(C)

 攻略 POINT

關係代名詞用在少了主詞或受詞的不完整子句前，而關係副詞則用在主詞與受詞皆具備的完整子句前。

核心理論

關係代名詞與關係副詞的區別

關係代名詞 who, what, which	可作為疑問詞，又可作為代名詞。這類的關係代名詞，後方通常接續少了主詞或受詞的不完整子句。
關係形容詞 whose, what, which	關係形容詞通常之後會立刻連接名詞，而後方子句為完整句。
關係副詞 when, where, why, how	可作為疑問詞，又可作為修飾動詞的副詞，後方通常接續完整子句。

Mr. White asked his immediate supervisor **who will lead the discussion on Monday**.

少了 will lead 主詞的不完整子句

White 先生詢問他的直屬上司，誰會在星期一帶領討論。

We are interested in **whose proposal will be reviewed at the board meeting**.

完整子句

我們好奇誰的提案將在董事會上被拿出來檢討。

We will notify you immediately **when we are able to arrange the delivery**.

完整子句

當我們可以安排寄送時，我們將會立刻通知您。

Step 3 　實戰演練

1 The company newsletter writer asked a participant ------- she had found the most valuable at the recent business seminar.

(A) that　　　　(B) how　　　　(C) what　　　　(D) when

2 Brendan Williams, the owner of the AOL Telemarketing Company, is ------- established a guideline stating that the average time for each call should be fewer than five minutes.

(A) how　　　　(B) who　　　　(C) regarding　　　　(D) concerning

▶答案與解析請參考解析本第 37 頁

Unit 64　複合關係代名詞

Step 1　實戰重點

解題策略　當選項中出現複合關係代名詞或是複合關係副詞時，若空格位於缺少主詞或受詞的不完整子句前方，選擇複合關係代名詞；若為完整句，則選擇複合關係副詞。

代表題型

------- orders one of the first 50 copies of the newly released book will get a free gift.

(A) Whoever　　(B) Wherever　　(C) Whenever　　(D) Whichever

攻略解題法

orders one of the first 50 copies of the newly released book will get a free gift.

動詞　名詞子句（主詞的位置）（少了主詞的不完整子句）　　　　動詞　動詞（get）的受詞

受詞

由於本句少了主詞，只有動詞與
受詞，因此須填入可作為主詞，
同時可連接句子的連接詞。

(A) Whoever　　(B) Wherever　　(C) Whenever　　(D) Whichever

無論何人　　　無論何處　　　　無論何時　　　　無論哪一個

文句分析　不定代名詞 one 的常見句型為「one of the ＋複數名詞」，表「～之中的某一個」，請記住，這個句型下，one 前方不可有 the 出現。

說明　　複合關係代名詞與複合關係副詞不同，前者作名詞用，後者作副詞用。並且，複合關係代名詞使用於缺少主詞或受詞的不完整子句中，而複合關係副詞則是用於完整句中。本題中，子句中少了動詞（order）的主詞，空格應為主詞的位置，因此可先將複合關係副詞 (B)、(C) 刪去，而「訂購」的主詞應為人物，因此答案為 (A) Whoever。

翻譯　　只要是訂購前五十本新書首刷的人，都可以獲得贈禮。

單字片語　order 訂購，命令／newly released 新出的

解答　　(A)

攻略 POINT

複合關係代名詞的結構為「關係代名詞＋ ever」，作名詞用，置於沒有先行詞的不完整子句前方。

核心理論

複合關係代名詞使用於缺少主詞或受詞的不完整子句中。

> whoever 無論何人　　whatever 無論什麼　　whichever 無論哪一個

People can find ~~whenever~~ they are seeking online these days.
　　　　　　 whatever 　　　　　　（find 的受詞）

近來，人們可以從路路上找到任何他們想找的東西。

▶ 多益考題中常會出現要辨別複合關係代名詞與複合關係副詞的題型，複合關係代名詞使用於缺少主詞或受詞的不完整子句中，而複合關係副詞則是用於完整句型中。

I'll take ~~some~~ is left after you make a choice.
　　　　 whichever 　　　（take 的受詞）

我會選你決定之後，剩下來的任何一個選項。

▶ 多益也會出現區分複合關係代名詞或是一般代名詞的考題，若子句有兩個，便無法使用一般代名詞。

The workshop is open to ~~who~~ wishes to improve their computer skills.
　　　　　　　　　　 whoever 　　　　　介系詞（to）的受詞

這個工作坊開放給任何想要增進他們電腦技巧的人。

▶ whoever 可以用 anyone who 代替。

Step **3** 實戰演練

1 ------- has a Bellasium membership card can receive airline miles for staying at hotel chains across the world.

(A) This　　　　　(B) He　　　　　(C) Everyone　　　　　(D) Whoever

2 Music in the Zukebox 8.1 program will play randomly, or you can choose ------- songs you prefer to hear with the program.

(A) when　　　　　(B) whichever　　　　　(C) however　　　　　(D) whoever

▶答案與解析請參考解析本第 37 頁

REVIEW TEST

1. ------- Jimmy wants is to take a break because he has been inundated with calls and emails during the high season.
   - (A) What
   - (B) That
   - (C) Instead
   - (D) Ahead

2. After the Fukushima radioactive leaks, people in Korea became concerned about ------- seafood imported from Japan was safe.
   - (A) if
   - (B) whether
   - (C) that
   - (D) which

3. We are pleased to announce ------- Globe Electronics has won the bid to make air conditioning systems for thousands of schools across Sudan.
   - (A) this
   - (B) that
   - (C) on
   - (D) what

4. When deciding ------- or not to invest in a company, you need to research the performance of the company and should speak with a trusted financial adviser.
   - (A) if
   - (B) that
   - (C) who
   - (D) whether

5. No one can tell ------- the Savannah branch manager will be able to arrive as scheduled because of the adverse weather conditions in Georgia.
   - (A) what
   - (B) which
   - (C) instead
   - (D) if

6. The Maintenance Department is required to check every cable and connection periodically to ensure ------- the emergency lighting equipment is working properly.
   - (A) which
   - (B) that
   - (C) prior
   - (D) before

7. After receiving several estimates, Mr. Kuten decided ------- company he would choose for the office renovation project.
   - (A) how
   - (B) which
   - (C) when
   - (D) who

8. ------- is necessary is to educate and train workers regularly for your company to maintain a high level of specialization.
   - (A) What
   - (B) There
   - (C) How
   - (D) As

9. City inspectors are considering ------- to permit developers to build a housing project in the farmland.
   - (A) if
   - (B) then
   - (C) whether
   - (D) and

10. ------- our business succeeds depends on our providing the best service of all hotels in the city.
    - (A) If
    - (B) Whereas
    - (C) Whether
    - (D) While

▶答案與解析請參考解析本第 38 頁

類型分析

14

形容詞子句連接詞

形容詞子句又被稱為關係子句，用來將兩個句子合而為一，讓句子看起來更簡潔。而用來修飾名詞（先行詞）的子句，就是形容詞子句或稱為關係子句，連接形容詞子句的詞彙，便是形容詞子句連接詞。

WARMING UP

01 文法概念前導 ·················· 正式進入文法單元前，先熟悉一下文法基本概念。

1) 形容詞子句連接詞的基本概念

形容詞子句連接詞又稱為「關係代名詞」或是「關係副詞」。當兩個句子之間有共同的要素，並利用該要素，將兩個句子合成一個句子時，所使用的詞彙便是關係代名詞或是關係副詞。

The man is the doctor. 該男子是醫生。　＋　He lives in Taipei. 他住在台北。

如同上方的兩個句子中，The man 與 He 指的是同一人，而這兩句中有共同的要素，因此我們可以將兩句結合如下：

He is the doctor who lives in Taipei. 他是醫生，住在台北。

此時，who 後方的「who lives in Taipei」便是形容詞子句，或稱關係子句，而 who 是關係代名詞。另外，用 who 後方一整個關係代名詞子句來修飾的名詞 the doctor，便是所謂的「先行詞」。

2) 形容詞子句連接詞的角色

形容詞子句連接詞，也就是關係代名詞或是關係副詞，是將一個完整的句子接續在文章內，擔任形容詞角色用來修飾名詞。

This is the document that I looked over. 這是那份我檢查過的文件。

3) 關係代名詞與關係副詞的差異

① 關係代名詞：同時代表了「連接詞＋名詞」的位置，可作為句子的主詞或受詞。

He hired a candidate who(that) has work experience. 他僱用了有工作經驗的求職者。

▶ 因為關係代名詞後方緊連了動詞，可知這裡的關係代名詞 who（that），為 has 的主詞。

The invoice which(that) you requested was sent to the wrong address.
您要的那份報價單被寄到錯誤的地址了。

▶ 關係代名詞的後方出現了主詞與動詞，但卻沒有受詞，由此可知關係代名詞 which（that）應為動詞 requested 的受詞。

② 關係副詞：同時代表「連接詞＋副詞」的位置，且關係副詞後方必定連接完整子句。

I remember the day when I met her. 我還記得遇到她的那一天。

▶ 關係副詞，是當先行詞表時間、緣由、地點或是手段時，所使用的連接詞，例句內的 when 後方句子，便是用來修飾表時間的先行詞 the day。

02 暖身例題

寫出底下句子中，何者為主詞、動詞以及連接詞。

1 The man who works in the Sales Department is kind.

→ _____

2 The staff member whom Steven is speaking with is the manager.

→ _____

3 He will manage the project which begins next month.

→ _____

4 We will give an award to any employee whose idea is good.

→ _____

03 例題解答

1 The man (who works in the Sales Department) is kind. 在業務部工作的那個男生很親切。
先行詞（主詞） → 主格關係代名詞　　　　　　　　動詞

▶ 從 who 開始的後方句子，用來修飾名詞 the man。如本例題般，who works in the Sales Department 這樣用來修飾前方名詞的子句，便稱為形容詞子句或是關係子句，而被修飾的名詞 the man，便稱為先行詞。

2 The staff member (whom Steven is speaking with) is the manager.
先行詞　　　　　關係代名詞　主詞　動詞1　　　　　動詞2
　　　　　　　　　　　　　　　關係子句

正在跟 Steven 談話的那位公司員工是經理。

▶ 通常關係代名詞的句型結構是「先行詞＋關係代名詞＋（主詞）＋動詞 1＋動詞 2～.」。
　　　　　　　　　　　　　　　　　關係子句

3 He will manage the project which begins next month. 他將會負責下個月開始的那個專案。
主詞　　動詞1　　　　先行詞　關係代名詞 動詞2
　　　　　　　　　　　　　　關係子句

▶ 也可能是「主詞＋動詞 1＋先行詞＋關係代名詞＋（主詞）＋動詞 2～.」的句型。
　　　　　　　　　　　　　　　　　　關係子句

4 We will give an award to any employee whose idea is good.
先行詞　　關係代名詞 主詞　動詞 形容詞
　　　　　　　　　　　　　關係子句

我們將會頒發獎項給任何一位有好點子的員工。

 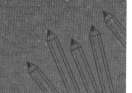

Unit 65 形容詞子句連接詞的種類 ①

Step 1 | 實戰重點

解題策略　若先行詞為人物，當空格位於少了主詞的「動詞＋受詞」的前方時，選擇主格；當空格位於少了受詞的「主詞＋動詞」的前方時，選擇受格；而「名詞＋動詞＋受詞／補語」的前方空格，則選擇所有格。

 代表題型

> Mr. Kim is the person ------- recently got promoted to team manager.
>
> (A) whose　　　　(B) whom　　　　(C) who　　　　(D) which

 攻略解題法

Mr. Kim is the person (------- recently got promoted to team manager.)
主詞　動詞　先行詞　主格關係代名詞（主詞＋連接詞）動詞　　　　介系詞片語

　　完整子句　　　　　　　　　關係子句（少了主詞的不完整子句）

修飾名詞 the person（先行詞），作為形容詞角色的主格關係代名詞子句

(A) whose	(B) whom	(C) who	(D) which
所有格	受格	主格	主格

文句分析　get promoted 表「升職」，與「get started、get settled」相同，都是句型 2 動詞＋ p.p.。

說明　　　根據先行詞種類的不同，使用的關係代名詞也會有所不同。簡而言之，就是根據先行詞為人物或是事物的不同，來決定使用的關係代名詞種類，若先行詞為人物，便要從 who、whose 或 whom 之中擇一。關係代名詞是用來代替子句中缺失的組成要素，若是少了主詞的不完整子句，要選擇主格關係代名詞，而少了受詞的情況，便是選擇受格關係代名詞。本例題中，先行詞為人物（person），而後方子句缺少的為主詞，可推測出應選擇主格關係代名詞 who。

翻譯　　　Kim 先生就是那位最近剛升為團隊經理的人。

單字片語　recently 最近／ promote 升職

解答　　　(C)

 攻略 POINT

> 當題目句型為「人物＋ ------- ＋動詞」時，空格內須填入 who。

核心理論

形容詞子句變化的原理

I know the man. + He is handsome. → I know **the man who** is handsome.

→ who 子句如形容詞般修飾 the man（名詞）。（主格）

I know the man. + She taught him. → I know **the man whom** she taught.

→ whom 子句如形容詞般修飾 the man（名詞）。（受格）

The artist **who**(= that) is working on the project is the owner of this company.

正在進行專案的那位藝術家，是這間公司的老闆。

▶ 先行詞為人物（artist），缺少主詞的不完整子句前方填入主格關係代名詞。

Our mechanics, **whose** responsibilities were to fix the drillship, failed due to the massive oil spill.

我們負責修理鑽井船的技工，因為大量漏油的緣故而失敗了。

▶ 先行詞為人物（mechanics），名詞（responsibilities）前方填入所有格代名詞。

The tourists **whom**(= that) James guided were my colleagues.

James 帶團的那群觀光客是我的前同事。

▶ 先行詞為人物（tourists），缺少及物動詞（guided）受詞的不完整子句前方，填入受格關係代名詞，此時的受格關係代名詞可省略。

That is the manager, **who** invited the clients to our plant.

那位是經理，是他邀請客戶來我們工廠的。

▶ 當先行詞跟關係代名詞中間有逗號時，稱為補述用法，補述用法中的關係子句，作用在於提供先行詞相關的補充說明。當句型為「先行詞（人物）＋逗號＋ ------ ＋動詞」時，空格填入主格關係代名詞。

1 She is the performer ------- was once well-known for her outstanding communication skills with her business associates.

(A) whom   (B) whose   (C) who   (D) which

2 We are looking for a staff member ------- thoughts are not only creative but also immediately practical.

(A) whom   (B) whose   (C) who   (D) that

▶答案與解析請參考解析本第 39 頁

Unit 66 形容詞子句連接詞的種類②

Step 1　實戰重點

解題策略　若先行詞為事物，當空格在於少了主詞的「動詞＋受詞」的前方時，選擇主格；當空格在少了受詞的「主詞＋動詞」的前方時，選擇受格；而「名詞＋動詞＋受詞／補語」的前方空格，則選擇所有格。

代表題型

Job seekers these days are searching for firms ------- are solid and provide good jobs.

(A) whose　　　(B) where　　　(C) which　　　(D) of which

 攻略解題法

Job seekers these days are searching for firms (------- are solid and provide good jobs).
　　主詞　　　　副詞　　　　動詞片語　　先行詞　　　關係子句（少了主詞的不完整子句）

修飾　　當先行詞為事物時，主格關係詞為 which

(A) whose　　　　(B) where　　　　(C) which　　　　(D) of which
　所有格　　　　　關係副詞　　　　　主格　　　　　　所有格

文句分析　不及物動詞 search 後方接介系詞 for，search for 作為及物動詞使用，此動詞片語後方具有受詞（firms），因此為主動語態。

說明　先行詞為事物（firms），並且空格後方為缺少主詞的動詞（are），可知答案為 (C) which。

翻譯　最近的求職者要找的是既穩定又能夠提供好工作的公司。

單字片語　job seeker 求職者／ search for 尋找〜／ solid 堅固的

解答　(C)

✎ 攻略 POINT
當題目句型為「事物先行詞＋ ------- ＋動詞」時，空格內須填入主格關係代名詞 which。

📖 **核心理論**

形容詞子句連接詞（＝關係代名詞）的種類			
	主格	受格	所有格
人物	who	who / whom	whose
事物、動物	which	who / which	whose / of which
人物、事物、動物	that	that	-

The project **which**(= that) is directed by Mr. Lee will be done by this weekend.
由 Lee 先生帶領的專案，將會在這週末完成。
▶ 先行詞為事物（project），缺少主詞的不完整子句前方填入主格關係代名詞。

The countries **whose** economies are growing fast should be prepared for sudden pitfalls.
經濟快速成長的國家，應該要對突如其來的危機做好準備。
▶ 先行詞為事物（countries），名詞（economies）前方填入所有格代名詞。

These are the items **which**(= that) I bought from our shop's online mall.
這些是我從我們的網路商店購買的商品。
▶ 先行詞為事物（items），缺少及物動詞（bought）受詞的不完整子句前方，填入受格關係代名詞，此時的受格關係代名詞可省略。

This is the copier, **which** was not easy to use due to its unfamiliar functions.
這就是影印機，因為還不熟它的功能，所以不好上手。
▶ 當先行詞跟關係代名詞中間有逗號時，稱為補述用法，補述用法中的關係子句，作用在於提供先行詞相關的補充說明。當句型為「先行詞（事物）＋逗號＋ ------ ＋動詞」時，空格填入主格關係代名詞。

1 The government announced a new project ------- will have a group of geologists investigating certain areas of the city which has not been developed yet.

(A) which   (B) whose   (C) of which   (D) whom

2 Mr. Lee and Ms. Wong, ------- new office building has been constructed near the former one, are now the co-representatives of the company.

(A) who   (B) whose   (C) which   (D) in which

▶答案與解析請參考解析本第 39 頁
類型分析 14 形容詞子句連接詞　209

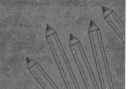

Step 1 ┊ **實戰重點**

解題策略　　請學會辨認用於不完整子句的關係代名詞，與用於完整子句的關係副詞。

 代表題型

> The new regulations were announced on the last day ------- our employees worked.
>
> (A) which　　　　(B) whose　　　　(C) when　　　　(D) where

 攻略解題法

The new regulations were announced on the last day ------- our employees worked.
　　主詞　　　　　動詞（被動式）　　　　先行詞　　連接詞　　主詞　　不及物動詞（無受詞）
　　　　　　　　被動語態所以沒有受詞　　　介系詞片語
　　　　　　　　　完整子句　　　　　　　　　　　　　　完整子句

(A) which　　　　(B) whose　　　　(C) when　　　　(D) where
　　主格　　　　　所有格　　　　關係副詞（表時間）　關係副詞（表場所）

文句分析　　本題為被動語態，因此後方沒有受詞。

說明　　　　關係代名詞用於缺少主詞或受詞的不完整子句，而關係副詞則用於主詞受詞皆具備的完整子句。本題空格後方連接的是主詞與動詞皆具備的完整子句（our employees worked），應填入關係副詞，因此可將 (A)、(B) 刪除。而先行詞為時間（the last day），所以空格須填入表時間的 (C) when。

翻譯　　　　新政策在我們的員工工作的最後一天發布。

單字片語　　regulation 規定／ announce 發表

解答　　　　(C)

 攻略 POINT

先行詞與完整子句之間，須填入關係副詞。

核心理論

先行詞	關係副詞	
表時間、場所、緣由、手段的相關名詞	時間→ when	理由→ why
	場所→ where	手段→ how

This is <u>the reason</u> **why** <u>he was late</u>. 這是他為什麼遲到的原因。

▶ 關係副詞前後皆為完整子句，why 後方的子句用來修飾 the reason。

It was <u>the day</u> **when** <u>he decided not to invest</u> in that company anymore.
那天正是他決定不再投資那間公司的日子。

▶ 時間先行詞（the day）後連接關係副詞 when。

We visited <u>the place</u> **where** <u>we will soon start our vineyard</u>. 我們造訪了我們即將開幕的葡萄園。

▶ 場所先行詞（the place）後連接關係副詞 where。

That is <u>the reason</u> **why** <u>we can't do business with you</u>. 這正是我們為什麼不能跟你做生意的原因。

▶ 原因先行詞（the reason）後連接關係副詞 why。

The report showed us <u>(the way)</u> **how** <u>we should target</u> certain customers.
這份報告讓我們知道我們該如何鎖定特定的客群。

▶ 手段先行詞（the way）後連接關係副詞 how。但關係副詞 how 不得與先行詞（the way）同時使用，句中只能擇其一出現。

He finally got the <u>office</u>, **where** <u>all the appliances he wanted are provided</u>.
他總算來到那間辦公室，那個提供所有他想要的設備的地方。

▶ 當先行詞跟關係代名詞中間有逗號時，稱為補述用法，補述用法中的關係子句，作用在於提供先行詞相關的補充說明。當句型為「先行詞（場所）＋逗號＋ ------ ＋動詞」時，空格填入關係副詞（where）。

1 Most of the industries were in the middle of a crisis ------- they all needed to set comprehensive and extensive but effective strategies.

(A) which   (B) whose   (C) where   (D) when

2 The J&W Corporation is the company ------- he worked as its in-house lawyer for five years and as the administrative consultant for the next twelve years.

(A) which   (B) where   (C) how   (D) whom

▶答案與解析請參考解析本第 40 頁

REVIEW TEST

1. The candidate ------- proposal has been accepted should bring his or her portfolio by next Wednesday.

   (A) whom   (B) who
   (C) that   (D) whose

2. Anyone ------- wants to participate in this year's environmental workshop program should fill out the form and submit it to the HR Department.

   (A) whose   (B) who
   (C) whom   (D) they

3. Our company forged an alliance with an airline, and we will close a deal with ------- travel agency provides us with lower prices.

   (A) whichever   (B) their
   (C) some   (D) that

4. SP Chemicals offers benefits to its employees ------- participate in various environmental groups at the company.

   (A) which   (B) who
   (C) where   (D) how

5. The current systems are suited for the equipment ------- is used in most of our factories, so it will cost both money and time if we change it now.

   (A) whose   (B) which
   (C) of which   (D) it

6. The supervisor revised the manual, ------- the employees could not fully understand, so the instructions in it have not been followed.

   (A) some   (B) their
   (C) every   (D) which

7. Ms. Yun, ------- was appointed to the position of vice president last year, is the youngest executive director ever at the company.

   (A) that   (B) how
   (C) who   (D) it

8. We make the workers use a pass card transcribing a record of the hours ------- they work so that they do not have to do any paperwork.

   (A) which   (B) who
   (C) when   (D) where

9. Mr. Larson went to Columbia, ------- is the place where he will meet the governor and discuss the development of the city.

   (A) where   (B) whose
   (C) it   (D) which

10. Unfortunately, we are short of employees, time, and supply, so we should increase everyone's working hours and stock up ------- products are available.

    (A) whatever   (B) its
    (C) how   (D) where

▶答案與解析請參考解析本第 40 頁

類型分析 15

副詞子句連接詞

副詞子句位於主要子句的前方或後方，同副詞角色，用來修飾主要子句，而副詞子句連接詞，便是用來連接副詞子句的連接詞。

WARMING UP

1) 副詞子句連接詞的基本概念

副詞子句連接詞，用來連接句型為「主詞＋動詞」並作副詞的子句，而副詞子句大多用來表「時間、條件、理由、讓步」等等的語意。

① He will be happy. 他將會很開心。　＋　She comes. 她來了。

▶ 首先要先思考上述這兩個句子的關聯性，「時間、條件、原因、讓步」哪個語意最為自然。

② If she comes, he will be happy. 如果她來了，他會很開心。

▶ 考慮了這兩個句子的關聯性後，發現以「條件」的語意連接最合適。這裡用 If 連接的子句，便稱為副詞子句，而連接該子句的 If，便是「副詞子句連接詞」。

2) 副詞子句連接詞的形態

副詞子句以「連接詞＋主詞＋動詞」的句型，置於句子內，是針對主要子句作補充說明的子句。作為從屬子句的副詞子句有著修飾文句的功能，因此無法單獨出現，必須搭配主要子句使用。

People arrived there early because there was no traffic.
      主要子句   副詞子句
因為沒有塞車，人們都提早抵達了。

3) 副詞子句連接詞的位置

副詞子句位於主要子句後方或前方，而當位於主要子句前方時，副詞子句後方必加上逗號。

① 當副詞子句位於主要子句前方

Although I am inexperienced, I did my best.

雖然我沒有經驗，但我已盡力了。

② 當副詞子句位於主要子句後方

He canceled the event because it is raining.

他取消了活動，因為正在下雨。

02 暖身例題

請在括號中寫出畫線部分的子句種類。

1 <u>While you are there</u>, Tom will keep you posted.
        (   )

2 Tom will keep you posted <u>while you are there</u>.
                          (   )

3 <u>When you register</u>, you will be given a key to the locker.
        (   )

4 <u>Although it looks expensive</u>, the hotel rates were reasonable.
           (   )

5 He couldn't control the machine properly <u>because he was not used to it</u>.
                                (   )

03 例題解答

1 <u>While you are there</u>, <u>Tom will keep you posted</u>.
    副詞子句（作副詞用）   主要子句
當你在那裡的時候，Tom 會持續向你更新情況。

> ▶ 此句的重點在於「Tom 會持續向你更新情況（Tom will keep you posted.）」，此為主要子句，而「當你在那裡的時候（While you are there）」是用來補充更新情況時間點的說明。

2 <u>Tom will keep you posted</u> <u>while you are there</u>.
      主要子句   副詞子句（作副詞用）
Tom 在你在那裡的時候，會持續向你更新情況。

> ▶ 當副詞子句在主要子句後方時，不使用逗號。

3 <u>When you register</u>, <u>you will be given a key to the locker</u>.
    副詞子句（作副詞用）   主要子句
你註冊的時候，會拿到一把置物櫃的鑰匙。

4 <u>Although it looks expensive</u>, <u>the hotel rates were reasonable</u>.
      副詞子句（作副詞用）   主要子句
雖然看起來很貴，但這飯店費用是合理的。

5 <u>He couldn't control the machine properly</u> <u>because he was not used to it</u>.
        主要子句   副詞子句（作副詞用）
他無法好好地控制那台機器，因為他還不習慣。

副詞子句連接詞的種類 ❶

 Step 1 | **實戰重點**

解題策略　當選項中出現表時間或是條件的連接詞，若題目中的主要子句為未來時態（will），則答案即為該選項。

 代表題型

------- you make a long-distance call, you will need to dial 1 and the area code first.

(A) So that　　　(B) Owing to　　　(C) When　　　(D) As though

✎ 攻略解題法

------- you make a long-distance call,
連接詞　主詞　動詞　　　受詞
────────────────────
　　　　　副詞子句

> 如同副詞會出現在完整句的前方或後方修飾句子，
> 副詞子句也會在主要子句的前方或後方作修飾

you will need to dial 1 and the area code first.
主詞　　動詞　　　　受詞
────────────────────
　　　　主要子句 ⋯> 對等連接詞

(A) So that　　　(B) Owing to　　　(C) When　　　(D) As though
　　以便～　　　　　因為～　　　　　當～的時候　　　　似乎～

文句分析　動詞 need 後方可接「to 不定詞」，也可接「受詞＋ to 不定詞」。

說明　　　當表時間或是條件的副詞子句情況發生於未來時，使用現在式。因此，當句型為「------
　　　　　＋主詞＋動詞現在式，主詞＋ will ＋動詞原形」時，空格填入表時間或是條件的連接詞。
　　　　　選項出現時間或是條件連接詞時，先不要試著翻譯成中文再找答案，請直接從句中線索解
　　　　　答，而線索就是主要子句中的動詞未來式 will。因此當選項中出現表時間或是條件的連接
　　　　　詞，主要子句又是未來時態（will），則該選項為答案，可知本題為 (C) When。

翻譯　　　當你要打長途電話時，你必須先撥 1 以及區碼。

單字片語　make a call 打電話／ dial 撥號

解答　　　(C)

 攻略 POINT

在時間與條件副詞子句中，以現在式代替未來式。

📖 **核心理論**

> 表時間、條件的副詞子句中，以現在式表未來式。
>
> | 時間連接詞 | before 在～之前　after 在～之後　when 當～的時候　while 在～的期間　until 到～為止　once 一旦～　as soon as 一～就～ |
> |---|---|
> | 條件連接詞 | if 如果～　unless 除非～　in case 倘若～　as long as 只要～　provided / providing 以～為條件下 |

When you leave tonight, the in-house technician **will inspect** the computers.
<u>　　　副詞子句　　　</u>

當你今晚離開的時候，內部的技術人員會檢查電腦。

▶ 時間（when）的副詞子句中，以現在式代替未來式。

All new hires **will meet** the CEO while they are attending the orientation session.

<u>　　　　　　　　副詞子句　　　　　　　　</u>

當所有新進員工參加員工訓練的時候，他們就會看到 CEO。

▶ 時間（while）的副詞子句中，以現在式代替未來式。

If you leave a message, I **will return** your call as soon as possible.
<u>　　　副詞子句　　　</u>

如果你留下訊息，我就會盡快回電給你。

▶ 條件（if）的副詞子句中，以現在式代替未來式。

Unless all of the products are packed carefully, they **will not be shipped**.
<u>　　　　　　副詞子句　　　　　　</u>

除非所有的產品都已經仔細包裝好了，否則它們不會被運送出去。

▶ 條件（unless）的副詞子句中，以現在式代替未來式。

Step 3 | 實戰演練

1 ------- a new telephone is installed, we will send all of our customers a text message to let them know what it is.

(A) Shortly　　　(B) Moreover　　　(C) Though　　　(D) As soon as

2 ------- the marketing director is on a business trip, all e-mails and calls will be forwarded to his assistant.

(A) While　　　(B) Since　　　(C) When　　　(D) Therefore

▶答案與解析請參考解析本第 41 頁

Unit 69 副詞子句連接詞的種類 ❷

解題策略　表讓步、原因、目的、結果的連接詞，以及複合關係詞等等，這些皆為副詞子句連接詞。其中，表讓步的副詞子句連接詞通常置於句首，並與 still 一同出現於考題中。

🎓 代表題型

------- Mr. Watanabe was offered a job by a competitor, he still wants to stay at our company.

(A) But   (B) Because   (C) Although   (D) Ever

✏️ 攻略解題法

------- Mr. Watanabe was offered a job by a competitor,
連接詞　　主詞　　　　動詞　　　受詞　　介系詞片語
　　　　副詞子句（句型 4 的被動語態）
he still wants to stay at our company. ──→ 請試著找出句型 4 動詞
主詞 副詞　動詞 動詞 want 的受詞　介系詞片語　　　offer 的直接與間接受詞
　　　　　　主要子句

(A) But　　　　　　(B) Because　　　　(C) Although　　　　(D) Ever
　但是　　　　　　　　因為　　　　　　　　儘管　　　　　　　在任何時候

文句分析　動詞 offer 屬於句型 4 的動詞，句型為「主詞＋ offer ＋間接受詞（對象）＋直接受詞（事物）」，轉換成被動式時，句型則為「人物＋ be offered ＋事物」。

　　例 A competitor offered Mr. Watanabe（間接受詞）a job（直接受詞）.

說明　　　表讓步的副詞子句連接詞有幾個特徵：通常置於句首、常與副詞 still 一起出現等等。本題由兩個句子組成，可先將副詞 (D) 刪去，而對等連接詞（But）不可置於句首，因此 (A) 也可刪除。最後，由空格位於句首，且句中出現 still 這兩個線索可知，答案為 (C) Although。

翻譯　　　儘管 Watanabe 先生獲得競爭對手提供的工作機會，但他仍然想要留在我們公司。

單字片語　offer 提供，提案／ competitor 競爭對手

解答　　　(C)

✎ 攻略 POINT

當句中出現與預期相反的結果時，請選擇表讓步的連接詞。

核心理論

常見的副詞子句連接詞一覽

表讓步的副詞子句連接詞	although, though, even if, even though 儘管〜
表原因的副詞子句連接詞	because, as, since, now that 因為〜
表目的的副詞子句連接詞	so that, in order that 為了〜

Although I was supposed to receive my shipment on April 11, it has <u>still</u> not arrived.

儘管我本來應該要在四月十一日拿到貨物,但它到現在都還沒送達。

▶ 當預期與最終結果相反時,請使用表讓步的連接詞(Although、Though、Even though、Even if)。

Because Mr. Taylor was <u>late</u>, the meeting couldn't start on time.

因為 Taylor 先生遲到了,所以會議無法準時開始。

▶ 說明前後句因果關係時,使用表原因的連接詞(Because、Now that、Since、As),這四個詞彙比較常見於考題中。主要的特點是,通常會伴隨帶有負面語意的子句出現,並多置於句首。

Ms. Ryu turned on the lamp **so that** she <u>could</u> read a book.

Ryu 女士為了閱讀書籍而打開了檯燈。

▶ 表目的的連接詞(so that、in order that)的語意為「為了〜」,考題大多以 so that 為主。另外表目的的副詞子句連接詞的特點,在於子句中通常會伴隨助動詞(can、may 等等)出現,而 so that、in order that 中的 that 是不可以省略的。

My business keeps me <u>so busy</u> **that** I can't talk to my colleague.

我的工作讓我忙到我沒辦法跟同事講話。

▶ 多益會出現「so +形容詞+ ------」的考題,此時就要選 that 填入空格,完成「so +形容詞+ that(因為太〜而……)」的句型。

Step 3 ┊ **實戰演練**

1 The communications channel between employees and employers should be open ------- employees can feel free to ask questions, to suggest ideas, and to point out errors.

(A) in order   (B) such   (C) even so   (D) so that

2 ------- effective a diet program is, it is essential to have healthy eating habits.

(A) But   (B) However   (C) Inasmuch as   (D) No matter

▶答案與解析請參考解析本第 41 頁

REVIEW TEST

1. Please wear a suit and tie with dress shoes at the business meeting ------- uncomfortable you may be.

   (A) provided   (B) given
   (C) however   (D) considered

2. The organization is in charge of maintaining historic castles in Scotland ------- tourists can enjoy them.

   (A) such as   (B) so that
   (C) even so   (D) so as

3. We expect to have a record harvest this year ------- the weather conditions in the western province have been favorable for the maturation of grapes.

   (A) only   (B) unless
   (C) since   (D) during

4. ------- you want to sign out a book or photocopied material from this office, please contact Linda and get her permission.

   (A) That   (B) Whether
   (C) As if   (D) If

5. The price includes the consultation fee, so please feel free to contact us ------- you want to know the details of our products.

   (A) whenever   (B) that
   (C) whether   (D) either

6. ------- he has traveled to Taiwan for business several times, this is the first time he has been accompanied by his employees.

   (A) While   (B) Because
   (C) As if   (D) Although

7. All of the new employees have to attend the welcome reception ------- they have an urgent personal matter to attend to.

   (A) in order   (B) since
   (C) unless   (D) without

8. This technology is so innovative ------- you will fall behind the competitior if you don't use it for your products.

   (A) what   (B) that
   (C) which   (D) such

9. ------- the new medicine has been approved by the FDA for use by adults, it is not recommended for pregnant females and children less than 1 year of age.

   (A) Rather than   (B) As long as
   (C) Following   (D) Even though

10. Mr. Bae is going to visit the store and ask for a machine replacement or a refund ------- the copy machine purchased two days ago doesn't work properly now.

    (A) moreover   (B) now that
    (C) besides   (D) owing to

▶答案與解析請參考解析本第 42 頁

類型分析

16

比較文法

比較文法亦即：有兩個比較對象相似時，使用原級文法；兩個對象有優劣高低時，使用比較級文法；比較對象為三個以上，其中之一特別顯著時，使用最高級文法。

WARMING UP

01 文法概念前導 ························ 正式進入文法單元前，先熟悉一下文法基本概念。

1) 比較文法的基本概念

比較文法用於表示多個比較對象之間是否相等，或是有高低多寡差別。大致上有原級、比較級，以及最高級三種類型。

2) 比較文法的種類

① 原級

表示相互比較的對象之間相等時。文法如底下所示：

比較對象 1 ＋動詞＋ as (so) ＋比較的性質＋ as ＋比較對象 2

The new copier works as well as the old one. 新的影印機跟舊的一樣好用。
　　比較對象1　　　　　　　比較的性質　比較對象2

這邊「比較的性質」只能代入形容詞或是副詞，而該使用形容詞還是副詞，則與動詞有關，若動詞為不需要接續補語的不及物動詞，填入副詞；若為需要補語的不及物動詞，則填入形容詞。

▶ 動詞 work 為不需要補語的不及物動詞，因此填入副詞。

② 比較級

表示相互比較的對象之間有優劣高低時。

比較對象 1 ＋動詞＋ more 形容詞（副詞）／形容詞（副詞）-er ＋ than ＋比較對象 2

This project is more difficult than the previous one. 這個企劃案比之前那個困難。
　　比較對象1　　　　　　比較的性質　　　　比較對象2

▶ 當形容詞（副詞）只有一個音節時，為「形容詞（副詞）＋ -er」；當形容詞（副詞）有兩個音節以上的時候，為「more ＋形容詞（副詞）」。

③ 最高級

相互比較的對象有三個以上，且其中有一個最為突出的對象時使用。

比較對象＋動詞＋ the ＋ most 形容詞（副詞）／形容詞（副詞）-est ＋ in ＋比較群體

This copier is the most expensive in the store. 這台影印機是店裡面最貴的。
　　比較對象　　　　　　　比較的性質　　比較群體

▶ 當形容詞（副詞）只有一個音節時，為「形容詞（副詞）＋ -est」；當形容詞（副詞）有兩個音節以上的時候，為「most ＋形容詞（副詞）」。

02 暖身例題

請選出下列何者為題目的正確翻譯。

1 This city is **as** large **as** Tokyo.
(1) 這個都市跟東京一樣大。
(2) 這個都市比東京還大。

2 The conference room is **larger than** its predecessor.
(1) 會議室比之前的大。
(2) 之前的會議室更大。

3 The new office is **more spacious than** the previous one.
(1) 新的辦公室比以前的寬敞。
(2) 以前的辦公室比新的寬敞。

4 Mr. Kane designed **the largest** restaurant in New York.
(1) 這間餐廳是 Kane 先生在紐約設計的餐廳中最大的。
(2) Kane 先生設計了一間紐約最大的餐廳。

5 This fax machine is **the most expensive** one in the store.
(1) 這台傳真機是店裡面最貴的。
(2) 這台傳真機是店裡面最不貴的。

03 例題解答

1 This city is **as** large **as** Tokyo. 這個都市跟東京一樣大。

▶ 當比較對象相等時，使用原級文法，句型為「as ＋形容詞／副詞＋ as」。

2 The conference room is **larger than** its predecessor. 會議室比之前的大。

▶ 當比較對象中的一方較為顯著時，使用比較級文法（-er than），句型為「形容詞／副詞＋ -er」或是「more ＋形容詞／副詞＋ than」。

3 The new office is **more spacious than** the previous one. 新的辦公室比以前的寬敞。

▶ 當比較對象中的一方較為顯著時，使用比較級文法，而用來作為比較的形容詞為兩個音節以上時，句型為「more ＋形容詞＋ than」。

4 Mr. Kane designed **the largest** restaurant in New York. Kane 先生設計了一間紐約最大的餐廳。

▶ 表示數個對象中，其中一個最顯著時，使用最高級文法，當表示該顯著特徵的形容詞只有一個音節時，句型為「the ＋形容詞＋ -est」。

5 This fax machine is **the most expensive** one in the store. 這台傳真機是店裡面最貴的。

▶ 表示數個對象中，其中一個最顯著時，使用最高級文法，當表示該顯著特徵的形容詞有兩個音節以上時，句型為「the most ＋形容詞」。

Unit 70 原級

解題策略　當出現將形容詞或副詞填入 as 與 as 之間空格的題型時，若前方為完整句型，空格填入副詞；若前方為不完整句型，則填入形容詞。

代表題型

Hopefully, the new chairs will be as ------- as the previous ones that lasted nearly 7 years.

(A) reliably　　　　(B) relies　　　　(C) reliable　　　　(D) reliance

攻略解題法

Hopefully, the new chairs will be as ------- as the previous ones that lasted nearly 7 years.

副詞　　　主詞　　　動詞　　　形容詞　　　修飾語句　　　修飾 ones 的關係子句

不完整句型　　　　　修飾

若想將副詞置於句首，後面必接逗號

as ＋形容詞＋ as，意為「如～一般」

(A) reliably　　　　(B) relies　　　　(C) reliable　　　　(D) reliance
副詞　　　　　　　動詞　　　　　　　形容詞　　　　　　名詞

文句分析　不定代名詞 ones，是相對於 new chairs 的代名詞。而 last 為不及物動詞，表「持續」。

說明　　　當題目的空格出現在 as 與 as 之間，請先將前後的 as 刪去，確認前方為完整或是不完整句型。若為完整句型，空格填入副詞；若為不完整句型，填入形容詞。所謂的完整句型，就是「主詞＋不及物動詞」或是「主詞＋及物動詞＋受詞」，而不完整句型，則是「主詞＋ be 動詞」。將本題中的前後 as 刪去後，可發現句型為「主詞＋ be 動詞」的不完整句型，因此答案為形容詞 (C) reliable。

翻譯　　　希望這些新椅子可以像之前那些用了將近七年的舊椅子一樣牢靠。

單字片語　hopefully 希望／ reliable 值得信賴的，牢靠的／ last 持續（功能），歷時

解答　　　(C)

攻略 POINT

將空格前後的 as 刪去後，若句子為完整句型，填入副詞；若為不完整句型，填入形容詞。

核心理論

> **原級比較句型**
>
> 1. 及物動詞＋受詞＋ as ＋副詞＋ as ＋比較對象 ▶ ～得如～一般
> 2. be 動詞＋ as ＋形容詞＋ as ＋比較對象 ▶ 跟～一樣～
> 3. 句型 5 動詞（make / keep / find / leave）＋受詞＋ as ＋形容詞＋ as ＋比較對象
> 4. once / twice / three times ＋ as ＋形容詞／副詞＋ as ＋比較對象 ▶ 比起～一／二／三倍～
> 5. as many ＋可數名詞複數形／ as much 不可數名詞＋ as ＋比較對象 ▶ 跟～一樣多

The new engineer works as efficiently [efficient] as the former one.

完整句

新的工程師工作跟前一任一樣有效率。

▶ 本句為具備主詞與不及物動詞的完整句型，因此 as 與 as 之間填入修飾動詞 works 的副詞。

This outdated copier is as efficient [efficiently] as the new one.

不完整句

這台舊型影印機跟新的一樣有效率。

▶ be 動詞後方須接續補語，因此 as 與 as 之間填入敘述主詞狀態的形容詞。

The newest computer systems will be twice as efficient as the current ones.

最新的電腦系統效率為現有的兩倍。

▶ 此文法語意為「比起～幾倍～」，用來表示比較對象之間的倍數。

People are purchasing twice as many [much] electronic products as they did 10 years ago.

相較於十年前，人們購買了兩倍以上的電子產品。

▶ as 和 as 之間不可單獨置入名詞，必須搭配 many 或 much 使用。many 後方接可數名詞，而 much 後方則接不可數名詞，這點請務必注意。

1 After 6 months of extensive renovations, the remodeled gallery and artist studios will make the museum twice as ------- as it used to be.

(A) more large   (B) larger   (C) largely   (D) large

2 The part designed like an airplane's wing can cut through the air and withstand winds as ------- as anything else can.

(A) ease   (B) easily   (C) easy   (D) more easy

▶ 答案與解析請參考解析本第 43 頁

Unit 71 比較級

Step 1 | 實戰重點

解題策略　比較級的句型為「形容詞／副詞＋er」或是「more ＋形容詞／副詞」，當形容詞或副詞為兩個音節以上時，使用後者句型。

 代表題型

Leather sofas are usually ------- and durable than sofas made of fabric because leather can resist dirt and stains better.

(A) comfort　　　(B) comforter　　　(C) more comfortable　　　(D) comfortably

 攻略解題法

修飾

Leather sofas are usually ------- and durable (than sofas made of fabric)
　　主詞　　動詞　副詞　　補語　　　　　修飾語句

because leather can resist dirt and stains better.
　連接詞　主詞　動詞　　受詞
　　　　　　　　副詞子句

(A) comfort　　　(B) comforter　　　(C) more comfortable　　　(D) comfortably
　原級　　　　　　名詞　　　　　　　比較級　　　　　　　　副詞

文句分析　副詞 usually（通常）、presently（目前）、currently（目前）主要用於現在式中。

說明　　　當形容詞或副詞只有一個音節時，句型為「形容詞／副詞＋er」，但當形容詞或副詞為「-able、-ful、-ous、-ive」等語尾的兩音節以上單字時，句型則為「more ＋形容詞／副詞」。本題中的 comfortable 為三音節以上，因此使用「more ＋形容詞」的句型，答案為 (C) more comfortable。基本上題型會以區分「more ＋形容詞」與「形容詞＋er」為主，請大家不要搞混。

翻譯　　　皮製沙發通常會比布製沙發來的舒服與耐用，因為皮革比較耐灰塵與髒污。

單字片語　leather 皮革／ be ＋形容詞比較級＋ than 比～更～／ durable 耐用的／ fabric 織品／ resist 抵禦／ dirt 灰塵／ stain 污漬

解答　　　(C)

 攻略 POINT

形容詞或副詞以「-able、-ful、-ous、-ive」等語尾結尾，為兩音節或三音節以上的單字時，比較級句型為「more ＋形容詞／副詞」。

📖 核心理論

主要題型在於區分「形容詞／副詞＋ er ＋ than」與「more ＋形容詞／副詞＋ than」。

比較級的要點

比較級的形態	比較級＋ than　比起～更～ （＝ more ＋原級＋ than） 首先必須要有比較對象，才能使用比較級。
比較級的強調	much、even、far、still、a lot 等等
比較級前方加上 the 的用法	The ＋比較級 , the ＋比較級　越～越～ <u>The more</u> you practice, <u>the better</u> you will become. 你練習得越多，你會變得越好。

The demand for organic produce among customers is **higher** than we expected.

消費者對於有機農產品的需求，比我們預期來得高。

▶ 當形容詞或副詞只有一個音節（high）時，句型為「形容詞／副詞＋ er」。

A cell phone with a camera is **more useful** than a camera.

一台具備相機功能的手機比一台相機來得有用。

▶ 形容詞或副詞以「-able、-ful、-ous、-ive」等語尾結尾，且為兩音節或三音節以上的單字時，句型為「more ＋形容詞／副詞」。

The newly released model is **much** <u>more</u> popular than the one which was released in the past.

新上市的型號比之前上市的更加有人氣。

▶ 想要強調形容詞或是副詞的比較級時，在比較級的前方加上 much、even、still、far、a lot、by far 等等。多益考題中主要出現 much、even，這些都是表示「更加」的意思。

Step 3 │ 實戰演練

1 Lonsdale International reported that this quarter's revenue of approximately $78.4 million was ------- than it had expected to get.

(A) high　　　　　(B) height　　　　　(C) highly　　　　　(D) higher

2 This car was ------- than the rest of the competition during the ambulance evaluation in Michigan.

(A) more speed　　　(B) speedier　　　(C) speediest　　　(D) speed

▶ 答案與解析請參考解析本第 43 頁

Unit **72** 最高級

Step **1** | 實戰重點

解題策略　形容詞或副詞為兩個音節或三個音節以上的單字時,句型為「the most ＋形容詞／副詞」。

🎓 代表題型

The ------- consideration when you choose your first job should not be the salary.

(A) more importantly　(B) importantest　(C) most important　(D) importantly

✏️ 攻略解題法

The ------- consideration (when you choose your first job) should not be the salary.
　　主詞　　　　　　副詞子句（作修飾用）　　　　動詞　　　補語

(A) more importantly　(B) importantest　(C) most important　(D) importantly
　副詞比較級　　　　沒有此種用法　　　最高級　　　　副詞

文句分析　本題目中的空格位於冠詞與名詞之間,可推測出空格需填入形容詞,最高級的句型為「the most ＋形容詞」或是「形容詞＋ est」。

說明　　當形容詞或副詞只有一個音節時,句型為「形容詞／副詞＋ est」,若形容詞或副詞為「-able、-ful、-ous、-ive」字尾的兩音節或三音節以上的單字時,句型為「the most ＋形容詞／副詞」。而 important 為三個音節以上的單字,因此使用「the most ＋形容詞」的句型,答案為 (C) most important。

翻譯　　當你在選擇第一份工作時,最重要的考量不應該是薪水。

單字片語　consideration 顧慮,考量／ choose 選擇

解答　　(C)

🗡 攻略 POINT

形容詞或副詞最高級只有一個音節時,句型為「the ＋形容詞／副詞＋ est」,若為「-able、-ful、-ous、-ive」字尾的兩音節或三音節以上的單字時,句型為「the most ＋形容詞／副詞」。

核心理論

> 主要題型在於區分「the most ＋形容詞／副詞」與「the ＋形容詞／副詞＋ est」。
>
> > **最高級句型**
> >
> > 1) 最高級＋ of all (the) ＋名詞複數形（對象）：～之中最～
> >
> > 2) 最高級＋ in (the) ＋名詞單數形（團體、機關、場所）：在～之中最～
> >
> > 3) 最高級＋ among / of ＋不可數名詞：～之中最～
> >
> > 4) 最高級＋ ever：目前最～
> >
> > 5) 最高級＋ (that) 主詞＋ have (ever) p.p.：曾經～之中最～
>
> 副詞 by far、quite、the very、much、only 可用來強調最高級。

China has **the highest** growth potential in the world.
中國具有全世界最高的發展潛力。

▶ 當形容詞或是副詞只有一個音節（high）時，句型為「形容詞／副詞＋ est」。

The most interesting book I've ever read is definitely 'The Dart.'
我讀過最有趣的書絕對是《The Dart》。。

▶ 形容詞或副詞以「-able、-ful、-ous、-ive」等語尾結尾，且為兩音節或三音節以上的單字時，句型為「the most ＋形容詞／副詞」。

This figure shows that the nation's economy is growing at **its** fastest pace in five years.
這個數據指出國家經濟在這五年間正以最快的步調成長中。

▶ 可用「所有格＋最高級」代替「the ＋最高級」。

We are dedicated to providing **only** the best service every day.
我們每天都致力於提供最好的服務。

▶ 強調形容詞或副詞的最高級時，請在「the ＋最高級」前方加上 by far、quite（相當地）、only（只）。

1 The ------- way to look for the nearest location is to type the name of the town on our website and to find the one you live in.

(A) more fast   (B) fasten   (C) most fast   (D) fastest

2 IN People & Solutions is a recruitment company specializing exclusively in medical and hospital employees, and we have worked for some of the ------- international and local hospitals.

(A) reputablest   (B) most reputable   (C) most reputably   (D) reputably

REVIEW TEST

1. E-Tax delivers ------- the most efficient and cost-effective solutions for real and personal property tax needs.

   (A) since
   (B) only
   (C) hard
   (D) ever

2. The comprehensive analyses performed by experts during the evaluations of new machines allows us to calculate their value as ------- as possible.

   (A) precisely
   (B) precise
   (C) precision
   (D) more precise

3. The results of the test conducted by EXPKrobit indicate that a device by CHIA is likely to be damaged more ------- than any other devices.

   (A) ease
   (B) easy
   (C) easily
   (D) easier

4. This is the ------- restaurant I've ever been to but only the third busiest in the whole country.

   (A) busy
   (B) most busy
   (C) busily
   (D) busiest

5. Nakasa's ------- novel is currently out of stock because more people than we had expected bought it.

   (A) most recent
   (B) recently
   (C) even recent
   (D) more recently

6. This is mainly used by small business owners who are looking for the ------- expensive method of shipping their finished products.

   (A) less
   (B) little
   (C) more less
   (D) least

7. The company she works for pays her a low salary, but her working hours are as ------- as she can make them.

   (A) flexibly
   (B) flexibility
   (C) flexible
   (D) much flexible

8. Due to the city's limited water supply, you are advised to have a rose garden, which needs ------- water than a lawn.

   (A) little
   (B) less
   (C) least
   (D) even

9. YesPoint collects your personal information, which is kept secure in compliance with the ------- guidelines.

   (A) strictly
   (B) most strictly
   (C) most strict
   (D) strictest

10. Mr. Jung, one of the ------- jazz pianists since 1980, is planning to play at the Seoul Jazz Festival next week.

    (A) influentially
    (B) most influential
    (C) more influential
    (D) influential

▶ 答案與解析請參考解析本第 44 頁

PART
5&6

VOCABULARY

Step 1 ┃ 100% 基本單字整理

☐ **notice** ⓝ 通知，啟事
　ⓥ notice 注意到
　ⓐ noticeable 引人注意的

without prior **notice**　沒有事前通知
until further **notice**　在進一步通知前

☐ **increase** ⓝ 增加
　ⓥ increase 增加
　ⓐⓓ increasingly 漸漸地

an **increase** in the total revenues　總收入的增加
a substantial **increase** in sales　銷售量的顯著增長

☐ **access** ⓝ 通道，存取
　ⓥ access 連接
　ⓐ accessible 可連接的

have **access** to the data　有權存取數據
access to the building　往大樓的通道

☐ **effect** ⓝ 效果，影響
　ⓐ effective 有效的，有力的
　ⓐⓓ effectively 有效地

have an **effect** on　對～有影響
the **effect** on total sales　對總銷售額的影響

☐ **request** ⓝ 要求，請求
　ⓥ request 要求～

upon **request**　根據要求
request for a salary raise　要求薪資調漲

☐ **addition** ⓝ 追加，附加
　ⓐ additional 附加的

a welcome **addition** to our team　我們小組歡迎的新成員
an **addition** of two bus lines　新增的兩條公車路線

☐ **charge** ⓝ 責任，費用
　ⓥ charge 向～收費

shipping **charge**　物流費用
at no additional **charge**　沒有額外費用

☐ **capacity** ⓝ 能力，容量
　ⓐ capacious 容量大的

expand the **capacity**　擴大生產能力
seating **capacity**　座位數

☐ **precaution** ⓝ 預防措施
　ⓐ precautious 警惕的

take safety **precautions**　採取安全預防措施
take every **precaution**　採取一切預防措施

□ **damage** ⓝ 損失，傷害，毀損
ⓥ damage 破壞
ⓐ damaged 遭受破壞的

extensive **damage** 巨大的損失
suffer minor **damage** 遭受輕微損害

□ **responsibility** ⓝ 責任，義務
ⓝ response 回答
ⓥ respond 回覆（to）

assume the **responsibility** 承擔責任
corporate social **responsibility** 企業社會責任

□ **confidence** ⓝ 信任，自信
ⓐ confident 確信的
ⓐ confidential 機密的

with **confidence** 有自信
have **confidence** in 對～有信心

□ **employment** ⓝ 僱用，工作
ⓝ employee 職員
ⓝ employer 僱主

long-term **employment** 長期僱用
temporary **employment** vacancies 臨時工作職缺

□ **approval** ⓝ 認同，許可
ⓥ approve 准許～（of）

obtain **approval** 獲得許可
final / official **approval** 最終／正式批准

□ **collection** ⓝ 收集，收取
ⓥ collect 收集，收取
ⓝ collector 收藏家，收集者

toll **collection** system 過路費收取系統
immense **collection** of product reviews 大量的產品意見函

□ **donation** ⓝ 捐贈，捐款
ⓥ donate 捐獻

make a **donation** 捐款
a generous **donation** 慷慨的捐贈

□ **description** ⓝ 說明
ⓥ describe 說明，敘述

give a full **description** 給予詳盡的說明
a detailed **description** 詳細的說明

□ **refund** ⓝ 退款
ⓐ refundable 可以退還的

a full **refund** 全額退款
demand a **refund** 要求退款

□ **observance** ⓝ 奉行，慣例
ⓥ observe 觀察，遵守
ⓝ observation 觀察

observance of the law 奉公守法
in **observance** of 遵循～

□ **commitment** ⓝ 忠誠，承諾
ⓐ committed 忠誠的
ⓥ commit 承諾，犯（罪）

a **commitment** to quality 對品質的承諾
make a **commitment** 致力於，努力於

1 Please register your product online to gain [access / approach] to important updates.

2 This hotel has the added [benefit / advantage] of links to the city center.

3 Jimmy will serve as the [alternative / replacement] for Kelly, who is scheduled to go on a business trip.

4 I wish to call [attention / concentration] to an important warning regarding the use of this equipment.

5 They have the [claim / authority] to allow special visitors to park in front of the building.

6 To build a factory near the greenbelt zone, you must obtain written [authority / authorization] from the mayor.

7 Four customers ordered several salads and decided on their [choices / options] of dressings.

8 It will take three weeks to repair the considerable [hurt / damage] to the roof.

9 The company will send the contract in [duplicate / double] for you to sign.

10 Heavy rain will have an [affect / effect] on sales at the restaurant.

▶答案與解析請參考解析本第 45 頁

1 The conference originally scheduled for this coming Friday has been postponed until further _____.
(A) notice
(B) advice

2 The company anticipates a fifty-percent _____ in profits by the second fiscal quarter.
(A) discount
(B) increase

3 The manager has decided to control _____ to information about the company's customers.
(A) approach
(B) access

4 We provide shipping and handling at no additional _____.
(A) charge
(B) fare

5 They do not take _____ for any belongings lost at the conference.
(A) response
(B) responsibility

6 Open communications can increase people's _____ in the new employee's performance.
(A) confidence
(B) ability

7 The document will be sent to the board for final _____ within a week.
(A) approval
(B) decision

8 The museum is going to exhibit a unique _____ from May 1 to August 31.
(A) information
(B) collection

9 If you're looking for a special dishwasher, go to our website for more extensive _____ of its features.
(A) publication
(B) description

10 We offer 20 percent discount on every bike in _____ of the twentieth anniversary of the company's founding.
(A) observance
(B) correspondence

▶答案與解析請參考解析本第 46 頁

 **Unit 74 名詞 ②**

Step 1 100% 基本單字整理

☐ **notification** ⓝ 通知
  ⓥ notify 通知

written **notification** 書面通知
prior / advance **notification** 事前通知

☐ **negotiation** ⓝ 談判，交涉
  ⓥ negotiate 談判
  ⓝ negotiator 談判者

initial **negotiation** 初步談判
after two years of lengthy **negotiation** 經過長達兩年的談判後

☐ **reservation** ⓝ 預約
  ⓥ reserve 預約
  ⓐ reserved 已預約的

make a **reservation** 預約
confirm a **reservation** 確認預約

☐ **production** ⓝ 生產（量）
  ⓥ produce 生產

production facility 生產設備
production figures 生產數據

☐ **performance** ⓝ 表現，成果
  ⓥ perform 進行，演出
  ⓝ performer 表演者

performance evaluation 績效評估
during the **performance** 演出期間

☐ **application** ⓝ 申請，申請書
  ⓝ appliance 家電用品
  ⓝ applicant 申請人

application form 申請表格
accept **application** 接受申請

☐ **excess** ⓝ 超出
  ⓥ exceed 超過
  ⓐ excessive 過度的

in **excess** of 超過～
excess baggage 超重行李

☐ **value** ⓝ 價值，價格
  ⓐ valuable 有價值的

increase in **value** 價值上升
of **value** = valuable 貴重的

☐ **withdrawal** ⓝ 撤回
  ⓥ withdraw 退出，取消

make a **withdrawal** 撤退，提款
withdrawal slip 取款單

☐ **consent** ⓝ 同意 ⓥ consent 同意（to）	without the written **consent**　沒有同意書 by unanimous **consent**　一致同意
☐ **reimbursement** ⓝ 給付，賠償 ⓥ reimburse 賠償，償還	request **reimbursement**　要求賠償 **reimbursement** for business expenses　公司報帳
☐ **combination** ⓝ 組合，聯合 ⓥ combine 結合	in **combination**　結合 in **combination** with　與～結合
☐ **regulation** ⓝ 規定，規則 ⓥ regulate 調整，校正	comply with current **regulation**　因應目前規定 under the new **regulation**　在新規定下
☐ **extension** ⓝ 延長，內線 ⓥ extend 延長 ⓐ extensive 廣泛的	**extension** on the deadline　延長截止期限 a visa **extension**　簽證延期
☐ **duplicate** ⓝ 副本，複製品 ⓥ duplicate 複製	make a **duplicate**　複製 submit the completed form in **duplicate**　提交填寫完的表單副本
☐ **personnel** ⓝ 職員，人事 ⓐ personal 個人的 ⓐⓓ personally 親自地	**personnel** department　人事部 security **personnel**　保全
☐ **variety** ⓝ 多樣性 ⓐ various 多樣的 ⓥ vary 有別於	a **variety** of colors and sizes　多種顏色與尺寸 a wide **variety** of delicious foods　各式各樣的美食
☐ **monopoly** ⓝ 壟斷 ⓥ monopolize 獨占	develop a **monopoly**　發展壟斷權 have a **monopoly** on　在～上擁有壟斷
☐ **processing** ⓝ 處理，加工 ⓝ process 過程，加工	data-**processing** software　數據處理軟體 food **processing** machinery　食品加工機器
☐ **advance** ⓝ 進步，發展 ⓐ advanced 進步的 ⓝ advancement 進步，升遷	in **advance**　先行，事前 **advances** in engineering　工程的進步

1 Based on the sales [scores / figures] for the past twelve months, the division decided to discontinue the CLK250.

2 The state is going to impose heavy [fines / charges] on vehicles parked on busy streets.

3 Westlines has decided to decrease its [air prices / airfares] for frequent flyers to retain its loyal customers.

4 Please take a few minutes off and fill out this survey [form / print].

5 The [establishment / foundation] of an online store in Bangkok requires the thorough study of several websites.

6 A large amount of investment is required for the [increment / improvement] of the facilities.

7 The results of the research are a good [indication / show] of the company's potential for future success.

8 I couldn't find an extensive [information / description] of the features on the box.

9 Before you start your own business, make a thorough [exploration / investigation] of the local business environment.

10 The salesclerk in the electronic store has a comprehensive [thought / knowledge] of the store's products.

▶答案與解析請參考解析本第 46 頁

1　The company needs a more experienced employee to deal with delicate contract _____.
(A) signatures
(B) negotiations

2　Let us know whether you would like to confirm your _____ and pay 20 percent of the total amount of your stay.
(A) relation
(B) reservation

3　The award for outstanding sales _____ will be presented to the top car seller.
(A) performance
(B) confusion

4　They will tell you whether your _____ for a car loan was successful or not.
(A) calculation
(B) application

5　Customers who make _____ on their birthdays will be sent a letter wishing them a happy birthday.
(A) vouchers
(B) withdrawals

6　When employees go on trips for the purpose of business, they have to comply with the company's _____ to be reimbursed.
(A) regulations
(B) preventions

7　Mr. Kim asked HBOL Bank to grant him a 2-week _____ on his loan.
(A) finance
(B) extension

8　This community provides a _____ of activities to keep you busy after retirement.
(A) material
(B) variety

9　More than half of the employees at LHA expressed _____ with their job security.
(A) satisfaction
(B) discussion

10　Many employers enable their employees to negotiate the terms of their _____ to make them fair.
(A) explanations
(B) agreements

Unit 75 名詞 ③

Step 1 | 100% 基本單字整理

☐ **impression** ⓝ 印象
- ⓥ impress 給～深刻印象
- ⓐ impressive 有深刻印象的

a lasting **impression** 持久的深刻印象
give a bad **impression** 留下不好的印象

☐ **confirmation** ⓝ 確認
- ⓥ confirm 確認

written **confirmation** 書面證明
a purchase **confirmation** number 購買確認單號

☐ **caution** ⓝ 注意，小心
- ⓥ caution 警告
- ⓐ cautious 小心的

use extreme **caution** 極其謹慎
proceed with **caution** 小心處理

☐ **reception** ⓝ 接待，歡迎會
- ⓝ receptionist 接待員
- ⓝ receptiveness 接受度

reception desk 服務處
an ideal location for a **reception** 歡迎會的理想地點

☐ **decline** ⓝ 減少，下降
- ⓥ decline （不及物）減少，下降
  （及物）拒絕

decline in sales 銷售量的減少
report a 10% **decline** in net income 回報淨利下降 10%

☐ **profit** ⓝ 利潤，營收
- ⓥ profit 獲益（from）

make a **profit** 賺錢
profits nearly doubled 利潤將近兩倍

☐ **accountant** ⓝ 會計師
- ⓝ accounting 會計
- ⓥ account 說明（for）

hire an **accountant** 僱用會計師
an inexperienced **accountant** 沒有經驗的會計師

☐ **fund** ⓝ 資金
- ⓥ fund 投資

generate **funds** 籌措資金
a lack of **funds** 資金的不足

☐ **alternative** ⓝ 替代方案
- ⓥ alternate 替代

alternative route 替代道路
alternative medicine 替代藥物

☐ **opening** ⓝ 空缺，開幕	job **openings** 職缺	
ⓐ open 開著的	the **opening** of the new theater 新劇院的開幕	
ⓥ open 開啟		

☐ **compliance** ⓝ 服從	in **compliance** with 遵守～
ⓥ comply 遵從（with）	ensure full **compliance** with the law 確保對法律的完全服從

☐ **expertise** ⓝ 專門技能，專長	a high level of **expertise** 高水準的專業知識
ⓝ expert 專家	areas of **expertise** 專業領域

☐ **indication** ⓝ 徵兆，跡象	a good **indication** of consumer confidence 關於消費者信心的好徵兆
ⓥ indicate 指出	an **indication** of economic growth 經濟成長的跡象
ⓐ indicative 表明的	

☐ **evaluation** ⓝ 評價	an extensive **evaluation** 廣泛的評估
ⓥ evaluate 評估	receive a favorable **evaluation** 得到一份好評
ⓝ evaluator 評估員	

☐ **hospitality** ⓝ 招待，好客	warm **hospitality** 窩心的招待
ⓐ hospitable 好客的	appreciate your **hospitality** 感謝您的招待

☐ **arbitration** ⓝ 仲裁	independent **arbitration** 獨立仲裁
ⓝ arbitrator 仲裁者	be settled by **arbitration** 通過調停解決
ⓥ arbitrate 仲裁	

☐ **dispute** ⓝ 爭論，紛爭	**dispute** concerning the topic 關於主題的爭論
ⓥ dispute 爭論	cause a **dispute** 引起紛爭

☐ **identification** ⓝ 身分證	present an **identification** card 出示身分證
ⓝ identity 身分	obtain a visitor's **identification** tag 得到訪客識別證
ⓥ identify 鑑定	

☐ **delay** ⓝ 延遲，耽擱	cause unexpected **delay** 導致未預期的延遲
ⓥ delay 延誤	without further **delay** 沒有進一步的延遲

☐ **participation** ⓝ 參加，參與	increase employee **participation** 增加員工的參與
ⓝ participant 參加人士	draw **participation** from many companies 吸引各家公司的參與
ⓥ participate 參加（in）	

1 If you add a new [material / ingredient] to the recipe, you can make a great seasonal meal.

2 A skilled manager can make a work [program / schedule] which is effective for all of us.

3 Before starting up your business in this town, seek [advice / proposal] from A to Z Consulting.

4 Unauthorized [duplicate / reproduction] of this software is prohibited.

5 In the [recollection / remembrance] activity, she missed the later part of the presentation.

6 The customer returned a defective [product / goods] and was fully refunded.

7 Five hundred dollars' [worth / value] of equipment has been purchased for each division.

8 We will gladly [exchange / change] this for something else in accordance with our return policy.

9 We need volunteers who have the [ability / interest] to work with people who have disabilities.

10 Our company is the best place for you to work as a [mentor / consultant].

▶答案與解析請參考解析本第 47 頁

1 To return the product you purchased online, we must receive _____ of your desire to do so within seven days of receipt of the item.
(A) convenience
(B) confirmation

2 The acquisition of the Real Corporation has been approved despite the _____ in the company's stock price.
(A) suggestion
(B) decline

3 Renting a car for the long term can be a less expensive _____ to owning a private car.
(A) replacement
(B) alternative

4 The Pacific Corporation is announcing an _____ for an assistant to the financial manager.
(A) open
(B) opening

5 You should know that it is not a good _____ of future performance.
(A) indication
(B) discussion

6 When you complete the _____ form, be sure you do not include your name.
(A) extension
(B) evaluation

7 One form of _____, such as a valid driver's licence or passport, is required.
(A) coalition
(B) identification

8 They strongly encourage the _____ of the executive directors in nonprofit organizations.
(A) participation
(B) production

9 Unless an individual possesses a related certification, he or she should be under the _____ of a physical therapist.
(A) supervision
(B) supervisor

10 Studies say that repeated _____ to sunlight can result in the production of melanin.
(A) application
(B) exposure

▶答案與解析請參考解析本第 47 頁

 Unit 76 動詞 ❶

Step 1 | 100% 基本單字整理

□ **complement** ⓥ 補充
  ⓝ complement 補充物
  ⓐ complementary 補充的

complement the menu　補充菜單
complement the building materials　補充建材

□ **devise** ⓥ 策劃
  ⓝ device 裝置

devise an innovative solution　構思創新的解決方法
devise a better regulation　設計更好的規範

□ **inspect** ⓥ 檢查，審查
  ⓝ inspection 檢查，審查
  ⓝ inspector 視察員，監工

be **inspected** frequently　常被審查
inspect the product thoroughly　全面地檢查產品

□ **solicit** ⓥ 徵求，懇求
  ⓝ solicitation 懇請

solicit proposal　徵求提案
solicit employee feedback　要求員工意見回饋

□ **generate** ⓥ 創造
  ⓝ generator 發電機
  ⓐ generative 有生產力的

generate profits　創造利潤
generate new ideas　想出新點子

□ **establish** ⓥ 建立
  ⓝ establishment 成立
  ⓐ established 既定的

establish stronger ties　建立更強烈的連結
establish a close relationship　建立親密關係

□ **conduct** ⓥ 進行，舉辦

conduct a survey　進行調查
conduct an inspection　進行審查

□ **exceed** ⓥ 超過，優於

exceed a sales target　超出銷售目標
exceed initial projection　超出最初的預測

□ **expect** ⓥ 期待
  ⓝ expectation 期待，預期
  ⓐ expected 期待中的

expect to be dismissed on Monday　預期在星期一解散
be **expected** to V　被預期要～

☐ **lower** ⓥ 降低（價格、量） ⓐ low 低的	**lower** expenditures　降低支出 **lower** the price　降低價格	
☐ **serve** ⓥ 服務，服役 ⓝ service 服務，勞務	**serve** as a professor　擔任教授 to better **serve** its customers　提供顧客更好的服務	
☐ **relieve** ⓥ 免除，緩解 ⓝ relief 緩解，解脫	**relieve** anxiety / stress　緩解焦慮／壓力 **relieve** traffic congestion　緩解交通堵塞	
☐ **restrict** ⓥ 限制 ⓝ restriction 限制 ⓐ restrictive 限制的	**restrict** the number of employees　限制員工人數 **restrict** visitor access　限制訪客出入	
☐ **assume** ⓥ 承擔 ⓝ assumption 假設	**assume** the title　擔任職位 **assume** a role　擔任角色	
☐ **reflect** ⓥ 反映	**reflect** the current strategy　反映現有策略 **reflect** the standards　反映標準	
☐ **consolidate** ⓥ 強化 ⓝ consolidation 強化	**consolidate** one's influence　強化～的影響力 **consolidate** one's position　鞏固～地位	
☐ **lead** ⓥ 領導，指揮	**lead** a discussion　帶領討論 **lead** a session　帶領會議	
☐ **diversify** ⓥ 使多樣化 ⓐ diversified 多變化的	**diversify** products　使產品多樣化 **diversify** one's source of income　使～的收入來源多樣化	
☐ **launch** ⓥ 發布 ⓝ launch 發布，進行	**launch** a new line of products　發布新產品系列 **launch** new construction projects　啟動新的建案	
☐ **instruct** ⓥ 指示 ⓝ instruction 指示 ⓐ instructive 有啟發性的	**instruct** sb to do sth　指示某人去做某事 be **instructed** to V　被命令去做～	

1   Analysts [expect / anticipate] sales of the equipment will gradually grow through next year.

2   Before you ask to [borrow / lend] an item from a coworkers, be prepared for the unexpected.

3   Mr. Kim will [assume / undertake] the title of Chairman of the Auditing Committee next year.

4   The pottery retailer will [reimburse / compensate] me for the damage incurred during shipping.

5   You need to [minimize / condense] your report from 10 pages into one for an abstract.

6   If wool is submerged in hot water, it tends to [decrease / contract].

7   [Connect / Contact] a sales representative if you have any questions about the product.

8   We will [demonstrate / show] a new machine in our showroom tomorrow.

9   Please be advised to [separate / divide] your trash from your food waste.

10   I have [encircled / enclosed] my resume and cover letter in response to your advertisement.

▶答案與解析請參考解析本第 48 頁

1 The Human Resources Department will hire an additional three employees to _____ the workers in the Marketing Department.
(A) compliment
(B) complement

2 People are not fully aware of the need to _____ rental cars thoroughly when they choose a car.
(A) insert
(B) inspect

3 Although the company was successful in the domestic market, it had a hard time _____ branches abroad.
(A) determining
(B) establishing

4 They could _____ to get a good result after going through a 3-4 month period of trial and error.
(A) expect
(B) anticipate

5 To _____ anxiety before an interview, a person should sleep soundly at night and take vitamin C.
(A) serve
(B) relieve

6 John Cage is supposed to _____ the title of personnel director after the current one retires next month.
(A) undertake
(B) assume

7 The company purchased some computer equipment to simplify and _____ the system into one comprehensive network.
(A) guide
(B) consolidate

8 The acquisition of the kitchen products' company ranging from cookware to ovens will _____ the company's product line.
(A) diversify
(B) recognize

9 We are going to _____ our newly upgraded model, the CDI-2000, on December 1.
(A) launch
(B) schedule

10 Flight attendants _____ passengers to turn off their electronic devices and to fasten their seatbelts during takeoff and landing.
(A) speak
(B) instruct

Unit 77 動詞 ②

Step 1 | 100% 基本單字整理

☐ **host** ⓥ 主辦
　　ⓝ host 主人，主持人

host a party　舉辦一個派對
host a talk show　主持一個訪談節目

☐ **allocate** ⓥ 分配，配給

allocate funds　分配資金
allocate more resources　分配更多資源

☐ **renew** ⓥ 更新

renew the contract　更新契約
renew the subscription　續訂訂閱

☐ **consult** ⓥ 協商，參照

consult with the legal team　向法務組諮詢
consult the e-mail　參照電子郵件

☐ **enhance** ⓥ 增進
　　ⓝ enhancement 增加
　　ⓐ enhanced 增強的

enhance working conditions　改善工作條件
enhance the efficiency　提高效率

☐ **release** ⓥ 推出，發布

release a report　發表報告
release a new line of products　推出新的產品線

☐ **resume** ⓥ 恢復

resume operation　恢復運作
resume regular activity　回復定期活動

☐ **impose** ⓥ 徵收
　　ⓝ imposition 徵收

impose the tax　徵收稅金
impose a fine　徵收罰鍰

☐ **process** ⓥ 處理

process an order　處理訂單
process data　處理數據

☐ **accommodate** ⓥ 容納	**accommodate** larger parties	容納更大的團體
	accommodate other facilities	容納其他的設施
☐ **reach** ⓥ 抵達，達到	**reach** capacity	達到容量
	reach a conclusion	達成結論
☐ **settle** ⓥ 解決 ⓝ settlement 解決 ⓐ settled 已解決的	**settle** the dispute	解決紛爭
	settle a longstanding argument	解決長久以來的紛爭
☐ **operate** ⓥ 操作 ⓝ operation 運轉	**operate** the new equipment	操作新設備
	operate more than 100 branch locations	經營超過一百多間的分店
☐ **accomplish** ⓥ 完成 ⓝ accomplishment 完成 ⓐ accomplished 已完成的	**accomplish** one's goal	完成某人的目標
	accomplish one's task	完成某人的任務
☐ **adhere** ⓥ 堅守 ⓝ adherence 嚴守	**adhere** to the regulations	堅守規定
	adhere to one's opinion	堅守某人意見
☐ **enforce** ⓥ 執行 ⓝ enforcement 執行	**enforce** a policy	執行政策
	enforce a new system	執行新的系統
☐ **indicate** ⓥ 指出 ⓝ indication 跡象 ⓐ indicative 表明的（of）	**indicate** an interest	表示出興趣
	indicate one's regret	表現出某人的遺憾
☐ **refuse** ⓥ 拒絕 ⓝ refusal 拒絕	**refuse** the invitation	拒絕邀請
	refuse to discuss the question	拒絕討論問題
☐ **promote** ⓥ 提倡，促進 ⓝ promotion 升遷，提升 ⓐ promotional 促銷的，晉升的	**promote** research	促進研究
	promote economic growth	促進經濟成長
☐ **authorize** ⓥ 授權，批准 ⓝ authorization 許可，授權 ⓝ authority 權力，權威	**authorize** the use of equipment	批准裝置的使用
	authorize overtime payments	批准加班費

1   The company urged the foreign workers to [insist / adhere] to the law.

2   Please read carefully and [follow / precede] the instructions on how to assemble your coffee table.

3   Please [answer / respond] to the questionnaire and return it before you leave.

4   The prosecutor refused to [indict / sue] him for fraud.

5   Some frantic fans [impeded / prevented] the movement of the performers.

6   The director had to [fire / lay off] 400 workers to cut the company's labor costs.

7   After visiting their factory, he decided to [agree / accept] the company's final offer.

8   It is believed that the study by Mr. Seo will [reveal / admit] the latest findings about stem cells.

9   I [assume / assure] you that your complaints will be sent to the investigator shortly.

10   We will continue to [multiply / broaden] our research activities and explore new programs.

▶答案與解析請參考解析本第 49 頁

1 They will _____ the 4th Annual Business Fair to promote business opportunities.
(A) participate
(B) host

2 The purpose of the training is to _____ cooperation among the employees.
(A) prevent
(B) enhance

3 They help _____ disputes between labor and management.
(A) success
(B) settle

4 To _____ more efficiently, the shop manager has strategically changed the business hours.
(A) operate
(B) compete

5 Special equipment and tools will be needed if you try to _____ your business goals in the gardening industry.
(A) feature
(B) accomplish

6 Fitzerland, Inc. will strictly _____ its new policies and procedures from now on.
(A) appeal
(B) enforce

7 If you _____ a preference for a particular role, our manager will take this into account.
(A) experience
(B) indicate

8 The supplier is expected to _____ the delivery of the merchandise by the next business day.
(A) send
(B) refuse

9 More companies are now asking advertising agencies to _____ their items and services.
(A) promote
(B) affect

10 The directors will _____ the use of the funds collected last year.
(A) agree
(B) authorize

▶答案與解析請參考解析本第 49 頁

Unit 78 動詞 ③

| Step 1 | 100% 基本單字整理 |

☐ **address** ⓥ 解決
ⓝ address 地址，演說

address customer requests　處理顧客的要求
have yet to be **addressed**　尚未處理

☐ **arrange** ⓥ 籌備，安排
ⓝ arrangement 安排，籌備

arrange an appointment　安排會面
arrange their own transportation　安排他們自己的交通方式

☐ **join** ⓥ 參加，合流
ⓐ joint 共同的，聯合的

join the company　加入公司
join the membership　加入會員

☐ **deserve** ⓥ 應得到
ⓐ deserved 應得的

deserve a promotion　應得到升職
deserve the same high-quality service　應該要得到相同的高品質服務

☐ **assess** ⓥ 評估
ⓝ assessment 評估，鑑定

assess the work　評估工作
assess the manufacturing process　評估製造過程

☐ **install** ⓥ 安裝
ⓝ installation 安裝，裝備

install the program　安裝程式
install the new security system　安裝新的保全系統

☐ **prevent** ⓥ 預防
ⓝ prevention 預防
ⓐ preventive 防止的

prevent delays from occurring　預防延期的發生
prevent perishable products from deteriorating
預防容易腐敗的產品變質

☐ **create** ⓥ 創造，產生

create new jobs　提供新的工作
create a warm atmosphere　打造溫暖的氣氛

☐ **resolve** ⓥ 解決
ⓝ resolution 解決，解答

resolve complaints　解決不滿
resolve many scheduling conflicts　解決很多行程上的衝突

☐ **achieve** ⓥ 達成，實現	**achieve** the sales goal	達到業績目標
ⓝachievement 成就，成果	**achieve** a double-digit increase	達到兩位數的增加

☐ **devote** ⓥ 貢獻於～	**devote** sufficient time to -ing	投入足夠的時間去～
ⓐdevoted 忠誠的	**devote** more resources to research	在研究上投入更多的資源

☐ **acquire** ⓥ 獲得，收購	**acquire** the corporation	收購企業
ⓝacquirement 取得	**acquire** the land	收購土地

☐ **recognize** ⓥ 認可，表揚	be **recognized** for	被認可為～
ⓝrecognition 承認，識別	**recognize** innovation in the field	認可該領域的創新
ⓐrecognizable 可識別的		

☐ **transport** ⓥ 運輸，輸送	**transport** the machine by air	以空運運送
ⓝtransport 運輸，輸送	be promptly **transported**	及時運送到
ⓝtransportation 交通，輸送		

☐ **describe** ⓥ 描述	**describe** the layout	說明設計圖
ⓝdescription 描述	**describe** the division of responsibilities	說明責任分工

☐ **notify** ⓥ 通知	**notify** the passengers of the delay	通知乘客誤點的事
ⓝnotification 通知，公告	**notify** the catering manager	通知餐飲經理

☐ **maintain** ⓥ 保持，維護	**maintain** relationship	維持關係
ⓝmaintenance 維護，保持，管理	**maintain** steady sales	維持穩定的業績

☐ **specialize** ⓥ 專精於	**specialize** in protective packaging	專精於保護性包裝
ⓝspecialization 專業化	**specialize** in overseas investment	專精於海外投資
ⓐspecialized 專門的		

☐ **outline** ⓥ 概述	**outline** the schedule	概述行程
ⓝoutline 大綱，要領	**outline** the refund policy	概述退款政策

☐ **commence** ⓥ 啟動，開始	**commence** production	開始生產
ⓝcommencement 開始	**commence** on June 1	六月一日開始

1　Adverse weather can [result / cause] delays in the delivery of supplies.

2　When you arrive at the laboratory, you will be asked to [comply / observe] with the rules.

3　We need to [cut / divide] the donated clothes into girls' and boys' clothes.

4　He is highly qualified and deserves to [earn / gain] a high salary.

5　They will [notify / announce] him that his membership will expire soon.

6　Material costs are expected to [rise / raise] sharply during the next fiscal quarter.

7　They seem finally to have [arrived / reached] an agreement today after the prolonged negotiations.

8　He will [amount / deposit] the check at the bank by 4 p.m.

9　Please [assure / ensure] that children are not left alone when you use this product.

10　During this special offer, we will [enclose / engrave] your name on your wallet for free.

▶答案與解析請參考解析本第 50 頁

1 The safety investigators advised our supervisor to ＿＿＿＿ the problem of removing hazardous waste.
(A) influence
(B) address

2 If you want to ＿＿＿＿ the team, please do not hesitate to send us an email.
(A) direct
(B) join

3 Please make an observational checklist and ＿＿＿＿ the safety conditions every day.
(A) operate
(B) assess

4 The company will ＿＿＿＿ the employees from using their smartphones while on duty from April 1.
(A) prevent
(B) abstain

5 Our team is going to participate in a seminar to learn how to make strategies and to ＿＿＿＿ issue.
(A) answer
(B) resolve

6 First, you have to ＿＿＿＿ your immediate supervisor that you want to relocate to another city.
(A) notify
(B) announce

7 Having your factory in New Delhi can allow you to ＿＿＿＿ a competitive advantage over your rivals than having it in Qingdao.
(A) maintain
(B) renovate

8 Some bookstores ＿＿＿＿ in college books and offer discounts to students.
(A) promote
(B) specialize

9 The orientation package includes guidelines that ＿＿＿＿ the procedures for fulfilling your responsibilities.
(A) deliver
(B) outline

10 The new software program training course will ＿＿＿＿ on June 1 at 6.30 p.m.
(A) finish
(B) commence

▶答案與解析請參考解析本第 50 頁

Unit 79 形容詞 ❶

Step 1 | **100% 基本單字整理**

☐ **temporary** ⓐ 暫時的，臨時的　　a **temporary** inconvenience　暫時的不便
　　　　　　　　　　　　　　　　a **temporary** discount　暫時的折扣

☐ **steady** ⓐ 穩定的　　　　　　　**steady** growth　穩定的成長
　ⓐⓓ steadily 穩定地　　　　　　a **steady** increase in productivity　穩定上升的生產率

☐ **adverse** ⓐ 相反的，不利的　　an **adverse** effect　負面影響，副作用
　　　　　　　　　　　　　　　　adverse economic conditions　經濟逆境

☐ **efficient** ⓐ 有效率的　　　　make **efficient** use of　有效運用～
　ⓝ efficiency 效率，能力　　　　in an **efficient** manner　以有效率的方法
　ⓐⓓ efficiently 有效率地

☐ **eligible** ⓐ 有資格的，合格的　be **eligible** for health insurance　具醫療保險資格
　ⓝ eligibility 適任　　　　　　be **eligible** to receive the award　有資格獲獎

☐ **qualified** ⓐ 有資格的，勝任　a **qualified** candidate　有資格的候選人
　ⓝ qualification 資格　　　　　be extremely well **qualified** for　就～來說，具有充分的資格
　ⓥ qualify 給予資格

☐ **responsible** ⓐ 有責任的　　　be **responsible** for the safety　對安全防護有責任
　ⓥ respond 回應　　　　　　　be held **responsible** for　必須對～負責
　ⓝ responsibility 責任，義務

☐ **subject** ⓐ 隸屬的，須經～的　be **subject** to approval　須經批准
　ⓥ subject 使遭遇～　　　　　be **subject** to delay　受到延誤
　ⓐⓓ subjectively 主觀地

☐ **regular** ⓐ 規律的　　　　　during **regular** working hours　在正常上班時間
　ⓐⓓ regularly 規律地　　　　on a **regular** basis　定期地 (= regularly)
　ⓝ regularity 規律性，整齊

☐ **preferred** ⓐ 偏好的 ⓥ prefer 偏好 ⓝ preference 偏好	**preferred** method of payment　偏好的支付方式 at one's **preferred** pace　就著某人喜歡的步調
☐ **dedicated** ⓐ 盡心盡力的 ⓝ dedication 貢獻，忠誠 ⓥ dedicate 奉獻	a **dedicated** assistant　一個盡心盡力的助理 a **dedicated** employee　一個盡心盡力的員工
☐ **rapid** ⓐ 快速的 ⓐⓓ rapidly 快速地 ⓝ rapidity 迅速，敏捷	**rapid** improvement　快速的改善 a **rapid** increase　急速的上升
☐ **relevant** ⓐ 相關的，適宜的	**relevant** experience　相關的經驗 a **relevant** receipt　一份相關的收據
☐ **comprehensive** ⓐ 全面的 ⓥ comprehend 包括	**comprehensive** information　全方位的資訊 a **comprehensive** study　一份綜合研究
☐ **broad** ⓐ 廣泛的 ⓥ broaden 擴大 ⓐⓓ broadly 寬廣地	**broad** knowledge　廣博的知識 a **broad** range of products　各式各樣的商品
☐ **professional** ⓐ 專業的 ⓝ profession 職業 ⓐⓓ professionally 專業地	**professional** assistance　專業的協助 seek **professional** advice　尋求專業建議
☐ **accessible** ⓐ 易接近的 ⓝ access 存取，通路 ⓥ access 連接	be **accessible** to members　會員可以利用 readily **accessible**　隨時可以訪問，隨時可以存取
☐ **affordable** ⓐ 可負擔的 ⓥ afford 足以承擔	at an **affordable** price　以可負擔的價格 **affordable** accommodation　價格實惠的住宿
☐ **promising** ⓐ 有希望的 ⓝ promise 承諾 ⓥ promise 承諾	the most **promising** candidate　最有希望的候選人 a **promising** company　前途光明的公司
☐ **damaged** ⓐ 被破壞的 ⓝ damage 損傷，破壞 ⓥ damage 損壞	**damaged** luggage　損壞的行李 **damaged** baggage report　行李毀損申告書

1 The terms and conditions of the renewal will be the same as the [early / previous] contract.

2 The employees only had a [marginal / pretty] interest in the news.

3 Because the restaurant fills up quickly, only a few seats remain [discarded / unoccupied] at 6 p.m.

4 We will open a beginner's course for the newly [connected / joined] members.

5 A [considerable / considerate] bonus will be provided when you reach three years of service.

6 He got out of his truck to check for [injured / damaged] goods.

7 Please be aware that to be reimbursed, you have to use a [designated / restricted] hotel.

8 Because the company developed an efficient strategy, it could make a(n) [enormous / dramatic] profit.

9 Please do not include [irrelevant / irrespective] information in your report.

10 The concert in the stadium is [possible / likely] to be postponed due to the weather conditions.

▶答案與解析請參考解析本第 51 頁

1 The monthly report shows there has been a _____ increase in sales.
(A) inclusive
(B) steady

2 There are still tickets _____ for the sessions on Friday and Sunday.
(A) capable
(B) available

3 Members of the board of directors finally reached a decision to choose a more _____ way.
(A) efficient
(B) guided

4 Mark Jones is _____ for promotion because of his distinguished performance.
(A) eligible
(B) special

5 Arendel Finance is looking for a _____ candidate for a bank teller.
(A) qualified
(B) described

6 Kevin Arnold is _____ for coordinating the activities of projects and supervising every procedure.
(A) responsible
(B) responding

7 To apply to be our store manager, you must have a _____ knowledge of computer systems.
(A) definitive
(B) comprehensive

8 As you know, Fine Painting is known to offer reliable service at _____ prices.
(A) affordable
(B) traditional

9 Mr. Irving was considered to be the most _____ member of the new generation of marketing strategy associates.
(A) specific
(B) promising

10 Before you ship something back, please ask us whether we can give a full or partial refund for the _____ item.
(A) appropriate
(B) damaged

Unit 80 形容詞 ❷

| Step **1** | 100% 基本單字整理 |

☐ **durable** ⓐ 耐用的，結實
　ⓝ durability 耐久力
　durable material　耐用的材料
　manufacture **durable** merchandise　製造耐用的商品

☐ **satisfactory** ⓐ 滿意的
　ⓥ satisfy 使滿足
　ⓐ satisfying 令人滿足的
　a **satisfactory** wage increase　令人滿意的薪資調漲
　a **satisfactory** result　令人滿意的結果

☐ **remarkable** ⓐ
　傑出的，不平常的
　ⓐⓓ remarkably 傑出地，不平凡地
　a **remarkable** growth　卓越的成長
　all the more **remarkable**　更令人驚豔的

☐ **extensive** ⓐ 廣泛的，廣大的
　ⓥ extend 擴展，延伸
　ⓝ extension 延伸
　perform an **extensive** review　進行大範圍的檢討
　extensive financial support　大規模的財務支援

☐ **indicative** ⓐ 表明的，指示的
　ⓥ indicate 指出
　ⓝ indication 跡象，表示
　be **indicative** of　表明～，暗示～
　be **indicative** of the lack of interest　暗示了不感興趣

☐ **substantial** ⓐ 大量的
　ⓐⓓ substantially 大量地
　a **substantial** reduction　大幅減少
　a **substantial** amount of time　大量的時間

☐ **worth** ⓐ 有價值的
　ⓐ worthy 有價值的
　ⓐ worthwhile 值得的
　be **worth** $500,000　價值五十萬美金
　be well **worth** the expense　花費很值得

☐ **considerable** ⓐ 相當的
　ⓥ consider 考量
　ⓐ considerate 體貼的
　ⓐⓓ considerably 相當地
　ⓝ consideration 考慮，體貼
　a **considerable** bonus　可觀的獎金
　considerable effort　相當大的努力

☐ **motivated** ⓐ
　有動機的，被刺激的
　ⓝ motivation 誘因，動機
　ⓥ motivate 刺激
　a **motivated** employee　有動力的員工
　seek **motivated** graphic artists　尋求積極的平面藝術家

□ **persuasive** ⓐ 有說服力的

⒜ persuasively 有說服力地
ⓥ persuade 說服

a **persuasive** argument　有說服力的主張
persuasive evidence　有說服力的證據

□ **numerous** ⓐ 龐大的

ⓝ number 數字，數值
⒜ numerously 龐大地

report **numerous** problems　回報眾多問題
attend **numerous** events　參加大量的活動

□ **spacious** ⓐ 寬敞的

⒜ spaciously 寬敞地

the **spacious** dining area　寬敞的用餐空間
reserve a **spacious** room　預定一間寬敞的房間

□ **conscious** ⓐ 意識到的

⒜ consciously 有意識地
ⓝ consciousness 意識，覺察

be **conscious** of　意識到～
safety-**conscious** client　有安全意識的客戶

□ **subsequent** ⓐ 隨後的

⒜ subsequently 隨後地

in **subsequent** years　接下來的幾年
subsequent to the appointment　會面之後

□ **extended** ⓐ 長期的，延長的

ⓥ extend 延長，擴展
ⓝ extension 延長，擴大

work **extended** hours　加班
the **extended** vacation request　長期休假申請

□ **transferable** ⓐ 可轉移的

ⓥ transfer 轉讓

be **transferable** to　可轉讓給～
This ticket is not **transferable**.　這張票券不可轉讓。

□ **reliable** ⓐ 可信賴的

ⓥ rely 依靠（on）
ⓝ reliability 信賴感

provide **reliable** service　提供值得信賴的服務
reliable inspection process　值得信賴的檢查程序

□ **protective** ⓐ 保護的

ⓥ protect 保護
ⓐ protection 保護

take **protective** measures　採取保護措施
wear **protective** gear　穿戴防護裝置

□ **specific** ⓐ 具體的，明確的

ⓥ specify 詳細說明
ⓝ specification 明細單

specific instructions　詳盡的說明書
due to a **specific** security alert　因為特定的安全警報

□ **detailed** ⓐ 詳細的

ⓝ detail 細節

for **detailed** information　為了詳盡的資訊
a **detailed** report　一份詳細的報告

1 Herne Technology Systems, one of the [prevalent / leading] companies in the world, is based in Essen, Germany.

2 If you fit the [required / obliged] profile for the job, please send an application to us.

3 The Carroll Historical Society will oversee the [preserved / reserved] historic buildings in the county.

4 I believe nothing is [superior / incompatible] with our existing system in terms of energy efficiency.

5 The Accounting Department sent a letter to request an [outdated / overdue] payment.

6 Boston Hospital was ranked first in position in the [modern / recent] evaluation of hospitals.

7 We have an [imaginative / imaginary] and innovative manager who researches new ways to approach problems.

8 The Internet is convenient but not a [dependable / reliable] source of information when you search for health and diet tips.

9 Several [averse / adverse] effects were reported by people after taking the new drug.

10 Part-time workers often work [expanded / extended] hours on weekends.

▶答案與解析請參考解析本第 51 頁

1 We are well-known suppliers that use very _____ material and highly scratch-resistant coating.
(A) durable
(B) confidential

2 The company made a _____ profit last quarter despite the sharp increase in raw material and energy prices.
(A) satisfactory
(B) satisfied

3 All our technicians have backgrounds in engineering and undergo _____ training to let them provide the best service.
(A) grateful
(B) extensive

4 Upgrading the existing machine will result in a(n) _____ improvement in efficiency.
(A) substantial
(B) usable

5 The Purchasing Department expects to reduce _____ expenses by placing bulk orders for cartridges.
(A) considerate
(B) considerable

6 The sales clerk in the ski equipment shop agreed to work _____ hours to get a special bonus.
(A) accustomed
(B) extended

7 Our water purifier will provide you with _____ service as long as you replace your water filter on a regular basis.
(A) reliable
(B) vulnerable

8 A visiting inspector was invited to observe our factory, and he urged us to take _____ measures.
(A) sincere
(B) protective

9 If you call Travel4U at 800-946-5956, we can provide you with _____ information about every country in the world.
(A) specific
(B) eager

10 We will confirm your reservation through an email that includes a _____ schedule of the seminar.
(A) visual
(B) detailed

Unit 81　副詞 ❶

☐ **promptly** ⓐⓓ 及時，立刻
　ⓐ prompt 立刻的
　ⓝ promptness 敏捷

answer **promptly**　及時回應
begin **promptly** at 1:00 p.m.　在下午一點準時開始

☐ **highly** ⓐⓓ 非常，高度地
　ⓐ high 高的
　ⓥ heighten 強化

highly recommended　高度推薦的
a **highly** profitable project　一件非常有利的專案

☐ **otherwise** ⓐⓓ 否則，反之
　ⓐ otherwise 不同的

unless **otherwise** noted　除非另作說明
unless **otherwise** stated　除非另有提及

☐ **directly** ⓐⓓ 直接地
　ⓥ direct 指導
　ⓝ direction 指導，控制，方向

report **directly** to　直接對～報告
leave **directly** after the show　表演結束後直接離開

☐ **dramatically** ⓐⓓ 引人注目地
　ⓐ dramatic 戲劇化的，引人注目的

grow **dramatically**　急遽成長
increase **dramatically**　急遽上升

☐ **adequately** ⓐⓓ
　足夠地，適當地
　ⓐ adequate 充足的，適當的

be **adequately** prepared　準備十足
wrap the package **adequately**　適當地包裝包裹

☐ **significantly** ⓐⓓ 顯著地
　ⓐ significant 重大的，重要的
　ⓝ significance 重要性

significantly improve　顯著地進步
significantly contribute to　對～有極大貢獻

☐ **heavily** ⓐⓓ
　在很大程度上，嚴重地
　ⓐ heavy 沈重的

rely **heavily** on　強烈依賴於～
heavily discounted airfare rates　折扣極低的機票

☐ **cautiously** ⓐⓓ
　小心翼翼地，謹慎地
　ⓝ caution 小心，注意
　ⓐ cautious 慎重的，小心的

be **cautiously** optimistic　審慎樂觀
ask a question **cautiously**　小心翼翼地詢問問題

☐ **currently** (ad) 目前 (a) current 現在的	**currently** under construction 目前正在施工中 be **currently** seeking temporary helps 目前正在尋求臨時雇員
☐ **immediately** (ad) 即時，立刻 (a) immediate 即時的	**immediately** 7 days from now 七天後立刻 must **immediately** report ~ 必須立刻回報~
☐ **regularly** (ad) 規律地，常常 (a) regular 規律的	a **regularly** scheduled event 定期舉行的活動 **regularly** perform maintenance checks 定期執行維護確認
☐ **rapidly** (ad) 急速地 (a) rapid 快速的 (n) rapidity 迅速	grow **rapidly** 急速成長 a **rapidly** growing economy 急速成長中的經濟
☐ **lately** (ad) 最近 (a) late 晚的	a **lately** installed generator 最近安裝的發電機 **lately** hired a full-time employee 最近僱用了全職員工
☐ **temporarily** (ad) 暫時地 (a) temporary 暫時的	be **temporarily** suspended 暫時中斷 be **temporarily** closed 暫時關閉
☐ **markedly** (ad) 顯著地，明顯地 (a) marked 顯著的，明顯的	rise **markedly** 明顯上漲 differ very **markedly** from 與~明顯地不同
☐ **efficiently** (ad) 有效率地 (a) efficient 有效率的 (n) efficiency 效率	work **efficiently** 有效率地工作 operate more **efficiently** 更有效率地運作
☐ **carefully** (ad) 慎重地，小心翼翼地 (a) careful 小心的	**carefully** review 慎重地檢討 read the safety procedures **carefully** 仔細地閱讀安全守則
☐ **approximately** (ad) 大約 (a) approximate 大概的	**approximately** 9:00 a.m 大約早上九點 **approximately** 500 employees 大約五百名員工
☐ **aggressively** (ad) 積極地 (a) aggressive 積極的	**aggressively** pursue new customers 積極地拓展新客戶 **aggressively** marketed products 積極行銷的產品

1 The factory admitted that they were [lastingly / continually] dumping pollutants into the lake.

2 Please enter the clients' data [accurately / assuredly] into the information database after meeting them.

3 The service representative [abruptly / promptly] answered the questions.

4 Gold and silver prices have [recently / soon] fallen sharply.

5 I would like to [personally / respectively] welcome all of the new members to our club.

6 The last customer service training was [high / highly] beneficial.

7 A flight attendant asked passengers to make sure their seatbelts were [adequately / tightly] fastened.

8 The bus stop is far [apart / distance] from the hotel we stay at.

9 The factory is located in a [sparsely / barely] populated area.

10 Our company predicts that revenue will increase [numerously / dramatically] by early June.

▶答案與解析請參考解析本第 53 頁

1 You should arrive early to register for the career development seminar, which starts _____ at 1:00.
(A) promptly
(B) temporarily

2 He must be _____ qualified to be the manager of the Planning Department.
(A) high
(B) highly

3 The manufacturing company can sell and ship products _____ to consumers.
(A) fully
(B) directly

4 Our sales have increased _____ since our advertising agency started using celebrities in advertisements.
(A) dramatically
(B) politely

5 To protect your computer from viruses, you are required to install this program _____.
(A) immediately
(B) especially

6 Ms. Kim is scheduled to be _____ relocated to fill in for an assistant manager who is out on maternity leave.
(A) differently
(B) temporarily

7 To allow the bus company to operate more _____, the city traffic authorities allowed it to change some of its lines.
(A) efficiently
(B) completely

8 If you have _____ checked the manual and there are still problems with the CLS250, please contact us.
(A) carefully
(B) markedly

9 They are going to hire _____ 30 new workers to respond to increasing inquiries.
(A) regularly
(B) approximately

10 The host is responsible to _____ promoting the events at the World Water Forum.
(A) necessarily
(B) aggressively

Unit 82　副詞 ❷

☐ **increasingly** (ad)
漸漸地，越來越～
　(a) increasing　正在增加的
　(a) increased　增加的

become **increasingly** popular　變得越來越流行
be **increasingly** reliant on donations　越來越依賴捐款

☐ **appropriately** (ad) 適當地
　(a) appropriate　適當的

appropriately address　適當處理
appropriately respond　適當回應

☐ **particularly** (ad) 特別地
　(a) particular　特定的

particularly small business owners　特別是那些小企業老闆
in **particularly** stressful situations　在特別有壓力的情況下

☐ **entirely** (ad) 完全地，全部地
　(a) entire　整體的，全部

entirely optional　完全任選
be made **entirely** of recycled materials　完全由回收材料製成

☐ **previously** (ad) 先前
　(a) previous　先前的

previously purchased items　之前購買的物品
as **previously** scheduled　依照之前安排的

☐ **nearly** (ad) 幾乎
　(a) near　相近的

nearly impossible　幾乎不可能
be **nearly** complete　幾乎要完成

☐ **clearly** (ad) 明確地
　(a) clear　明確的

speak **clearly**　明確地說
be **clearly** visible　清晰可見的

☐ **securely** (ad) 牢固地，安全地
　(a) secure　安全的
　(n) security　安全

securely mounted　牢牢地固定住
lock the door **securely**　牢牢地鎖上門

☐ **briefly** (ad) 短暫地，簡要地
　(a) brief　短暫的

be delayed **briefly**　延後一下子
speak **briefly** and clearly　簡潔扼要地說

☐ **severely** ⓐ嚴重地，嚴厲地 ⓐ severe 嚴重的，嚴苛的	be **severely** damaged　嚴重受損 a **severely** critical report　一份嚴厲批判的報告
☐ **routinely** ⓐ定期地，日常地 ⓐ routine 日常的	visit the factory **routinely**　定期拜訪工廠 requires feedback from customers **routinely** 要求顧客定期回饋意見
☐ **closely** ⓐ密切地，謹慎地 ⓐ close 近的	examine **closely**　謹慎地檢查 be **closely** related to　與～非常有關聯
☐ **exclusively** ⓐ單獨地，僅僅 ⓐ exclusive 獨有的 ⓝ exclusion 排除	deal with **exclusively**　專門去處理～ **exclusively** to the healthcare industry　僅針對醫療保險產業
☐ **politely** ⓐ有禮貌地 ⓐ polite 有禮貌的，和氣的 ⓝ politeness 禮貌	interact **politely** with customers　客客氣氣地接待顧客 **politely** tell customers that　有禮貌地告訴顧客～
☐ **thoroughly** ⓐ徹底地 ⓐ thorough 徹底的	research the company **thoroughly**　徹底地調查公司 be **thoroughly** inspected　被徹底地檢查
☐ **consistently** ⓐ一貫地 ⓐ consistent 一致的	be **consistently** late for work　工作一直遲到 at prices **consistently** lower than our competitors 以總是比我們競爭對手更低的價格
☐ **relatively** ⓐ相對地 ⓐ relative 相對的	**relatively** low compensation　相對低的賠償 a **relatively** new firm　相對新的公司
☐ **instantly** ⓐ立即，即刻 ⓐ instant 立即的	take effect **instantly**　立即生效 an **instantly** recognizable landmark　立刻可以認出來的地標
☐ **strictly** ⓐ嚴格地 ⓐ strict 嚴格的	be **strictly** limited　嚴格限制 be **strictly** enforced by　被嚴格強制執行
☐ **evidently** ⓐ明顯地，顯然 ⓐ evident 明顯的 ⓝ evidence 證據	underestimate **evidently**　明顯低估 drop **evidently**　明顯下降

1 The dress will be [exclusively / extremely] designed for you after measuring your exact size.

2 We need to change the management system to survive in a(n) [consecutively / increasingly] competitive market.

3 Most of the workers at the company commute [only / exceptionally] by car.

4 The company's event was rescheduled [primarily / firstly] because of budget concerns.

5 Even though it was raining [quite / heavily], the conference started on time.

6 The supply of office space in Tokyo is [rapidly / extremely] decreasing.

7 Safety precautions must be [strongly / stringently] observed.

8 The blue shoes you ordered are not in stock now; [but / however], black is available in your size.

9 They have [yet / still] not released the much anticipated test results.

10 An opinion survey is [normally / once] conducted after the regular seminar.

▶答案與解析請參考解析本第 53 頁

1 The manager will _____ handle the complaints about the parcel that was sent from China to North America.
(A) securely
(B) appropriately

2 If you become a member, you can _____ receive new material from us.
(A) progressively
(B) routinely

3 Before you reach a conclusion concerning the statistical analysis study, you are advised to look into the data _____.
(A) closely
(B) narrowly

4 The Neppia Company has focused _____ on improving its technology because of lack of funds.
(A) cordially
(B) exclusively

5 It is important to make sure that you read the instruction manual _____.
(A) thoroughly
(B) regionally

6 A _____ sustained commitment to high-quality standards let MagMag remain one of the leading companies.
(A) consistently
(B) sensibly

7 Although the Alan Paradise Hotel is _____ more expensive, they offer far better service.
(A) relatively
(B) promptly

8 We asked the company to create a logo which would be _____ recognizable to potential customers.
(A) absolutely
(B) instantly

9 The dress code for salesclerks is _____ enforced to look professional and to ensure customer satisfaction.
(A) strictly
(B) indifferently

10 They can _____ repair the damaged door if some parts are replaced.
(A) unfairly
(B) evidently

▶答案與解析請參考解析本第 54 頁

REVIEW TEST

1. Not all employees are satisfied because some think some of the women will not ------- competently under the new male-centered company policy.

    (A) request
    (B) support
    (C) release
    (D) function

2. All staff members are required to ------- the regulations to maintain peace and order in the company.

    (A) capture
    (B) follow
    (C) attract
    (D) value

3. Using a website to renew a(n) ------- to a magazine is much easier than mailing a form to an office.

    (A) prevention
    (B) organization
    (C) problem
    (D) subscription

4. People doing teleworking will be able to ------- the company's database from their homes through computer link-ups.

    (A) conform
    (B) renovate
    (C) access
    (D) restrict

5. Carlson Health's new dietary supplements are ------- with customer demand, and it aims to export them all over the world.

    (A) consistent
    (B) desirable
    (C) predictable
    (D) common

6. The meeting will begin ------- at 2:30, so make sure that Mr. Brooks arrives at the conference room at least 10 minutes early.

    (A) easily
    (B) seemingly
    (C) extremely
    (D) promptly

7. This program is not only designed ------- for children but also for adults with symptoms of ADHD.

    (A) specifically
    (B) fully
    (C) frequently
    (D) rarely

8. Ever since the company's foundation, it is ------- unusual for her to hire someone who is relatively inexperienced.

    (A) recently
    (B) highly
    (C) technically
    (D) widely

9. Some video footage aired on AKL, a TV station, are easily ------- to anyone through a simple process if it will not be used commercially.

    (A) cautious
    (B) accessible
    (C) necessary
    (D) national

10. The ------- of Food Project is to create a thoughtful and productive community of factory workers from diverse backgrounds.

    (A) mission
    (B) consideration
    (C) designation
    (D) impression

▶答案與解析請參考解析本第 54 頁

PART
6

從屬連接詞 &
填入正確句子

Unit 83 填入連接詞

解題策略　填入連接詞的題型解題重點在於，把握好前後兩句之間的關聯性。

 代表題型

Milton Allison Magazine's new head office was eventually completed last week.

Each employee's move-in time can be checked on the company's website.

Even though it is expected to take over two months to relocate, employees can take advantage of a number of benefits. -------, those employees in divided offices do not have to move across town for interdepartmental meetings anymore, which will lead to an even more efficient business.

Q. (A) Therefore

　　(B) Nevertheless

　　(C) For example

　　(D) However

✐ 攻略解題法

說明　　從選項可以推測出，本題型應該是選出用來連接句子與句子，最適當的連接副詞。空格前方語意是在說明，雖然遷移辦公室要花很多時間，但員工可以在遷址後從中得到益處。而空格後方則是舉出，未來員工不需要再為了跨部門的會議而在市區奔走的例子，由此可知答案為 (C) For example。

翻譯　　Milton Allison 雜誌總公司的新辦公室，總算在上週完工了。每位員工搬遷的時程，可以在公司網站上確認。雖然預計要兩個月以上才能搬遷完畢，但員工可以從中獲得不少好處。例如，不同部門的員工們，以後不需要再為了跨部門的會議而往返於市鎮間，這樣一來將會提高工作效率。

單字片語　move-in 搬入／relocate 搬遷／take advantage of 從～獲得好處／interdepartmental 部門之間的／lead to 導致～

解答　　(C)

🏷 攻略 POINT

1. 先確認題目是否為找出適當的連接詞，再確認前後文句的語意。
2. 找出前後文句的關聯性，再選出選項中適合的連接詞。

核心理論

在 Part 6 的四題中，固定會出一到兩個連接副詞的題型。

連接詞（連接副詞）的題型重點在於，透過前後兩句的關聯性找出答案。

對照關係	however 然而　in contrast 相反地　on the other hand 另一方面
因果關係	therefore = hence 因此　as a result 所以　consequently 因此 eventually 最後
附加說明	moreover = furthermore 並且　in addition = besides 此外 in fact 事實上
表時間	meanwhile 同時，另一方面　in the meantime 同時，另一方面
表讓步	nevertheless = nonetheless 不過，然而
表選擇	otherwise 否則　instead 反而
舉例	for example = for instance 例如

Milton Allison Magazine's new head office was eventually completed last week. Each employee's move-in time can be checked on the company's website. Even though it is expected to take over two months to relocate, employees can take advantage of a number of benefits. -------, those employees in divided offices do not have to move across town for interdepartmental meetings anymore, which will lead to an even more efficient business.

關於本題目，我們知道的資訊有：「告知新辦公室落成的消息」，與空格前方「雖然搬遷要花一段時間，但員工在遷址後可以獲得好處」的這件事。而 ------ 後方，列出了員工未來要開跨部門會議的時候，不用再穿梭於市區間的例子。也就是說，這是舉例說明前方提及員工可獲得的好處之一。

Q. (A) Therefore　因此（因果關係）　　(B) Nevertheless　然而（對照關係）

(C) For example　例如（舉例）　　(D) However　然而（對照關係）

Dear customer,

Thank you for purchasing the Gusto Espresso Coffee Machine ITL200.

When it is accompanied with a valid receipt, the product is warranted for twelve months from the date of purchase. According to the terms of the warranty, we will repair or replace your product free of charge. -------, the warranty does not cover defects caused by improper use, incorrect maintenance, or unauthorized modifications to the original product.

(A) Therefore　　　(B) Thus　　　(C) However　　　(D) as a result

▶答案與解析請參考解析本第 56 頁

Unit 84 填入正確句子

解題策略　　掌握好空格前後文章的脈絡後，一一檢查選項文句與文章的關聯性。

 代表題型

> PIONEER (21 July) - Pioneer Natural Resources (NYSE) and Eagle Ford Shale (EFS) will be merging into one company. The merger is effective as of 1 September. The newly created company will be operating under the name Enterprise Products Partners. -------. In a joint statement, the CEOs, Kristine Solis of NYSE and Donna Fields of EFS, assured customers they will see no service changes. They also said there will be no employee layoffs.
>
> Q (A) Enterprise Products Partners expects to hire more employees.
>
> (B) The energy sector is vital to Enterprise's development.
>
> (C) Both companies have a grasp of the international financial market.
>
> (D) Both companies have an excellent reputation in their respective industries.

✏️ 攻略解題法

說明　　空格前方的句子提及了兩間公司的名字，可以推論出，後方的句子也應該是與兩間公司有關的內容。然而 (C) 選項中，提到兩間公司皆為金融業，與事實不符，因此答案為 (D)，而用來代指前方公司的形容詞 Both，是本句的關鍵字。

翻譯　　PIONEER（7 月 21 日）—— Pioneer Natural Resources (NYSE) 與 Eagle Ford Shale (EFS) 兩間公司將進行合併。本合併將在 9 月 1 日生效，而新公司將會以 Enterprise Products Partners 的名稱繼續經營。兩間公司在各自的業界中都頗負盛名。在聯合聲明中，NYSE 的 Kristine Solis 與 EFS 的 Donna Fields 兩位 CEO 向顧客保證，他們的服務將不會有任何變化。他們也提及了不會解僱任何員工。

單字片語　　merge 合併／ effective 有效的／ as of 從～起／ operate 運作／ under the name 以～名／ joint statement 聯合聲明／ assure 保證／ lay off 解僱／ energy sector 能源領域／ vital 重要的／ development 發展／ grasp 掌握，支配／ international 國際的／ financial market 金融市場／ excellent 優秀的／ reputation 名聲／ respective 各自的／ industry 產業

解答　　(D)

🏹 攻略 POINT

1. 請確認將選項帶入文章後，文意是否流暢。
2. 先確認選項中的指示代名詞（it、that、these 等）與連接詞（however、therefore、also 等），再掌握句子與前面文句的關聯性。

核心理論

1. 題型
❶空格位於文章一開始
❷空格位於文章中間
❸空格位於文章最後

▶空格位於文章一開始的情況非常罕見，大多數題目都是位於文章的中央。

2. 解題攻略
❶先確認空格前後方的文意，預測空格可能出現的內容。
❷空格後方句子中出現的（指示）代名詞、連接詞或是關鍵字，都有可能為解題線索。
❸確認各個選項的語意後，選出適合填入空格的選項。
❹要注意的是，選項中的句子出現跟文章相關的字彙時，有可能是陷阱。

PIONEER (21 July) - Pioneer Natural Resources (NYSE) and Eagle Ford Shale (EFS) will be merging into one company. The merger is effective as of 1 September. The newly created company will be operating under the name Enterprise Products Partners. -------. In a joint statement, the CEOs, Kristine Solis of NYSE and Donna Fields of EFS, assured customers they will see no service changes. They also said there will be no employee layoffs.

(A) Enterprise Products Partners expects to hire more employees.
Enterprise Products Partners 預計招募更多員工。
(B) The energy sector is vital to Enterprise's development. 能源領域對 Enterprise 的發展很重要。
(C) Both companies have a grasp of the international financial market. 兩間公司都掌握著國際金融市場。
(D) Both companies have an excellent reputation in their respective industries.
兩間公司在各自的業界中都頗負盛名。

▶ 空格前方的句子提及兩間公司的名字，可以預測後方內容也應與兩間公司有關。
▶ 從文章脈絡來看，空格中應該會出現 both 來代指兩間公司，並且提及兩間公司在各自領域都獲得好評的事情。
▶ 確認在空格填入 (D) 選項後，語意連接順暢。

Step 3 | 實戰演練

Bath (7 May) - Although only 20 percent of the cars on Bath city streets are electric, this number is changing at a rapid pace. This is due to the city's generous tax benefits offered to electric car drivers. According to Martin Freeman, President of Bath Green Businesses, more attractive designs and longer-lasting batteries have also made a difference. Mr. Freeman predicts the number of electric cars in Bath will more than double in the coming years. -------.

Q (A) Moreover, he likes the convenience of having recharging stations on highways.

(B) In fact, he believes that in 20 years only electric cars will be sold here.

(C) Therefore, he feels that the price of electric cars is too high.

(D) He notes that the population of Bath has been decreasing steadily.

▶答案與解析請參考解析本第 56 頁

REVIEW TEST

Questions 1-4 refer to the following e-mail.

To: Frances McDormand
From: Max Lloyd-Jones
Re: Registration for Food Industry Professionals Conference
Date: 2 August

Dear Mr. McDormand,

Thank you for 1. ------- for the Food Industry Professionals Conference in Vancouver on 19-22 August.

Approximately 150 food representatives are expected to share their ideas on food safety as well as new technology in food preparation and packaging. We 2. ------- more detailed information to all participants at least two weeks before the event.

Unfortunately, one of the seminars you selected, Advances in Food Packaging, has been canceled. 3. -------, I have transferred you to Safe Food Preservation, which is scheduled for the same time slot.
4. -------.
I am looking forward to seeing you in August.

Sincerely,

Max Lloyd-Jones
Event Organizer

---

1. (A) forwarding
(B) developing
(C) cooperating
(D) registering

2. (A) will send
(B) sent
(C) have sent
(D) were sending

3. (A) All the same
(B) By comparison
(C) For this reason
(D) Above all

4. (A) Inform the hotel that you are a registered conference attendee.
(B) You will receive an e-mail shortly confirming your registration fee.
(C) If you are not satisfied with this, please contact us to choose a different topic.
(D) Therefore, the conference will be held in three different venues in Sydney.

Questions 5-8 refer to the following e-mail.

To : undisclosed-recipients
From : robert.sheehan@maxmedia.com
Date : September 1
Subject : Payment Policy

Dear Writers,

We 5. ------- our process for paying our freelance writers for their articles. Rather than issuing a payment for each article, we will make payments only once a month. I know this may be an 6. -------. However, it has become too time-consuming to process individual invoices each week. Starting now, do not submit an invoice for each article you write. 7. -------, please submit one itemized invoice each month for all articles written during that month. Please sign the attached form and return it to me by Friday, September 7. 8. -------.

We appreciate your cooperation in this matter.

Robert Sheehan, Human Resources
Max Media

5. (A) are changing
   (B) should change
   (C) may be changing
   (D) would have changed

6. (A) alternative
   (B) exaggeration
   (C) opportunity
   (D) inconvenience

7. (A) In that case
   (B) Instead
   (C) Based on that
   (D) Likewise

8. (A) This is necessary because we want to make sure that you agree to our new process.
   (B) Articles will be reviewed by our editorial team.
   (C) Your payment will be remitted immediately after you submit your article.
   (D) There are some small details that have been overlooked.

REVIEW TEST

Questions 9-12 refer to the following memo.

To: Box Office Staff

From: Jaremy Ray Taylor, General Director

Date: 15 November

Subject: Policy Update

I am writing to inform you of a change in the 9. ------- policy for our classical music series, effective immediately.

There have been many requests on the day of the concert from patrons who prefer to sit on the aisle because there is more leg room. From now on, we will accept such requests 10. ------- at the time tickets are purchased. Subsequently, audience members 11. ------- extra space may ask for a seat in the back two rows, as those are not usually filled. 12. -------. This policy should help us avoid complaints once a performance has begun.

9. (A) refund
　(B) pricing
　(C) seating
　(D) recording

10. (A) only
　(B) less
　(C) very
　(D) late

11. (A) needed
　(B) who need
　(C) they need
　(D) having needed

12. (A) Many people prefer to sit there, near the orchestra.
　(B) Saturday evening performances attract the largest crowds.
　(C) Ticket holders may not enter the theater after the performance begins.
　(D) It is further from the stage, but it is more comfortable there.

▶答案與解析請參考解析本第 57 頁

PART

7

閱讀文章類型分析

WARMING UP

1 Part 7 閱讀題型種類

Part 7 從電子郵件（email）、廣告文（advertisement）、信件（letter）、備忘錄（memo）、公告（notice）、報導（article）、訊息對話（text message chain）、表格（form）或其他類型（導覽文、講稿、說明）等等文章中出題，分為單篇閱讀（Single Passage）、雙篇閱讀（Double Passage）以及三篇閱讀（Triple Passage）三種題型。其中，電子郵件、報導、廣告與公告等等是最常見的類型。

要能夠在 Part 7 獲得高分並不容易，但終歸是要克服的難題。因此，只要熟讀了本書中仔細整理出的各種文體出題方向，以及針對不同題型的解題攻略（skill），就能慢慢發現解題速度會越來越快。Part 7 就是一場與時間的戰爭，就算閱讀解題能力再怎麼好，若是解題時間分配上產生失誤，一樣拿不到好成績。所以從現在起，系統性地掌握出題趨勢分析以及題型分析，並反覆練習，相信就能考取比預期更高的分數。

2 Part 7 文章的閱讀技巧

1. 必須具備足夠的字彙數量

閱讀理解能力與解題能力都同等重要，但如果字彙量不足，這兩種能力也是無用武之地。考生如果能夠一個個記下閱讀中常見的單字、片語，那麼相當於向自己的目標分數又往前跨了一大步，因此一定要熟記大量豐富的單字。

2. 每篇文章都要讀三遍，是鐵則而非選擇

「請將一篇文章讀三遍。」這樣一說，總是會被大家回問「為什麼？」因為大家會覺得已經讀過的文章，有再三閱讀的必要性嗎？然而事情要經歷過了才知道，只要那些對提升分數心急如焚的人試著將「讀三遍原則」實踐後再赴試，就會了解為什麼要這麼做了。與其做了 100 道選擇題，倒不如將 10 篇文章讀三遍來得有效。將一篇文章反覆閱讀後，可以發現不僅閱讀速度提升了，對於文章內容的掌握度也更高，還能夠發現之前沒注意到的細節。

多益閱讀題目的文章都大同小異，所以只要經常練習閱讀，就會在考場上遇到相似的文章，讓人產生似曾相識的感覺，閱讀速度變快，也可以更全面地掌握內容，就更容易發現解題的線索。因此比起練習一堆例題，考生每天持續固定練習閱讀一到兩篇文章，慢慢地就會發現，當初開始練習閱讀題時，那道名為「閱讀」的障礙已經自動消失不見。

3. 必要的解題技巧（skill）可以幫助減少閱讀花費時間

當單字量與閱讀理解能力累積到一定程度，就該開始培養解題技巧。但是並非了解所有的解題技巧後就能所向無敵，重點是加強練習如何運用在實際題目裡。根據題型不同，總共有 21 種解題技巧，其中有幾種比較符合初學者（basic）實力，屬於必須得分的題型，只要能夠熟練這些題型，全部拿下分數後，就能提升自己在閱讀部分上的自信心，所以希望考生們能夠將這些技巧好好熟讀於心。

3 Part 7 閱讀常見文章類別

除了底下列出的這些，當然還有其餘不同的文章類型，但多益考題大多與下列類型相同。雖然這些類型並沒有太大的差異，但根據每種文章的特性，要注意的重點、提及的位置都有所不同，將這些小技巧記下，更能有策略性地著手解題。近期的考題中，閱讀文章的類型豐富度也越來越高，因此更需要多加留意。

1. 電子郵件／信件	7. 信件
2. 報導	8. 備忘錄
3. 訊息對話	9. 導覽文
4. 公告	10. 其他（報價單、網站、傳單、宣傳冊、表格等等）
5. 廣告	11. 雙篇閱讀
6. 資訊情報	12. 三篇閱讀

4 Part 7 閱讀常見題型

1. 細節資訊掌握	5. 掌握同義詞
2. 類推／推論	6. 掌握意圖
3. 事實確認	7. 空格內容推理
4. 主旨＆目的	8. 要求＆提議

Unit 85 電子郵件 E-mail

Step 1 模擬例題

解題策略 | 請記住電子郵件的基本架構為：郵件寄送目的在信件開頭，文章中間部分為補充資訊，請求或要求事項放在結尾。

Questions 1-2 refer to the following e-mail.

To: Mrs. Laura Parker
From: Star Boutique
Subject: Grand-Opening Sale at the Third Star Boutique

We are pleased to inform you that the third branch of the Star Boutique has opened on Park Avenue. There is a whole new selection of party and bridal wear along with accessories. The store has its own designers; hence there is an exclusive selection of formal wear.

This coming July 7, we will hold a grand-opening sale along with a cocktail party, which will be a black dress affair. The items on sale will include all accessories, formal wear, and women's and men's wear. There will be discounts of up to 20%.

Please print the invitation which is attached to this e-mail and bring or wear something black to the event.

We are looking forward to your attending the party. Thank you.

Peter Stacy

1. Why was the e-mail sent to Mrs. Parker?
(A) To invite her to a new branch store
(B) To describe a bridal dress
(C) To provide information about some new items
(D) To inquire about some accessories

2. What is Mrs. Parker asked to do?
(A) Print an e-mail
(B) Arrive before 10 a.m.
(C) Attend a concert
(D) Come in a black outfit

▶ 中譯請參考解析本第 59 頁

To: Mrs. Laura Parker   ➡ 收件人
From: Star Boutique   ➡ 寄件人
Subject: Grand-Opening Sale at the Third Star Boutique   ➡ 郵件主旨

1 We are pleased to inform you that the third branch of the Star Boutique has opened on Park Avenue. There is a whole new selection of party and bridal wear along with accessories. The store has its own designers; hence there is an exclusive selection of formal wear.   ➡ 郵件寄送目的

This coming July 7, we will hold a grand-opening sale along with a cocktail party, which will be a black dress affair. The items on sale will include all accessories, formal wear, and women's and men's wear. There will be discounts of up to 20%.   ➡ 細節與補充事項

2 Please print the invitation which is attached to this e-mail and bring or wear something black to the event.   ➡ 要求或請求

1 We are looking forward to your attending the party. Thank you.

Peter Stacy

Q1. Why was the e-mail sent to Mrs. Parker?

「Why was ~ sent?」為詢問主旨，請勿誤認為詢問理由的題型。必須先詳細閱讀文章第一段內容，通常在第一段中含有 inform 的句子，即為信件主旨。而本題中的「We are inform you that the third branch of the Star Boutique has opened on Park Avenue.」，告知了「新店開幕」的消息，並且在末段的句子「We are looking forward to your attending the party.」，提到期待對方來訪，可知答案為 (A)。

Q2. What is Mrs. Parker asked to do?

「is 主詞 asked」為詢問要求或請求的問題，通常這類題型的答案線索位於末段之中，特別是在 if 句中或是命令句（Please ＋動詞原形）中出現。因此只要確認是這類題型後，就可以直接從末段的 if 句或命令句中找答案。本題使用的是命令句「Please print the invitation which is attached to this e-mail and bring or wear something black to the event.」，請對方將邀請函印出，並穿著或攜帶黑色服裝出席，答案為 (D)。

🔖 攻略 POINT

請熟記電子郵件的寄送目的、補充訊息以及要求事項的相關題型特徵。

1   We are pleased to inform you that the third branch of the Star Boutique has opened on Park Avenue.

> We are pleased to inform you (that the third branch of the Star Boutique
> 主詞　　　　　　動詞片語　　　　間接受詞　　　　　　　　　直接受詞
>
> has opened) (on Park Avenue).
> 　　　　　　　　　介系詞片語

動詞 inform、notify、tell、remind、advise、assure、convince 等動詞，皆為套用「對象＋ that 子句」句型的句型 4 動詞，其中的對象為間接受詞（向～、對～），而 that 子句則為直接受詞。

2   There is a whole new selection of party and bridal wear along with accessories.

> There is a whole new selection of party and bridal wear (along with
> 虛主詞 動詞　　　　　　　　　　　主詞　　　　　　　　　修飾語（介系詞片語）
>
> accessories).

There 本來是地方副詞，此處則作為句型 1 的虛主詞，句型結構為「There ＋動詞（is、remain、exist）＋主詞＋修飾語」，請注意，這裡的動詞與主詞間須保持主詞動詞一致性。「There ＋ be 動詞＋名詞＋介系詞片語」的意思為「在～有～」，there 在此用來引起聽眾注意力。

3   This coming July 7, we will hold a grand-opening sale along with a cocktail party, which will be a black dress affair.

> This coming July 7, we will hold a grand-opening sale (along with a cocktail
> 　　　　　　　　　主詞　　動詞　　　　受詞　　　　　修飾語（介系詞片語）
>
> party), (which will be a black dress affair).
> 　　　　　　　　關係子句

關係代名詞的前方，必須出現先行詞，而後方則必須接續缺少了主詞或是受詞的不完整子句。關係子句分為限定用法與補述用法兩種：沒有逗號，且句型為「先行詞＋關係代名詞＋不完整子句」，為限定用法；而包含逗號的句型「先行詞＋逗號＋關係代名詞＋不完整子句」，則為補述用法。補述用法與限定用法不同，句子完全按照順序翻譯即可，例如上方句子，即可翻譯為「在即將到來的 7 月 7 日，我們將會舉辦開幕特賣以及雞尾酒派對，派對的服裝要求為黑色。」

1　I am writing to 不定詞 寄信目的

I am writing to inform you that we received our order today.

我來信是為了告訴您，我們今天已經收到訂購的貨物了。

I am writing to inquire about the position posted in *The Daily Mail*.

冒昧來信向您詢問關於 The Daily Mail 上刊登的職缺。

2　This e-mail is to 不定詞 寄信目的

This e-mail is to confirm that you will be dismissed from the company on October 14.

此信通知您將於 10 月 14 日被解僱。

3　Thank you for your e-mail of 日期

Thank you for your e-mail of September 16, which had samples and a price list enclosed.

感謝您 9 月 16 日附上樣本與價格表的來信。

4　attached 附加檔案

Please find **attached** the file you requested.　附件檔案為您所要求的，請查收。

Attached is the sample.　附件檔案為樣本。

5　Could you 要求或是囑咐事宜

Could you come to see me tomorrow?　你明天可以來找我嗎？

Could you let me know what is going to happen at the workshop after lunch?

你午餐後可以告訴我研討會上將會是什麼情況嗎？

6　I/We would be grateful if you could 要求或是囑咐事宜

I would be grateful if you could send me your latest catalogue and price list.

如果您可以寄最新的目錄與價格表給我，我會非常感激。

I would be grateful if you could send me a copy soon.

如果您可以儘快寄複本給我，我會非常感激。

7　Please 要求或是囑咐事宜

Please contact us if you have any more questions.　若您有其他疑問，請您與我們聯繫。

Please do not hesitate to contact me if you want the replacement goods.

若您想要更換商品，請放心與我聯繫。

Questions 1-2 refer to the following e-mail.

To: William Mach
From: Elizabeth Swan
Date: October 5
Subject: Letter of Recommendation

Dear Professor Mach,

I greatly enjoyed and benefited from the four classes which I took with you over the past four years. I hope that you know me well enough and have a high enough regard for my abilities to write a general recommendation for me.

As you can see from the attached cover letter, I am targeting positions in the design industry which need my drawing and editing skills. I have included a summary sheet to refresh your memory about some of my key papers, including my senior thesis. I have also attached my resume, which lists some of my accomplishments outside the classroom.

Thanks so much for all you have done for me and for taking the time to review this request.

Sincerely,

Elizabeth Swan

1. What is the purpose of the e-mail?
   (A) To ask about a new position
   (B) To inquire about a new class
   (C) To report on an accomplishment
   (D) To request a recommendation letter

2. What is being sent with the e-mail?
   (A) A job description
   (B) A summary of the papers
   (C) A job application form
   (D) A letter of recommendation

Questions 3-5 refer to the following e-mail.

To: Anna Moon
From: Fortune Company
Date: July 3
Subject: Welcome to Fortune!

Dear Anna,

It is a pleasure to welcome you to the Fortune Company. We are excited to have you join our team, and we hope that you will enjoy working at our company. Before you join our team, you must participate in the new staff training program. The program will be held on July 21, and you will stay at our company's hostel for one week. There, you can learn more about our company's rules and working systems before you start working on August 1.

On the last Saturday of each month, we hold a special staff party to welcome all new employees. Please be sure to come next week to meet all of our senior staff members as well as the other new staff members who have joined Fortune this month.

If you have any questions during your training period, please do not hesitate to contact me. You can reach me at my e-mail address or on my office line at 000-0001.

Warm regards,

Rebecca Brown, Manager

3. What is the purpose of the e-mail?
   (A) To describe a company policy
   (B) To provide information about a staff training program
   (C) To mention the location of the company
   (D) To introduce some company products

4. When will the staff training end?
   (A) August 1
   (B) July 30
   (C) July 27
   (D) July 21

5. What is implied about Ms. Moon?
   (A) She will be a manager at the company.
   (B) She will not be able to commute from home during the program.
   (C) She will receive a fax with the same message that is in the e-mail.
   (D) She will start work on July 21.

Unit 86 報導＆新聞 Article & News Report

解題策略　閱讀題的報導多以新聞文章為主，解題時，要詳細閱讀作為主旨的第一段內容。另外，由於此類文章中，經常會出現較困難的單字片語，因此也要多多增進自己的字彙能力。

Questions 1-2 refer to the following press release.

New Britney Wilson Book Finally Becomes a Bestseller

LONDON - Britney Wilson's latest novel has quickly climbed up the bestseller lists now that it's finally available for purchase on Amazon.com. -[1]-.

Britney's romance novel True Love was in the top 100 by late Monday for both print and e-book sales. She wrote it under the pen name Olive Gratel. -[2]-.

Monday was the book's official publication date, but it couldn't be ordered from Amazon before then because the online retailer and Britney's U.K. publisher, the Suria Book Group, are arguing over e-book terms. -[3]-: Customers were told delivery of the book would likely take 2-4 weeks. -[4]-.

Ronnie's website currently ranks True Love number one for printed books and number 5 for e-books.

---

1. What is the purpose of the article?
   (A) To announce that some novels can be purchased online
   (B) To report that True Love is ranked number one by a website
   (C) To inform readers that a novel has climbed up the bestseller lists
   (D) To provide information on a new book

2. Who is Olive Gratel?
   (A) A designer
   (B) A writer
   (C) A director
   (D) An inspector

3. In which of the marked [1], [2], [3], and [4] does the following sentence best belong? "In addition, buying True Love in hardcover comes with its own frustrations."
   (A) [1]
   (B) [2]
   (C) [3]
   (D) [4]

▶中譯請參考解析本第 61 頁

New Britney Wilson Book Finally Becomes a Bestseller

LONDON - 1 Britney Wilson's latest novel has quickly climbed up the bestseller lists now that it's finally available for purchase on Amazon.com.

➡ 主旨

Britney's romance novel *True Love* was in the top 100 by late Monday for both print and e-book sales. 2 She wrote it under the pen name Olive Gratel.

➡ 深入說明

Monday was the book's official publication date, but it couldn't be ordered from Amazon before then because the online retailer and Britney's U.K. publisher, the Suria Book Group, are arguing over e-book terms. In addition, buying *True Love* in hardcover comes with its own frustrations: Customers were told delivery of the book would likely take 2-4 weeks.

Ronnie's website currently ranks *True Love* number one for printed books and number 5 for e-books.

Q1. What is the purpose of the article?

報導類的文章中，最重要的內容在第一段，因為此段不僅是主旨所在，同時也可以藉由第一段落來把握通篇文章的內容結構。所以針對詢問主旨的題型，將第一段仔細閱讀過即可。本題中，從「Britney Wilson's latest novel has quickly climbed up the bestseller lists now that it's finally available for purchase on Amazon.com.」，意為「由於 Britney Wilson 的最新小說終於可以在 Amazon.com 上購買，目前已迅速竄升至暢銷榜上。」由此句可知本篇為宣傳行銷用報導，因此答案為 (A)。

Q2. Who is Olive Gratel?

報導類閱讀題中，詢問人物題型的相關線索通常位於第二段，因此只要遇到報導文章並詢問「該人物為下列何者？」的題目時，從第二段文字下手即可。本例題中，雖然第一段文字中也有線索可循，但第二段裡的「She wrote it under the pen name Olive Gratel.」，「她以 Olive Gratel 的筆名撰寫該小說。」可明顯發現 Olive Gratel 為作者筆名，因此答案為 (B)。

Q3. In which of the marked [1], [2], [3], and [4] does the following sentence best belong? "In addition, buying True Love in hardcover comes with its own frustrations."

本題是詢問該文句適合插入於文章中四個位置中的何處，而由該文句中的連接詞 In addition（此外），可得知該句應是用來補充前方的內容。題目的文句內容是「購買《真愛》精裝版時有遇到問題。」能夠將第三段中「雖然書籍上市日期為星期一，但由於規範問題，在此之前都無法在 Amazon 上購買。」以及「消費者被告知書籍配送時間可能要花費二至四週。」順暢地連接起來，因此答案為 (C) [3]。此類選出插入文句最適合位置的題型，在單篇閱讀中，約莫會出現一題。

> 攻略 POINT
>
> 報導類文章中的第一段，是能夠掌握整篇文章大意與脈絡的重要部分，請仔細閱讀。

1 Britney Wilson's latest novel has quickly climbed up the bestseller lists now that it's finally available for purchase on Amazon.com.

> Britney Wilson's latest novel <u>has quickly climbed up</u> the bestseller lists
>   主詞   動詞   受詞
>
> <u>now that</u> it's finally available (for purchase on Amazon.com.)
> 連接詞 主詞動詞   補語   介系詞片語（介系詞＋名詞）

最高級文法為「the ＋最高級（最～的）」，不過其中的 the 可以用所有格代替，例如本句中可以「Britney Wilson's latest 或是 their latest」代替 the latest。另外 now that 形同 because，用來連接表理由副詞子句的連接詞，其他類似的連接詞還有 since、as 等，請務必牢記。

2 Britney's romance novel *True Love* was in the top 100 by late Monday for both print and e-book sales.

> Britney's romance novel *True Love* <u>was</u> (in the top 100) (by late Monday)
>   主詞   主詞的同位語 動詞 介系詞片語   介系詞片語
>
> (for both print and e-book sales).
>   介系詞片語

by 介系詞在多益測驗中，常見用法為「by ＋時間點（到～為止）、by ＋場所（～的旁邊）、by ＋數量（大約～）、by ＋ -ing（以～）、be ＋過去分詞＋ by（被～）」這五種，其中最頻繁出現的是第一種，此處的 by 與 no later than 作相同解釋。

3 buying *True Love* in hardcover comes with its own frustrations:

> buying *True Love* (in hardcover) <u>comes</u> (with its own frustrations):
> 主詞 buy 的受詞 介系詞片語   動詞   介系詞片語

動名詞是在動詞後方加上 -ing 的詞性，如名詞般可作主詞或受詞，同時也保留動詞特性，可連接受詞。將上方例句分析後，可發現動名詞（buying）如名詞置於主詞，也同動詞般，後方保有受詞（True Love）。而當動名詞作為主詞時，視為單數，因此後方動詞也須以單數形（comes）出現。

1 人物／團體／機關／公司 announced that 依據發表的內容

The board of trustees **announced that** Stanford will not make direct investments in coal-mining companies.

董事會宣布 Stanford 將不會直接投資礦產公司。

2 人物／團體／機關／公司 pointed out that 內容

Critics of these studies **pointed out that** people would have to drink 800 cans of diet soda per day.

這些研究的評論者指出，人們一天必須喝八百罐的無糖汽水。

3 人物／團體／機關／公司 reported that 報導內容

A British newspaper **reported that** an increasing number of cinemas have been banning the eating of popcorn in their theaters.

一份英國報紙報導說，有越來越多的電影院禁止在廳內食用爆米花。

4 商品 come with 附加品

The device will also **come with** the same 2-megapixel front-facing camera.

本裝置也會附帶相同的兩萬畫素前鏡頭。

5 商品 appear on 上市地點、時間

The A-776 will **appear on** the market at the end of August.

A-776 將會在八月底上市。

6 公司 has recently been expanding 事業體／產品／職缺

The Linux Foundation **has recently been expanding** into new markets very quickly.

Linux Foundation 近期非常快速地擴展了新的市場。

7 公司 acquire 併購（目標公司）

SAP announced it will **acquire** a Boston-based e-commerce software company.

SAP 宣布他們將會併購從 Boston 起家的一間電子商務軟體公司。

Questions 1-3 refer to the following article.

Summer has arrived early in Japan this year as the weather has been unusually warm in June. -[1]-. While it provides more opportunities for people to engage in outdoor activities and sports, the warm weather also increases the prevalence of summer diseases. -[2]-.

The Ministry of Health says it is particularly important to be aware of illnesses such as eye infections and mosquito-borne diseases as well as food-borne illnesses. -[3]-.

The best way to avoid eye infections and food-borne diseases is to wash your hands properly and regularly. In order to avoid catching these diseases, it is important to ensure that food is cooked thoroughly, the Ministry of Health said. -[4]-.

"Cook food thoroughly, especially meat and seafood," a spokesman for the Ministry of Health said. "Make sure that you wash your hands before you start cooking."

1. What is the main topic of the article?
(A) The dangers of outdoor activities
(B) The risk of being infected by mosquitoes
(C) Awareness of summer diseases
(D) The weather forecast for Japan

2. According to the article, what action will NOT prevent summer diseases?
(A) Washing one's hands on a regular basis
(B) Cooking meat until it is halfway done
(C) Cooking meat until it is completely done
(D) Washing one's hands before starting to cook

3. In which of the positions marked [1], [2], [3], and [4] does the following sentence best belong?

"In some cases, the initial symptoms may be followed by more serious symptoms, such as paralysis, later."
(A) [1]
(B) [2]
(C) [3]
(D) [4]

Sutera Opens Sales Office in Korea

The Sutera Hotel Corporation has opened a sales office in Seoul that links Sutera Hotels around the world with Korean travelers planning business and leisure trips. The regional sales office is the fifth in Asia, following ones located in China, Japan, Hong Kong, and Singapore. The Seoul office deals mostly with big enterprises and wholesale tour operators in Korea.

Jason Pang, the vice president of global sales for the Asia-Pacific region, said the Korean office is expected to reach its goal of 10-percent sales growth in the coming month.

"Korea is one of our top five markets in the Asia-Pacific region. We see huge potential in the country," Pang said.

According to Pang, the Korean inbound and outbound markets have grown 25 percent from the years 2012-2013 in terms of room nights and revenues while the Asia-Pacific region saw sales growth of 10 percent during the same period.

4. What is the purpose of the article?
   (A) To advertise the opening of a new hotel
   (B) To describe Sutera hotel's business
   (C) To announce the opening of a new sales office
   (D) To notify managers about the hotel's new plan

5. Who is Jason Pang?
   (A) A sales vice president
   (B) An assistant manager
   (C) A customer service manager
   (D) A general manager

6. What is NOT mentioned about the Korean office?
   (A) It has attained a growth rate of 25%.
   (B) It will reach its sales goal next month.
   (C) It is the company's fifth office in Asia.
   (D) It is in a market with a huge amount of potential.

Unit 87 廣告 Advertisement

解題策略　這類文章，必須要先確認是徵人廣告，或是一般商業廣告。若是徵人廣告，首先要掌握的資訊是工作內容與應徵資格；若是一般商業廣告，則先從標題下手，確認商品的種類，再去了解商品的特徵、折扣活動或是購買方法等等。

Questions 1-2 refer to the following advertisement.

Studio/Project Manager at Luxury Interiors Studio

Luxury Interiors Studio is looking for an organized and diligent studio coordinator. The studio specializes in branding, interior architecture and design, and development for high-end hotels, restaurants, bars, and residences.

The studio/project manager will ensure that all projects run under budget and on schedule and will do the following:

• Assist in scheduling the studio's resources and booking external resources.
• Monitor hours spent on projects and ensure that the work is done under the budget.
• Be fully briefed at all times on the stages of all of the ongoing projects.

The manager should have an adaptable working style. Experience or a background in architecture or interior design is essential. The manager will be proficient at using AutoCAD, MS Project, Photoshop, Illustrator, and Excel.

If you meet these requirements, please apply on our website: www.STUDIO.com.

---

1. What is the purpose of the advertisement?
   (A) To invite people to an opening ceremony
   (B) To apply for a position
   (C) To introduce a new product
   (D) To seek a new staff member

2. What is NOT mentioned as a responsibility of the job?
   (A) Making sure the projects are done under budget
   (B) Planning the studio's resources
   (C) Reporting on the completion of projects
   (D) Helping to book external resources

▶中譯請參考解析本第 63 頁

Studio/Project Manager at Luxury Interiors Studio ⇒ 標題

1 Luxury Interiors Studio is looking for an organized and diligent studio coordinator. The studio specializes in branding, interior architecture and design, and development for high-end hotels, restaurants, bars, and residences. ⇒ 徵才職缺

The studio/project manager will 2(A) ensure that all projects run under budget and on schedule and will do the following: ⇒ 工作內容
- 2(B), (D) Assist in scheduling the studio's resources and booking external resources.
- 2(A) Monitor hours spent on projects and ensure that the work is done under the budget.
- 2(C) Be fully briefed at all times on the stages of all the ongoing projects.

The manager should have an adaptable working style. Experience or a background in architecture or interior design is essential. The manager will be proficient at using AutoCAD, MS Project, Photoshop, Illustrator, and Excel. ⇒ 資格條件

If you meet these requirements, please apply on our website: www.STUDIO.com. ⇒ 應徵方法

Q1. What is the purpose of the advertisement?

通常廣告的主旨與目的都會寫在第一段文字中，因此，詢問廣告目的或主旨的題型答案，請從包含標題的第一段文字中找尋。本題答案為 (D)。

Q2. What is NOT mentioned as a responsibility of the job?

遇到題目中出現 NOT 的題型，通常答案的相關資訊會位於有項目符號或是記號之處。再加上本例題中，剛好第二段有項目符號，又是在描述業務內容的段落，完美符合解題所需的線索。NOT 題型可以說是所有題型中最麻煩的，一定要詳加閱讀內容。可以先閱讀選項，再回去文章中找相關情報。(A) 和文章中的 ensure that all projects run under budget and on schedule and will do the following 與 Monitor hours spent on projects and ensure that the work is done under the budget. 相符，而 (B) 則是與 Assist in scheduling the studio's resources and booking external resources. 相符。然而文章中 Be fully briefed at all times on the stages of all the ongoing projects. 其中的「時常回報（at all times）」，與 (C) 描述不符，因此答案為 (C)。

攻略 POINT

徵才廣告中，必須先確認業務內容以及應徵條件。

1 The studio specializes in branding, interior architecture and design, and development for high-end hotels, restaurants, bars, and residences.

The studio specializes in (branding, interior architecture and design, and
主詞　　　　　　動詞　　　　　　　　　　　動詞的一串受詞
development)(for high-end hotels, restaurants, bars, and residences).
　　　　　　　　　　　　　介系詞片語（介系詞＋名詞）

specialize in 表示「專門從事～」，是多益考題中常見的動詞片語。而雖然不及物動詞後方不可接續受詞，但只要「不及物動詞＋介系詞（specialize in）」就等同及物動詞，後方可接受詞。因此這類「不及物動詞＋介系詞」的組合，要好好掌握。

2 The studio/project manager will ensure that all projects under budget and on schedule and will do the following:

The studio/project manager will ensure (that all projects run under budget
主詞　　　　　　　　　　　　動詞　　　　動詞（ensure）的受詞（名詞子句）
完整子句（主要子句）
and on schedule and will do the following):
　　　　　　　　　　　動詞　　受詞

所謂的分詞構句，是將「連接詞＋主詞＋動詞（完整子句），主詞＋動詞」的連接詞與主詞省略後，將動詞轉化為 -ing 或 -ed 形態的句型，分詞可置於完整子句（主要子句）前方或後方。此句的 that all projects run under budget and on schedule and will do the following 作為受詞，其中以 and 連接，要注意的是，雖然 and 是用來連接修飾語，但 on schedule 和 will do the following 不能互換位子，因為 on schedule 是用來修飾 all projects，而 will do the following 則是用來帶出下方的列點事項。

3 The manager will be proficient at using AutoCAD, MS Project, Photoshop, Illustrator, and Excel.

The manager will be proficient at using AutoCAD, MS Project, Photoshop,
主詞　　　　動詞　　補語　介系詞　動名詞（at 的受詞）　動名詞（using 的受詞）
Illustrator, and Excel.

介系詞後方必定連接受詞，受詞詞性主要以名詞與動名詞為主。請注意，介系詞後方的動名詞必為現在式。

1 公司 is looking for 職缺 某公司正在招募某職缺

Luxury Interiors Studio **is looking for** an organized and diligent studio coordinator.
　　公司名　　　　　　　　　　　　　　　　　　　　職缺

Luxury Interiors Studio 正在招募有條理又勤奮的工作室統籌。

2 應徵者 will be responsible for 業務內容

Candidates **will be responsible for** planning specific products.
　應徵者　　　　　　　　　　　　　　　　業務內容

應徵者將會負責企劃特定的產品。

3 應徵者 should have 資格條件

A candidate **should have** a degree in planning or geography or a closely related field.
　應徵者　　　　　　　　資格條件

應徵者須具備企劃、地理學，或是相近領域的學位。

4 職缺 is required to have 資格條件

The person apply for the position **is required to have** a minimum of two years of work experience.
　　　　　　　　　　職缺　　　　　　　　　　　　資格條件

應徵本職缺的人至少要具備兩年以上的工作經驗。

5 應徵者 should send 應徵資料

Candidates **should send** a CV and a PDF portfolio of their graphic design work.
　應徵者　　　　　　　　　應徵資料

應徵者須寄送簡歷以及視覺設計作品集的 PDF。

6 Please 應徵方式或是遞交應徵資料

For more information, **please** visit our website at www.pbavenues.com.
　　　　　　　　　　　　應徵方式

欲知更多資訊，請上我們的官網 www.pbavenues.com。

Please send a resume, a cover letter, and the names of two references.
　　　　遞交應徵資料

請寄送履歷、求職信以及兩位推薦人的姓名。

Questions 1-2 refer to the following advertisement.

A Teaching Post at a University

Hours: Full Time
Salary: £28-36K per year

A great opportunity has arisen for a professor to work at an outstanding independent college in London. The college has a real commitment to sciences, which is shown by both its popularity with students and the achievements of its graduates.

The resources and facilities available at the college are excellent. In addition to its excellent academics, the college has a friendly and lively atmosphere, and it has a wide range of sports and extracurricular activities in which students can get involved.

The successful applicant will teach either physics or chemistry at a very high level. A desire to be involved in the entire college life and to contribute to its lively community will be an advantage. The main requirements for this role are a passion for science and a commitment to making it an exciting and rewarding subject.

If you would like to know more about this opportunity, please submit your CV (curriculum vitae) to the address listed below.

1. What position is being advertised?

(A) Technician
(B) Lecturer
(C) Scientist
(D) Librarian

2. What is NOT mentioned as a requirement for the position?

(A) A specialization in chemistry
(B) A major in science
(C) A specialization in biology
(D) A major in physics

Do you want to start or build a career in exhibition and event sales?

We are looking for sales executives with 6-12 months of sales experience. It is your sales skills and ability we are the most interested in. It is not a requirement that you have any relevant experience. So this could be the perfect job if you are considering changing careers.

Selling high-value exhibition packages will be an exciting challenge for your sales skills.

Who is qualified? A person with:
• Innovative sales skills
• Ideally, 6-12 months of sales experience
• Competent communication skills
• An A-level education; a degree is preferred but not essential.

The salary is dependent on experience. It starts at £18,000 and can go as high as £35,000 for a more experienced person. This does not include commission!

Apply now by visiting our website at www.eae.co.uk.

3. What position is being advertised?
   (A) Accountant
   (B) Salesman
   (C) Negotiator
   (D) Cashier

4. What is NOT mentioned as a requirement for the position?
   (A) An ability to make sales
   (B) Experience in sales
   (C) A degree
   (D) Proficiency in communication skills

5. How should a candidate apply for the job?
   (A) By mailing an application
   (B) By meeting the person in charge
   (C) By visiting a website
   (D) By contacting the office

Unit 88　書信 Letter

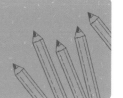

解題策略　書信的基本結構為「寄件人－收件人－信件主旨－細節內容與補充說明－要求事項－結尾問候語」。

Questions 1-2 refer to the following letter.

J&J Store
42 Gaya Street, Sabah
Tel: 755-4254

June 20

Ms. Stella
20 Pitt Street, Sabah

Dear Ms. Stella,

Our records show that you have been a customer at J&J's since our grand opening last year. We would like to thank you for your support by inviting you to the opening of our second shop, which will happen on June 25.

As you know, our store offers a complete and diverse line of computers, software, and hardware packages for both personal and business applications. All of our stock, including all of electronic equipment and hardware & software packages, will be marked down by 30-50%. In addition, please accept the enclosed $20 gift voucher to use with your purchase of $200 or more worth of products at our store.

We look forward to seeing you at J&J's new shop this coming June 25. The opening sales event is invitation only. Please bring this invitation with you and present it at the door.

Lilly Lohan
Store Manager

1. What is the purpose of the letter?
   (A) To describe a company's business
   (B) To invite a person to the opening of a store
   (C) To ask for an opinion
   (D) To thank a customer

2. What is enclosed with the letter?
   (A) $200 in cash
   (B) $20 in cash
   (C) A discount coupon
   (D) An invitation card

▶中譯請參考解析本第 65 頁

J&J Store
42 Gaya Street, Sabah
Tel: 755-4254

➡ 寄件人資訊

June 20

➡ 寄件日期

Ms. Stella
20 Pitt Street, Sabah

➡ 收件人資訊

Dear Ms. Stella,

➡ 信件主旨

Our records show that you have been a customer at J&J's since our grand opening last year. 1 We would like to thank you for your support by inviting you to the opening of our second shop, which will happen on June 25.

As you know, our store offers a complete and diverse line of computers, software, and hardware packages for both personal and business applications. All of our stock, including all of electronic equipment and hardware & software packages, will be marked down by 30-50%. In addition, please accept 2 the enclosed $20 gift voucher to use with your purchase of $200 or more worth of products at our store.

➡ 細節內容與補充說明

We look forward to seeing you at J&J's new shop this coming June 25. The opening sales event is invitation only. Please bring this invitation with you and present it at the door.

➡ 要求事項

Lilly Lohan
Store Manager

寄件人姓名
寄件人職稱／公司

Q1. What is the purpose of the letter?

由於第一段即為信件主旨,因此詢問主旨的題型,解題線索通常要從文章第一段內容中找尋。本題中第一段第二句提及「第二間分店開幕」,加上「We would like to thank you for your support by inviting you」,表達「想要招待您前來」的句子,可知本信件為邀請信函,因此答案為 (B)。

Q2. What is enclosed with this letter?

出現「is enclosed」的題型,旨在詢問附件,通常相關的資訊會在第二段中被提及,因此從該段落中即可尋獲答案。本題中,第二段落最後一句為「the enclosed $20 gift voucher」,可得知折價券也同時附在信中,答案為 (C)。

攻略 POINT

請務必掌握信件的主旨、補充訊息以及要求事項的相關題型特徵。

1 Our records show that you have been a customer at J&J's since our grand opening last year.

Our records <u>show</u> (that you <u>have been</u> a customer at J&J's since our grand
　　主詞　　　動詞　　連接詞 主詞　　動詞　　　　　　補語　　　　　　　　介系詞片語
　　　　　　　　　　　　　└───── 動詞（show）的受詞（名詞子句）─────┘

opening last year.)
　　　副詞

that 相關文法非常重要，that 既可作為名詞子句連接詞，也可作為關係代名詞。作名詞子句時，意思為「～的事情」，可置於主詞、受詞與補語的位置。如上方例題中，that 位於及物動詞（show）後方作受詞，可知此處為連接詞，此時 that 後方必須接續主詞與受詞／補語皆具備的完整子句。另外，that 作關係代名詞時，句型則為「先行詞＋that＋少了主詞或受詞的不完整子句」。

2 As you know, our store offers a complete and diverse line of computers, software, and hardware packages for both personal and business applications.

As　you <u>know</u>, <u>our store</u> <u>offers</u> (a complete and diverse line of computers,
連接詞 主詞 動詞　　　主詞　　　動詞　　　　　　動詞（offers）的受詞

software, and hardware packages) (for both personal and business
　　　　　　　　　　　　　　　　　　　　　　　　　介系詞片語

applications).

配對連接詞 both... and 句型為「both A and B」，表「A 和 B 都～」，此處的 both 為副詞，and 為對等連接詞。類似的配對連接詞還有 either A or B（A 或 B 其中之一）、neither A nor B（A 和 B 皆不）、not only A but also B（不只 A，B 也）等等用法。

3 All of our stock, including all of electronic equipment and hardware & software packages, will be marked down by 30-50%. In addition, please accept the enclosed $20 gift voucher to use with your purchase of $200 or more worth of products at our store.

<u>All of our stock,</u> (including all of electronic equipment and hardware &
　　主詞　　　　　　　　　　　　　　　　介系詞片語

software, packages,) <u>will be marked down</u> by (30-50%.) In addition, please
　　　　　　　　　　　　　　動詞　　　　　　　　　　　　　　連接副詞

<u>accept</u> the enclosed $20 gift voucher <u>to use</u> (with your purchase)
　動詞　　　　　　受詞　　　　　　　　 to 不定詞　　　介系詞片語

(of $200 or more worth of products at our store).
　　　　　　　　　介系詞片語

雖然連接副詞確實跟連接詞意思相同，也常置於句子與句子中間，但連接副詞就是副詞，尤其是 however 雖為副詞，卻容易因意思與 but 相同，而被誤認為連接詞。in addition 也是，請記住它是副詞而非連接詞。in addition 表「此外」，是用來補充前方句子的內容。如上方例題，in addition 前方提及優惠相關內容，後方也是說明優惠內容，因此中間使用 in addition 連接。

Step 4 　書信中的常見句型用法 ＊書信中的常見句型用法，與電子郵件相同。

1 I am writing to 不定詞 寄信目的

I am writing to inform you that we received our order today.

我來信是為了通知您，我們已經收到訂購的貨物了。

I am writing to inquire about the position posted in *The Daily Mail*.

冒昧來信向您詢問關於 The Daily Mail 上刊登的職缺。

2 This letter is to 不定詞 寄信目的

This letter is to confirm that you will be dismissed from the company on October 14.

本信通知您將於十月十四日被解僱。

3 Thank you for your letter of 日期

Thank you for your letter of September 16, which had samples and a price list enclosed. 感謝您九月十六日附上樣本與價格表的來信。

4 enclosed 附件

Please see the **enclosed** contract. 請確認附件的合約。

Enclosed are the samples. 附件為樣本。

5 Could you 要求或是囑咐事宜

Could you come to see me tomorrow? 你明天可以來找我嗎？

Could you let me know what is going to happen at the workshop after lunch?

你午餐後可以告訴我研討會上會有什麼情況嗎？

6 I/We would be grateful if you could 要求或是囑咐事宜

I would be grateful if you could send me your latest catalogue and price list.

如果您可以寄最新的目錄與價格表給我，我會非常感激。

I would be grateful if you could send me a copy soon.

如果您可以盡快寄複本給我，我會非常感激。

7 Please 要求或是囑咐事宜

Please contact us if you have any more questions. 若您有其他疑問，請與我們聯繫。

Please do not hesitate to contact me if you want the replacement goods.

若您想要更換商品，請冊需猶豫與我聯繫。

Questions 1-2 refer to the following letter.

Dear Ms. Stella,

We are pleased that you chose J&J's for your laptop purchase. Our sales staff was delighted to be of help you. We hope you are enjoying the convenience and quality of your new laptop.

Let us also remind you that we are offering some special gifts for anyone who buys the laptop you did. Your free laptop accessories, including a laptop case, screen protector and mousepad, have arrived. These accessories are a gift from us to you. Drop by any time this month to pick them up.

Are you aware that we sell bed tables for laptops? A new shipment of bed tables in many beautiful colors and elegant styles has just arrived. Come to see our selection. We would like to help you find the perfect table to match your laptop.

If you have ever have any questions, please call us at 755-4254.

Sincerely,

Michael Jones
Director of Sales

1. What is the main purpose of the letter?
   (A) To describe some features of a product
   (B) To remind a customer to stop by the store
   (C) To ask for a customer's opinion
   (D) To provide some information about a new laptop

2. What is indicated about Ms. Stella?
   (A) She bought some accessories for her new laptop.
   (B) She will visit J&J's soon.
   (C) She recently purchased some electronic equipment.
   (D) J&J's will provide her with a laptop table.

Questions 3-5 refer to the following letter.

Anita Yong
514 Main Street, Los Angeles

Mr. Eric Park
Human Resources Manager, Pacific Hotel

Dear Mr. Park,

I wish to apply for the position of front desk manager at the Pacific Hotel since my qualifications and work experience satisfy all the eligibility criteria mentioned by you in the job advertisement. As requested, I am enclosing a completed job application form, my certification, and my resume.

I have a master's degree in hospitality management from Los Angeles University. Since I graduated, I have a year of experience doing an internship at the BAC Hotel in Australia. I have been working at Khan's Hotel in L.A. for the past 5 years. In addition, I have experience managing a team of 8 people. I have good communication skills as well. The responsibilities mentioned in your job advertisement are quite similar to the ones that I currently have.

Please see my resume for additional information regarding my experience. In case you need to get in touch with me, please feel free to contact me at the phone number listed on my resume anytime between 1 p.m. and 7 p.m.

Thank you for your time and consideration. I look forward to speaking with you about this employment opportunity.

Anita Yong

3. Why was the letter written?
(A) To schedule a job interview
(B) To decline a job offer
(C) To submit a job application
(D) To describe some job qualifications

4. How long has Ms. Anita Yong worked for the BAC Hotel?
(A) One year
(B) Five years
(C) Eight years
(D) Two years

5. What is NOT mentioned about Ms. Anita Yong?
(A) She has submitted a job application form.
(B) She worked at the BAC Hotel as a manager.
(C) She can be reached at 3:00 p.m.
(D) She applied for the front desk manager position.

▶答案與解析請參考解析本第 66 頁

Step 1 模擬例題

解題策略　備忘錄的基本架構為「收件人－寄件人－主旨－內容主旨－詳細說明」。

Questions 1-2 refer to the following memo.

To: Marketing Teams
From: Richard Picker
Date: July 25
Re: Revised Marketing Plan Meeting

On July 28, we will hold a divisional meeting from 1:00-5:00 p.m. in the manager's conference room to discuss the revised strategic marketing plan that we have to submit to the president by August 15.

Please closely examine these documents and prepare your initial presentations in the following areas:

Product development manager: The needs of healthcare companies and their present levels of satisfaction and threats.

Marketing manager: The products, pricing, promotions, and distribution strategies of key competitors.

International sales manager: Sales organizations and strategies, including improvements in the relationships with other healthcare concerns.

1. What is the purpose of the memo?
   (A) To invite staff members to a seminar
   (B) To introduce a new employee
   (C) To inform people of the exact date of a meeting
   (D) To provide some details about a meeting

2. According to the memo, what are the managers asked to do?
   (A) Be on time at the meeting
   (B) Get their presentations ready
   (C) Submit some documents before the meeting
   (D) Complete a questionnaire about the meeting

▶ 中譯請參考解析本第 67 頁

To: Marketing Teams ➡ 收件人
From: Richard Picker ➡ 寄件人
Date: July 25 ➡ 日期
Re: Revised Marketing Plan Meeting ➡ 主旨

1 On July 28, we will hold a divisional meeting from 1:00-5:00 p.m. in the manager's conference room to discuss the revised strategic marketing plan that we have to submit to the president by August 15. ➡ 內容主旨

2 Please closely examine these documents and prepare your initial presentations in the following areas: ➡ 詳細說明與要求事項

Product development manager: The needs of healthcare companies and their present levels of satisfaction and threats.

Marketing manager: The products, pricing, promotions, and distribution strategies of key competitors.

International sales manager: Sales organizations and strategies, including improvements in the relationships with other healthcare concerns.

Q1. What is the purpose of the memo?

本題意在詢問備忘錄的主旨，除了特殊情況外，通常相關解題線索會位於第一段內容中。本題中，文章第一段開頭就說「On July 28, we will hold a divisional meeting from 1:00-5:00 p.m. in the manager's conference room」，可以得知這是在通知員工「會議的日期、時間與地點」，因此答案為 (C)。

Q2. According to the memo, what are managers asked to do?

詢問要求事項（are asked）的題型，通常要從最後一段尋找資訊，因為備忘錄的要求事項大多寫於最後一段，尤其是 if 子句或是命令句中的內容。如本題中末段的第一句便是命令句，解題線索從該句挖掘即可。「Please closely examine these documents and prepare your initial presentations in the following areas」可得知「準備提案報告」的要求，因此答案為 (B)。

攻略 POINT

先掌握左上方的收件人、寄件人與主旨，預測備忘錄內容後再行閱讀。

1 On July 28, we will hold a divisional meeting from 1:00-5:00 p.m. in the manager's conference room to discuss the revised strategic marketing plan that we have to submit to the president by August 15.

(On July 28), we will hold a divisional meeting (from 1:00-5:00 p.m.)
介系詞片語　主詞　動詞　受詞　介系詞片語

(in the manager's conference room) (to discuss the revised strategic
介系詞片語　to 不定詞

marketing plan) (that we have to submit to the president by August 15.)
關係代名詞（that）的先行詞 ─────── 關係子句 ───────

完整句子後方的位置為副詞，因此置於此處的 to 不定詞，在此作副詞用。多益考題中可能出現的副詞用法，大致可分為「目的、結果、理由」三大類，最常出現的為目的用法（為了～）。作副詞用的 to 不定詞，可置於完整句前方或後方。另外，表目的用法需要加強語氣時，可用 in order to 不定詞代替，而表目的的連接詞還有 so that、in order that 等等。

2 Please closely examine these documents and prepare your initial presentations in the following areas:

Please (closely) examine these documents and prepare your initial
副詞　動詞　受詞　動詞　受詞
────── 動詞片語 ──────　────── 動詞片語 ──────

presentations (in the following areas):
副詞片語

對等連接詞常見的句型，即為並列表現的句型。對等連接詞中，有 and、but、or、so 等等這幾種，而 and、but、or 可以放在單字間、片語間以及子句間作連接，但 so 只能用來連接子句。上方例題中，並列連接的是動詞片語，因此中間用對等連接詞（and）連接。

1 We regret to inform you that 通知內容

We regret to inform you that we cannot offer you the job.

在此遺憾地通知您，敝公司無法提供您職位。

We regret to inform you that your application has been rejected.

在此遺憾地通知您，您的申請已遭拒絕。

2 I'm sending this memo to 備忘錄主旨或是收件人

I'm sending this memo to the entire staff. 我將這個備忘錄寄給全體員工。

3 The work schedule for ~ will change.

The work schedule for the book **will change**. 本書的出版時程將會調整。

4 人物 be responsible for 負責業務

You will **be** primarily **responsible for** writing the advertising content for our company website. 你主要將會負責撰寫我們公司網站的廣告文案。

You will **be responsible for** delivery of the package. 你將會負責包裹運送。

5 I'd like to ask you to 要求事項

I'd like to ask you to keep my valuables. 我希望你可以幫忙保管我的貴重物品。

I'd like to ask you to refrain from checking your e-mail throughout the day.

我希望你可以不要一整天都在確認你的電子信箱。

6 The 12th annual 活動 will take place 時間

The 12th annual BIO Investor Forum **will take place** on October 8-9 at the Palace Hotel. 第十二屆的年度 BIO 投資者論壇，將會在十月八日至九日，於皇宮飯店舉行。

The 10th annual Sydney Fair **will take place** this Friday.

第十屆的年度雪梨博覽會將在這週五舉行。

Questions 1-2 refer to the following memo.

To: All Secretaries

From: Management Team

Date: June 5

Subject: Not Wearing the Prescribed Uniform; Cause for Dismissal from Service

We had our executive conference last week. Supervisors from various overseas corporations participated in it. We were expected to attend the conference in proper uniforms. But our boss was disappointed that only some of us wore our uniforms. Our boss has therefore ordered all of us to wear our new uniforms starting on July 1.

He wants me to remind all of you of the corresponding penalties for noncompliance with this order. For the first offense, a reprimand shall be given. For the second offense, the offending person will be suspended anywhere from 1 to 30 days. And a person will be dismissed from the job for the third offense.

Let this be a reminder to all of us that a simple act of negligence can be a reason for dismissal. Have a nice day!

1. Why was the memo written?

(A) To notify employees that some staff members have been dismissed

(B) To announce that the new uniforms have arrived

(C) To remind staff members to wear their designated uniforms

(D) To give some information about a staff policy

2. What is NOT a possible punishment?

(A) The staff member's salary will be lowered.

(B) The staff member will be suspended.

(C) The staff member will be fired.

(D) The staff member will receive a rebuke.

Questions 3-5 refer to the following memo.

To: Sales Staff
From: Management
Date: Monday, July 1
RE: New Quarterly Reporting System

We'd like to quickly go over some of the changes in the new quarterly sales reporting system that we discussed at Monday's special meeting. First of all, we'd once again like to stress that this new system will save you a lot of time when reporting future sales.

Here is a look at the procedure you will need to follow to complete your area's client list:

1. Log on to the company website at http://www.salesandgoods.com.
2. Enter your user ID and password. These will be issued by next week.
3. Once you have logged on, click on "New Client."
4. Enter the appropriate client information.
5. Repeat steps 3 and 4 until you have entered all of your clients.

As you can see, once you have entered the appropriate client information, processing orders will require NO paperwork on your part.

3. What is the purpose of the memo?
(A) To advertise a new reporting system
(B) To give instructions on how to use a new reporting system
(C) To introduce the new reporting system
(D) To give some information about the company's website

4. According to the memo, when will each staff member get an ID and password?
(A) On July 1
(B) On July 8
(C) On July 18
(D) On July 28

5. What are the employees being asked to do?
(A) To fill out their client lists on a new system
(B) To create their IDs and passwords by themselves
(C) To write all of their client information on paper
(D) To provide some feedback on the new system

▶答案與解析請參考解析本第 68 頁

Unit 90 公告 Notice

解題策略　公告的基本架構：前半部內容為主旨，中間部分為時間、方法、要求事項，而後半部則為聯絡資訊等等。

Questions 1-2 refer to the following notice.

Notice about Office Uniforms

Attention, all staff members. This notice is regarding staff uniforms. As mentioned last week, all staff members are required to wear their uniforms while in the office. Most staff members are complying with the regulation, however, there are still some staff members who are not wearing the proper uniform.

PROPER STAFF UNIFORMS ADD REPUTATION & DIGNITY TO THE OFFICE AND TO THE PERSONALITY OF STAFF, TOO.

All staff members are requested to strictly adhere to the dress code. Disciplinary action will be taken against offenders at the start of next month. All supervisors are also requested to send a daily report to the administration that states the names of the members of their departments who are not following the dress code.

Thank you for your help.

For any inquiries, contact the Human Resources Department at 386-2678.

---

1. What is the purpose of the notice?
(A) To notify staff members that they must wear their uniforms
(B) To provide information on how to purchase an office uniform
(C) To inform the staff about a company policy
(D) To advertise the company's new uniforms

2. What is mentioned in the notice?
(A) All staff members must send a report to the administration.
(B) Most staff members are not wearing their uniforms at work.
(C) Staff members will be penalized if they do not follow the dress code.
(D) Some staff members are required to wear uniforms.

▶ 中譯請參考解析本第 69 頁

Notice about Office Uniforms ➡ 標題

Attention, all staff members. This notice is regarding staff uniforms. 1 As mentioned last week, all staff members are required to wear their uniforms while in the office. Most staff members are complying with the regulation, however, there are still some staff members who are not wearing the proper uniform.

➡ 主旨

PROPER STAFF UNIFORMS ADD REPUTATION & DIGNITY TO THE OFFICE AND TO THE PERSONALITY OF STAFF, TOO.

➡ 細節說明與要求事項

All staff members are requested to strictly adhere to the dress code. 2 Disciplinary action will be taken against offenders at the start of next month. All supervisors are also requested to send a daily report to the administration that states the names of the members of their departments who are not following the dress code.

Thank you for your help.

For any inquiries, contact the Human Resources Department at 386-2678.

➡ 聯絡資訊

Q1. What is the purpose of the notice?

本題型意在詢問主旨，公告的主旨通常寫於第一段。只要閱讀首段一兩句，不僅可以了解公告的主旨外，還可掌握整體的文章脈絡，因此公告文章一定要從頭仔細閱讀。例題中第一段第二句「all staff members are required to wear their uniforms while in the office」，提到所有的員工皆被要求穿著制服上班，可知答案為 (A)。

Q2. What is mentioned in this notice?

「is mentioned」為詢問事實與否的題型，屬於複雜難解的題型。尤其每種閱讀文章類型不同，沒有辦法鎖定答案線索可能出現的位置，因此建議將此題型留到最後再解，因為通常回答完同系列的其他題目後，就可以大致掌握住本題型的解題線索了。而本文中第三段「Disciplinary action will be taken against offenders at the start of next month.」，提到下個月起違反者將予以懲戒，因此答案為 (C)。

攻略 POINT

先透過首段掌握公告的主旨後，便可進一步預測細節說明與要求事項的內容。

1 As mentioned last week, all staff members are required to wear their uniforms while in the office.

> As mentioned last week, all staff members are required to wear their
> 連接詞＋過去分詞　　副詞　　　　主詞　　　　　動詞　　補語　wear 的受詞
>
> uniforms (while in the office).
> 　　　　　　介系詞片語

as 的用法非常多元，可作為介系詞，句型為「as ＋身分／資格（以～）」，或作為連接詞：狀態連接詞＋過去分詞（如同～）、時間副詞子句連接詞（當～的時候）、表理由的副詞子句連接詞（因為～）等等。本例句中的 as 作狀態連接詞用，只是句型上較為複雜，雖然連接詞後方必須為完整子句，但此處的狀態副詞子句連接詞，則是接續了省略「主詞＋ be 動詞」的分詞構句，也就是轉化為「as ＋過去分詞」的句型。可能有很多考生會將這邊的 as 誤認為介系詞，然而，若考題中 as 後方接的不是身分／資格，則有非常大的可能性是作狀態連接詞用，尤其是「as ＋過去分詞」的句型。

2 Most staff members are complying with the regulation, however, there are still some staff members who are not wearing the proper uniform.

> Most staff members are complying with the regulation, however, there are
> 　　主詞　　　　　動詞片語　　　　　受詞　　　連接副詞　　　動詞
>
> still some staff members who are not wearing the proper uniform.
> 　　　先行詞　　　　關係代名詞　動詞片語　　　　受詞

副詞 however 可作為連接副詞（然而），或是複合關係副詞（無論如何）用。連接副詞的用法，如同上方例句，用於對照前後兩個句子時，請注意這邊的 however 不是連接詞，而是連接副詞。很多人容易將 however 誤認為連接詞。而若是作複合關係副詞時，句型為「however ＋形容詞／副詞＋主詞＋動詞」。所以大家不要一見到 however，就直覺地將其翻譯為「然而」，也請記住複合關係副詞「無論如何」的用法。

Step 4 　公告中的常見句型用法

1 We are pleased to announce 公告主旨

We are pleased to announce that nine companies earned good reviews in every
category. 　非常榮幸在此通知，這九間公司在每個領域都獲得好評。

We are pleased to announce that we are building a new facility in New York.

非常榮幸在此通知，我們將要在紐約新建一個設施。

2 Please be aware that 注意事項

Please be aware that the regulations will change on the first of next month.

請注意規則將於下個月開始變更。

Please be aware that the conference lasts only until July 21.

請注意，會議只持續到七月二十一日。

3 Please note that 注意事項

Please note that these dates are tentative. 　請注意這些日期只是暫時的。

Please note that we have extended our store hours on weekdays.

請注意，我們已延長平日的營業時間。

4 人物 is requested to 要求事項

Property owners who live in this city **are requested to** pay their taxes.

住在這城市的不動產所有人被要求繳稅。

5 Please contact 聯絡處（人、部門、公司）

Please contact one of our sales representatives. 　請聯絡我們其中一名業務代表。

Please contact Mr. McKenzie concerning this matter.

關於本事宜，請聯絡 McKenzie 先生。

6 There has been a change in 場地

There has been a change in the location of our December event.

我們十二月的活動地點有所變更。

There has been a change in the boarding location. 　登機口有變動。

Questions 1-2 refer to the following notice.

Notice Concerning Reductions in Staff Salaries

It is with regret that our company needs to announce that we have decided to reduce staff members' salaries. These reductions will take effect on January 1.

As is well known, due to the recession, the company is losing money and has not been able to meet its target for the last 2 years. The company has also lost some of its big clients. Due to this, the management has decided to reduce all staff members' salaries. Senior managers will take the lead by having their pay reduced by 20%. All non-executives' salaries will be reduced by 10%.

The board will continue to monitor the situation. Salaries will be restored to their previous levels if the company's financial performance improves in the next 2 quarters.

To learn more about this and to get answers to your queries, you may contact the Recruitment Department.

1. Why was this notice written?
   (A) To announce to the staff that their salaries will be slashed
   (B) To invite people to the meeting about salary reduction
   (C) To describe the company's financial problems
   (D) To mention several benefits for employees

2. By what date does the notice suggest that the company will restore employees' salaries?
   (A) On April 1
   (B) On May 1
   (C) On June 1
   (D) On July 1

Questions 3-5 refer to the following notice.

Announcement for Employee Training

In order to continue improving our customer service and to expand your skills, an employee training session has been scheduled. This training will take place from September 10 to 13, and the training session will be repeated to start at 10 a.m.

Thank you for being a valued member of our team here at the 7 Days Company. We have been in this business for quite some time, and we have always managed to stay ahead of our competitors. This is not possible if not with all of your support to our business.

If you attend this training session and take notes, the things you learn will be a huge help to boost the productivity of our organization. In the meantime, thank you again for all you do on behalf of the 7 Days Company. I look forward to seeing you at the training session.

Department Manager

---

3. What is the purpose of the announcement?
   (A) To ask for feedback on the training session
   (B) To notify employees about the dates of their vacation
   (C) To inform employees that they will have a training session
   (D) To announce that a new employee has started working at the company

4. What is indicated about the employee training session?
   (A) It will be held on January 10 and 13.
   (B) It is for employees to improve their customer service.
   (C) Only managers may attend it.
   (D) It will be repeated at noon.

5. What are the employees asked to do?
   (A) Prepare to give their presentations
   (B) Leave early on the last day of the training session
   (C) Arrive on time at the training session
   (D) Leave a note during the training session

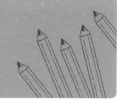

Unit 91 訊息對話 Text Message Chain

Step 1 | 模擬例題

解題策略　本類型的文章內容，多為公司內部關於會議、日程安排、業務等等的訊息對話，或是網路軟體上的對話，因此要多多熟練日常口語表現，並且掌握住對話對象以及對話內容。

Questions 1-2 refer to the following text message chain.

Sarah Paulson	[11:23 A.M.]

Bruce, this is just to let you know I'll be in Amsterdam next Friday.

Bruce Greenwood	[11:25 A.M.]

What's going on?

Sarah Paulson	[11:26 A.M.]

Our Amsterdam office requested a safety training for its employees. One of their instructors has to take an unexpected business trip, and they need a substitute.

Bruce Greenwood	[11:26 A.M.]

Did you manage to book a flight?

Sarah Paulson	[11:27 A.M.]

Not on such short notice. I'll drive.

Bruce Greenwood	[11:28 A.M.]

OK, good luck!

1. What will Ms. Paulson do next Friday?
   (A) Teach a training course
   (B) Meet an instructor
   (C) Go on a trip
   (D) Apply for a job

2. At 11:27 A.M. what does Ms. Paulson mean when she writes "Not on such short notice."?
   (A) She will not arrive on time.
   (B) She will not travel by plane.
   (C) She cannot accept an invitation.
   (D) She cannot make a payment.

▶中譯請參考解析本第 71 頁

Sarah Paulson	[11:23 A.M.]
1 Bruce, this is just to let you know I'll be in Amsterdam next Friday.	

➡ 對話目的

Bruce Greenwood	[11:25 A.M.]
What's going on?	

Sarah Paulson	[11:26 A.M.]
1/2 Our Amsterdam office requested a safety training for its employees. One of their instructors has to take an unexpected business trip, and they need a substitute.	

➡ 詳細內容

Bruce Greenwood	[11:26 A.M.]
Did you manage to book a flight?	

Sarah Paulson	[11:27 A.M.]
2 Not on such short notice. I'll drive.	

Bruce Greenwood	[11:28 A.M.]
OK, good luck!	

Q1. What will Ms. Paulson do next Friday?

此為推論題型，推論題目主詞 Paulson 女士下週五將要做什麼。由 11 點 26 分，Sarah Paulson 傳的訊息「Our Amsterdam office requested a safety training for its employees. One of their instructors has to take an unexpected business trip, and they need a substitute.」中，得知阿姆斯特丹辦公室的一名講師因為臨時出差，無法前往指導安全講習，因此需要一名代課者。可推測出 Paulson 女士應該會前去代課，因此答案為 (A) Teach a training course。

Q2. At 11:27 A.M. what does Ms. Paulson mean when she writes "Not on such short notice."?

此題旨在詢問，透過「Not on such short notice.」這句話，Paulson 女士想要表達何種意圖。針對 Bruce Greenwood 提出是否訂好機票的問句「Did you manage to book a flight?」Paulson 女士回覆「Not on such short notice.」（通知太臨時了，沒辦法訂）後，又立即加上一句「I'll drive.」（我會開車去），可以得知她並不會搭飛機前往，因此答案為 (B) She will not travel by plane。

 攻略 POINT

1. 要懂得正確掌握訊息對話的脈絡。
2. 只要熟悉了對話雙方提出要求或是給予提案時常用的語句，就能更快掌握。

1 Bruce, this is just to let you know I'll be in Amsterdam next Friday.

> Bruce, this is just to let you know (that) I'll be in Amsterdam next Friday.
> 　　　　　　主詞　　　　使役動詞　　動詞原形　　　　　　名詞子句

使役動詞 let 的意思為「讓他人去做～」，沒有強制或是拜託的意思，反而是有點獲得他人准許的語感。例如 Just let me~，意思為「就讓我～」，比起命令句來說，語氣較委婉一些。若要讓語氣不那麼強硬，尋求對方許可時，可在命令句前方加上 just。要注意的是，Just let me 後方動詞須為原形。

2 Our Amsterdam office requested a safety training for its employees.

> Our Amsterdam office requested a safety training for its employees.
> 　　　　　主詞　　　　　　動詞　　　　　受詞　　　　　介系詞片語

request 同時是動詞也是名詞，作動詞使用時，常見句型為「request ＋受詞＋ to 不定詞」或是「request that ＋主詞＋ （should）動詞原形」。特別是將 to 不定詞作為受詞補語的句型「request ＋受詞＋ to 不定詞」，常轉化成被動語態「be requested to 不定詞」使用。而作名詞使用時，多益中常見的用法有 upon (on) request「根據要求」，或是 address customers' requests「處理顧客要求」等等。

3 One of their instructors has to take an unexpected business trip, and they need a substitute.

> One of their instructors has to take an unexpected business trip, and they
> 代名詞　　介系詞片語　　　　動詞片語　　　　　　受詞　　　　　對等連接詞 主詞
> need a substitute.
> 動詞　　　受詞

one of the（所有格）＋複數名詞，意思為「～的其中之一」，作為句子主詞時，由於前方為 one，因此動詞須為單數形。多益考題中，常見「all / some / most of the（所有格）＋複數名詞／不可數名詞」的表現方式，但要注意的是，除了 one 之外，all、some、most 作代名詞時，of the（所有格）後方可以連接可數或不可數名詞，而作句子主詞時，動詞必須要與 of the（所有格）後方的名詞達到單複數一致性。

That's a relief. 那真是太好了。

It's settled. 都準備好了。

Please do 請您～

I'm just looking around. 我只是看看而已。

I will give you a good deal on it. 我會給你一個好價錢的。

Let me think about it. 讓我考慮一下。

I'm just getting by. 我就老樣子吧。

Put yourself in my position. 你站在我的立場想想看。

Don't take it too hard. 你不要想太多了。

I like it just the way it is [you are]. 我就喜歡（你）這樣。

It comes in handy. 這派得上用場。

There's a way to do things. 做事是有方法的。

I'll transfer you. / I'll contact you. 我會再聯絡你。

No means no. 我說不就是不。

His plan is beyond challenge. 他的計畫太完美了，挑不出什麼毛病。

It would have been nice. 那就好了。

I'm up to my ears in work. 我埋首於工作中。

I'm all tapped out. 我錢都花光了。

You drive a hard bargain. 你還真是會談判。

Don't let it get to you. 別讓這件事影響你。

It's the thought that counts. 禮輕情意重。

Don't even bring that up. 別再提這件事。

I'll come after I finish what I'm doing. 我處理完手上的事就過去。

It stands up to complain. 到哪都不遜色。

What's the occasion? 有什麼特別的事嗎？

Give me a break! / Give it a rest! 夠了！

I've been let go. / I've been laid off. 我被辭退了。

Nothing can excuse this. 不得有任何藉口。

Take it or leave it. 不要就拉倒。

You see..., I told you so. 看吧，早就跟你說了……。

It'll go down to the wire. 直到最後一刻才能見分曉。

Is this in addition? 這是額外的嗎？

That's apples and oranges. 這根本沒辦法比較。

Questions 1-2 refer to the following text message chain.

Karen Gillan	[2:14 P.M.]
Hi, are you still at the printing office?	

Bobby Cannavale	[2:15 P.M.]
Traffic was really terrible, so I actually just got here.	

Karen Gillan	[2:16 P.M.]
That's a relief. Ms. Pyle just emailed me, saying that there will be 20 people at the board meeting tomorrow, not 12.	

Bobby Cannavale	[2:17 P.M.]
OK. Anything else you need me to pick up while I'm here?	

Karen Gillan	[2:18 P.M.]
No, thanks.	

1. At **2:16** P.M., what does Ms. Gillan most likely mean when she writes, "That's a relief"?
   (A) She is glad that she is no longer driving in traffic.
   (B) She still has time to give Mr. Cannavale some information.
   (C) She thinks she can attend the board meeting after all.
   (D) She is pleased with the most recent financial statement.

2. What will Mr. Cannavale most likely do next?
   (A) Order more copies of a document
   (B) Purchase binders and notepads
   (C) Schedule a board meeting
   (D) E-mail a colleague

Questions 3-6 refer to the following online chat discussion.

Adam Driver   [10:15 A.M.]

Hi, Do you guys know if a parcel has arrived for me? I was supposed to get a delivery of some articles today, but I think they were sent to someone else by mistake. It's from Tatum's Financial Times and should be labeled "urgent."

Seth MacFarlane   [10:17 A.M.]

There's nothing for you here at the reception desk. You might want to check with the editorial department on the second floor.

Riley Keough   [10:18 A.M.]

There's a parcel from Tatum's Financial Times here in the mail room, but there's no name on it.

Adam Driver   [10:18 A.M.]

That must be the one for me. Could you look at the shipping label again?

Riley Keough   [10:19 A.M.]

Sorry, it does have your name on it. It was so small that I didn't notice it.

Adam Driver   [10:20 A.M.]

Great! Could you have the parcel sent up to my office please?

Riley Keough   [10:20 A.M.]

No problem. I am going upstairs in a minute anyway.

---

3. Why did Mr. Driver start the online chat discussion?

(A) He received a damaged parcel.

(B) He has a meeting with a client soon.

(C) He is expecting some important articles.

(D) He delivered a shipment to the wrong person.

4. What does Mr. MacFarlane recommend doing?

(A) Calling Tatum's Financial Times

(B) Changing a meeting place

(C) Going to the reception desk

(D) Checking a different location

5. At **10:19** A.M., what does Ms. Keough most likely mean when she writes, "Sorry"?

(A) She misplaced a delivery slip.

(B) She arrived late to work today.

(C) She would like Mr. Driver to repeat his instructions.

(D) She made a mistake reading a label.

6. What will Ms. Keough probably do with the package?

(A) Take it to Mr. Driver

(B) Send it out by express mail

(C) Leave it at the reception desk

(D) Remove the items from it

▶答案與解析請參考解析本第 72 頁

雙篇閱讀
Double Passages

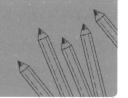

解題策略
1. 此部分需要閱讀兩篇文章，回答五題，每次考試都會有兩大題、十小題（題號 176-180 以及 181-185）。
2. 主要由電子郵件（書信）、公告、廣告、報導、表格等等文章類型聯合出題。
3. 其中約有三題詢問單篇內容，有一到兩題為綜合題型。
4. 題目順序幾乎會跟文章描述順序相同，因此建議先閱讀題目再回過頭去文章中找答案。

Question 1 refers to the following notice.

To whom it may concern,

I have made many purchases from Vitra Furnishings in the past, and I am consisently pleased with the high level of quality the product. However, one of the pieces I ordered (#39293) didn't come with any instructions. My order ID is 3929, and my customer ID is 2324. You'll find a copy of my invoice enclosed with this letter.

If you could send the appropriate directions to my e-mail address at aperry@bmail.com, it would be appreciated.

Regards,
Amanda Perry

Vitra Furnishings
859, Maplethorpe Avenue, Chicago

CUSTOMER INVOICE

ORDER DATE : May 4
ORDER ID : 39293
DATE : May 10

Products Purchased

Item No.	Item Description	Quantity	Unit Price	Total Price
12421	Bedside Table	1	$150	$150
34789	Table Lamp	2	$70	$140
39293	Clothing Chest	1	$350	$350
72648	Drawing Table	1	$280	$280

Subtotal : $920
Shipping : $50

1. Of the pieces Ms. Perry ordered, what items didn't come with any instructions?

(A) Bedside Table
(B) Table Lamp
(C) Clothing Chest
(D) Drawing Table

▶中譯請參考解析本第 73 頁

To whom it may concern,

I have made many purchases from Vitra Furnishings in the past, and I am consisently pleased with the high level of quality the product. ❷ However, one of the pieces I ordered (#39293) didn't come with any instructions. My order ID is 3929, and my customer ID is 2324. You'll find a copy of my invoice enclosed with this letter.

If you could send the appropriate directions to my email address at aperry@bmail.com, it would be appreciated.

Regards,
Amanda Perry

❷ 先找第一個線索。
可從此處得知 Perry 要的產品編號。

Vitra Furnishings
859, Maplethorpe Avenue, Chicago

CUSTOMER INVOICE

ORDER DATE : May 4
ORDER ID : 39293
DATE : May 10

Products Purchased

Item No.	Item Description	Quantity	Unit Price	Total Price
12421	Bedside Table	1	$150	$150
34789	Table Lamp	2	$70	$140
❸ 39293	Clothing Chest	1	$350	$350
72648	Drawing Table	1	$280	$280

Subtotal : $920
Shipping : $50

❸ 找第二個線索。
單據中可以從產品目錄上，看到編號 #39293 的產品為 Clothing Chest。

1 ❶ Of the pieces Ms. Perry ordered, what items didn't come with any instructions?

在 Perry 女士訂購的產品中，哪一項產品沒有附說明書？

(A) Bedside Table
(B) Table Lamp
(C) ❹ **Clothing Chest**
(D) Drawing Table

❶ 掌握題目主旨。
題目問的是 Perry 訂購的商品中，未附有說明書的為何者。

❹ 綜合以上的線索後，選出答案。
透過第一以及第二個線索，可以知道沒有附上說明書的商品為 (C)。

▶ 本題要綜合兩篇文章的資訊，才能進行解答。首先要先了解題目的主旨，接著找出答案的線索在哪一篇文章中，若是類似本題的綜合題型，通常兩篇文章中各會有一條線索，利用這兩個線索，綜合推論出正確答案。

▶ 首先，按照步驟❶，了解題目主旨，接著透過步驟❷找到第一個線索，以及步驟❸的第二個線索，最後由兩個線索可推敲出步驟❹的答案為 Clothing Chest，因此選擇 (C)。

Questions 1-5 refer to the following e-mails.

From: Miriam Chance <chancem@stjudithmedassociation.com>
To: Daniella Poisson <dpoisson@1medsupplies.com>
Date: April 7
Subject: Pre-OP series

Dear Dr. Poisson,

It was a wonderful experience to have met you at last week's conference in Riverbank. Your presentation was very impressive, and I could learn much about your company's new Pre-OP series of medical instruments.

For this reason, I am wondering whether you would be willing to travel to San Andreas and give us a more detailed presentation about the item. I am currently out of the state, but will return on April 17, and April 23 would be an ideal date for us since all hospital staff in Burbank are asked to come to the San Andreas office on the 23rd for a quarterly staff meeting.

Have a great day and I look forward to hearing from you.

Miriam Chance, MD
Saint Judith Medical Association

From: Daniella Poisson <dpoisson.@1medsupplies.com>
To: Miriam Chance <chancem@stjudithmedassociation.com
Date: April 8
Subject: Re: Pre-Op series
Attachment: Pre-Op series specifications

Dear Dr. Chance,

Thank you for your invitation. Unfortunately, I have a prior arrangement with Medical Tech Forum in Markstown on the specific date you mentioned. However, I will be back in your area at a conference in Golden Bay on April 26, so I will be available either the day before or after the 26th.

I am excited to realize that the Pre-Op series caught your interest, so I have attached a file that shows the dimensions of the instruments. I will be more than happy to present these instruments at your office for you and your colleagues. Contact me anytime and let's come up with an appropriate date.

Sincerely,

Daniella Poisson, MD

1. What is indicated about Saint Judith Medical Association?
   (A) It has offices in more than one location.
   (B) One of its dentists is a designer of medical instruments.
   (C) Its dentists organized a conference in Riverbank recently.
   (D) Its staff meetings occur once a month.

2. Where is Dr. Poisson scheduled to be on April 23?
   (A) In San Andreas
   (B) In Burbank
   (C) In Markstown
   (D) In Golden Bay

3. What has been included with the second e-mail?
   (A) A list of Dr. Poisson's professional accomplishments
   (B) A document showing the sizes of dental instruments
   (C) A draft of an agenda for an upcoming forum
   (D) A recording of a presentation given by Dr. Poisson

4. Why was the first e-mail written?
   (A) To place an order for new equipment
   (B) To promote a doctor's services
   (C) To publicize a professional conference
   (D) To propose an informational meeting

5. How did Dr. Chance first learn about the Pre-Op series?
   (A) By visiting a medical practice in another state
   (B) By hearing about it from another doctor at her medical practice
   (C) By attending a presentation by Dr. Poisson
   (D) By participating in a survey for doctors

▶答案與解析請參考解析本第 73 頁

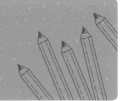

Step 1 | **模擬例題**

解題策略
1. 此部分需要閱讀三篇文章，回答五題，每次考試都會有三大題、十五小題（題號 186-190、191-195、196-200）。
2. 通常由一般類型的文章搭配單據、表格或是行程表等等，可以快速掌握資訊的文章類型聯合出題。
3. 跟雙篇閱讀相同，約有三到四題詢問單篇內容，有一到兩題為綜合題型。
4. 題目順序幾乎會跟文章描述順序相同，因此建議先閱讀題目再回過頭去文章中找答案。

Question 1 refers to the following letter & reviews.

Kitchenware Utopia Food Processor - Model C3

Our best-selling model, the C3, is made of high-quality plastic and easy-to-clean stainless steel.

Features: The unique blade design and powerful motor make this a professional-grade appliance, ideal for busy restaurants of all sizes.

Warranty: We include a seven-year warranty on all parts and labor.

Regular purchase price: $319.00 / KU Club Members: $299.00

---

www.kitchenwareutopia/review/c3/454			
HOME	**PRODUCTS**	**REVIEW**	**FAQ**

Rating : ★★★★★

This product is amazing. I'm a caterer, and I've used a lot of food processors, but this is by far the best one. The price is a little expensive, but it is worth the investment. Since I have a membership, I got the discount. The only complaint I have about it is that it is heavy, so it wasn't as portable as I had hoped. However, overall, I am very satisfied with the product.

Posted by Ellis Perls
March 27

---

www.kitchenwareutopia/review/c3/CR121			
HOME	**PRODUCTS**	**REVIEW**	**FAQ**

We are glad to hear you are happy with our C3 food processor. We would like to respond to your complaint and provide a suggestion regarding your concerns. Our C2 processor might be better suited to your professional needs. The C2 offers the same motor size as the C3, but it is much smaller than the C3. However, this model does cost slightly more than the C3.

Posted by Kitchenware Utopia Customer Service on March 28.

---

1. Why would the C2 processor likely be recommended as more suitable for Mr. Perls?

(A) It is inexpensive.

(B) It is dishwasher proof.

(C) It is easy to assemble.

(D) It is lightweight.

▶中譯請參考解析本第 75 頁

Kitchenware Utopia Food Processor - Model C3

Our best-selling model, the C3, is made of high-quality plastic and easy-to-clean stainless steel.

Features: The unique blade design and powerful motor make this a professional-grade appliance, ideal for busy restaurants of all sizes.

Warranty: We include a seven-year warranty on all parts and labor.

Regular purchase price: $319.00 / KU Club Members: $299.00

www.kitchenwareutopia/review/c3/454			
HOME	PRODUCTS	REVIEW	FAQ

Rating : ★★★★★

This product is amazing. I'm a caterer, and I've used a lot of food processors, but this is by far the best one. The price is a little expensive, but it is worth the investment. ❷ Since I have a membership, I got the discount. The only complaint I have about it is that it is heavy, so it wasn't as portable as I had hoped. However, overall, I am very satisfied with the product.

Posted by Ellis Perls
March 27

❷ 先找第一個線索。
可從此處得知 Perls 唯一不滿的是產品太重不好攜帶。

www.kitchenwareutopia/review/c3/CR121			
HOME	PRODUCTS	REVIEW	FAQ

We are glad to hear you are happy with our C3 food processor. We would like to respond to your complaint and provide a suggestion regarding your concerns. Our C2 processor might be better suited to your professional needs. ❸ The C2 offers the same motor size as the C3, but it is much smaller than the C3. However, this model does cost slightly more than the C3.

Posted by Kitchenware Utopia Customer Service on March 28.

❸ 找第二個線索。
提及 C2 比 C3 更小且更輕的資訊。

1. ❶ Why would the C2 processor likely be recommended as more suitable for Mr. Perls?

為什麼會推薦 C2 食物調理機，並說它更適合 Perls 先生？

(A) It is inexpensive.
(B) It is dishwasher proof.
(C) It is easy to assemble.
(D) ❹ It is lightweight.

❶ 掌握題目主旨。
題目問的是 C2 食物調理機適合 Perls 的理由。

❹ 綜合以上的線索後，選出答案。
透過第一以及第二個線索，可以得知 C2 食物調理機被推薦的理由為 (D)。

▶ 雖說此大題包含了三篇文章，但並不會出現要綜合三篇資訊才能解題的題型。如同雙篇閱讀大題，約有三到四題詢問單篇內容，有一到兩題為綜合題型，因此解題方法同雙篇閱讀即可。

▶ 此題為綜合題型，首先按照步驟❶，了解題目主旨後，再決定要從哪篇文章找答案，如本題中的關鍵字為 C2 processor 跟 Perls 先生，因此先從 Perls 先生寫的評論開始閱讀。從第二篇❷找到第一個線索，以及第三篇❸的第二個線索，最後綜合兩個線索可知道 C2 比 C3 合適的理由為❹。

Questions 1-5 refer to the following article, schedule, and e-mail.

City to Upgrade Aging Gas Pipes

(September 1) - During the month of October, Nairobi Energy Services, Inc., plans to replace two kilometers of cast-iron underground gas pipes with plastic-coated steel pipes as a part of its commitment to maintaining the city's energy infrastructure.

"The increase in pressure provided by the new pipes will better support today's high-efficiency furnaces, water heaters, clothes dryers, and other gas appliances," said Ms. Esther Cheptumo, the gas company's vice president. "The new system will ensure safe and reliable gas delivery for years to come."

Some streets in Nairobi will be closed to traffic between 11:00 A.M. and 4:00 P.M. while pipes are replaced. The gas company is working with city officials to develop a schedule that will minimize the inconvenience. The schedule will be updated daily on the company's website as well as in all local newspapers. Customers who experience a significant problem due to the work schedule should contact the gas company with their concerns.

Gas Service Upgrade Schedule

Monday	Oct. 16	Wallastone Street
Tuesday	Oct. 17	Moringa Street
Wednesday	Oct. 18	Blackstone Avenue
Thursday	Oct. 19	Stainwood Street
Friday	Oct. 20	No work scheduled (National holiday)

When work on your street has been completed, a NESI technician will come to your house to connect your service line.

To: Peter Abonyo <pabonyo@mailergrip.com>
From: Judith Kamau <jkamau@nesi.co.ke>
Re: Account No. A0194
Date: October 12

Dear Mr. Abonyo,

Your street is scheduled for gas pipeline replacement on Tuesday, October 17. Technicians will be available to reconnect your gas lines between 3:00 P.M. and 8:00 P.M. Please call us at 555-0181 to schedule a time for the work to be completed. Gas service to your home will be interrupted for about one hour while the reconnection work is done.

Thank you.

Judith Kamau

1. According to the article, what is true about the pipes?
   (A) They will help new appliances run better.
   (B) They will be installed more quickly than cast-iron pipes.
   (C) They will be replaced in several years.
   (D) They will be installed at night.

2. What does the article indicate about the work schedule?
   (A) It will not be approved by city officials.
   (B) It has been posted by Ms. Cheptumo.
   (C) It contains several errors.
   (D) It has not been finalized.

3. What will happen on October 16?
   (A) A meeting of NESI officials will be held.
   (B) A national holiday will be celebrated.
   (C) A street will be closed to traffic.
   (D) A NESI customer's complaint will be resolved.

4. What is suggested about Mr. Abonyo?
   (A) He requested some information.
   (B) He lives on Moringa Street.
   (C) He recently spoke with Ms. Kamau.
   (D) He is not home in the evening.

5. Who is most likely Ms. Kamau?
   (A) A city official
   (B) An NESI employee
   (C) An appliance technician
   (D) An executive at a factory

REVIEW TEST

Questions 1-2 refer to the following memo.

Memo

To: All employees
From: Sales Department Manager
Re: Meeting on July 18

There will be a staff meeting at 10:00 a.m. on Friday, July 18. Attendance at this meeting is compulsory for all employees in the Sales Department. The meeting will last for 3 hours, and there will be a discussion regarding the reduction of customer complaints in the coming month. The details of the staff meeting are provided below.

Venue: Dream Conference Hall, Main Office
Time: 10:00 a.m. to 1:00 p.m.
Meeting to Be Presided By: Mr. Bill Williams

Please ensure that you are on time for the meeting. Attendance will be recorded by Alice Smith, the personal assistant to the CEO. We are looking forward to discussing how to reduce customer complaints at the staff meeting. Please make sure that you bring your tablet PCs to the meeting so that you can take notes on all of the suggestions and recommendations regarding the items that are discussed.

---

1. What is the purpose of the memo?
 (A) To give information about the Sales Department
 (B) To notify the staff of a voluntary meeting
 (C) To announce a mandatory meeting to the staff
 (D) To ask for agenda requests for the meeting

2. What are the employees asked to do?
 (A) Bring their laptops to the meeting
 (B) Bring their handheld computers to take notes
 (C) Suggest at least one topic to be discussed
 (D) Take note of who attends the meeting

Questions 3-4 refer to the following notice.

Attention to All Staff

We will be holding a retirement ceremony in the staff room at our restaurant in honor of Mr. Paul on July 30 at 9 p.m. Sandwiches will be served along with cocktails. Please join us to congratulate Mr. Paul, who is retiring from his position as head chef on July 31. During his retirement, Mr. Paul plans to open his own Italian restaurant. We extend our best wishes to him as he enters this new stage of his life.

Mr. Paul started at the Little Italy Restaurant at the May Hotel in 1984, where he was hired as a junior staff member. He eventually worked his way up to head chef. I have enjoyed working with Mr. Paul over the years and have valued his friendship and support on many occasions. I'm sure all of us can say the same thing. I look forward to seeing everyone there to give a toast to this wonderful co-worker, friend, and mentor. Mr. Paul is a person whom we will all miss.

3. What is being announced?
   (A) A tea party for the staff
   (B) A cocktail party
   (C) The grand opening party at a restaurant
   (D) A retirement party

4. What is indicated about Mr. Paul?
   (A) He started working as the head chef in 1984.
   (B) He has worked at the restaurant for more than 20 years.
   (C) He is retiring to open an Italian restaurant.
   (D) He wants to work at the Little Italy Restaurant as a junior staff member.

Questions 5-6 refer to the following text message chain.

Spencer Walton [1:15 P.M.]

Hi, Betty. Mr. Wellinton just told me that he can't make it to the conference next month because of a scheduling conflict.

Betty Stone [1:18 P.M.]

Would you like me to ask the organizing committee to find a replacement?

Spencer Walton [1:20 P.M.]

I can recommend Dr. Lane from Ford Association. She's an excellent speaker, but I don't know if she's available at such short notice.

Betty Stone [1:21 P.M.]

I'll find out.

Spencer Walton [1:22 P.M.]

Great. If she's not available, I'll ask around and check.

Betty Stone [1:23 P.M.]

Sounds great.

5. Why did Mr. Walton send the message?
   (A) To ask for contact information
   (B) To report a cancellation
   (C) To confirm an event's location
   (D) To request an updated schedule

6. At 1:21 P.M., what does Ms. Stone mean when she writes, "I'll find out."?
   (A) She will ask whether the conference can be rescheduled.
   (B) She will find the time to meet with the organizing committee.
   (C) She will check on Dr. Lane's availability.
   (D) She will get information about the Ford Association.

To: Mr. Danson
From: Eric Watson
Date: September 17
Subject: Invitation to a business meeting

Dear Mr. Danson,

This email is regarding the business summit which is being organized by the JBC Corporation in order to announce and discuss trade possibilities for business expansion. We are inviting all of our business partners to the event. Kindly find the attached invitation that will allow you to take part in this meeting.

We request that you bring all of the necessary documents, which you will find on the second list attached to the invitation. Please join us with the innovative ideas and plans as we need to finalize certain strategies to spread business on the international platform. Furthermore, we will announce the concerned partners to take care of new business units along with responsibilities & duties. The JBC Corporation is looking forward to your attending to make this meeting fruitful.

If you have any questions, feel free to contact me at my office number during regular working hours.

7. Why was the email sent?
(A) To join the JBC Corporation
(B) To invite a person to a business meeting
(C) To announce the expansion of a business
(D) To discuss a business partner

8. According to the email, who most likely is Mr. Danson?
(A) A competitor
(B) A cooperator
(C) A supplier
(D) A colleague

9. What is Mr. Danson asked to do?
(A) Start working at the JBC Corporation as a manager
(B) Invest in the JBC Corporation to help it expand
(C) Bring some needed equipment
(D) Come up with some original ideas

Questions 10-12 refer to the following information.

The Almond Hotel has all the facilities you expect from a luxury hotel. Whether you're staying with us for business or leisure or if you are attending or organizing an event, you will have access to a range of superb comforts and amenities to provide you with an effortless, enjoyable stay.

- With free Wi-Fi Internet access available throughout the hotel, it's easy to keep in touch with home, the office, and the entire world.
- In-room dining is available 24 hours a day for all our guests. We have a wide range of meals and beverages on offer.
- The Almond Hotel has its own gym, and, as a guest, you will have free, unlimited access.
- Instead of taking the subway or a taxi, why not treat yourself to a limousine ride between the Almond Hotel and the airport?

Please ask the concierge for more details about our limousine service. If there is anything we can do to make your stay at the Almond Hotel more comfortable, please don't hesitate to ask any member of our staff.

10 What is the purpose of the information?
(A) To promote the opening of a new hotel
(B) To announce some new facilities at a hotel
(C) To provide some information about a hotel's facilities
(D) To notify employees of some new benefits

11 According to the information, what is NOT mentioned as being available at the hotel?
(A) Free Internet
(B) Free, unlimited use of a gym
(C) Limousine service from the hotel to the downtown area
(D) Room service 24 hours a day

12 What are the customers asked to do?
(A) Create an ID and password to access the Wi-Fi
(B) Pay for the in-room dining service
(C) Contact the hotel to make a reservation
(D) Inquire about the hotel's transportation service

Lamada Hotel Launches Private Yacht

The Lamada Hotel has launched a private yacht service for customers who are looking for a luxury travel experience. -[1]-. The private yacht was renovated to have its seating capacity reduced from 20 passengers to 10. By reducing the yacht's seating capacity, the Lamada Hotel was able to add a few soft mattresses for passengers to enjoy sailing on the ocean.

-[2]-. It boasts individually handcrafted leather seats, serves international cuisine, and significant service of Lamada. It offers two tour packages to coincide with the yacht lunch. -[3]-.

The Sunset Cruise package tour stops at five destinations, all of which are exotic islands. The package includes two glasses of red wine or two martinis as well as some snacks so that passengers can enjoy the beautiful sunset while on board. -[4]-. The Unlimited Wine package tour stops at one exotic island and provides passengers with a mini semi-buffet and unlimited wine and draft beer while on board.

For inquiries and reservations, call 000-1456 or visit the website www.lamadahotel.com.

13. What is the purpose of the article?
   (A) To offer a free tour package
   (B) To announce that a new hotel facility has been launched
   (C) To advertise the opening of a new hotel
   (D) To describe a new online booking system

14. What is indicated about the yacht?
   (A) It was renovated to reflect an exotic island.
   (B) It is a totally new yacht the hotel had made.
   (C) It is large enough to accommodate ten people.
   (D) It is only for customers who want to travel in luxury.

15. According to the article, where most likely is the hotel located?
   (A) Near a river
   (B) Near a mountain
   (C) Near the sea
   (D) Near a field

16. In which of the positions marked [1], [2], [3], and [4] does the following sentence best belong?
   "The yacht was renovated to reflect the iconic Lamada Hotel's facilities and service."
   (A) [1]
   (B) [2]
   (C) [3]
   (D) [4]

To : Dylan O'Brien
From : Kaya Scodelario
Subject : legal assistant

It has come to attention that we are in desperate need of a new legal assisting service. If you're having trouble finding applicants, an old colleague of mine recommended that we try Pados Legal Assisting. It seems that the legal assistants we have been hiring on our own have not been working out. Either they turn out to be unfamiliar with any of the processes or they are unable to handle the fast-paced environment that you and I have been working in for quite some time now.

I'm in no way blaming you for these unsuccessful hires, but we really need to find legal assistants that will be able to stay with our company for a while.

I am looking forward to hearing from you.

To : Kaya Scodelario
From : Dylan O'Brien
Re : legal assistant

Kaya,

I agree entirely that these latest hires have been unacceptable. We've been using Goldsmith Legal Assisting Services for a long time, and they used to send us only the best people. Since September, though, there has been a decline in the quality of those they've sent.

I will look into Pados legal assisting and try to find out as much as I can. Hopefully they will be able to help us out. I'll make this my top priority and get this taken care of as soon as possible.

Sincerely,
Dylan

17. What is the purpose of the memo?
    (A) To announce a conference
    (B) To inform of new guidelines
    (C) To request a meeting
    (D) To recommend a service

18. What is indicated about Pados legal assisting?
    (A) They are trustworthy.
    (B) They are unreliable.
    (C) They are expanding.
    (D) They are unsatisfying.

19. What is suggested about Ms. Scodelario?
    (A) She works in a hospital.
    (B) She is Mr. O'Brien's boss.
    (C) She works in marketing.
    (D) She is a new legal assistant.

20. According to Dylan O'Brien, what happened in September?
    (A) Mr. O'Brien was hired.
    (B) There was a decline in quality.
    (C) Ms. Scodelario was promoted.
    (D) They started using Goldsmith Legal Assisting Services.

21. Who most likely is Mr. O'Brien?
    (A) A sales representative
    (B) A hiring supervisor
    (C) A consultant
    (D) An engineer

From:	Pavel Sebastian <psebastian@swanhotel.com>
To:	Liu Kang <lkang@mkmail.com>
Date:	February 3
Subject:	Your stay at Swan Hotel

Confirmation Number: 5889500
VIP Members Number: 245094FT

Dear Mr. Kang,

Thank you for choosing Swan Hotel! Details of your hotel reservation are attached. Please e-mail us at reservations@swanhotels.com if you need to make any necessary changes to your reservation. All cancellations must be made at least one week in advance to avoid losing your deposit.

Please contact our front desk at services@swanhotel.com for services such as ordering tickets, booking tours, or transportation requests.

CONFIRMATION

Hotel location	55 Tulegatan St. 114 98 Stockholm
Room	Two double-size beds, 10th floor
Check-in	After 4:00 P.M., Friday, 18 February
Checkout	By 1:00 P.M., Sunday, 20 February
Number of people in room	2
VIP Member price	$270/night (Orignal price: $350)

We hope you enjoyed your stay!
We would like to ask you to take a moment to complete this survey.

1. How did you hear about Swan Hotel?

TV _____ Magazine _____ Travel agent _____ Internet __X__ Other _____

2. What was the purpose of your trip? _____Vacation_____

3. If you dined at Restaurant Frantzen, how would you rate the restaurant?

Outstanding _____ Good __X__ Fair _____ Unsatisfactory _____

4. How would you rate the quality our housekeeping service?

Outstanding __X__ Good _____ Fair _____ Unsatisfactory _____

5. Name and e-mail address (optional) Liu Kang. lkang@mkmail.com

If you are not a Swan Hotel VIP member, join today! All our VIP members receive a 20% off their room rates and are eligible for exclusive benefits only for VIP members. For more information, call us at 717-7755-5775 or visit our website at www.swanhotel.com.

22. What is the purpose of the e-mail?

(A) To promote a travel-rewards program

(B) To offer a larger room to a hotel guest

(C) To request participation in a survey

(D) To confirm accommodation arrangements

23. On what date did Mr. Kang most likely arrive at Swan Hotel?

(A) February 3

(B) February 11

(C) February 18

(D) February 20

24. What is suggested about Mr. Kang?

(A) He ordered theater tickets.

(B) He received a reduced room rate.

(C) He used the services of a travel agency.

(D) He changed his date of departure.

25. What is indicated about Swan Hotel?

(A) It has a restaurant.

(B) It opened in February.

(C) It primarily serves business travelers.

(D) It advertises on the radio.

26. What does the survey indicate about Mr. Kang?

(A) He received helpful information from the concierge.

(B) He was very happy with the cleanliness of his room.

(C) He appreciated having free internet access.

(D) He is a frequent visitor to Stockholm.

▶答案與解析請參考解析本第 77 頁

PSV 0029

一次戰勝新制多益 TOEIC 必考閱讀攻略＋解析＋模擬試題

作　　者 — SINAGONG 多益專門小組、金富露（Peter）、趙康壽
譯　　者 — 林雅雯
主　　編 — 林菁菁、林潔欣
編　　輯 — 黃凱怡
校　　對 — 曾慶宇、劉兆婷
企劃主任 — 葉蘭芳
封面設計 — 江儀玲
內頁排版 — 張靜怡

董 事 長 — 趙政岷
出 版 者 — 時報文化出版企業股份有限公司
　　　　　　108019 臺北市和平西路三段 240 號 3 樓
　　　　　　發行專線 — (02) 2306-6842
　　　　　　讀者服務專線 — 0800-231-705・(02) 2304-7103
　　　　　　讀者服務傳真 — (02) 2304-6858
　　　　　　郵撥 — 19344724 時報文化出版公司
　　　　　　信箱 — 10899 臺北華江橋郵局第 99 信箱
時報悅讀網 — http://www.readingtimes.com.tw

法律顧問 — 理律法律事務所　陳長文律師、李念祖律師
印　　刷 — 和楹印刷有限公司
初版一刷 — 2019 年 8 月 9 日
初版二刷 — 2021 年 10 月 1 日
定　　價 — 新臺幣 599 元
版權所有・翻印必究
（缺頁或破損的書，請寄回更換）

時報文化出版公司成立於 1975 年，
並於 1999 年股票上櫃公開發行，於 2008 年脫離中時集團非屬旺中，
以「尊重智慧與創意的文化事業」為信念。

一次戰勝新制多益 TOEIC 必考閱讀攻略＋解析＋模擬試題 /
SINAGONG 多益專門小組、金富露（Peter）、趙康壽作 .
-- 初版 . -- 臺北市：時報文化 , 2019.08
　432 面；19×26 公分 . -- (PSV；29)
　ISBN 978-957-13-7873-2 (平裝)

1. 多益測驗

805.1895　　　　　　　　　　　　　　　　108010684

Original Title: 시나공토익 BASIC READING
SINAGONG TOEIC Basic Reading by SINAGONG TOEIC Institute & Peter Kim & Jo gang-soo
Copyright © 2018 SINAGONG TOEIC Institute & Peter Kim
All rights reserved.
Original Korean edition published by Gilbut Eztok, Seoul, Korea
Traditional Chinese Translation Copyright © 2019 by China Times Publishing Company
This Traditional Chinese edition published by arranged with Gilbut Eztok through Shinwon Agency Co.

ISBN 978-957-13-7873-2
Printed in Taiwan